To Win His Wayward Wife

Rose Gordon

TO WIN HIS WAYWARD WIFE

© 2011 C. Rose Gordon
Front cover image © 2011 LFD Designs
Back cover design © 2014 Aileen Fish
All rights reserved.

ISBN 9781938352430

Published by Parchment & Plume, LLC
www.parchmentandplume.com

Parchment
& Plume LLC

Other Titles Available by Rose Gordon

SCANDALOUS SISTERS SERIES
Intentions of the Earl
Liberty for Paul
To Win His Wayward Wife

GROOM SERIES
Her Sudden Groom
Her Reluctant Groom
Her Secondhand Groom
Her Imperfect Groom

BANKS BROTHERS BRIDES SERIES
His Contract Bride
His Yankee Bride
His Jilted Bride
His Brother's Bride

OFFICER SERIES (AMERICAN SET)
The Officer and the Bostoner
The Officer and the Southerner
The Officer and the Traveler

GENTLEMEN OF HONOR SERIES
Secrets of a Viscount
Desires of a Baron
Passions of a Gentleman

For my youngest son, who wakes me up every Saturday morning at quarter to seven so I can make Belgium waffles, by coming into my room and screaming, "It's time to make the muffles, muffle maker!"

And to my husband, who has encouraged me in all of my hobbies, including painting; and allowed me to display the painting I did of him even after our oldest son looked at the picture and said, "That doesn't look like Daddy. It looks like the teacher from Brown Bear!" (Just in case you don't know, the teacher from *Brown Bear, Brown Bear What Do You See?* is a woman...)

Chapter 1

August 1813
London, England

"Dearly beloved, we are gathered here today…"
Madison Banks knew it was her brother-in-law, Paul Grimes, who was speaking. She heard his voice and tried to listen to his words, but she couldn't seem to force herself to focus on them. Instead, her focus was directed solely on her groom.

He was tall, handsome, titled and wealthy. Every girl's dream come true. Except hers. To be honest, he gave her the chills. And not the good kind, either. No, these chills were the kind that sent people into hiding. He sent *her* into hiding. Not to say he was mean to her, because that would actually be a lie. He had been extremely nice to her at one point—which was part of the reason she now found herself standing up in front of hundreds of people pledging her life to him.

It all started eight short weeks ago, when her parents had just left for America to make arrangements to have their household moved to England, her father's homeland. Her sister, Brooke Black, Lady Townson, along with her husband Andrew, Lord Townson, stepped in to act as her chaperone and guardian while her parents were away.

At first, things had gone well; very well, in fact. Brooke played her chaperone's role in regular Brooke fashion. In short, she wasn't a very good one. She often allowed Madison to go on unchaperoned carriage rides in the park and would leave the room for half-hour

1

intervals to check on her newborn while Madison was left unattended with a gentleman. Madison hadn't complained about such things. She rather enjoyed that Brooke gave her the freedom Mama hadn't allowed.

However, it wasn't Brooke's lack of chaperoning skills that led to Madison's demise. That was completely her own doing.

A month ago, she'd been at a ball surrounded by countless gentlemen fawning over her bright blonde hair, clear blue eyes and porcelain skin; all the while, she was thinking what a lot of simpletons they all were. Couldn't anyone notice anything deeper about her than her outward appearance, she wondered. She knew she'd acted shy and withdrawn the previous Season, but she'd been dancing waltzes and going to numerous social events for the past few months and all anyone could notice was her looks.

No one cared about the charitable works she did for others. Nor did anyone see her personal talents. No; all anyone saw was her striking beauty, and they were all so struck dumb by it, they couldn't function properly in her presence.

Annoyed with the inane comments of the imbeciles around her, she decided it would be best to dance and endure the company of only one dullard instead of a dozen. The orchestra started playing the opening strains of a waltz and Madison caught sight of her brothers-in-law walking across the ballroom. Curious, her eyes shifted to search the direction they were walking, and that's when she thought her world was about to collapse around her.

Directly across the ballroom from Andrew and Paul, stood Robbie Swift, the no-good, filthy cad who ruined her life. No, wait, that wasn't entirely true. Her family may blame him for ruining her life, but they knew just as well as Madison did that she was just as responsible.

Robbie was a local banker's son from Brooklyn, New York. He was tall, handsome and undeniably charming. He had all the makings of a young girl's fairy tale husband.

He was only two years older than Madison, and when she and Brooke were young girls, the three of them would play together (when they could manage to ditch their youngest sister, Liberty, that is). As they entered their teenage years, Robbie was no longer a playmate but just another acquaintance. He attended her father's church and played the flirt to all three of the Banks sisters. Unfortunately—or fortunately, depending on who you ask—Madison was the only member of the Banks family who could abide him.

Brooke could hardly tolerate him as a playmate when they were younger, and her feelings for him didn't change as they grew older. Only because of Madison's never ceasing protests, did Brooke finally quit trying to fling rocks at him with a makeshift slingshot.

Liberty wasn't much better at hiding her dislike for Robbie. However, instead of hurling rocks at him or pouring large quantities of salt into his tea as Brooke had, she'd drone on and on about how much she didn't enjoy his presence and wished he'd either marry Madison or go find another girl to annoy.

Mama and Papa were the only ones who attempted to hide their dislike for him. They'd casually have conversations with her, dropping hints about other eligible gentleman or suggesting she take a break from the courtship with Robbie to see what would happen.

But no, Madison didn't want their advice. She wanted Robbie. She had to have him no matter what. For a brief time, she considered taking her parents advice and focusing on another gentleman, but when she'd heard he'd made some unflattering remarks about her, she strengthened her resolve and started to pursue Robbie like a cat chasing a mouse.

The problem was she, being the cat, had been declawed, not that such a thing was possible, mind you, except metaphorically, of course. She could chase him into a corner and almost have him in her clutches, then he'd scurry away and she'd be on the chase again. This cat and mouse game, where she chased him and he escaped her grasp at the last minute, went on for five years. Yes, that's right, five *years*! Now some would say, a courtship is usually about five months. Or some might even be five weeks. And then, of course, there are the ones that are rather odd at five days. But five years? That's unheard of. And yet, that's how long the cat chased the mouse. Actually, cat and mouse is a bad analogy. A better analogy would be a puppeteer and puppet. In this analogy, Madison would undeniably be termed the puppet.

For five years, she danced to his tune in hopes of becoming Mrs. Robert Swift. And in the end, that honor went to a weak ninny named Laura Small.

Laura was a spoiled southern girl who had never so much as seen needle and thread in a person's hand as they weaved it in and out of cloth. She'd grown up in southern Georgia on a booming cotton plantation. She flounced her way into New York spending money as if it grew on a cotton plant. She used her sugary-sweet southern voice to get the men to do her bidding with nothing more than a few compliments and a sickening grin. Within a week, she was the belle of all the balls. Within another week, she was Mrs. Robert Swift.

While Madison and Robbie had an unusually long courtship of five years that led nowhere, Laura and Robbie had an unusually short courtship of five days that led to the altar. Talk about the injustice of the world!

Only a month after the blessed event of two heartless,

coldblooded creatures becoming one, Madison's family decided it was time to visit Papa's family in England.

Their intention was only to stay a few months, but when her older sister, Brooke, married an earl and announced a few months later she was in the family way, her parents decided to stay a bit longer. Then had come the unexpected marriage of her younger sister, Liberty, to a country vicar named Paul Grimes. When it turned out that two of their three daughters were happily married in England, Mama and Papa decided it would be best if they took up residence in England as well, which was why they were absent from the ball.

She'd been in England over a year now and had attended more balls than she cared to count. Not that she didn't like to dance, she did. The problem was she didn't want to marry. Robbie's betrayal had cut deep, deeper than she thought possible. So brutal was his treatment of her, she didn't think she could ever trust a man again.

She'd lived her life constantly lost in a daydream for nearly a year, before allowing herself to open up and enjoy life again. She'd erected walls around her heart and vowed she'd never be so careless as to trust another with it again.

So naturally, when she saw that miserable scoundrel who had the nerve to call himself a man, she started to panic. Hundreds of questions swirled around in her head, but they all came down to: what did he want now? She knew he hadn't come here for anyone else. He only knew one other person in England besides her family, and that person was a commoner. Robbie wasn't here for Liberty or Brooke, she was certain of that, which meant he was here for her.

Knowing he'd probably spotted her already, she fought to keep her calm as she weighed her options. She could dance the night away with any number of gentlemen who were currently swarming around her like bees to a hive and ignore him in hopes he'd leave. She could make her way to seek refuge with her sisters and wait for their husbands to toss him out like she knew they were about to do. Or, she could slip out of the ballroom and run to her bedchamber, remaining there for the remainder of the night.

Glancing at the herd of sheep dressed as gentlemen who surrounded her, she ruled out option number one. Shifting her gaze to where Brooke and Liberty were, she saw she'd have no choice but to walk directly in front of him as she walked to the staircase that led to Brooke's look-out. That only left retiring for the evening. That wouldn't be a bad option, she supposed. She'd just have to make her way to the side doors and walk through the gardens to get into the main part of the house.

Plan in place, she excused herself from her adoring pack and started to walk in the direction of the gardens. With each step she took, she felt her blood pumping faster through her veins. She could feel his razor sharp blue eyes staring at her as she made her way to the edge of the ballroom. Reminding herself to breathe and stay calm, she forced a smile to her lips as she passed a handful of curious guests. She heard footsteps behind her and almost froze. He was following her. Had Andrew and Paul not been able to rid this place of his unpleasant presence?

Willing herself once again to calm down, she reached out her shaking, clammy hand to open the door. Her palm so sweaty she could barely hold onto the knob as she gave it a twist. Swallowing the lump of panic that had formed in her throat, she tried again. Relief temporarily flooded her when the door swung on its hinges and she was able to slip outside.

Though the gardens were dimly lit, Madison had been in them enough that she could navigate them with a blindfold. All but running, she scurried down the steps, around the shrubs, through the bushes and over a concrete bench in an effort to get to the door. She grasped the brass knob to open the door just as she heard her name being called.

Her hands froze. Her heart froze. Her blood froze. It was *his* voice. The voice that used to whisper in her ears words of love and affection. The one that made promises of a future filled with love, happiness and children. The voice she'd tried for so long to forget.

"Madison," he called, turning her skin to gooseflesh.

Ignoring him, she tried to open the door. There were no lights around the door, if she could just slip in and lock the door behind her, he wouldn't be able to find her. But that was the problem, she couldn't slip in. The knob wouldn't turn. It was locked.

"Blast," she exclaimed quietly through clenched teeth. She remembered she'd once swiped a key to the front door and kept in her reticule. She just hoped it would work for this door.

"Oh, Madison darling, where are you?" Robbie drawled, causing her fingers to tremble as she dug for her key. "I know you're out here."

She wanted to yell. She wanted to scream in frustration. She wanted to get this blasted door open. Her fingers closed around the key and she held it tightly as she pulled it from her reticule.

"You know you want me," he said, his voice sounding closer than before.

Her fingers shook as she tried to jam the key into the keyhole. Every time she came close to getting the tip in, her shivering hand would miss and she'd scratch the knob with the end of the key.

"You know, those two bodyguards you've got in there should have known better than to just escort me out," he said with a chuckle. "They have no idea of our feelings for each other, eh? Oh well, who could fault them for thinking I'm too much a gentleman to jump a fence to get to the woman I love. That's right, Madison, I said love. I love you. Now come out of hiding, so we can talk."

Madison's hands briefly stilled from their mission of trying to get the key into the lock. She closed her eyes and shook her head. Love. Did the man really think after all this time, he could prance back into her life to say he loved her, and everything would be all dandy between them? If that was his great plan at winning her back, he was completely addled.

"Now come on, pet," he drawled again, making her blood curdle. "Get your luscious derriere out here, so we can talk."

His words shocked her and the key she'd been holding slipped to the ground to make a light ringing *clink* on the flagstones. All the blood seemed to rush from her head and she began to panic again. What if he'd heard the key hit the ground and came closer? Numbly, she tried to bend down to pick it up. Halfway to the ground, she saw a shadow that caused her to freeze in place.

Too dark to make out the face of the man next to her, she stared in silent shock as a giant hand reached down and picked up the brass key. The man stood up and slipped the key into the lock with extraordinary ease, before putting his hands on her waist and helping nudge her into the dark house.

No lamps were lit inside and the pair stood in complete darkness. "Thank you," she said at last.

"You're welcome," a vaguely familiar voice returned behind her.

They stood together in silence for another moment, while Madison waited for her heart to slow down to normal. But the longer she waited, the more she realized it wasn't slowing down. Robbie was still outside yelling for her and becoming crasser each time he spoke.

"Oh, why is he here?" she muttered to herself. "Why can't he just leave me alone?" She brought her hands up and covered her face. She felt like she was going to faint. Just as she could feel herself about to crumple to the floor, two strong hands came up and pulled her backward to rest against his hard body.

"It's all right," the stranger murmured in her ear. "I told Townson I saw the scoundrel jump the rock wall. He'll take care of him in a minute."

"Thank you," Madison said softly. Robbie was right when he pegged Andrew as too good a gentleman to guess Robbie would come back. Andrew was the sort that stayed calm and always gave people the benefit of the doubt—at first. Then, if they betrayed his trust, they normally regretted it.

She'd heard tell from more than one source that he'd been involved in a number of fisticuffs. His most notorious partner being the Duke of Gateway, the man who'd tried to pay him last spring to ruin her sister Brooke. Those two had apparently had their share of scrapes over the past fifteen years and had each broken the other's nose at one point. She had no doubt that, with Andrew being built like a tree the way he was and Robbie being no bigger than a twig, Andrew could easily break him. "I hope he doesn't kill him," she remarked when she heard Andrew's angry voice.

"He won't," the voice behind her said. "Do you love him?"

"Who? Andrew?" she asked, automatically ruling out the chance he could be asking about Robbie. "Of course. Why wouldn't I? He's always been kind to me." Not to mention, he was her brother-in-law.

"What of Mr. Swift?"

Madison closed her eyes. "No."

"Then why don't you want him hurt?"

"I didn't say that," she corrected. "I said I hoped Andrew doesn't kill him. In case you didn't see him, Robbie is as big as a quill. All Andrew has to do is hit him once and he'll snap in half."

The man chuckled. "You think they're unevenly matched, do you?"

"Of course," she burst out with a nervous giggle. "I'm not a coldblooded monster or anything, but I wouldn't be opposed to seeing Robbie roughed up a little. At the same time, I don't want his blood on Andrew's hands. Anyone who's ever seen Andrew knows it wouldn't take any effort on his part to hurt Robbie."

"Do you think Mr. Swift is a weakling who cannot defend himself?"

"Yes," she answered bluntly. "I mean no offense to him in that regard, but the truth is I've seen the man felled by a pebble my sister shot at him from a makeshift slingshot."

"Was this a reenactment of David and Goliath put on for your father's church?" the man asked, his chest rumbling with a chuckle.

"No." She shook her head and tried not to giggle at the memory. "Robbie tried to flip Brooke's skirt up one Sunday after church, and after she kicked his hand away, he got angry and tripped her. That's when she ran inside and took off who knows what piece of her clothing and used it to hurl a rock no bigger than her pinky nail at his head. He fell to the ground like he was a lead weight."

The stranger laughed quietly and his hands squeezed her a little tighter. "That must have been quite a sight."

"Oh, it was. But his wailing wasn't. He moaned and groaned in pain for nearly five unbearably miserable minutes before he realized nobody was paying him any mind. Except me, of course. I was the only one stupid enough to fall for his theatrics."

"You're not stupid," his calm voice said behind her.

Silence fell over them once again, as they listened to heated exchanges and what Madison would swear were sounds of an impending fight outside.

A sudden unmistakable crack followed by the loud thump of a body hitting the ground nearly made Madison jump out of her skin. "Perhaps I should go out there before something else happens," she said hastily, trying to turn around.

His hands tightened. "No," he said softly in her ear. "You're not needed out there."

"Excuse me?" she asked in disbelief. "Who are you to tell me where I am or where I'm not needed?"

He didn't answer.

Who was this man anyway? Who was he to tell her what to do? Did he not realize how much worse it would all be if she didn't stop Andrew before it was too late? "I really think I need to get out there," she said again, trying to break his grasp. "Robbie isn't like Andrew's other opponents have been. He's not able to hold his own in a fight."

"So you want to rescue the man who loves you?" he said bitterly.

"No," she burst out. "I've no romantic notions about Robbie. I just don't want to see him dead, that's all."

"Because then Townson would go to prison or be exiled. Is that it?" He wrapped his arms around her waist and pulled her back against his hard body.

"Yes," she said sharply, trying to free his fingers from the hold they had on her. "I care far more for Andrew than I do for Robbie. I have to stop their fight. Please?"

His hands loosened a fraction, but stayed in position. "I don't hear either of them anymore," he said after a minute.

She heard them though. She could pick out Robbie's pathetic whimpers anywhere. They were distant, but she could hear them all the same. "I think Andrew's loading him into a carriage."

"Yes," the man agreed. "Mine."

"Yours? Why?"

He didn't answer her. Instead, he released his hold, and from somewhere Madison couldn't place, the mysterious gentleman lit a short candle and reached around her to hand it to her. "I promised Townson to keep you out of the way," he explained. "You may go wherever it was you were headed. Just don't follow me."

"Why?" she asked, attempting to turn around to face him.

"No." He gripped her waist again, intent to keep her from turning to face him.

"Who are you?" she asked, truly curious. She'd just spend the last five or ten minutes in the dark with this man and she had no idea who he was. She'd somewhat recognized his voice, but she couldn't place it. Not that that meant much. She'd met so many men since she'd come to England, it was nearly impossible to keep them all straight when she could see their faces. Their voices were even more difficult for her to place. As odd as it was, she thought a lot of them sounded alike with their English accents and it was hard to tell them apart, especially in the dark.

"Don't worry about that. Just go."

She didn't budge. Curiosity may have been rumored to have killed the cat, but she was no weak, declawed cat anymore; she wanted to know who this man who had been holding her in the dark was. "No," she said defiantly. "I'm not leaving until I know your identity."

"Who do you think I am?" His voice was so close she could feel his breath fan her ear and blow her hair, making her shiver.

"I don't know," she said honestly. "I'm not good with voices. But I know for certain you're not Lord Wray, Lord Drury, or Mr. Chapman. I'd know those three voices anywhere with how much I have to hear them wax and spout ridiculous poetry about my blue eyes looking like endless skies. I know you've spoken to me before though. I just don't know where."

"You don't need to remember where. You just need to go. Now."

"Not until I have your name." She looked down at the candle stub she was holding. It hadn't been very large to start with and now it looked no larger than an acorn. She really needed to get walking if she wanted to have enough light to guide her to a lighted hall. "Please, tell me. My candle is about to burn out. I need to start walking, but I won't leave until I have your name."

"That's unwise," he stated. "You need to go before someone finds us. Townson or your sister will be looking for you soon and it would be best they don't find us like this."

Madison fought the urge to snort. "You clearly don't know my sister." If Brooke found them alone in the dark, she'd turn her eyes and pretend it never happened. If Madison asked her to, that is. First, Brooke would probably try to talk her into letting the rumor slip, if the match was to Madison's advantage.

"I know her husband well enough," the man countered. "He wouldn't be happy about this."

"He'd handle it however Brooke told him to." Andrew wasn't one for gossip in the first place, and he loved his wife and her family well enough that she was certain he wouldn't call this man out or start rumors about them, especially if he was the one who asked him to keep her out of his fight with Robbie.

"That's because she leads him around by his prick," the man said, his voice full of disdain.

If the statement had been made about anyone else, she would

have dissolved with laughter on the spot. But she knew better than anyone that Andrew truly loved his wife and Brooke undoubtedly returned his love in equal measures. "That was a nasty thing to say. I demand you apologize."

He grumbled something she couldn't understand, then mumbled, "Sorry, I forgot for a second that I was in the presence of a lady. I'll choose my words more carefully in the future."

"That's not what I meant, and you know it," she shot back hotly. "Apologize for your unflattering remark about my sister and her husband."

He scoffed. "Fine, I apologize. From now on I'll say, 'Of course he will, he's the most besotted man in England.' Does that meet with your approval?"

"You're rather rude, did you know?" she asked sarcastically. Of course he knew he was rude. He probably prided himself on it.

"Thank you. You may not believe this, but you just complimented me."

"It wasn't meant as such," she retorted. "Now, tell me who you are, so I can go before my candle burns out. The flame is already burning the tips of my fingers because it's so close to where I'm holding it on the bottom."

"Then you'd better start walking," he said, giving her a gentle shove forward.

Thinking she was going to outwit him, she quickly whipped back around to get a peek at his face. But in her haste, she made an error in judgment. She forgot to block the candle flame when she spun, and the quick spinning motion put out the flame right before she was able to get a glimpse of him.

"Good work," he said sarcastically.

She ground her teeth. This man was absolutely intolerable. Why on earth had Andrew asked him to keep her occupied while he took care of Robbie?

Either he must be a mind reader or she'd spoken her thoughts aloud, because the infuriating man said, "Because I was—"

The rest of his words were abruptly cut off, when the door behind him suddenly swung open and revealed a very displeased Andrew. "What are you doing?" he hissed at her companion.

"Exactly what you told me to do. I kept her away from him," the mystery man said calmly. His back was to the gardens and the only light streaming into the room was behind him, making it possible for her to see his form, but not his face.

Andrew being directly underneath a lamp was fully visible and Madison was sure she'd never seen him so angry. "Well, you've done your job. Now let her go. Madison, come with me. I'll take you to

Brooke and she can see you to your room, if you'd like."

Madison went to sidestep the mysterious man, discreetly trying to glance up to see who she'd been with. Almost out of the doorway, she froze when another voice, one that she and every member of the Banks family knew well, entered the scene. "Well, what do we have here?" Lady Algen said waspishly.

Madison noticed she wasn't the only one who stiffened at the comment. Lady Algen, who was London's—no, England's—no, the continent's—most vicious gossip hungry harpy, stood with her hands on her hips, grinning like a jackal. This did *not* look good. Turning her eyes from Andrew to the back of the man she hadn't been able to glimpse on her way out the door, she knew trouble was about to ensue and all three of them were powerless to stop it.

"What irony," Lady Algen declared, licking her lips. "I was present at the ruination of your sister with this man," she gestured to Andrew, "I believe I also brought to light your other sister's scandalous ways." She shook her head and clucked her tongue. "I just had no idea it would come to this. Miss Banks, I honestly thought you were better than this."

"That's enough," Andrew said. His voice was so hard, both Madison and Lady Algen froze in terror. "Nothing is going on here. Go back and enjoy the ball while I return Madison to her sister."

Lady Algen snorted. "I don't think so. I shall escort her to her sister. Your wife will be in need of a shoulder to cry on when she finds out her husband has been trysting with her sister in the corners of her own gardens, during a ball *she's* hosting no less."

Madison gasped. Lady Algen thought she and Andrew were trysting? Did that mean she hadn't seen the man in the doorway? She peeked over to the open door and he was no longer standing there. The hall was so dark, she couldn't see if he was even in there or not. Blast the man.

"My wife will not require a shoulder to cry on," Andrew said smoothly. "There is nothing going on between Madison and myself that my wife is not aware of."

"So she approves of your activities, then?"

"There are no 'activities', real or imagined, between us," Andrew said defensively.

"So are you denying that the two of you were trysting in the dark?" Lady Algen asked.

"Come along, Madison," Andrew said, ignoring Lady Algen and offering his arm to Madison.

Wearily, she took his arm and barely made one step when Brooke came running up. "Thank goodness," she said excitedly as she ran to embrace Madison. "Don't worry, everything's fine now."

"Is that so?" Lady Algen asked archly. "Are you aware that your husband and sister have been keeping each other company tonight?"

"No, they haven't," Brooke said fiercely, putting her hands on her hips. "My husband was disposing of some rubbish, so to speak and Madison was with—"

"Me," growled an angry voice that belonged to the unidentified man coming out of the doorway, grabbing Madison's attention and making her gasp. "Townson asked Madison and me to wait over here until he came to collect us to formally announce our engagement."

"Your engagement?" Lady Algen gasped, her eyes darting back and forth between the four of them.

"Yes, our engagement," he confirmed. "Now, shall we all go back into the ballroom and allow Townson to make the announcement? Come, sweet," he finished, offering his arm to Madison.

Madison stood numb. Closing her eyes, she silently prayed the ground would suddenly open and swallow her whole while an angel came down from heaven and wiped clean the memory of anyone that knew her. This was bad. This was beyond bad. This was catastrophic proportions bad. This was attempting to swim across the ocean back home to New York bad.

Catching sight of Lady Algen's skeptical stare, she swallowed the uncomfortable lump in her throat and linked arms with the man she was about to become formally betrothed to. If she had been anyone else watching the scene, or even if it had been anyone else she had just become engaged to, she would have laughed at the twin looks of horror both Andrew and Brooke sported.

"Well, I never," Lady Algen said, shaking her head. "I didn't believe she'd go through with it."

Madison's escort stopped and turned to face Lady Algen. "Madam, you'd be wise to hold your tongue," he counseled in a low, sharp tone. "The only thing you witnessed here tonight was a formal engagement announcement. Nothing else. If I hear even a hint of a rumor circulating suggesting anything else, you and anyone associated with you, will be finding out just how exciting the wilds of Australia really are." He paused for a minute to let her brain work out his words. "Don't think I don't know of your involvement in the incident that took place at my house more than six years ago."

Lady Algen took in a sharp intake of air and ran off as if she were being chased by a lion.

Turning back to face Madison, her nearly betrothed sent her a devious smile. "You just had to see my face, didn't you," he drawled tauntingly. "And now, you'll get to see it every day for the rest of your life."

Madison and Brooke gasped in unison at his cruel remark.

Andrew, however, was not one to stand idle and watch while someone was taunted. Instead, he grabbed the man's arm, spun him around and delivered a swift, hard punch to the other man's midsection, making him gasp at the sudden loss of air, but showing no other signs of distress.

"Take that as a warning," Andrew said evenly. "Come, ladies, let's go announce this confounded engagement before Lady Algen does."

That was it. That was how Madison now found herself, four weeks, two over-chaperoned carriage rides, and six obligatory waltzes later, looking into the cold blue eyes of her bridegroom.

And all she could think was in a way he was right, if she hadn't been so blasted interested in discovering his identity, she wouldn't be here taking vows to look at his unyielding, handsome face for the rest of her life.

Curiosity may not have killed the cat, but it sure didn't do her any favors.

Chapter 2

The groom, Benjamin Archer Leopold Charles Robert Collins, Duke of Gateway, swallowed nervously as he stared into the uncertain eyes of the woman who was now repeating her vows to be a faithful and loving wife to him until death do them part.

She was so beautiful, he thought as he watched her pretty pink lips move as she repeated Paul's words. Her magnificent blonde hair was piled high atop her head with two sets of ringlet curls spiraling down to rest on either side of her face. Her gown was a gorgeous shade of sea foam green. It had capped sleeves, a moderately swooped bodice and long, flowing skirts that swished when she walked down the aisle to him.

That's right, to him! He was the luckiest man in England. Today, right now, he was making Madison his wife. He'd never again have to go to another ball and watch her from the corner of the room as men danced attendance on her. After today, she'd be his and only his. He fought to keep the smile off his face as he thought what that meant. No other man would get to hold her and kiss her. No other man would get to claim her as his. She belonged to him; and no matter how many times he and Townson came to blows over that fact, she would still belong to him.

He cast a glance at the uneasy look on Townson's face. He'd actually been a good sport about it, Benjamin allowed. He couldn't fault the man for being angry things had worked out the way they had. Not that he was complaining; it had benefited him greatly. He'd been hoping for this moment for more than six years. *Six bloody years!* Had it really been six years since he'd met her? He turned his head and thought about it, rolling back the mental calendar in his head. Yes, it had been six years, almost six and a half actually.

At eighteen, he'd gone on Tour around the continent and spent a year seeing sights, tasting delicacies, and experiencing things he'd never imagined possible. But that trip paled in comparison to the one he took to the United States. In March of 1807, at three and twenty, he'd decided to go on Tour again, this time to America.

He'd once heard of a distant relation he had through his mother's side of his family who lived in Brooklyn, New York. His whole life, he'd grown up knowing he was a marquis and would one day be a duke. Everyone in Europe seemed to know about him and his scandal ridden past. But not in America, he thought. Over there, people held no stock in titles. Heck, the founders had gone so far as to make a public declaration for the whole world to know they thought all men equal with equal rights and positions. Thus, he surmised, it would be a perfect place to go.

Leaving behind his fashionable (but not dandified, thank you) clothing, he took what would pass as commoner clothing, grew a scraggly if not somewhat patchy beard, and set sail for America. He was fairly certain he wouldn't be recognized by his name, Benjamin Collins, but just to be safe, he chose his third most hated middle name and shortened it to Leo.

Knowing for sure nobody would equate Leo Collins with Channing, his courtesy title at the time, he slouched his shoulders and sought entry into the Swift household.

The family welcomed him with open arms, as he knew they would, since he'd corresponded with them for two months before he'd offered to send them a sizable amount if they'd agree to house him and not breathe a word of his title.

To his good fortune, the first night he was in the States, the family had been invited to a ball given by some wealthy client of Mr. Swift's. Eager to go and experience the American way, he dressed in clothes that would have been the height of fashion—ten years prior— and eagerly attended the ball.

This ball was like nothing he'd ever seen before. The rules were more relaxed, but at the same time, the dances weren't as progressive. This intrigued him. He sat on the side of the ballroom and watched as couples did the quadrille and a few different reels, but no waltzes.

He was lost in a trance, tapping his toe and watching the sea of young girl's flounces rise and fall as they danced when two young ladies passed right in front of him, breaking his line of vision.

His eyes left the dance floor and traveled to the duo who dared end his mesmerizing entertainment when his breath caught. They were both beautiful, but one was so stunning she was arresting. Her blonde hair and pale skin were stark opposites of the emerald green gown she wore. He only had a profile view of her, but it was enough to know everything about her was dainty and quaint. He'd later find out that her looks belied her real personality, which would only serve to intrigue him more.

The beautiful blonde and her raven haired companion stood only ten feet away from him talking and giggling about who knew what. Frankly, he didn't care what they were doing just as long as they stayed right there so he could watch her.

He crossed his arms and leaned back to make his staring less obvious, not that it did any good.

"Something caught your eye?" Robbie Swift, his annoying younger cousin, asked before taking a seat.

"Someone," Benjamin corrected with a nod in her direction.

Robbie scoffed. "Madison Banks?"

Benjamin turned his eyes back to Madison. She had a name now. She was no longer the beautiful blonde wearing green. She was Madison. Not Miss Banks. Not Miss Madison. Just Madison.

"You're wasting your time," Robbie said, breaking into his thoughts. "Her father's my minister. You'll never stand a chance."

"Men can change. *I* can change," Benjamin told him solemnly. For her, he could, and would, change anything. He'd move mountains for her if it were the least bit possible and she asked it of him.

Robbie laughed. "Even you can't change that much," he said, shaking his head. "Madison and Brooke, those two girls you're looking at, were brought up to be all that is prim and proper. If you don't believe me, ask anyone who knows them. Their youngest sister even totes around a notebook filled with the rules to every game she's ever been allowed to play."

Benjamin shook his head. "Rules are meant to be broken."

"Not by them," Robbie said again. "If you're looking for a girl to lift her skirts, and I think you are, look no further than the door. You see her?" He nodded in the direction of the door. "The one wearing the blue dress with the white lace? She's got what it takes to tickle your fancy."

Benjamin scowled. He had no interest in a quick tumble in the storage closet. "No, thank you." He turned his eyes back to Madison.

"You'll not get it from her, I guarantee it," Robbie said. "You'd be more likely to charm her sister into lifting her skirts than her."

Benjamin turned a cold look to Robbie. "Is that all you think about?"

"Yes," Robbie said instantly.

16

Benjamin rolled his eyes. "You've got a lot to learn. There's more to women than tupping."

Robbie snorted. "Yes, spoken like the wise old man you are. What are you two and twenty?"

"Three and twenty," Benjamin corrected, shifting his gaze back to the sisters who were now surrounded by a pack of slobbering potential suitors.

"All right, and are you going to try to convince me you live the life of a monk?"

Not taking his eyes off Madison as she was led to the floor, he said, "No. But I could become one if it meant I could have her."

Robbie let out a harsh bark of laughter. "Don't bother. She's already in love with someone else."

"Who?" Benjamin demanded, spinning his head around to face Robbie.

But Robbie didn't speak. He didn't need to. His knowing grin said it all. Madison was in love with Robbie. Benjamin's heart sank and he shifted his gaze back to where she was being twirled around the floor. Just then, her partner spun her around to face them and he caught a glimpse of the smile she sent Robbie.

Jealousy like he'd never known before ate at him. The only woman he'd ever wanted would never be his. "Are you going to offer for her, then?" he asked raggedly, resigning himself to the bitter pain of being too late to catch her attention.

"No." Robbie shook his head with vigor. "She may love me, but I've no need for her."

"Right; because she won't lift her skirt," Benjamin returned with a sneer. "You don't deserve her."

"Maybe not," Robbie conceded with a lopsided shrug. "But that doesn't change how she feels about me."

Turning to walk away, Benjamin caught sight of Madison walking their way and froze. She was beautiful as she came toward him, her dress swaying back and forth with each step. She flashed him a bright smile before turning to Robbie. "Good evening, Robbie," she said with a blush.

"Good evening, Madison," Robbie returned, beaming. "Care to dance?"

"I'd love to." She accepted his arm and flashed Benjamin a weak smile.

Benjamin watched them take to the floor. Robbie was an awful dancer. He stepped on her toes and twirled her too fast, heedless as to who or what she'd hit in the process.

Scowling, Benjamin took a seat to watch the awful spectacle that was presented before him.

"I have no idea what she sees in him," a female voice muttered.

"Nor do I," Benjamin agreed with a quick glance to his right to see who the woman he was now talking to was.

"She's always been the one bound to find the good in everyone," Madison's sister, Brooke, said, shaking her head. "I think she's found one that has no good, and she wants to be his saving grace."

"Why?" Benjamin asked, idly scratching his unkempt beard.

She shrugged. "That's just Madison, I suppose."

"She could do far better than him," he declared. "There are many lost souls more worthy of her than him."

"Are you applying for the job, then?" Brooke asked with a smile.

"Absolutely."

"Hmm, as Madison's older sister and her most trusted confidant, I need more information about you before I can recommend you," she said; a twinkle in her eye.

Benjamin laughed. "My name's Leo. I'm visiting from England. I'm a bounder of the worst sort and I'm desperately in need of saving. But, I am savable. I guarantee it. I can dance better than he can. I have higher brain function than he does. And, I can tell just by looking at her, there's more to her than just her beauty."

"Yes, there is," Brooke confirmed, nodding her agreement. "I shall be happy to pass on my highest recommendation for you. Whether she'll take it or not, I don't know. Let's just hope for the best."

The dance ended and the sisters scurried off to join their friends, leaving Robbie and Benjamin to stare at each other.

Over the next three weeks, Benjamin spent enough time in Robbie's presence to know he not only was unworthy of Madison's love, he was unworthy to lick her boots. He was a womanizer of the worst sort.

Fortunately, he'd learned although Madison may have her cap set on Robbie, they weren't even courting. Hope filled his heart and he attended more social events, and even her father's church services in hopes of seeing her again.

He felt confident he could have made a good impression on her and won her from Robbie, except every time he'd start to talk to her, or even just go near her, Robbie would suddenly show up and pull her away. It was infuriating. In three week's time, he'd spoken to her less than half a dozen times for periods of about two minutes each.

During the entire twelve minutes of shared conversation, he'd learned she sewed for the needy, volunteered to tutor children at an orphanage, painted, and enjoyed topics of conversation that were not suitable for young ladies. He was certain there was a lot more to her, but bloody Robbie and his bloody presence prevented him from finding out more.

Thinking back, he should have sought out Brooke and tried to make his appeal to her. But he hadn't, and instead, he had to sit back and watch as Madison tried in vain to vie for Robbie's attention, only to be treated poorly when he graced her with it.

At the end of March, her father had announced a church outing to the Hudson River. The weather was nice enough, perhaps a little breezy. But that didn't matter. He was too awestruck by Madison to know or care about anything else. His eyes were trained on her nearly the whole time.

When she'd finally broken free of her crowd and started to walk in his direction, he moved away from the tree he'd been standing against and went to meet her. Only ten yards separated them, when a hand clapped him on the back. "Care to go fishing?"

"Not now, Robbie." There wasn't any way he was going to let Robbie interfere this time.

"Madison, would you like to fish?" Robbie called as she was approaching.

"I'd love to." She flashed a bright smile in their general direction.

Unable to know who the smile was meant for, Benjamin pretended it was for him and returned it. "Leo here has no interest, so it'll just be us," Robbie said, grabbing her arm.

Madison sent Leo what he'd interpreted as a disappointed smile. Oh, who was he trying to fool? It had been nothing more than a friendly smile. She had no interest in him joining their fishing and flirting.

Arms crossed, he let out an annoyed sigh and watched in irritation as Robbie draped himself over Madison trying to show her proper fishing technique.

Ten minutes was all he could stand of that, so he turned to walk away when he heard a startled scream come from their direction. Turning back, he noticed the hem of Madison's gown was wet and she looked to be rather distraught. He wanted nothing more than to go to her side and rescue her from his cousin's clutches but stayed put and watched with annoyance as Robbie scooped her up and carried her away.

The next night turned out to be his last night in America. He'd finally come to the conclusion he was not going to get to talk to her if he was associated with Robbie. Thus, he decided to see if she had any interest whatsoever in him. If she did, he'd rent his own apartment in Brooklyn; and if not, he'd go home.

That night another local family hosted a dinner party the Swifts and Banks had been invited to join. All through dinner he cast glances down the table at Madison. She didn't return any though. She was too busy chatting and socializing to notice him.

After dinner, they all gathered in the drawing room, where the hostess insisted they play nursery games. The first few weren't too intolerable. However, he nearly jumped up and down with enthusiasm when she suggested everyone hide and she'd seek them out. This would provide the perfect opportunity to talk to Madison, he thought as he followed her out the door. With all the people present, he lost sight of her in the hallway but felt confident he knew the direction she was headed.

He wandered around for nearly ten minutes before he caught sight of her gown atop a lighted balcony. Looking around for stairs or a ladder that would lead to the balcony, he heard a male voice whisper something he couldn't make out. Unable to find stairs, he grabbed hold of the textured bricks and started to climb up. Just as he reached the top, he turned his head and watched in the shadows as a somewhat unsettled Madison whispered, "Not him, only you," before she wound her arms around Robbie's neck and he lowered his lips to hers.

Benjamin tore his gaze away and dropped to the ground like a lead weight had been lowered on his stomach, which it had. He was certain of it. He felt worse than ever before. He'd just witnessed confirmation that she'd never feel for him what he did for her. All her love was for Robbie, not him.

The next day, he traveled home and swore never to even think of America again.

That goal was achieved for little more than five years. Then, one mid-April day in 1812, he walked into a ballroom and his eyes immediately landed on a group of three young American girls.

They hadn't recognized him right off. Actually, they still hadn't, even after a year. It had been five years since they'd met, after all. His horrible attempt at a beard was now gone. His clothes were now the height of fashion (still not dandified though). Most everyone now called him by his ducal title, except the few who were close enough to call him by his Christian name, Benjamin. Of course, Madison and her sisters wouldn't pick up on his name since they'd known him as Leo. For all anyone knew, they were meeting for the first time.

And now, more than a year after their second "first" meeting, they were taking vows and becoming man and wife.

Six years of miserable longing were over and they were now moments away from her becoming his wife.

Not that he had planned for it to happen the way it had. That was just a stroke of luck. He'd actually commissioned an engagement ring the morning after he'd first seen her in London. He'd carried it in his pocket like a besotted man for a few weeks at first. Then, when they'd been here a few weeks and he noticed she was still withdrawn and rumors circulated she had no interest in men or marriage, he put the ring back in its box and stood content to watch her from the shadows.

Before the start of this Season, he'd brought the ring to London to be fixed. It would seem in all his nervous excitement at the beginning of last Season, he'd clutched the ring too tightly and accidentally broken one of the prongs that held the diamond in place.

His plan was to try and charm his way through her wall of defenses in order to win her hand. But when he arrived in London this Season, he was shocked and slightly unsettled to find her wall of defenses and haze of uncertainty were already gone. Instead of being quietly lost in her daydreams, she was surrounded by every eligible—and a few ineligible—gentleman from ages twenty to eighty.

With his plan ruined, he decided once again to watch her from the shadows and look for an opportune time to present himself to her. He knew she wouldn't be very accepting of him at first due to her sister and brother-in-law's past history with him. What an idiot he'd been to offer Townson money in exchange for orchestrating the ruination of Madison's sister, he thought closing his eyes to block out the memory.

The time for him to present himself to her hadn't arrived before she'd left to attend her increasing sister's grand event. When she came back a few weeks later, the timing was even worse. Her parents had left for America and made Townson her guardian in their stead. This was not good news for Benjamin. Townson and he had an uncomfortable past which was all his doing. There was no way Townson would give his permission for Benjamin to marry her. Nor court her. Nor even call on her. In fact, he was absolutely stunned when Townson allowed him into her mere presence when he'd asked him to keep her occupied so he could dispatch Robbie.

He would have been content to stay in the shadows when they were caught by Lady Algen. He'd been prepared to wait for Mr. Banks to return before asking for her hand. The only reason he could no longer wait in the dark for everyone to leave was the three of them had done enough suffering at his hands, and he couldn't stand idle as the family faced yet another scandal created by him. He was just fortunate Madison swallowed her shock and took his arm.

He'd done his best to postpone the wedding until her parents could return. But fear of rumors convinced them all to hold the wedding on the date originally set: four weeks from the engagement announcement. With her parents not yet returned, Townson stepped in and walked her down the aisle. He'd even gone so far as to keep a scowl off his face, except for a split-second when he placed Madison's hand in Benjamin's.

"I now pronounce you man and wife. You may now kiss your bride," Paul Grimes said, drawing Benjamin back to the present.

Slowly, reverently almost, and definitely tenderly, Benjamin reached his free hand up to cup Madison's cheek as he lowered his head to press his lips against hers.

Under his, her lips briefly softened before exerting the same amount of pressure he had and returned the kiss.

Straightening, he looked down at her to memorize exactly what her face looked like after their first kiss.

"Ladies and Gentlemen, I now present to you the Duke and Duchess of Gateway," Paul said proudly as the grinning couple turned to face the clapping audience.

Chapter 3

Madison peeked up at her bridegroom through her lashes. He was startlingly handsome when he grinned, she thought before she turned her eyes back to the sea of wedding guests. She'd personally never seen His Grace beam like this before. Brooke had once told her she'd only seen him truly smile once and though it was an absolutely beautiful sight, it seemed to foreshadow something unpleasant.

Blinking to rid herself of that disheartening thought, she turned her smile up to a full beam and allowed him to escort her down the aisle.

Their wedding had taken place in St. Gregory's church with the breakfast to follow at her sister's townhouse.

Gateway led her to his carriage and wordlessly helped her up. "Thank you, Your Grace," she murmured when she got settled.

"You're welcome." He sat down next to her. "You're a beautiful bride, Madison."

Her eyes locked on his still grinning face. "Thank you again, Your Grace." Was he just like all the others? Could he only see her superficial beauty? "You're rather handsome yourself," she said with a weak smile. She hadn't lied. He was handsome. He was one of the handsomest men in England and everyone, including himself, knew it. At close to, if not exactly, six feet tall, he was taller than most. His hair was light blond and kept clipped reasonably short. His face was full of hard planes and angles that made him look like he was chiseled from stone. His eyes also resembled stones, the sapphire kind. They were a color of blue that assumed many different hues. She'd noticed at times they were pale blue like the sky and at other times they were a few shades darker like blue flame on a candle. Where his nose had once been a slim line, it now had a permanent knot toward the top and looked slightly lopsided. His mouth was usually clamped shut in a straight line with his slightly red, neither thin nor thick lips pressed together in twin rows. This was the first time she'd seen him smile in a way that didn't make him appear to be sneering, snarling or grimacing. He actually looked exceedingly handsome just now.

"I'd say thank you, but we all know that would just lead to more useless small talk."

She smiled up at him. "I believe you're right."

Silence filled the carriage. Though she hadn't gotten to know him very well in the past few weeks, she'd gathered he wasn't one for small talk and pleasantries. Whether it was because he just wasn't interested in her or because by nature he was just a quiet sort, she didn't know.

The ride to her sister's didn't usually feel as long as it did this time, but sure enough only a half hour had passed before she was disembarking Gateway's carriage and was on her way inside.

Their breakfast went faster than she imagined possible and she soon found her nervous self being loaded once again into her husband's silence-filled carriage.

Due to the haste of their wedding, they'd decided to wait until spring to go on their wedding trip, provided she wasn't breeding. Madison gulped. Breeding? Surely not; they barely knew each other. They wouldn't be having relations often enough for her to be breeding. Or would they? She'd been told men could take anything in a skirt to bed. For them it was just physical, not emotional. But for her, like most women, marital relations fell into the emotional category.

Looking at him now, she could tell he was expecting to visit her room tonight and the thought made her stomach clench. They barely knew each other. Perhaps she should ask for more time. No, that wouldn't matter. He didn't seem the sort to be denied, especially if she were to tell him she wanted to get to know him better first. She'd just have to swallow her fear, close her eyes, endure the activity and be thankful when he left.

"You look nervous, Madison," Gateway said, breaking into her thoughts.

"I'm not," she lied. "All right, I am."

A smile tugged at his lips. "There's no need. I'm not as bad as they say."

"Right," she chirped. The whole country had something unpleasant to say about him. How could he possibly be nearly as bad as everyone claimed? But even if he was only half that bad, that was bad enough.

"I know we don't know very much about each other," he intoned, causing her eyes to meet his. "I'd like that to change. I think I can be a good husband to you, but you'll have to let me in."

Her eyes went wide. What was he talking about? Let him in? Let him in where? Her bed? Of course she was going to have to let him in there. She couldn't deny him his husbandly rights any more than she could have denied his abrupt announcement of their engagement. It just wasn't done. "All right, Your Grace," she agreed with a tense nod. This was going to be a long night.

"Good, I'm glad that's settled. Now, if only I could stop you from calling me 'Your Grace'."

She swallowed. "What would you prefer? Gateway?"

"No," he burst out. "Never. I despise being called by my title. You may call me Benjamin or Ben, whichever you prefer."

She stared at him. Of course she knew what his name was, but she'd never considered he'd ask her to use it. "Benjamin," she said, testing it on her lips.

He smiled at her. "It looks like we're here."

He helped her descend the carriage then escorted her to the front door where all the servants were assembled to greet their new mistress.

One by one Benjamin introduced her to each of the servants, surprising her that he knew them all by name. She wasn't bad with names necessarily, but when meeting so many at one time, she knew she'd never remember them all without having to ask again. She did make a point to remember Todd, the butler, Mrs. Potts, the cook, Mrs. Landry, the housekeeper and Lottie, the lady's maid Benjamin had hired for her. Beyond that, she couldn't keep up with all the Marys, Johns and Sarahs.

In an odd twist of events, Benjamin dismissed Mrs. Landry when she offered to give Madison a tour of the house and insisted he'd show her around himself.

Perched on his arm, she listened with great interest as he led her around the house and pointed out each room explaining why it was the way it was. She was quickly learning her husband had a great interest in both art and history. He'd admitted he couldn't paint a square without messing it up and she'd almost told him she'd once had a great passion for painting before deciding he probably didn't care about such things.

After he'd taken her through all of the common rooms in the downstairs, they climbed a great marble staircase that had beautifully carved mahogany banisters and a bright red carpet running down the center of the stairs.

Idly, she trailed her fingers up the smooth wood as they climbed the stairs to where she presumed their rooms would be located.

Taking a deep breath as they reached the top landing, she stood quietly while he opened the first door and put his hand on the small of her back to encourage her to go forward.

The room she entered was clearly a sitting room. There were two large royal blue settees positioned close to a large window with beautiful cream colored drapes. On the far wall, under a small window was a petite secretary stocked with fresh quills, inkpots and vellum. Soothing pale green wallpaper covered the walls and gave the room a softer touch. She roamed around and ran her fingers along all the surfaces, noting the feel of the fabric and the hard edges of the planes as she went. He must have talked to Brooke to know she wasn't a fan of pinks and purples, she mused to herself. Smart man.

"As I'm sure you've guessed, this is your sitting room. Through that door," he gestured to a door on the wall without windows, "is your bedchamber. You can also reach it through the hallway, if you'd prefer."

She nodded. If she went to her bedchamber now, would he follow her? A shiver skated down her spine. Perhaps she'd wait until he found something else to occupy his time before she explored her bedchamber.

"I've some letters to write," she said abruptly, hoping he'd take the hint and leave.

He looked slightly disappointed, but didn't argue. With a nod, he accepted her statement, informed her dinner would be served at eight and departed, making only a soft click as he shut the door.

Madison waited only a minute or two before opening the door and walking into what would now serve as her permanent sleeping location in London.

Awe swept over her as she inspected the masterfully carved scrolls on the poles of her canopy bed. Running her fingers along the fringe of the deep crimson counterpane, she walked to the head of the bed where a little side table was positioned. After inspecting the odd little table that was perfectly polished and held a five candle lamp and a small clock, she went to the wardrobe. Her clothes had all been delivered the day before and it appeared Lottie had already put them away for her.

With nothing else to do, she sat in solitude and waited for dinner. Solitude was no stranger to Madison. She'd spent nearly a year in that state after the bitter end of her relationship with Robbie. However, during that year, she'd always had her sisters nearby, and even if they hadn't been talking to her, at least she'd known they'd been there. Now she had no one near her, leading her to feel lonelier than ever before.

Dinner came soon enough and was an extraordinary feast she was certain she would have enjoyed had she been able to eat a bite. Nerves were getting the best of her. All day today, she'd been a bundle of nerves; first with the wedding, then with worries of the wedding night. There was no denying he intended to visit her room tonight. His whole body screamed it. From the look in his eyes to the knowing smile that touched his lips, she could tell he had plans to devour her as soon as he was done devouring his evening meal.

Knowing this only made her gut clench tighter.

"I think I shall retire now," she blurted out as she set her napkin on the table and stood to depart.

She hurried up the stairs and slipped into her room before exhaling a deep, nervous breath. Lottie was waiting for her in the corner and quickly helped her take off her dress before handing her a white cotton nightrail. Brooke had gone with her to the modiste to pick her trousseau. Of course Brooke, having a love match, suggested all sorts of filmy negligees. To appease Brooke, she'd ordered a few with the sole intent not to wear them. Ever. Brooke and her husband may enjoy bed play, but she was certain she and Benjamin would not find the activity nearly as enjoyable.

Dismissing Lottie, Madison blew out all the candles, leaving her room lit only by a little sliver of moonlight that peeked in through the break in the curtains. Shakily, her fingers went to the buttons at the top of her nightrail. As quickly as she could, she undid the first five before pulling her counterpane down and crawling into her bed. Once comfortable on the bed, she hiked the hem of her gown up to pool just above her waist, exposing the necessary parts for his easy accessibility. Content he'd not find her nightrail impeding him in any way, she raised her hands to her chest and repositioned her gaping bodice so the fabric was spread far enough to expose most of her breasts, but not far enough to show her nipples.

Resting her hands by her sides and reminding herself to take deep breaths, she heard him walking around in his room and knew it was only a matter of minutes before he would knock on her door.

Those few minutes felt like hours as she laid there in the poorly lit room waiting for his discreet knock. Finally when she thought she could take it no longer, the knock came.

"May I come in?" Benjamin asked, opening the door.

Her mouth went dry and her throat tightened in such a way that no matter how hard she tried, she couldn't form a single coherent noise.

Taking her silence as an affirmative, Benjamin started walking in her direction. He wore only a dark dressing gown as he moved silently across the carpet in his bare feet, holding a single candle in his right hand.

When he reached her side, he put the candle on table before turning his gaze to her. She watched as he swallowed before letting his eyes travel down her body. To fight the instinctive urge to cover herself from his gaze, she fisted her hands in the sheets, twisting them into tight coils with her fingers.

His gaze drifted past her nearly bared breasts and down to her waist before snapping back to her face. "What's the meaning of this?" he demanded angrily.

She stared at him in shock. What did he mean? What was the meaning of what? He'd obviously come to her room with the intent of bedding her, did he not recognize she was in ready position? "What do you mean?" she asked, swallowing convulsively.

"Why are you presenting yourself to me like a whore?" he spat.

Her eyes went wide and the burning heat of hot tears pricked the backs of her eyes. She opened her mouth to speak, but no words would come out. She mentally told herself to cover up, but her body must have been in too much shock because she didn't move. She couldn't move. She could do nothing more than just lie there and stare at him, her mouth fruitlessly trying to work.

His hard blue eyes bored into her, demanding an answer. An answer she couldn't give. At last, he shook his head, grabbed the counterpane and carelessly flung it over her. "That was a disgusting display, madam," he hissed with a snarl. "I never want to see it again, do you understand? That's how a whore presents herself to a man who uses her body with little regard for her. Is that what you want?"

Wide eyed, she continued to stare at him, unable to respond.

He shook his head. "Believe me when I tell you that no woman wants to be treated that way. Heed my warning; don't ever do anything like this again."

In silent shock, she watched him leave her side. The hard crashing slam of the door broke her shock and made room for mortification and hurt.

Under the covers, she righted her nightrail and waited until he stopped slamming things in his room. A few minutes later, she heard him slam another door, presumably the one to the hall. Against her better judgment, she crawled out of bed and bent down to look out the keyhole in her door. She could see him in the hallway. He was dressed in evening clothes. It appeared he was going out. She caught sight of another man in the hall, Benjamin's valet perhaps. He mumbled something she couldn't understand to the other man before dashing to the stairs. Less than a minute later, she heard the front door shut.

He'd left. He'd left her on their wedding night. Not only had he left her room after saying nasty things to her, he'd actually left the house on their wedding night to spend it with someone else.

Never one to be given to fits of vapors, Madison found it odd when one hot, salty tear slipped from her eye and left a wet path down her cheek before dropping off the edge of her chin, only to be absorbed by the thick carpet at her feet.

Chapter 4

"Where's my wife!" Benjamin demanded as soon as Townson stepped foot into his own study. Benjamin had gone out for a carriage ride around the city last night to think things through and when he'd returned ready to apologize, he'd found his wife missing.

"I don't know what you're talking about," Townson said evenly.

Benjamin crossed his arms so he wouldn't strangle the insolence right out of Townson. "Yes, you do. She's here. I know she is, and so do you," he said through clenched teeth.

"No, I don't." Townson took a seat behind his massive desk. "I have no idea what you're talking about. Madison isn't here."

"Where else would she be?" he snapped.

Townson gave him a dubious look. "I don't know, at your house perhaps. She is *your* wife, not mine. I may not be a genius but that makes perfect sense to me."

Benjamin ground his teeth. "Call *your* wife in here. I'd like to ask her a question."

"You have no business commanding me in my own house, Gateway. I'll not remind you of your manners again," he said, piercing him with his steely stare. "But since I have nothing to hide, I'll call Brooke in here and *I'll* ask her if she knows anything."

"Fine." Brooke would be more likely to be honest with her husband than him anyway.

Townson went to the hall for a minute before coming back to sit behind his desk. "Addams is on his way to get her. Don't worry, I told him not to mention your presence."

Benjamin nodded.

Silence filled the room as they waited for Brooke's grand entrance. Benjamin scanned Townson's impassive face. Was it possible he was telling the truth? Perhaps Madison wasn't here after all. It was dark when he'd gone into her room early this morning. She could have been completely buried under the covers, trying to hide in case he was looking for her.

His stomach tightened into an uncomfortable knot. He'd been wrong to be so hateful to her the night before. He should have just righted her gown and eased her fears, rather than let his mouth run away from him. She hadn't deserved his brutal words. She'd been nervous and uncertain. It had shown on her face for all to see.

The unmistakable sound of slippers sliding along the hardwood floor brought Benjamin back to the present and he sat in silence as the door opened and Brooke walked in.

"Andrew, I'm glad Addams found me. I need to talk to you—" Her voice died on the spot when she saw Benjamin sitting by her husband's desk.

Thankfully Townson was no fool, and after an extended blink, he looked back at his wife and drawled, "I believe you're not the only one. Go find Madison and send her down."

"No," Brooke said, shaking her head in defiance.

"No?" Townson echoed. "Brooke, listen to me. I know your intentions are good, but I cannot continue to harbor her here when her husband has every right to have her in his house."

"How can you speak of her as if she's a fugitive? He's the one in the wrong," she accused, pointing a finger at Benjamin.

"Darling, I know you don't like him, and that's your right, but the fact is, she's his wife. Legally, she cannot stay here," Townson responded quietly.

Brooke crossed her arms. "But—but—but he—"

"What she means to say is he doesn't want me," Madison said, walking into the room.

"That's not true," Benjamin said hastily, leaping from his seat.

"Really?" Madison inquired with cool reserve. "Then why did you go seek out the company of another on our wedding night?"

Every eye in the room turned toward Benjamin. Brooke's were full of accusations. Townson's full of fury and questions. And Madison's were full of hurt. Hurt he'd caused by his harsh words and careless actions. The hurt he saw in her eyes hit him harder than any punch Townson had ever thrown him, including the one that broke his nose.

"Answer her," Townson barked.

"I didn't," Benjamin bit off. "I went for a ride, nothing more. I didn't even speak to another person except Billings, my coachman." He was relying on her being able to read the honesty in his eyes because that was all he could offer her just now.

She shrugged. "It's of no consequence," she said flippantly. "Your nighttime activities are of no interest to me."

"Oh, yes, they are. You're to be a major part of those activities. Therefore, they'd better be of some interest to you."

She leveled a cold stare at him. "Do you honestly expect me to share your bed after last night?"

Heat crept up Benjamin's face. Surely she did not wish to discuss this in front of her family. Turning to their audience, he said, "Can you please excuse us?"

"Don't bother," Madison said while the earl and countess shook their heads, denying his request for them to leave the room. "Nothing more needs to be said on the subject. I shall stay here. That way you are free to come and go as you please without concerning me."

"Madison," he said tightly, "I'm sorry, but that option is not available to you."

Madison ignored him and turned toward her sister and brother-in-law. "Can I stay in my old room?"

Brooke nodded enthusiastically and Townson slowly shook his head. "I'm sorry, Madison, but I cannot let you stay here against his wishes."

"But—but—but," Madison sputtered.

"Grab your things and let's go," Benjamin said, coming to her side.

Madison shifted her eyes from her sister's direction to his. Her eyes were reminiscent of looking out a ship's porthole while sailing across the ocean during a storm. So much hurt and fury swirled together, Benjamin was almost hesitant to touch her elbow and steer her from the room.

Just as his fingers brushed her delicate elbow, her fiery eyes snapped back to Townson. "I'd like to collect my favor now, Andrew."

"Pardon?" Townson asked; his face was expressionless except for one quirked eyebrow.

Madison nervously licked her lips. "You owe me a favor. I'd like to collect."

"Madison, I don't mean to sound like a braggart, but I don't believe I'm in your debt."

"Yes, you are," she countered with a pointed glance at Brooke.

Townson looked to Brooke and then to Madison and back to Brooke once more before comprehension lit his features. "That was you?" he whispered.

Madison nodded.

Benjamin and Brooke exchanged confused looks before Brooke broke eye contact and turned to her husband. "What is she talking about?"

"Er...as it turns out..." he cleared his throat and fidgeted with his cravat for a second.

"Oh, please," Madison said, rolling her eyes. "Brooke, do you remember when Andrew showed up at Covent Garden?" When Brooke nodded once, Madison continued. "I'm the one who told him to go there."

"That was *you*?" Brooke squealed before turning to her husband.

"I thought you said it was a servant."

"I never said that. I said I *thought* it was a servant. That's completely different. She stood in the corner of my dark study wearing a hood."

"Sounds more like a woman of ill repute," Brooke quipped.

"I actually thought she was at first," Townson admitted.

"Seems to be a common misconception," Madison muttered, making a new wave of remorse wash over Benjamin.

Thankfully, her sister hadn't heard that remark because she said, "Wait, you went to welcome a prostitute into your bed before I'd even left the country?" Her voice had taken on a sharper edge and her eyes were boring into her husband in a way that made Benjamin glad he hadn't married her.

"No," Townson said defensively. "In fact, if you ask her, she'll tell you I wasn't overly welcoming."

"That's true. He wasn't. He actually was rather rude at first. And, if that's not convincing enough, he kept readjusting his dressing robe. As if I'd be interested in what it covered," she said sarcastically, rolling her eyes again.

"You'll never know," Brooke said smugly, making her husband shake his red face in embarrassment. "But why did you make me embarrass myself by going to his townhouse when you knew he'd be at the garden?"

Madison looked at her sister like she was a simpleton. "I didn't intend for you to embarrass yourself. I told him where we were going and assumed he'd try to catch you outside the house where he'd been sitting on a bench for the previous two days. When we went outside and I didn't see the lummox there, I worried he'd stayed home and decided to try a different tactic. I just wanted to make sure he wasn't home first. Sorry, I didn't know you were going to get a set down by the holier-than-thou 'butlering' footman."

Brooke laughed. "All is forgiven."

"Now that we've established who came to my house that night, that I had no intentions to be unfaithful to my wife, I was uncomfortable being dressed in only my dressing robe in the company of another woman *and* that Madison thinks I'm a simpleton who cannot follow simple directions," he flashed her a quick smile, "we need to discuss what will happen now. Madison, being the one I owe the favor to, what do you want me to do?"

"Let me stay here."

Townson let out a pent up breath. "Trust me when I say I'd love nothing more than to keep you safely here and away from him." He sliced a sharp glance at Benjamin. "But I cannot do that. Legally, I have no right. I can use physical force to temporarily keep you here, but he'll just take me to court."

"Fine. We'll let the courts decide it."

"The courts are going to decide you must return," Townson said gently. "Unless he seeks an annulment," he flickered a hopeful glance to Benjamin who shook his head in return, "you'll have to return to his house eventually."

"What if I seek an annulment? Could you help me petition?"

"I can help you petition, but it won't do any good. You won't be granted one unless he agrees to it. And since he won't, the courts will then force you back to his house."

Madison nodded and shot pleading eyes at Brooke and Townson. Benjamin almost felt sorry for her. So much so, that if he'd been an onlooker in this situation, he would have taken up in her defense and fought anyone who wanted to take her away against her will. But since he was the one that wanted her returned to his home, he just shot her a triumphant smile. "Let's go," he said quietly in her ear.

"Wait a second," Townson called, standing. "Ladies, why don't you go wait in Brooke's sitting room, we'll join you in a minute. I want to speak to Gateway alone."

Benjamin didn't want to let her go. He was ready to haul her out to his carriage right this minute. Unfortunately, Madison took Townson's suggestion to heart and scampered from the room faster than he could react.

"This had better be important," Benjamin ground out after Brooke followed her sister out.

"It is," Townson said, resuming his seat. "You realize she's scared of you, don't you?"

"Why?" Benjamin demanded, flabbergasted. "She has no reason to be weary of me. I've never done anything to her to make her scared."

Townson raised an eyebrow at him.

"All right, with the exception of last night, I've never done anything to affect her so," he allowed.

"Really?" Townson drawled. "You don't think she might fear you because you hired a man to ruin her sister and to make her flee the continent?"

Benjamin snorted. "You're the man I hired and she seems to trust you just fine."

"That's because I've proven myself to her. She's spent enough time in my company to know she has nothing to fear from me."

"What are you suggesting?" Benjamin asked, knowing he probably wasn't going to like the answer.

"Court her," Townson returned with a shrug. "She barely knows you. Let her stay here at night and take her out during the day so she can get to know you. Take her for a ride in the park or to the British Museum. Just spend time with her and let her learn she can trust you."

"Absolutely not," Benjamin said firmly. "She's my wife. I'll not have rumors circulating that we're living apart after only a day."

"What if we go to Rockhurst?"

Benjamin crossed his arms. "If I don't want her to live separate from me in London, what makes you think I'd let her go there?"

"We'll all go," Townson returned, folding his hands and resting them in his lap. "She can stay at Rockhurst and you can stay in the gamekeeper's cottage."

"I beg your pardon?" Why was he being made to stay in the

gamekeeper's cottage while his wife was to be a guest in a house that he knew had at least seventy-five bedchambers?

Townson shrugged. "I've just renovated it. What's the problem?"

"I don't care about how quaint the cottage is. I want to know why I'm to stay in it while Madison is kept somewhere else."

"Because it's what I'm offering," Townson said, his lips twitching.

"You're enjoying this too much." This was retribution for what he'd put Andrew through last spring when he'd hired him to ruin Brooke. Damn if life didn't have a way of sneaking up on a person and biting him in the arse.

"Anyway," Townson continued, "you'll be close enough to see her every day and nobody will be the wiser."

Benjamin ground his teeth. He wanted her back right now. He didn't want to court her. But what if Townson was right? They all knew she wouldn't be happy about going home with him today. Would she be more accepting of him if he played her game and courted her?

"Fine," he ground out at last. "But if one word of this leaks out, she'll be back in my home before nightfall. Am I clear?"

Townson nodded. "Would you like to tell her or shall I?

"I will."

Chapter 5

Madison blinked. That's all she could do. She'd once again been rendered speechless by her husband. He seemed to have a knack for this sort of thing.

He wanted to *court* her? Surely she'd misheard him. Was this the same man that was so cruel to her last night and demanded she return to his home at once, not more than ten minutes ago? "Could you please repeat that, sir? I'm quite certain I misheard," she said.

Now it was his turn to blink at her. Opening his eyes after an extended blink, he calmly said, "First, please don't call me 'sir'. I admit it's slightly better than Your Grace or Gateway, but not much. Yesterday you called me Benjamin, and I would like you to continue doing so. Second, you did not misunderstand. I would like to court you."

"Why?" she asked, uncertainty filling her voice. Why did the man want to court her? Couldn't he just leave her alone? Many couples lived in separate residences, why couldn't they?

Benjamin swallowed uncomfortably. "It's been brought to my attention that we didn't court, therefore, we don't know each other well enough. I would like to change that."

"Someone had to bring it to your attention that we don't know each other as well as other married couples," she said dubiously.

He sent her a lopsided smile. "I feel I know enough about you. But yes, someone had to remind me that you may not know enough about me to be comfortable with me."

Of course he felt he knew enough about her already. He, like most men, was willing to take anything in a skirt to bed regardless of his knowledge of, or feelings for, the woman. He'd just confirmed that suspicion for her for the second time now. "All right, I'm free every Wednesday afternoon from one to three thirty. Provided Brooke is available to chaperone, I'll plan to see you then."

"Not so fast," he said quickly. "I'm not some lapdog like another man we both know who lives here. I'll not be given a two and half hour window once a week. I'm compromising by agreeing to do this and not dragging you home right this minute. Therefore, you'll be doing some compromising, too."

Madison crossed her arms. "Name your terms, Benjamin."

"First, you must call off your watchdogs. I require our outings to be unchaperoned. Stop shaking your head. I'm playing your game, and you'll play mine. No chaperones. Second, I understand you like to participate in several charitable organizations. I'm not going to stop you from that, but you'll allow me at least two and a half hours each day."

"Absolutely not," she said sharply, shaking her head. "I can understand your concerns about Brooke and Andrew being overprotective, but I cannot give you so much time. That's more than any couple, married or not, spends together."

"That's doubtful," he said with a scoff. "I imagine one day you'll think two and a half hours with me is not long enough."

"Now, *that's* doubtful," she said, curling her lip in disgust at his innuendo. "Do those two and a half hours each day have to be exclusive?"

"No," he said quietly. "I'd like it to be. But we can include family activities as well. Just as long as half the time is exclusive, I'll be satisfied."

"Fine." At least part of the time, she'd have others present to help keep him pleasant. "Any other demands?"

"We'll be leaving for Rockhurst after lunch. I've already sent a note to direct Lottie to pack your things. You'll ride with me in my carriage," he announced, standing to leave.

Madison blinked at him again. They were going to Rockhurst? He was coming, too? And they were to be alone in his carriage for the ride? "All right," she replied in mock cheerfulness. She knew she'd have to ride with him anyway, but at least this way she got to pretend she agreed with him even if she didn't.

After that lone tear hit the plush carpet the night before, Madison had made up her mind not to let him play her the fool the way Robbie had. Granted, he was not nearly as close to her as Robbie had been, but that didn't mean he couldn't take what power he did have over her and use it against her.

Quite honestly, she was rather surprised when he showed up this morning. Not that she thought he wouldn't come, his pride demanded it. She was just shocked he'd discovered her missing so soon. How had he even known? Did he go searching for her? It really didn't matter, she thought dismissively.

Last night, she'd waited until well after the household had

become silent before making her quiet escape. Obviously not a stranger to donning a dark cloak and hiring a hack, she'd easily made it to Brooke's and used her key to let herself in before retiring to the bedchamber she'd previously occupied. It hadn't been until about thirty minutes before her husband had arrived that she'd first seen Brooke.

Brooke had once poured out her marital troubles to Madison, and she thought it only fair to dump her bucketful of woes out for Brooke to help her wade through them. She knew Brooke and Andrew couldn't hide her. She had no intention of asking them to until she saw the raw anger in Benjamin's eyes. She'd planned only to seek Brooke's counsel on the matter. She'd been brutally rejected once already in her life, and that was one time too many for her liking. She wasn't going to stand idle while it happened again.

She would have returned, she reminded herself again as she dug through her sewing box. She would have gone back to his house and been the perfect cool, impassive wife. But no, he had come and acted all high-handed, which only served to infuriate her more. Then she let her fear of him and his reputation for being the Dangerous Duke get in the way, and she'd acted like a ninny and pleaded for Andrew's help. Not that she minded the recent developments, mind you. She only wished she hadn't revealed her vulnerability to him.

The morning passed swiftly and Madison once again found herself facing a table full of food with no desire to eat. She excused herself and waited in the drawing room for Benjamin to show up.

Just as her hopes were rising that he'd changed his mind and wasn't coming, his carriage stopped out front.

~*~*~*~

Benjamin stared at her from across the carriage. She *was* scared of him. He could see that now. It all made sense. The uncertainty he thought he'd glimpsed in her eyes several times the day before, her loss of appetite at their wedding meal and then again at dinner, and of course, her trembling half-dressed body complete with tight hands fisting the sheets when he'd joined her in her room. He'd thought it was all bridal jitters, but now it was plain as day, she was terrified of him. What the blazes for? He'd never done anything to her to give her a reason to fear him.

"What has you scowling?" she asked suddenly.

"Nothing," he said, shaking his head. "I just don't understand you, that's all."

"What's there to understand? You made some unflattering remarks and then you left me. Was I not entitled to do the same?" Her voice was smooth and calm and held no hint of fear or uncertainty.

"I came back," he pointed out. "That's the difference."

"And I would have, too," she countered, plucking at a pleat in her skirt. "You just didn't give me the chance."

"I don't believe you."

She looked up at him with cool eyes. "Believe what you wish, but that's the truth. In case you don't know, allow me to inform you, I may come across as docile as a lamb, but I'm not. I'm not as outspoken about things as my sisters may be, but I do not take kindly to being treated poorly and I will not stand by while you make a mockery of me."

"I didn't make a mockery of you," he replied defensively.

She shrugged. "Benjamin, I don't care if you keep your wedding vows to me. I know you probably won't and that's fine. However, leaving me on our wedding night was the cruelest thing you could have done. I know now you didn't seek the company of another woman, but I didn't know it then."

He stared at her in disbelief. She didn't care if he kept his wedding vows? "Do you intend to keep yours?" he choked out, heart racing in anticipation of her answer.

"Of course," she said with a dim smile.

He felt a bit of relief at her answer, but not much. He reached up and rapped on the top of the carriage.

"What are you doing?" she asked, blinking at him

"Directing the coachman to take us home," he replied easily.

"No," she snapped, her eyes narrowing. "You promised to take me to Rockhurst. That's where we're going."

"You just said you would have come home anyway, so I see no reason to go to Rockhurst."

"That was before."

"Before what? Before I agreed to dance to your tune like some trained monkey in a traveling circus sideshow?" he asked sarcastically.

"Don't speak to me that way," she said evenly, belying the fire in her eyes. "I didn't ask you to court me. You suggested it and I agreed. To be honest, I think it's a rather good idea."

"You would," he retorted before leaning out of the carriage and yelling to Billings, his artifact of a coachman, to go on to Rockhurst.

"I don't know what that snide comment was about, but if you want to share my bed at any point in the future, you'd better woo me as if your life depends upon it."

He let out a harsh bark of laughter. "You make it sound like you have a choice."

"Don't I?" she countered with what he knew to be false bravado.

"No, actually you don't. I don't know the marriage rules in America, but I know them well enough for England. And since you married an Englishman, who happens to have an English title, in a ceremony that took place in England, thereby, making you English now, you shall have an English marriage. And in England, the husband does not get denied entry into his wife's bed."

"Is that so?" she returned haughtily.

"Yes, that's so," he mocked. "It's only due to my generosity that I have agreed to this madness and have not demanded my husbandly rights." He knew that was a cruel card to play, he just didn't care.

"Then perhaps you'd like to just flip my skirt up right here and now," she suggested coolly.

He clenched his jaw. "What did I tell you last night?"

"You said not to *act* like a whore," she corrected. "I'm not. I'm merely suggesting that since you seem so overly concerned about your 'husbandly rights', you should just take them now."

He ground his teeth. "I'm not 'overly concerned' as you put it. I'm just telling you that you cannot deny me your bed."

"Fine," she ground out, leaning forward. "I've accepted that. My acceptance is why I made my suggestion. However, if you want a wife who is *willing* to accept your presence in her bed, I suggest you mend your ways. Otherwise, you're going to be bedding a woman who is the equivalent of a cold fish. I may not be able to deny you entry, but I can deny you my willingness and participation."

He was at a loss for words. This was not how he'd envisioned the conversation. Not that he'd planned to force her, he'd never do that. He just wanted to explain it was only because he cared for her that he'd agreed to do this. Although her last words may not have come out exactly right, he understood their meaning. She'd let him use her body, but she wouldn't enjoy it; therefore, he wouldn't, either. He'd only enjoy sharing her bed if she was willing and participated in equal measure. He'd be lying if he said otherwise.

"I see I've made my point," she said evenly, breaking into his thoughts for a second.

She'd made her point all right. She'd made it loud and clear. And now it was up to him to determine how he was to win her affections.

Chapter 6

Madison tried in vain not to fidget in her seat. It was the one nervous tendency she had that was always guaranteed to give away her anxiety. Something about Benjamin unsettled her and put her off. She couldn't describe exactly what it was though. At least she'd been able to get through her speech with a bravado she hadn't felt. She'd doubted a few times he'd believed her, but now she could tell by the look carved into his marble face that he'd believed every word. Good. She didn't want him to think her a doormat he could walk all over. She'd have to allow him into her bed at some point, but at least she could put him off for a while as he tried to gain her approval.

The ride to Rockhust passed quickly enough. Madison kept herself occupied with sewing while her husband brooded in silence. They arrived just after dark to find a small supper had been prepared. Having not eaten more than a handful of crumbs in two days, Madison had to remind herself not to act the part of a glutton. She could raid the kitchen later.

After dinner, the uncomfortable situation intensified. It was no secret there were hard feelings between her husband and Brooke and Andrew. And it was also no secret who was the cause of all those hard feelings: Benjamin.

"Perhaps we should all retire," Brooke said tentatively, swaying back and forth while holding Nathan, her three month old son, trying to get him to sleep.

"I agree," Andrew added, shooting a pointed look at Benjamin.

Relieved she hadn't had to be the one to suggest it; she gave an exaggerated yawn and said, "I'm exhausted. I think I just might sleep 'til noon."

Brooke nearly stopped mid-sway and made a little high pitched urp sound in her throat before resuming her sway, while Andrew bent his head to study the floor, presumably to hide his grin. These two may know she was an early riser, but Benjamin didn't. If she could just slip out before he awoke, she could hide from him all morning.

"Let's be off before I have to carry you to bed, then," Benjamin said lightly, offering her his arm.

Madison lightly placed her fingers next to his elbow and allowed him to walk her to the end of the hall. "I know the way from here," she said, loosening her grip on his arm.

His free hand came to settle on top of her hand that was trying to break free, keeping it firmly on his arm. "I'm sure you do. All the same, I'll escort you there."

"There's no need. It will take you far longer to get to the gamekeeper's cottage than it will for me to get to my room. Perhaps you should head there before all the wild animals come out for the night."

He gave her a half smile. "I appreciate your concern for my safety and wellbeing. However, I assure you, if there are wild animals out there looking for dinner, which I'm certain there are not, they're already out, so an extra ten minutes will not make a whit of difference. And, if there are wild animals out there looking for dinner, which as I already said, I'm sure there are not, I will gladly brave them for the honor of walking you to your room. Now, which way is it?"

Madison shook her head. The man was determined, she'd give him that. "To the right, then to the left, then up the stairs, then take the west hall until it splits, then go north until it dead-ends, then go left and my room is the third door on the right," she said with a bright smile. Just see him bungle those directions.

But he didn't. He led her straight to her room. "You do know it would have been easier if at the top of the stairs we'd just gone left, then taken the first right, don't you?" he asked with a teasing smile.

"I know."

"Do you?" he asked, leaning closer to her.

She shifted positions so her back was against her door and she was looking at him directly. "Yes, I just hoped you'd get lost and give up," she admitted with a teasing smile of her own.

"I don't think that's what it was," he mused aloud, cocking his head in feigned contemplation. "I think you wanted to spend more time with me."

She swallowed.

"I think you weren't ready for me to leave yet," he continued. "I think you enjoy my company more than you want to admit. I think you'd also like to enjoy my company further by allowing me into your room…"

She opened her mouth to deny his charge.

"…but I'm not going to come in. No, I think I shall go examine the renovated gamekeeper's cottage instead."

She glared daggers at him. He was far too arrogant.

"Perhaps we should strike a compromise," he said with mock deliberation. "What do you say we both indulge our inner desires and settle for a goodnight kiss, hmm?"

She stared at the cocky man. He honestly thought to accuse her of practically begging him to stay for a night of heated passion and then he suggests a kiss to tide her over. He was cracked. "I think not," she said.

"Why not? Are you afraid you won't be able to stop at one?" he taunted, a corner of his mouth tipping up.

Fighting the urge to slap the smug look off his face, she went up on her toes and pressed a quick peck against his handsome, hair bristled cheek before moving back against the door. She thought he'd frown and demand she kiss him again, on the lips this time. But instead, she noticed his face broke out into a wide grin like she'd seen at their wedding and he said, "That'll do."

She blinked at him. That wasn't expected. What was he up to?

"Good night, Madison," he said softly before leaning over and brushing a warm kiss over her brow.

Too stunned to say anything in return, she watched as he walked away whistling. When her mind was finally able to form a rational thought, she reached for the door handle and found it was already opened. He must have turned it for her when he leaned in for the kiss, she thought, bringing her cool fingers to where her skin still felt like it was on fire from his kiss.

~*~*~*~

Benjamin felt wealthier than a king as he walked away from Madison. She'd kissed him. It may not have been on the lips. It may not have been out of love and adoration. It may not have been because of any great passion she felt for him. It may have only been to rid her of his presence. But it didn't matter. She'd kissed him. And he'd liked it.

He liked that he could still feel the scorching heat of her lips on his cheek branding him far more than if she'd slapped him. He liked that she'd had the spunk to act that way with him. She could have denied his request completely or just stood there rigidly while he pressed his lips to her. Instead, she'd completely surprised him with her cheeky peck on his cheek.

Downstairs, he was walking out of the house when he caught sight of Townson holding his little boy against his shoulder. "Thank you," Benjamin said softly, trying not to wake the baby.

"You're welcome," Townson said quietly, seeming to understand what Benjamin was thanking him for. "Would you care to sit a minute?"

He really didn't want to. He'd rather be alone planning his next move. And yet, he found himself taking a seat across from Townson and his sleeping son. How fortunate he was, and he probably didn't even know it, Benjamin thought. To wake up every morning next to the one you love and have a child with her. A wave of jealousy similar to the one he'd experienced more than fifteen years ago bubbled inside him.

He'd once let his jealously of Townson get the better of him and no good had come of it. The two shared a common relation (of sorts): Townson's mother. Lizzie, the dowager countess, raised both of them. She raised Andrew as her son, he was, and him as her brother, he wasn't. Through sloppy genealogy and several sordid affairs, Benjamin and Elizabeth Black shared a common connection: the previous Duke of Gateway. When the old duke was a green lad, he had a liaison with a maid that resulted in Lizzie's conception. Fortunately for Lizzie, the current duke at that time (Benjamin's ostensible grandfather) took her in as a ward against the wishes of everyone else in the family.

Before she came of age to be introduced to society, which her grandfather fully intended to do, the man died, leaving her a ward to the subsequent duke, her newly married biological father. Her father had been forced to make a match for her in order to receive his funds. So he matched her with the first wastrel who asked: Thomas Black, the former Lord Townson.

Immediately after Lizzie and Thomas's marriage, the new duchess inadvertently exposed Lizzie's bastardy, thus causing Thomas to exile his breeding countess to Essex. Lizzie would have spent the rest of her days in the country raising Andrew and forgetting all about her previous ties if not for Benjamin's mother's adultery with a footman and presenting her husband with an undeniable cuckoo. The duke had no choice but to accept Benjamin legally, but refused to accept him otherwise. Instead, after his wife ran off with her lover to Italy, he contacted Lizzie and asked her to raise Benjamin in Essex. With no other source of income, she agreed and Benjamin was bundled off to Essex.

Benjamin's and Andrew's respective fathers, the duke and the old earl, had demanded they not share company past age five. Consequently, Benjamin went to live with his nanny and Lizzie visited him every afternoon. It really was rather confusing and convoluted, but when one doesn't know any different, one grows accustomed to the idea.

Benjamin knew that Lizzie, who as Andrew once so eloquently put it, was neither his sister of blood nor paper, had a son and since he didn't have a mother himself, jealous feelings formed.

Those jealous feelings came to the forefront when they began school and Lizzie informed him he couldn't acknowledge her in public. He'd sat in silence as he watched the woman he'd grown to love hug and kiss Andrew goodbye, not doing more than sending him a small glance. Jealousy gave way to bitterness that night and in all his thirteen year old wisdom, he'd mentioned rumors about Andrew's parentage. Word quickly spread and as Benjamin predicted, Andrew was the outcast at school. However, what he hadn't counted on was the bullying to become as bad as it had. With some quick thinking and skillful manipulation, Benjamin was able to offer Andrew protection from a disaster he'd thoughtlessly created.

Benjamin was fairly certain that to this day Andrew didn't know Benjamin was the one behind the initial rumors. He'd like to keep it that way, too. He'd created enough problems with his petulant jealousy and any mention of it now would only cause more problems that neither of them needed. However, that didn't help Benjamin's current jealous state. It only helped to remind him to think before he acted.

"What are your plans?" Townson asked, bringing him out of his fog.

"You mean with Madison?"

Townson nodded.

Benjamin blinked. He'd once had a similar conversation with Townson, except the roles had been reversed. "I'm not sure yet."

"Would you like some advice?" Townson asked, repositioning Nathan in his arms.

"Since the general consensus around here is that you're the best husband there ever was, please," Benjamin returned somewhat sarcastically.

Townson grinned. "With you as my competition, I'm a certainty."

"Thank you for the reminder," Benjamin returned dryly.

"You're welcome. Now, what I was going to suggest is to take it easy with her. She's not delicate necessarily, but she's not very trusting, either. That horse's arse she was courted by in America was one of the worst kinds."

"I know," Benjamin told him solemnly. He remembered his month in Robbie's company; that was bad enough, who knows how much worse he'd gotten in five year's time.

"You do?" Townson asked, not just with his voice, but with his eyes, too.

"Yes," Benjamin confirmed. He'd bet he knew more of her situation with Robbie than Townson did. He'd received several rather explicitly detailed letters from Robbie describing his and Madison's courtship.

"All right," Townson said quietly. "Just treat her right, please."

"I will," Benjamin vowed, standing up to take his leave. "I know my actions in the past haven't always been respectable, but I promise I will do right by her."

"See that you do," Townson said gruffly, his concern for his sister-in-law's happiness plain as day in his eyes.

Chapter 7

Benjamin slept a whole fifteen minutes before it was time to get up. He'd spent most of the night thinking of ways to woo his wife. Love matches were rare and elusive, but he couldn't help wanting one. The problem was convincing his wife she wanted one, too. What a cruel twist of fate, he thought, rolling out of bed. Most times it was women who longed for love matches and tried to get their husbands to love them, and yet, not his wife. No, his wife seemed to have as much interest in love as he did in hair ribbons, which, just to clarify, wasn't much.

After he dressed and broke his fast alone in Rockhurst's giant breakfast room, he decided to go to Bath. He'd never been a welcome guest at Rockhurst, and it felt uncomfortable roaming the halls in search of his wife when he was clearly unwanted. To be fair, he'd told her he wouldn't impose on her charitable activities, which seemed to be what she was up to this morning. He'd walked in and found Madison and her younger sister, Liberty, with a few other ladies sewing clothes for the needy.

In her usual polite way, she'd sweetly offered to teach him how to sew. And in his usual not-interested-in-female-pursuits way, just as sweetly declined and informed her he'd be back for lunch and she'd be spending the afternoon with him.

For now, he'd go to Bath. He remembered from his brief time in America that she'd liked to paint. He'd caught Brooke on her way up to the nursery, and after he'd nearly beat Madison's whereabouts out of her, he'd casually asked if Madison needed any painting supplies. Brooke then informed him she hadn't seen Madison paint since before they'd left New York. Thus, he was on his way to buy painting supplies for her.

The selection in London would be better, but surely he could gather enough of the basics in Bath to occupy her for now.

It was a perfect plan, he mused as he rode Greer, his stallion, to Bath. She could teach him how to paint this afternoon. Not that it would do any good; he was abysmal at the hobby. But that wouldn't matter. They'd be spending time together doing something she liked. And if he proved to be as bad of an artist as he imagined, he'd pose for her. He liked that idea even better. If he posed for her, she'd have to touch his body to position him perfectly for her portrait. Perhaps he'd even suggest she paint him nude.

He shifted uncomfortably in his saddle. He better put a cap on these lusty thoughts before his trousers got any tighter.

At a little shop in Bath, he bought every painting supply he could find. With his purchases in hand—literally—he ran into his other brother-in-law—once again, literally. "Sorry, Paul," he called.

"It's all right." Paul ducked his head so he wouldn't get the glass poked out of his spectacle with the corner of a very large canvas. "Can I help you?"

"No, I don't think so." Benjamin laid half of his canvases across the saddle then stuffed the smaller packages into his saddle bag.

"I didn't realize you lived so close," Paul mused.

"I don't. I—we're visiting Brooke and Townson."

"Are you on your way to Rockhurst, then?" Paul asked, catching the stack of canvases before the wind blew them to the ground.

"Thank you," Benjamin said, taking the canvases back. "Yes, I'm on my way back. We're to have lunch there."

"I'm headed that way, too. Why don't I help you manage those canvases on the way?"

Benjamin shot him a slight smile. "Thank you. It seems I bought more than I can hold."

Paul nodded. "I understand better than anybody what it's like trying to win the affections of one of the Banks sisters."

"You have no idea," Benjamin muttered, shaking his head.

"I bet I do," Paul stated flatly, jumping on his horse. He took the three large canvases from Benjamin, leaving him to juggle only the seven smaller ones. "On more than one occasion, I've thought Andrew got off easy. He may have been the only one who got married due to a true scandal, but he also never had to do much work to gain his wife's affections."

"Amen, Preacher," Benjamin cheered as he got on his horse. "That man should be kissing my feet."

"Would you really want him to?" Paul teased, curling his lip.

"Not really." He guided his horse down the lane. "But if he'd encourage his sister-in-law to, I'd be obliged."

Paul chuckled. "Surely, you'd rather she not kiss your feet though," he said, waggling his bows.

"No, there are many other places I'd prefer. But I'd be happy

with her kissing me anywhere at this point, feet notwithstanding."
He'd let her kiss his feet if that's where she was willing to kiss him,
though he seriously doubted that was the case.

"I've only one piece of advice. Gaining her approval might be
difficult, but you'll be glad you did," Paul told him with a genuine
smile.

"I know," Benjamin said before he could stop himself.

Paul turned his curious, bespectacled green eyes on him, and
Benjamin pretended to take a keen interest in the scenery. He didn't
care to reveal that he'd spent the past six years in love with a woman
to whom he'd barely spoken.

Not wanting Madison to see her present until after lunch, he let
Paul go inside Rockhurst while he dropped off the painting materials
in his cottage before joining everyone for lunch.

Benjamin felt like an outsider walking through the halls and
found the dining room only by the noise floating down the hall leading
him there. He stepped in and saw everyone was already assembled.
They were milling around the far end of the room, talking and waiting
for him before taking their seats. Nobody was looking in his direction
as he took his time walking the length of the room.

The room had to be forty feet long and about half as wide, and
right in the center was a little oval table that had exactly six chairs
and six place settings. Benjamin had never seen such small dining
accommodations. Perhaps Townson had once been more impoverished
than he'd thought.

Approaching the group, Townson's voice floated to his ears.
"Now, ladies, you'll each be seated with your husbands for this meal.
The three of you together almost proved to be fatal last time," he said
with mock reproof. "Especially you," he added with a pointed look to
Madison that made Brooke and Liberty burst into giggles and Madison
do a perfect curtsy.

"See, I told you she was proud of herself," Liberty told her
husband. "He didn't believe me when I told him."

"No, what I didn't believe was that Andrew complimented her
after he nearly choked to death," Paul corrected. "I fully believed she
was proud she'd caused such an event."

"Oh really? I specifically remember you saying, 'Madison said
that?'" she said, doing her best imitation of her husband's voice. "Then
you burst into howls of laughter."

"That had nothing to do with me doubting she was proud she'd
said it," Paul gently countered with a secret smile for his wife. "At that
time, I was just shocked she'd said it at the table. You forget, before
we married, I spent a lot more time in her company than yours. Trust
me; I've borne witness to many shocking statements that have passed
her lips."

Feeling like he was eavesdropping on a conversation he was
present for, Benjamin asked, "What did she say?"

Madison visibly tensed. Liberty bit her lip. Brooke developed a
curious fascination in the flatware. Andrew tried not to snicker; and

Paul, being a minister, had the hardest time of them all. He smiled and said, "I'd tell you, but you'd never believe it."

"Shall we sit," Brooke said suddenly with a bright smile.

Benjamin felt even more the outsider as he took his seat next to Madison. He knew every family had their inside jests, but why couldn't they share them with him? He was part of the family now, wasn't he? Would it always feel this way, he wondered, looking at his wife. Would he always be the outsider? The one who merely had to walk into the room and all fun and conversation died on the spot.

"Am I interrupting anything?" asked a familiar voice from the hallway, eliciting six identical answers of: "No!"

"Come in, Mother," Townson said, getting out of his chair. "Take my seat, and I'll get Stevens to get another setting."

Lizzie greeted each one of them before taking the empty seat next to Brooke. "I see you've been doing a good job taking care of two of my boys."

Benjamin fought to keep a scowl off his face at being referred to as one of her two boys that Brooke was taking care of, then he remembered Nathan and realized Lizzie was complimenting Brooke on being a wonderful wife and mother.

"I'd be lying if I didn't admit one's easier to keep satisfied than the other," Brooke said with a faint smile.

"I have a feeling I know to whom you refer," Lizzie said, smiling. "I suppose I was fortunate in that regard. I may have had two little boys to tend, but at least my stallion—and I don't mean that as a compliment—had exited the stable."

Benjamin shook his head. Leave it to Lizzie to act uncouth at the table. She'd always been blunt and somewhat brutally honest. That's one of the things that made their relationship so strong. They both had that characteristic. Neither gave a hang how Society viewed their words or actions.

"Nicely put, Mother," Andrew said dryly, coming back into the room with an empty chair. A servant was right behind him, holding the pieces for another place setting.

"Actually, that was rather nicely put," Lizzie argued.

"Yes, it was actually a better description than she told me," Liberty added.

"And me," Brooke commented.

"And me," Madison said with a shudder, catching Benjamin's attention. Was that at the root of her apprehension? He'd have to ask her about it later.

"For goodness' sake, Mother," Andrew burst out in mock agitation. "It's a miracle Brooke and Liberty consummated their marriages after hearing your Tales of the Terrible Townson's Bedchamber."

"To be fair, Andrew, I was a little late on meeting Brooke before the consummation," Lizzie countered. "However, I understand the conversation would have done little good for her anyway."

"What is that supposed to mean?" Andrew demanded irritably.

"It was a compliment," Lizzie said defensively. "You apparently did a satisfactory job the first time; which is a good thing, since she didn't conceive on your wedding night."

Andrew put his fork down with a sharp clip. "We're not discussing this any further."

"I believe the appropriate response should have been, 'Thank you, Mother'," she said with a smile. "However, I long ago gave up on instilling manners in you. That's Brooke's responsibility, now." She turned to Brooke. "Good luck, dear. You'll need it." Then she flashed a smile in the direction of Benjamin and Madison. "And when will you two be giving me my next grandchild?"

"Grandchild?" Madison asked before Benjamin could comment.

"I may not be his mother, or his sister for that matter, but I consider myself the closest thing he has to a mother. So yes, I'd consider his child in the same category as Andrew's," Lizzie explained.

Benjamin watched Madison nod her understanding. Why did she look so unsettled? Did she not want a baby? Or was it *his* baby she didn't want?

Thankfully, Lizzie turned her baby talk attention to Liberty, who was already expecting, and left him and Madison to eat in silence.

Benjamin's excitement at spending the afternoon alone with Madison abruptly crashed, when Lizzie invited Madison to go visit her cottage for the afternoon. Madison sent him an uncertain glance that he couldn't interpret. Extracting a promise that she'd spend the whole day with him tomorrow, he let her go and spent the rest of the day in solitude.

Chapter 8

Madison grabbed her sketchpad along with two quills and went for a walk. Being early morning, the August sun hadn't made it unbearable to be outside yet. She found the well walked path she knew led to a stream. She'd promised she'd spend the whole day with Benjamin, and she intended to, after she had a little time to think.

She'd actually been disappointed when she hadn't gotten a chance to spend time with him the previous day. Not that she hadn't enjoyed Elizabeth's company, because she had, but she would have preferred Benjamin's. Eventually they'd have to go home together. She'd have to be his wife and live in his house, and the sooner she got to know him, the easier it would be.

Stripping off her slippers and stockings, she put her feet into the cool water and sat on the grassy edge. This part of the stream was an optical illusion, if there ever was one. The water was so clear it looked like it was no more than ankle deep. However, one only made that assumption once, she'd learned. The first time she'd come to sit here, she'd scooted off the steep embankment, thinking to stand in the water. Instead, she scooted so far forward trying to touch the rocks, she'd slipped and ended up in water up to her neck. Groping the high sides, she had to walk a good twenty feet before finding part of the embankment that sloped enough for her to climb up.

Picking up her quill and pad, she placed them on her lap and started sketching. It had been a while since she'd sketched. Six years to be exact. And even then, it had only been for a very brief time. Of course she'd drawn outlines of figures when she'd painted, but not in near as much detail as she was using today. Today, she was capturing every single detail, all the lines, slopes, planes, ridges, and curves of her feet. Yes, her feet! Goodness, what had her life come to that she was sneaking off to sit by a stream and sketch her feet?

Seeing the feet on the paper looked identical to the two that were currently in the water, she added some rocks around them then drew the current view of her skirt-covered legs. Still not satisfied she'd made the best use of her piece of paper, she drew a big rectangle that looked like her drawing pad on top of her skirt. On the piece of paper in the sketch, she drew a smaller version of her feet-in-water sketch before adding one hand holding the pad and the other a quill. Pausing from her fifteen minutes of hard work, she cocked her head to the side and studied the image. As ridiculous as it was to draw one's own feet, she had to admit the images were actually quite good.

Fingers in ready position to rip the page off and make a ball of it, a low voice whispered in her ear, "Is there any room in that sketch for another pair?"

Her heart almost stopped. And it had nothing to do with the fact that Benjamin had just crept up on her and very nearly scared the wits out of her. No, it was a combination of his mere presence, scent, closeness and the velvety sound of his voice. "That depends," she teased.

"On what?" he asked, taking a seat next to her. He took off his coat and cravat before bringing his hands down to his boot laces.

"On how handsome your feet are, of course," she said lightly, flashing him a smile.

"I won't lie," he said, removing one boot. "Mine aren't grand; certainly not worthy of a picture. But," he paused to take off the other boot, "they won't give you nightmares, either." He yanked off his stockings and shoved them into his boots before plunking his feet into the water right next to hers.

Together they stared down at their feet. Hers were small and slender, his long and wide. His toes were long and blunt, curling down a little at the ends. Hers were short and petite with pink ends. Even though they were bigger, his would be much easier to draw with all the hard lines and edges. A vein that ran from his ankle to his toes was distinctly visible and his arch was a perfect curve.

"Are they worthy of your ink and paper?" Benjamin asked, making her blush. He'd just caught her staring at his feet!

"As you said, they're not great, but I won't be having nightmares, either," she said simply with a shy, embarrassed smile. "Actually, they're too big."

"Too big?" He looked down at his feet, frowning. "If they were as small as yours, I'd never stay upright."

She laughed. "No, I mean there's not enough room on the paper. I'd have to make them smaller than mine to get them to fit. See?" She turned the paper toward him so he could see how little room there was on the paper for her to add his feet.

"Pity," he said, smiling. "You'll just have to start over, then."

She flipped to the next page. "All right, hold still."

"How long have you been sketching?" Benjamin asked as she went about sketching.

"For only about fifteen or twenty minutes before you walked up. I was going to spend the day with you, I promise," she said, glancing up at him.

He waved a hand dismissively. "It's all right. We are spending the day together. But I meant how long, as in days, weeks, months, years, have you been sketching?"

"Not long. I started about six years ago, but it was a short-lived endeavor. Today was the first time since then." She scratched her quill on the paper a few seconds. "You're going to have to stop kicking your feet, Your Grace," she said, sending him a governess-type stare.

"Did you sketch feet back then, too?" he asked with a smile she could hear instead of see.

"No," she said laughingly. "Actually until today, I was a virgin foot sketcher, I'm afraid."

He chuckled. "What's that little smile about, Madison?"

She looked up at him. "What do you mean?"

"I mean, even though your head was bent and some of your hair was falling forward shielding your face, I could see you smiling. And I know better than to think you're laughing at your own joke," he said, inching a little closer to her side.

"Your feet," she said simply, turning back to her paper.

"My feet?" he asked dubiously. "What's so humorous about them? They're just feet, everyone has a set."

"I know," she said, shrugging. "It's just your toes are odd, that's all."

"My toes?" he repeated, frowning down at his toes. "What's wrong with them? There are five of them on each foot. They're all intact. And none of them have black toenails. What do you find funny about them?"

"Nothing," she said evasively. "I wasn't laughing at them. I was just smiling."

"Why?" he demanded, exasperated.

"Your second toe," she pointed down at the toe next to the big one, "is a little longer than the first one."

"So? What's wrong with that?"

"Nothing," she said, choking on a giggle. "I didn't say anything was wrong with it." Who knew he'd be so fun to bait?

"Then why are you laughing about it?"

"I already told you, I wasn't laughing," she repeated, looking up into his deep blue eyes. "I was just smiling. There's a difference."

"All right," he allowed. "And why are you smiling?"

"As I said, your second toe is slightly longer than your first."

"And?" he prompted.

She shrugged. "And nothing."

He cocked his head and stared at her curiously.

"Oh, all right, I'll tell you," she said, putting her quill down and turning to look at him. "There was a half-Indian woman that lived down the street from us in Brooklyn and she used to tell us that her tribe had some legend concerning people who had a longer second toe."

"And?" he prompted again.

"She seemed convinced the length of the second toe compared to the first had a direct correlation with one's intelligence," she said and tried not to laugh at his flabbergasted expression.

"And?" he prompted once again.

"Oh, you want to know if the legend is in your favor or not?"

He rolled his eyes playfully. "And?"

"I shall not tell you," she exclaimed and burst into peals of laughter when his arm snaked around her waist and brought her with him as he fell backwards onto the soft grass to lie side by side.

Turning his face to her as they lay in the grass with their feet still together in the water, he said, "That is the most ridiculous thing I've ever heard. Did this woman really believe it?"

"No," Madison said, shaking her head wildly. "But I think that was only because the legend wasn't in her favor."

Benjamin laughed. His hand was still around her waist and he gently pulled her closer to him. "I don't care about any legend," he said softly. "I already know I'm the smartest man that ever lived."

"Mighty cocksure, aren't you?" she teased. From what she could tell, every man thought he was the smartest man in creation.

"You bet I am," he said solemnly. "I'm the one who got to marry you."

She knit her brows. "What does that have to do with intelligence?"

"I could have stayed hidden in that doorway, you know."

She smiled. "Yes, I know. You also could have just told me your identity thirty seconds earlier. Had you done so, I would have scrambled down that hall so fast you would have thought the flames of hell were nipping my heels."

He shook his head and laughed. "You're not really scared of me, are you?"

"Not scared, just unsure."

"Why?" He brought his hand up to caress her cheek as he pushed a blonde ringlet away from her face.

She closed her eyes. "Why not?" she countered.

"I don't think I've ever done anything to give you reason to be scared or uncertain of me. I know I've done some bad things to your family. But not you, never you."

She brought her hand up to settle on his wrist, holding his hand where it rested on her cheek. Beneath her fingers, she could feel the strong rhythm of his blood as is passed through his body. "I'm trying," she whispered at last. "I've been hurt before, Benjamin."

"I know," he whispered against her hair, right before he pressed a soft kiss to her temple.

She doubted he did know, but it felt good all the same to have him be so tender with her.

They lay in the grass in their quiet, gentle embrace while several minutes passed, each left to their own thoughts. While she couldn't claim to be a mind reader, she assumed by the furrow of his brow that Benjamin was lost in deep contemplation about something. She wouldn't dare ask him what it was because she didn't want to be forced to share what she was thinking.

A little *Ker plunk* sound from the water startled them both and brought her out of her moment. Together, they sat up and looked to where their feet were still in the water.

"Look, there's a fish," Madison said, pointing to a bluish green fish that was swimming away.

"Sure is," Benjamin agreed. "He's a fast swimmer, isn't he?"

Madison nodded. "Fish are so lucky, swimming comes naturally to them."

"I should hope so," he said dryly, giving her a look like she'd just said the stupidest thing ever, which she had.

"What I meant was that fish are naturally good swimmers, whereas some other beings, myself included, are not," she clarified.

He cocked his head to the side in interest. "You don't know how to swim?"

Madison shook her head. "No. The only body of water close to us in New York was the Hudson River. And to be frank, you couldn't pay me to willingly step foot in that cesspool."

Benjamin gave her a curious look before shaking his head. "Would you like me to teach you to swim?"

"Would you?" she asked, grinning at him like an idiot. She'd always wanted to learn to swim.

He grinned in return. "Of course, take off your gown."

Chapter 9

"Absolutely not," Madison shrieked, scrambling off the embankment they'd been sharing. "If you think after only a handful of conversations and one tender moment with you, I'm going to change my mind and strip naked in front of you, you're daft."

"I didn't ask you to strip naked," Benjamin countered, getting up to stand next to her. "You can wear your chemise."

She turned her eyes up to the sky and let out an exaggerated sigh. "Yes, because that serves as an excellent covering," she said sarcastically. "Once it gets wet, it becomes transparent," she further explained in a way a tutor would speak to his pupil.

"You'll be submerged in water by then, so what will it matter?" he countered. For a woman who wanted to learn to swim, she was sure full of complaints.

"And what will you wear?"

Nothing. "My smalls." He watched her as she shifted from one foot to the other and made little clicking noises with her nails. "You've nothing to fear, I'm not going to do anything to you."

She made eye contact with his chest. She was obviously struggling with whether or not to trust him.

"Madison," he said softly, bending his knees so his head would be lower and he could look into her eyes.

She smiled tentatively at his gesture. "It's not you. I have a hard time trusting men," she said in a voice that was barely audible.

"You seem to trust Townson just fine." His tone held more bitterness than he'd intended.

"I'm sorry," she whispered. "but I don't know you very well."

"And how do you propose to get to know me if you refuse to do anything but put your feet in the water next to mine and sit next to me from time to time?" he asked, agitated. Why could she trust Townson but not him? He wasn't even as scary looking as Townson. That man was built like a Clydesdale.

"You're right," she conceded. "I'll remove my gown."

Benjamin grinned at her. "Do you need any help?"

"No. I'll just go behind the bushes if you don't mind."

He did mind, but he wasn't going to say anything. If it made her feel better to go behind a few paltry plants in order to remove her gown, then so be it. "All right, I'll get in the water and wait for you."

It took him less than fifteen seconds to strip to his smalls and get into the water. Thankfully the water was blessedly cool, helping to suppress his ardor. It wouldn't do for her to get too close to him and be able to feel his reaction to her.

Timidly, she walked toward him wearing only her chemise. Suddenly he didn't think the water was cool enough. Her chemise hung loosely on her shoulders by two thin strips of lace edged fabric. The front had a low swoop, offering him a generous view of the tops of her breasts. He was expecting it to fall around or below her knees, but instead it only came to mid-thigh, exposing the creamy curves of her legs. She crossed her arms nervously under her breasts and fidgeted while he swept her with his eyes.

Realizing that he was causing her undue discomfort, he murmured a quick apology then said, "You have two choices. You can come in down that muddy slope over there," he pointed to a spot about thirty yards away where a muddied rocky slope led to the water, "or you can jump in from there."

"Jump in?" she gasped. "Have you forgotten I don't know how to swim? I can't just jump in."

"Sure you can. I'll catch you," he said with a grin. "Just jump right here," he pointed to the water in front of him, "and I'll catch you." He opened his arms wide and waited for her.

She hesitated only for a second before walking to the edge and with a small noise of trepidation, jumped straight into his waiting arms.

"Good job." He slowly lowered her down the rest of the way into the water until her feet were on the rocks. "It's rather deep right here. Let's move over a bit where it won't be so deep."

"Thank you. I don't like how deep it is, either. Last time I was in here, I thought I might drown."

"I thought you said you hadn't been swimming before," Benjamin said, carrying her to a shallower spot.

"I haven't. But that doesn't mean I haven't accidentally found myself in the water. It was so clear I believed the water to be shallower than it was and before I knew it, I was in up to my neck because I wanted to put my feet on the rocks."

"Were you alone?" he asked, setting her down in a place that was no deeper than her waist.

"Yes," she said, nodding.

He didn't like the sound of that. She could have easily drowned and nobody would have known it. "In that case, I'm not letting you out of this water until I'm satisfied with your swimming skills."

She shot him a laughing smile. "We might die here, you know."

"Nonsense, and if it does take that long for you to learn to swim, I'll die a happy man."

She looked at him curiously. "And why is that?"

"Because I'll die with you," he answered, not caring if he sounded like a lovesick imbecile.

"And you claimed Andrew was the one led around by his genitals."

"I didn't say that to get you to lift your skirt," he said slowly. "You're my wife. I like being around you. Is it so wrong for me to enjoy your company?"

"No," she said, shaking her head. "I rather enjoy yours just now, too."

He grinned. It positively thrilled him that she would admit to enjoying his company. "All right, let's swim. First, lie down on your back." He moved to her side, and with one arm wrapped around her shoulders, he pulled her backwards toward the water. "You're all right. I've got you. Both my arms are under you, you're not going to sink. Just relax. Now, we need to see if you sink or float."

"You just said you wouldn't let me sink," she panicked, trying desperately to put her feet back on the bottom.

"Hold still," he commanded gently as he held her firmly so she couldn't get up. "I'm not going to let you drown, Madison. Trust me. Please." He looked into her eyes to let her see he meant his words. "I'm just going to relax my hold on you a little to see if your body stays on top of the water or starts to go under. Most people float, but some don't. If you are a sinker, you'll have to work a little harder when you swim."

"Great," she muttered, "with my luck, I'll sink like a bag of bricks."

He chuckled. "Are you ready?"

She nodded and clenched her hands into fists.

"You'll be all right. Just relax. Look up at the sky and study the clouds. What do you see?" he asked soothingly as he relaxed his hold on her.

"Oh, please," she said with an abrupt laugh. "I'm not eight. I don't study clouds in hopes of seeing bunnies and turtles."

"And why not?" he demanded in mock indignation. "I do that and I'm not eight."

She laughed. "You do not. You're just saying that. No grown man goes around staring at clouds to see what they resemble."

"I do," he said solemnly. He looked up in the sky and scanned the clouds. "That one over on the far right looks like a cat. Oh, and that one, on the left near where those trees are visible, that looks exactly like a side profile of Prinny."

"Oh, stop it," she said laughingly. "It does not. Prinny isn't that thin."

"No, he's not, is he?" Benjamin mused.

"Not by half. The last time I saw him, he looked like a hippopotamus."

"And how many hippopotami have you seen?"

"Well, none," she admitted. "But I've seen drawings and murals of them though."

"Very well," he allowed. "You're in luck, you're a floater."

"What?" she asked, turning her face toward his. "How did you determine that?"

He shrugged. "While you were waxing about hippos and Prinny, I let you go and you stayed afloat."

"You tricked me," she mused with a smile.

"Yes, I did," he conceded. "I knew if I told you when I was going to let you go, you'd get nervous and tense up."

"Very sneaky of you, Your Grace."

"All right, now that you know the depth of my deception, let's swim. You're going to bring this arm," he grabbed her right arm that was by her side and brought it up, rotating it as he went, "up and bring it around until it meets the water. You want it turned, so that when it goes in your hand goes in first, using the side of your hand and fingertips to break the water." He held her arm and helped her make a few more rotations. "Very good; now, you'll alternate first your right, then your left."

"My feet are sinking," she fretted a minute later.

He looked down at her dainty feet that had slipped below the surface of the water enough that only her toes were still above. "That's normal. But if you'd like, I'll move down and hold them up." He scooted down a bit and supported her ankles with his palm.

"Am I doing this right?" she asked, making another perfect stroke.

"Perfect." He moved the arm he'd kept under her back for support and slowly walked with her as she swam along the water. "If you really want to move, you can kick your feet, too."

"You're holding them."

"I know. And I have no intention of letting them go, either," he said, rubbing her anklebone with his thumb. "I was just telling you that you could use them if you needed to. But you're just frolicking, there's no need to use them now."

"Just like a man," she muttered.

He laughed. "How did you get your scar?" he asked to make idle conversation. He liked having her in the water. She was relaxed and seemed to be more trusting of him.

"The one on my ankle?"

He frowned and turned her foot over. Sure enough there was a large a scar that was two inches long and half an inch wide. "I was actually talking about the one here." He brushed his thumb across a little knick that was down by her toes.

"Oh, that," she said dismissively. "When I was younger, maybe nine or ten, Brooke and I were sitting together in Mama's Sunday school class. That wasn't usually the case, I assure you, especially after the incident that led to the scar. Anyway, there were two rows of chairs and Brooke and I were in the second row with Liberty right in front of us in the first. Bored from hearing of Noah and the flood for the thousandth time, Brooke and I quietly untied the bow on the back of Liberty's dress. Then we each took our end and tied it around each side of her chair. You know that little piece of wood that connects the seat to the back support plank?" She turned her head as best she could to look down at him and waited to see him nod his understanding. "When class was over, Liberty stood up, taking her chair with her of course, and the sharp edge at the bottom of the leg scratched my foot."

He chuckled. "Was that the only damage done that day?"

"Do you mean did we get in trouble when we got home? No. Mama used to carry around a tin of sweets and she'd let us have one at the start of church service. That week, she gave mine and Brooke's to Liberty and banned us from sitting together in class ever again. It was nearly two years before we were allowed to even be within arm's length of each other at church. But to be honest, I think Mama found it just as funny as the rest of us."

"Do you and your sisters often play jokes on each other?" he asked as he mindlessly traced the surfaces of her ankles and feet with his fingers.

"Yes," she said, giggling, "except not as much since Brooke got her drawers in a twist after a game of charades."

"Charades?" he echoed in disbelief. "You mean the game where you act out a play or poem or something equally ridiculous?"

"We didn't," she said plainly. "We acted out a scene about her life that I daresay was more embarrassing for her to watch than participate in."

"Did you do it to be cruel?" he asked, moving to stand by her bare knees.

"No. Though I'll say I was surprised at the time, when Andrew continued courting her. Men don't usually like tears, and if I'm not mistaken, I think she was on the verge of them that night."

Silence hung in the air. They both knew why Townson had continued to court Brooke after her near fit of vapors. He hadn't had a choice. He was indebted to Benjamin to ruin her and vapors weren't going to put him off. Benjamin swallowed uncomfortably. "What of the other?" he asked suddenly.

"What other?" she asked, reaching the edge of the water and moving to stand up.

"The scar on your ankle," he clarified, trying to look anywhere but where her chemise was billowing up around her waist.

"Oh," she said with a blush. "You don't want to know."

"Yes, I do," he encouraged with a smile. "Your blush is telling me I want to know."

"No, you don't."

"Why not?"

"Because that story isn't one that you, my husband, would like to hear," she explained.

"Please? I promise not to react poorly."

She picked up a leaf that was floating in the water and wound it around her finger before looking up into his eyes again. "All right, I was trying to catch the attention of a gentleman by going fishing in the Hudson and I slipped on a rock and gashed my foot on the sharp edge of a nearby rock as I fell."

A knot formed in his gut. Robbie was the gentleman she'd been trying to impress by fishing. He remembered that day like it was yesterday; Robbie draping himself all over her, her startled scream, the wet hem on her skirt and Robbie carrying her off to safety. "I see," he said slowly, forcing a thin smile to his lips.

"I told you that you wouldn't want to hear it," she said, throwing the leaf into the water.

"Perhaps in the future, I'll believe you," he said, reaching for her hands. "Now that you've learned the backstroke, let's try some forward swimming." He started pulling her down the stream by her hands. "Kick your feet."

"Like this?" she asked, kicking her feet under the water.

"I guess," he said with a shrug. "They're under the water so I can't see them. However, since I'm not aware of a wrong way to kick feet, you're probably doing it right." He sent her a grin and kicked his own feet to help give them more propulsion.

"You're a cheeky one, did you know that?"

"No," he muttered honestly. "Normally people think I'm an ass."

"That's because you usually are," she pointed out dryly.

"Thank you."

"You're welcome," she said pertly, making his smile brighten. Nobody ever had the nerve to call him an ass to his face; behind his back, definitely. But to his face? Never; except maybe Townson, but that was different, Townson was a man.

"Madison, I wanted to talk to you about something serious," he said gravely, bringing her laughing eyes to his for a second before uncertainty entered them again. "I wanted to talk to you about our wedding night."

Her eyes dropped to his chin and he felt her hands tense. "I'm sorry," she said quietly. "I know you thought I wasn't coming back, but I was. I was just angry about what happened."

"I know," he said, gently pulling her to him. "Look at me, Madison." He wrapped one arm around the middle of her back to pull her to a standing position and held her close to him. With the other, he cupped her cheek. "I'm the one who should be sorry. I shouldn't have acted that way with you. To say I wasn't shocked or even hurt when I saw you that way would be a lie. But that does not excuse the way I treated you. As soon as I left your room, I knew I'd done everything wrong. That's why I went out. I went for a ride to think of how to apologize and make things right. I know we don't get a second wedding night, but I want you to know I'm sorry for making such a mess of the one we had."

"Why were you hurt?" she asked, her eyes searching his face.

"I'd been looking forward to that night for a long time." No need to tell her just how long he'd been looking forward to it. She probably didn't even remember the scruffy bearded man in pauper's clothing that she'd barely noticed in America. "But that doesn't matter. You deserved better. That was not very well done of me. I'll never do anything like that to you again. I promise."

She nodded quietly and stared at his shoulder.

"I'll never force you," he murmured in her ear, rubbing his hand along her back. "Would you like to get out for a while?"

Chapter 10

M adison hesitantly walked out of the water to where Benjamin was standing in the grass with his hands on the drawstring to his smalls. Now that he'd apologized—which she thought was rather sweetly done considering who he was—did he expect her to perform her wifely duties? Is that why he was fumbling with the tie on the front of his tented drawers and staring at her?

Trying not to let her nerves show, she walked up to stand across from him. "Having trouble?" she teased.

"Yes," he said hoarsely.

"I'm rather surprised," she mused aloud. "I always thought men had the problem of keeping their drawers on, not taking them off."

"I was trying to untie the knot when you came out of the water, and ugh, I looked up and got distracted by you, and um, stopped paying attention to what I was doing and knotted it," he said uneasily, his face turning red as he directed his gaze down to the knot he'd inadvertently put in the drawstring.

She tried not to laugh. The Dangerous Duke, as he was known to some, or The Great Gateway, as he was known to others, couldn't even get his drawers down because he'd bungled the knot in his drawstring! "Then I guess you'll just have to leave them on," she said, taking a seat on the soft grass.

"I'd prefer not to," he said with a frown. "Like you, I normally don't wear them. I only put them on because Brooke mentioned you were by the water and I thought I'd ask you to swim."

Forgetting that he'd been considerate enough to put them on in anticipation of taking her into the water, she said, "How do you know

I don't normally wear them?"

"I just saw you wearing only your chemise. If you wore drawers, I would have seen them," he said with a grin.

Her face turned crimson and she jerked her eyes away from him. No wonder he'd been so intent on holding her feet. He'd been peeking at her privates!

As if reading her thoughts, he said, "Don't worry, I didn't look. I spent the whole time trying *not* to look."

"Thank you," she said uncomfortably. "Just quit playing with them and sit down."

"No," he said defiantly. "I don't like them to begin with, and now that they're wet, they're cold."

"Who cares?" she burst out. "So is my chemise, but you don't see me trying to take it off."

"Then take it off," he said with a shrug, still picking at the knot he'd put in the string.

"You'd like that, wouldn't you?" she retorted.

"Of course I would," he returned automatically. "Any man would."

She rolled her eyes and gained her feet then walked over to where his fingers were only making the knot worse by pulling on the string and tightening it. "I hate to be the bearer of bad news—"

"Sure you do," he muttered.

"—but it appears these will have to be cut," she finished.

"Then cut them," he said tersely.

"With what, oh wise one? A rock?" she asked sarcastically.

"My knife."

She stared blankly at him.

"In my trousers."

She cast a look a hundred yards away to where his trousers rested in a pile next to the place they'd been sitting earlier. "Truly?" she muttered.

"Yes, please go get them."

"Fine," she huffed, walking to his trousers. It took her nearly two minutes to dig through everything in his pockets before finding a slim penknife. Walking back up behind him, she said, "Do you always carry every small possession you own around with you?"

"No, only the basics," he replied. "I used to have a candle stub in there, but someone I know wasted it."

"Oh, for goodness' sake," she sighed, pulling the blade out on the knife. "That thing was less than an inch tall to begin with."

He shrugged and tried to take the knife from her.

"I don't think so," she said triumphantly, pulling the knife back. "I had to go fetch the knife. I get to sever the string."

"Just don't sever anything else," he muttered, moving his hands away from the string to hold onto the waistband.

"Don't worry, I'll not knick your tallywhacker," she told him, causing him to choke on his laughter as she cut the string. "There you go. Now you can run naked through the field like the little boy you long to be."

His abdomen was contracting in laugher and his face took on a look she'd never seen before. "You're great," he said, brushing a kiss on her cheek. "Do you want to turn around while I take these off?"

Did it matter? He was about to be intimate with her; she'd see it then. Perhaps he was shy, she thought with a shrug before turning around. "Just let me know when I can turn back around."

Ten seconds later, he grunted and said, "All right, Madison, you can turn around, but no laughing."

No laughing? Surely he wasn't *that* small. Maybe that was a good thing. Perhaps the smaller it was, the less it would hurt. Taking a deep breath and steeling herself for what sight lay ahead of her, she turned around and gasped in shock. "Why—what—ugh…" She trailed off, staring at the lily white arse that was pointed straight at her while its owner laid on his stomach on the green carpet of grass.

"The red line?" he asked, turning his head to look over his shoulder at her innocently. "That's the product of the too tight drawers I've been wearing for the past few hours."

"No," she said, flabbergasted. "I wasn't talking about the line around your waist. I didn't even notice it. I was startled that I turned around to be greeted by your blinding white hind end."

"And what did you expect to be greeted by?" he asked, blinking owlishly at her.

"Your—your—your…"

"Oh, I know what you were expecting," he said, understanding making his eyes light up. "Well, I thought there should still be some mystery about me for you to discover later."

Now she blinked at him.

"You've already seen everything else today. I've got to leave you in suspense for what you'll find tomorrow," he said with a grin, patting the ground next to him. "Come, lie with me."

"Literally or biblically?" she asked tentatively.

"Literally," he said, patting the ground again. "For today, anyway," he added after she'd taken her spot next to him.

"It's my turn," she said abruptly, looking into his handsome face.

His eyes went wide. "Please don't make me turn around," he pleaded.

"What are you talking about?"

"When you take your chemise off," he said simply with a wolfish smile.

"I'm not taking my chemise off," she said, giving him a playful swat on the shoulder.

"Pity," he twisted his lips in disappointment.

She reached her hand to his face and ran her slender fingers along his hard jaw. "I answered your questions, now you'll answer mine."

"Fair enough," he agreed.

"Why did you try to pay Andrew to ruin Brooke?" she asked. She'd always wondered about that. Her sisters had, too. At first, she'd just assumed it was because Brooke had rebuffed his advances. But

Brooke said she didn't think that was the case, because the two of them had done nothing more than share a close waltz and a few paltry kisses in the garden. When they'd asked Andrew, he'd said he hadn't known Benjamin's reasons and they'd believed him. But Benjamin knew.

A dark shadow crossed his eyes. "Pick another question," he said gruffly.

"No. Answer me, please," she said, pulling her hand away from his face.

"Not today," he said, taking her hand and returning it to his face. "I'll tell you, but not today. Ask me an easier question. I asked you easy questions."

"Fine." She idly ran her finger along the length of his nose. "Why did Andrew break your nose?"

"Because I said some rather unflattering remarks about Brooke," he said evenly. His eyes looked straight into hers and she could tell he was telling the truth.

"Why?"

He blinked. "Truthfully, it was never really about Brooke. I was angry he hadn't done what he'd agreed to do."

"Because he married her?" she asked, tracing the knot at the top of his nose.

"Yes."

"Did you want to marry her?"

"No," he said softly, shaking his head, "only you."

She smiled. "Why did you break his?"

"Jealousy."

"You were jealous of Andrew? Why?" she asked in disbelief. Andrew was a nice enough man, but truth be known, he lacked several attributes that were part of Benjamin's appeal.

"As you know, Lizzie was paid to raise me. When we went to school, she told me I couldn't mention her or write to her. I was hurt that the only person who I'd known ever wanted me suddenly didn't.

"At thirteen, I didn't fully understand why she couldn't associate with me. And out of jealousy that he was still able to maintain a relationship with Lizzie while I wasn't, I started rumors to get Andrew teased. I know he's a big man now, and don't get me wrong, he was big at thirteen, too, but he was no match for an entire group of taunting boys. Fortunately, none of the older boys ever took interest in our juvenile squabbles, so I was able to help end the bullying and taunting. But only at the cost of his pride and both of our good names."

"You regret it, don't you?"

"More than you know. I regretted it only a day or two after I did it, and I still regret it today." He pursed his lips and blew out a breath. "The way I thought to set it to rights back then was to set into motion a chain of events that made it appear as if I was a bully and Andrew my accomplice. With Andrew's size and my skillful manipulation, the two of us managed to keep everyone from crossing us. But that's not what you asked is it?" he asked flashing her a thin smile. "You asked why

I broke his nose, which, I must admit, came about quite by accident actually. As you can guess, our former arrangement made us appear as friends, but we really weren't. He resented me for my schemes.

"At the end of our final term, I missed a mathematics exam because the night before I'd been on a wild-goose chase trying to run down my real mother. Andrew told the professor I'd been out drinking and consorting with women the night before and the professor failed me. Angry, I hired a group to rough him up then I jumped him."

He held his hand up. "I know it sounds bad. But you wanted the truth. Anyway, I thought it would be a fairer fight if he'd already been worn down by the others. You might not believe it, but at the time, I was as thin as your Mr. Swift fellow, if not thinner. However, I think it just made him more agitated because he gave as good as he got. Fortunately for me, I was able to get one solid punch to his nose, temporarily stopping him so I could run off."

Madison smoothed his hair back and twirled a silky lock between her fingers. "I'd say I'm surprised you've ever been jealous. But I'm not. You had reason to be. Thinking of it from your perspective, I understand your motives."

"You do?"

"Yes," she said with a gentle smile. "Are you still jealous of him?"

He nodded. "Of course. But for an entirely different reason."

"Because he has Brooke and Nathan?"

He nodded again. "Those are two things I'd give anything for, a wife who loves me and a child we created together."

Madison felt her heart squeeze. He wanted love. Love from a wife. Love from a child. He'd said a child. Not an heir, a son or a daughter. But he wouldn't find those things with her. He didn't love her and she couldn't love him. Love was such an elusive emotion; one that caused a person to hurt something fierce when it wasn't returned. And at the same time, an emotion that once it had been destroyed, was nearly impossible to have again.

"Can I ask you something else?"

"Sure," he said, plucking at the blades of grass by his fingers. "You can ask as many questions as you want. But I can't guarantee I'll answer all of them. Not today anyway."

"If everything was never really about Brooke, why don't you apologize to her?"

He snorted. "You think she'd accept?"

She bit her lip and looked up to the sky. "Yes. She doesn't usually hold grudges. The only person I remember her holding one against is that vermin Robbie Swift. The whole time we courted, she didn't like him and made sure I knew it. But what you did was not nearly as bad as what he did."

He lowered his lashes to look at the grass for a minute before raising them so he could look back up at her. "Would you like me to apologize?"

"Yes," she said honestly. With Benjamin as her husband, they were bound to spend time in each other's company. "Andrew, too."

Benjamin's eyes went wide. "I don't think it's wise to mention our school days, Madison. That part of the past is best left where it is."

"I know," she said, bringing her hand to rest on top of his. "I meant about Brooke."

He nodded. "All right, anything else?"

"Yes. I noticed when you were talking earlier, you referred to Andrew as Andrew, but you always call him Townson. Why?"

He shrugged. "It's his title. He calls me mine, even though I despise it and have asked him not to. So I call him his."

She buried her head in the grass. "For two men who are coming up on their thirtieth year, you two are awfully immature. Start calling him Andrew and I'm sure he'll follow suit."

"I don't want to be called Andrew," he teased with an overdone frown.

"You're ridiculous."

"I know. All right, I'll do it. But only because you asked it of me." He turned his hand over so their hands were palm to palm. "Anything else to please the duchess?"

She smiled at his use of her title. Not because she was a title-hungry harpy like some, but because her title was a direct connection to him and for some reason she liked that. "Not just now. But when I think of it, I'll let you know," she said with a cheeky smile.

"You do that. I'll be waiting."

Chapter 11

Benjamin stared at his sleeping wife. Even when she slept, she was enchanting. Her mouth hung open slightly, revealing her pretty white teeth. Her hair hung lazily over one of her eyes in the most seductive manner he'd ever seen. She was still clad in her chemise, but the front now gaped from her lying on her side with both hands resting under her head.

Silently, he rolled away from her and walked over to get their clothes. They'd been asleep in the sunshine for at least an hour and her shoulders were beginning to turn pink. He imagined his backside was, too, but considered that a small price to pay for being allowed to spend so much time in her presence. He hadn't wanted to expose his past with Andrew. It showed him in the most unfavorable light possible. But she'd asked, and compared to telling her why he'd wanted her family shamed off the continent last year, it seemed the better choice.

At least she'd understood, or said she had anyway. She had a point though. At nearly thirty, it was time for him and Andrew to put the past behind them and act friendlier toward each other, for the sake of their wives if for no other reason. For some reason, telling her the story and admitting his jealous feelings aloud almost made them all vanish. Andrew may have known both of his biological parents, but his relationship with them wasn't any better than Benjamin's. As for being jealous of Andrew for having a wife who loved him and a child—that wasn't even jealousy, it was longing. Thinking about it logically, Andrew really didn't have anything Benjamin couldn't acquire, except Madison. And that was the crux of his newfound jealously of the man.

In his early twenties, the young girls used to chase Benjamin in throngs and declare their undying love and adoration for him. Now, in his late twenties, most women still pursued him. He just didn't care about it now like he did then. He could have married any one of those women and had a wife who loved him the way Brooke loved Andrew. But none of those girls were Madison. And to be frank, he'd be lying if he didn't admit that he believed Madison had romantic feelings for Andrew.

It was in the way she talked to and about him. The way she'd appealed to Andrew to rescue her from her own husband. The way the two talked and teased in the dining room about some family joke they wouldn't share with him. How she'd dressed like a nightwalker and met him in his study. All the other reasons: the mother who loved him, the wife who loved him, the son he created out of love, he could dismiss his jealous feelings over. But not Madison, she was *his* wife. *He* deserved her love. And as long as Madison continued to entertain romantic notions of Andrew, he, Benjamin, her husband, was left out in the cold.

He could always shed light on the ways Andrew was not a candidate for sainthood. But if he did, he'd always feel like he'd only won her by default. He had no intention of winning her that way. He'd rather lose her altogether than win her like that.

He pulled on his trousers and scooped up his discarded clothes before going behind the bushes and grabbing her gown and sketch pad. Arms full of their clothes, he walked back to where Madison still lay asleep on the grass. He dropped all the clothes to the ground and reached down to grab his shirt. He shook out his shirt and draped it over Madison's exposed skin to keep her from burning.

"How long have I been asleep," she asked sleepily after he'd finished positioning his shirt over her.

"An hour," he said quietly. "You can close your eyes and go back to sleep if you'd like."

"Are you leaving?" she asked, turning her head to see his face.

He brushed her hair out of her blue eyes. "No. I'll be here."

"Why am I wearing your shirt?" she asked, fingering the edges of the shirt that was draped over her.

"You were starting to burn," he explained. "So I covered you up."

"Thank you. Do you burn?"

"Not usually, but I might have today," he said as he repositioned himself on the grass.

"That's good," she said sweetly as she lowered her eyelids.

"Good?" he echoed. Perhaps his enchanting wife had a penchant for talking nonsense in her sleep.

"Yes, you could use some color in your cheeks," she mumbled sleepily.

He let out a shout of laughter. "You're being rather naughty."

"Yes, I know," she admitted. "Very naughty. I have a feeling that's why you like me."

He smiled. At least she knew he liked her. "You're right, it is.

Well, part of the reason anyway."

She rolled over onto her back and looked up at his downturned face. "Do you want to know the reason I like you?"

His breath caught. She actually liked him? "Yes," he said solemnly, nodding.

"You've been very patient with me," she said, settling her head on his lap.

"I don't want you to fear me, Madison." He ran his fingers through her somewhat tangled hair. "I don't know why you do."

"Yes, you do," she said ruefully. "It's because of what happened with Brooke."

Should he tell her? Just blurt it out? What would it hurt at this point? She was already his wife. Just because she didn't have any interest in him before didn't change the fact that she'd married him anyway. "The reason I hired Andrew to ruin Brooke is—"

"Excuse me, are you Gateway?" interrupted a fellow carrying a messenger's bag.

"Yes," Benjamin said, eyeing him curiously.

"I've a note for you." The messenger held out a missive.

"Thank you." He frowned when he saw the writing on the outside of the missive. His estate manager at Glenbrook must be having problems. He'd attend to it later.

"Aren't you going to read it?" Madison asked when he tossed it on the ground.

"No. There'll be plenty of time for that later. Right now, I'm spending time with you."

"What if it's important?"

"It's not," he said in a way he hoped she'd interpret as final. "Nothing is more important than you at the moment."

"Thank you," she said, moving her head closer to his abdomen. "Oh, am I hurting you?"

"No, why?"

"Your face changed when I moved my head," she said, moving to sit up.

He pushed her back down. "My facial expression was not one of pain. Not the kind you'd understand anyway."

She smiled at him and slightly moved her head around.

"Don't tease," he warned.

"Sorry," she said with a wink. "You're actually rather fun, did you know?"

"Once again, no. Nobody thinks I'm fun."

"Well, I do."

"Well, you're the only one," he returned, running a finger down her cheek.

"That's not true. Lizzie likes you."

He shook his head. "Yes, much to Townson's dismay, she does."

Madison smiled up at him. "See, I'm not the only one." She turned her head and faced the water. "Thank you for teaching me to swim. I know I was rather shabby at it, but thank you."

"You weren't shabby at all." He rubbed his knuckle back and forth across her upturned cheek. "Your backstroke was perfect."

"Is that the only stroke you know?"

"No. I also know the breaststroke."

She whipped her head around to face him. "Did you just say what I think you said?"

"Yes," he answered with a grin.

"Why do I get the feeling you made that up?"

He shrugged. "I don't know. But I didn't."

She shook her head, causing him more discomfort than before. "Surely it was a man who thought of it."

"Probably," he conceded. "Some call it the front crawl. Perhaps you've heard of it by that term?"

"No," she murmured. "Dare I ask why it's called the breaststroke?"

"Because when you do it, you feel the muscles pulling right here."

~*~*~*~

Madison froze. His hand was most definitely resting right at the top of her left breast. His gentle but firm fingers were scorching her skin and sending the most unusual sensations skidding through her body. She shifted her eyes to his and saw a look she'd never seen before. She'd seen hunger and desire before, but she'd never seen such tenderness.

The tender look in his eyes was far more unsettling than him touching her breast.

"Perhaps I'll teach you another day," he said, moving his fingers away.

The absence of his touch was chilling. She'd noticed when he'd put his hand there, and yet, she'd noticed it more when it was gone. How bizarre. "Another day?" she repeated. She wasn't sure what he'd planned, but she didn't intend to live out the rest of her days swimming in her sister's stream.

"It will have to be another day. I can't get back into the water today," he said with a pointed glance at his drawstringless drawers.

"Right, because you want to keep me interested," she teased. Although truly, how could any woman find interest in *that*.

"Exactly," he agreed, humor dancing in his eyes.

"It's probably time for lunch anyway," she said, wiggling around and trying to get back up.

"You're right. I cannot wait to hear the topic of conversation today," he muttered, taking to his feet.

"I'd say you were rather fortunate, actually. The conversation at luncheon was mild compared to what she had to say in her cottage," Madison said, slightly blushing.

"My sincerest apologies; if I had known she was taking you off to elaborate more on her horrendous wedding night, I would have interfered," he said quickly, putting on his shirt.

Madison scooped up her gown. "No, I'd heard all about that after our engagement was announced."

Benjamin's head snapped in her direction. His eyes searched her face. "She didn't scare you, did she?"

"Oh, no," Madison said laughingly, trying to pull her gown on. "And yesterday we actually talked exclusively about you."

"Me?" he repeated, jabbing a finger toward his chest.

Madison righted her sleeves. "How else do you think I knew you liked to run around in the field naked?"

Benjamin groaned.

"And," she said, coming up to him to button up his shirt for him, "that was one of the less amusing things she had to say about you."

Chapter 12

"What are your plans for tomorrow," Benjamin asked Madison quietly as they took their seats at the table for their evening meal.

Madison leaned down to fix her skirt that seemed to be snagged on the heel of her slipper. "I plan to go to Bath to tutor a group of illiterate bastards."

"Excuse me?" he burst out, drawing all attention to him and Madison.

"I believe you heard me."

Benjamin stared at her and shook his head. "I don't believe I did," he said honestly. There was no way she'd just said what he thought he'd heard.

"No, you heard her correctly," Brooke said, trying not to laugh. "Although I believe Liberty calls them illegitimate illiterates."

Madison shrugged. "Illegitimate illiterates, illiterate bastards, it's the same thing."

"Say, Gateway, you're a bastard, why don't you go, too?" Andrew said, his lips twitching.

Benjamin shot him a peeved stare. "I'd love to, Andrew. But I wasn't invited."

"You are now," Madison said with a smile that made his heart skip a beat.

"All right," he agreed. "But only if you'll spend the rest of the day with me in Bath." He'd planned to ask her to go there with him tomorrow anyway. He was worried she'd refuse or her watchdogs wouldn't approve, but her plans to go there already worked to his advantage.

"All right," she said quietly. "You do know there's not a lot to do there."

"There's enough," he said with a wolfish smile. Yesterday he'd made plans for them in Bath that would be met with an automatic "no" if he told her now. Knowing this, he wisely decided to keep quiet about his secret plans.

After dinner was cleared and he'd walked Madison to her room and asked for his obligatory goodnight kiss, which was met with a quick peck on the cheek—again, he went in search of Andrew and Brooke. Madison was right; he owed them both an apology for what he'd done. Not that he really thought it was so bad, since it did end in their happy marriage. But all the same, he shouldn't have interfered the way he had.

Stevens, the butler, told him they were in a private sitting room upstairs and Benjamin made his heavier-than-lead feet carry him there. After a light knock on the door, Andrew's curious face greeted him. "May I talk to you?" Benjamin asked quietly.

Andrew's body stiffened and his gaze turned hard. "What's wrong?" he demanded.

"Nothing; I owe Brooke an apology for something and I've come to make it."

"Yes, you do," Andrew said, opening the door all the way and allowing Benjamin to come inside.

Brooke was sitting in a rocking chair holding her infant, unaware he'd entered the room. "Brooke," he said softly, sitting down in the chair next to hers.

Brooke started. "Gateway."

"Sorry, didn't mean to startle you," he murmured.

"It's all right," she said uneasily, her eyes shifting from him to her husband.

Running a hand through his hair, Benjamin said some words she should find somewhat familiar, "I'm a bounder of the worst sort, Brooke. But I'm savable. Part of being savable is admitting when I'm wrong. And I admit I was wrong last spring when I contracted someone to ruin you. I apologize."

Brooke's dark brown eyes searched his face. "I don't understand," she said at last.

"I know," he said quietly. "One day you will, but I cannot explain it to you until I've told Madison. It's only fair."

She nodded. "Gateway, I—"

"Benjamin," he corrected.

"Benjamin," she said, shaking her head a little. "I don't hold what you did to me against you. I let go of that long ago. Actually, I should thank you for it. I'd still be kissing bounders like you in the shrubs if it hadn't been for you and your harebrained scheme," she said with a grin. "I just don't know you well enough to trust you with my sister. I know you're not as dangerous as the *ton* thinks, but I just don't know you."

"I know," he allowed.

She sighed. "As long as you tell Madison everything, that's all I ask."

"I will," Benjamin said, standing.

"Oh, Benjamin," Brooke said quietly. "One more thing," she closed her eyes for a minute and twisted the edge of Nathan's baby blue blanket before looking at him again. "I think she likes you. Please be careful with her. She's been through a lot."

"I know," he said solemnly. Brooke didn't look like she believed him, but he didn't want to expose his relation to Robbie. Then, he'd have no choice but to tell her the reasons he'd hired Andrew to ruin her, and Madison deserved that explanation first. "I care more for her than you can possibly understand."

"I hope so," Brooke said, cocking her head in interest.

Benjamin walked across the room to where an interested Andrew stood with his arms crossed, leaning against the door. "In case you haven't determined my motives already, Andrew, the reason I chose you to be the one to ruin her was because of Lizzie. I knew you weren't aware of my connection to her at the time—per her request, of course. I also knew you were impoverished and were about to lose that estate in Essex. That's why I leant you the money. I had no intention of actually repossessing it. But when you defaulted and insisted you owed it to me, I was in a position to think of another way to let you keep that house so Lizzie would have a home.

"The simple solution was to give her one of my estates. But she refused because it would lead to unnecessary gossip and questions. My only other option was to give you a bank draft, but everyone knows no self-respecting man would accept that much money." He shrugged. "When another possibility presented itself—one I cannot mention just now—it seemed the best solution. It would give you an income and Lizzie a place to live."

Andrew nodded. "I drew a similar conclusion shortly after I married. I believe I was sitting on a hard bench reading a newspaper and waiting for my irate wife to emerge from her holdings when everything fell into place." He sighed. "I know I wasn't very gracious the day I found out about our bizarre connection, but I want you to know I appreciate what you've done."

"No need to thank me, just forgive me."

~*~*~*~

They were in the carriage on their way to Bath to help the illiterate bastards learn to read. As shocked as he first was to hear Madison say that, he had a feeling he was actually going to enjoy the activity. But not as much as he was going to like the activity that followed, of that, he was certain.

"You look awfully excited to go help a group of outcasts learn to read," Madison mused as she sat next to him in the carriage.

"Seeing as I'm going to help my own kind—bastards and outcasts—I should be excited," he quipped. "I just had no idea Liberty was involved in such an organization."

"She didn't either at first," Madison said evasively. "You seem rather accepting of your position."

"I'm not." He knew she was alluding to the fact Andrew had pointed out his bastardy for all and sundry the night before. "If Andrew had been anyone else, I would have called him out. The fact is, most marriages among the nobility are not love matches and infidelity is very common. I'd estimate at least two third of the second born are bastards and at least a quarter of the first. Unfortunately, I fall into that category. I don't like it, but I can't change it. However, I do not advertise it and I would have been rather displeased if Andrew had made that comment in front of anyone who didn't already know."

"It's ironic how you spread rumors at school about him being a bastard, when he's not, and in the end, you're the one who is and hardly anyone knows it."

He nodded sadly. "I know. But in my own defense, I was only thirteen. Not to mention, in a legal sense, I'm not a bastard. The duke did claim me as his."

She smiled at him. "There's no need to defend yourself, Benjamin. As I said yesterday, I do understand your side of the tale where Andrew is concerned and I sympathize with you."

He smiled weakly at her.

"Anyway, Andrew didn't mean anything by his comment last night," she said nonchalantly. "I realized very early on in his courtship with Brooke that he'd never intentionally be cruel."

Benjamin shrugged. Quite honestly, his dealings with Andrew in the past ten or more years had been so limited he really couldn't comment.

The literacy meeting was held in the common room at Paul's church. Which was a vast improvement from where meetings were originally held, or so he'd been told. There were about thirty students ranging in age from children as young as five or six all the way to adults who were in their forties. It was actually a rather humbling sight to behold. All his life he'd held a title and been an heir to a dukedom, never denied anything money could buy, and yet, he still felt empty; whereas, most of the people here had next to nothing but were much more content than he'd ever been.

Lizzie caught sight of him after he'd walked in and directed him to help his wife with whatever group she joined. That was an instruction he didn't need to hear twice. He remained on the side of the room where the children were and watched for Madison. He assumed she'd join the children's group. She seemed the sort that would want several children clutching her skirts and calling her Mama. He smiled; she'd make a great mother.

Madison came to his side. "Come on, we'll go to the back corner."

Benjamin frowned. The back corner? That was where all the oldest people were. "Why?"

She shrugged. "Because they need to learn penmanship."

"And you're going to teach them?"

"No. We are," she said, pulling on his sleeve.

He tried not to groan. He'd never liked practicing his letters as a child and now to volunteer to sit with a group while they did such a tedious task felt like pure torture. Why did people who were that age need to learn to write anyway? They'd already survived forty years without the skill, why start now?

"Because people who are illiterate often get taken advantage of," Madison explained, startling him. She laughed. "You must not have realized you were mumbling under your breath."

"Sorry," he muttered. "What do you mean they get taken advantage of?" He ran a duchy and he was quite certain many of his tenants couldn't read or write, but they'd never complained about being taken advantage of. They'd complained about a great many other things, but never that.

"Think about it. If you cannot read or write and you get a bill from the local smithy, how in the world are you supposed to know if he's taking advantage of you?"

That brought him up short. He had no idea how someone would know if they were being openly robbed. "You make a good point," he conceded.

"Thank you." She took a seat at the table full of adults. "Good morning," she said to the group who had missed work or abandoned their household duties in order to come to the meeting. "I'm Mrs. Grimes' sister, Madison and this is my husband—"

"Benjamin," he cut in. Not that he'd care if society found out he, a duke, volunteered to help a group of people born on the wrong side of the blanket, but if she was going to be informal, so was he.

"Right," she continued. "Well, we're going to work on letters today. I've brought a stack of…"

Benjamin leaned back in his chair and watched her as she explained what she'd brought for them to use to write their letters. She got up and walked around to look over each of their shoulders as they practiced. Only once did she require his help and that was to ask him to sharpen a quill. She worked so well with them, helping them hold their quills better so their letters would come out more smoothly and teaching them tricks to remember the difference between a "b", being a line with a belly, and a "d", being a line with a derriere. She was amazing.

Six years ago during one of their brief conversations, she'd told him she volunteered at an orphanage to help teach children to read and write. He'd had a hard time picturing it then. She'd been so young, it was difficult envisioning her demanding attention and controlling the lesson. But now, seeing her actually do it, he was in awe. All the people at the table watched her as if they were just as fascinated by her as he was.

"Are you ready to go?" she asked, gaining her feet.

Benjamin nodded. "You're quite good with them."

"Thank you," she said with a blush.

He helped Madison put away a few stray books and papers

before returning to the carriage. "Are you hungry?" he asked, leaning back against the squabs of the seat across from her. He would rather have sat next to her, but she'd arranged her skirt in a way there was no room to sit next to her without sitting on it.

"Famished," she said with a smile. "The people I've been staying with—don't tell them I said this—have been starving me." Her eyes were positively sparkling with laughter.

He chuckled. "I won't tell them that if you don't tell them I think their overall hospitality is lacking where I'm concerned."

"Hmm. That seems odd. I'd think they'd welcome *you* with open arms. Perhaps you should write a letter to the master of the house complaining of poor treatment," she mused, her traitorous lips twitching.

"I doubt it would do much good," he responded casually. "However, I've a few coins to my name and I know an excellent place to eat in Bath. Would you care to go or shall I return you to Rockhurst to feast on gruel?"

She bit her lip and rolled her eyes up to study the top of his carriage. "Gruel does sound delightful, I must admit. However, the company would positively ruin it for me. So, I think I shall endure your company alone and suffer a far less tasty meal."

"Very well," he said with a grin. He liked playing these games with her. It made him feel like they finally had something that was just between them. "Can I tell you a secret?"

"Please do," she said, leaning her whole body forward, bringing her face scant inches from his.

He leaned forward, too. Closing the space to two inches between them, and in a stage whisper said, "I love waffles and chocolate."

Her eyes grew wide and she looked like she was trying not to laugh. "You do?" she whispered in feigned surprise. "Though I'm rather surprised to hear you love something in general, I'm more surprised that it's waffles."

"And chocolate."

"Even I love that," she whispered dismissively. "I drink it all the time for breakfast."

"I wouldn't know," he said dryly. "You seem to have eaten and have vanished by the time I reach the breakfast room at the advanced hour of seven."

She shook her head. "No. I usually eat and vanish around eight. But the difference is I eat from a tray in my room."

That was rather odd, he thought. But then again, eating every meal with one's sister and brother-in-law had to be tiresome. "Perhaps tomorrow you can join me for breakfast."

"Perhaps I will," she said thoughtfully. "Will you be requesting waffles for this grand meal on the morrow?"

"No," he said, shaking his head. "I doubt Cook would care about my wishes. However, I know a great place here in Bath to get waffles."

"What?" she questioned with excitement in her voice. "You want to travel forty minutes to Bath tomorrow morning in order to eat waffles?"

"No," he said, shaking his head again. "I'll eat coddled eggs or porridge or whatever Cook prepares for us for breakfast tomorrow. I want to eat the waffles now."

"Now?" she asked dubiously. "But it's lunchtime."

"Who cares?" he said with a shrug. "There's no law saying, 'Thou shalt not eat waffles once the clock strikes noon'."

She giggled and shook her head. "Only you would think of such a thing. I honestly doubt there are any laws regarding waffles."

Benjamin leaned even closer to her, their faces barely an inch apart now. "You do, do you? And what would you do if I told you there was?"

"You mean besides laugh at the absurdity?"

He nodded. "Yes. Would you give me a kiss if such a law existed?"

She licked her lips. "I suppose."

"As it happens, such a law does, or should I say did, exist," Benjamin said with an easy smile. "During the medieval times in France, waffle vendors would actually wait outside churches on religious holidays and such to sell their waffles. As you can imagine, competition among the venders was fierce since little money was to be had among the lowest class at the time. With all the vendors out there competing with each other and trying to grab the attention of potential customers, chaos broke out. Vendors were fighting with each other about stealing customers or having a better location to the point it became a rather large problem and King Charles IX had to create a law dictating just how far apart waffle vendors were to be spaced."

"That's ridiculous," Madison said, shaking her head in disbelief.

Benjamin shrugged. "I know. Now, about that kiss."

She leaned forward to press her lips to his cheek and he pulled back to avoid it. "No," he said, putting a finger on her puckered lips. "I want a real kiss and I want it when I choose."

She looked at him curiously. "I wasn't aware that that wasn't a real kiss. I always assumed a kiss was a matter of puckering one's lips, pressing them against something—preferably a body—and exerting pressure."

"You're correct," he allowed. "But I want a kiss on the lips this time."

She blinked then said, "As long as you keep your lips shut during the kiss, I shall kiss you on the mouth at the time of your choosing."

"Of course," he said, trying not to laugh. "It usually works best that way anyway."

She cocked her head a little and gave him an expressionless stare. "I meant—"

"I know what you meant, Madison," he said softly. He had no desire to hear her recount the gruesome details of the sloppy kisses she'd shared with Robbie. He'd happily kiss her with a closed mouth for now and gracefully introduce her to deeper, more passionate kisses later.

"Since you told me your secret, do I owe you one of mine?"

"Of course," he said even though he'd never have asked her to share one in return.

"Mine is more of a confession really," she said shyly.

His eyes went wide and he gave her the ducal stare he'd perfected that usually made people turn to icicles. "Do tell," he drawled, trying not to crack a smile.

"I've only had waffles once, maybe twice."

"Pity," he said, dropping his head and shaking it in mock sadness. Or was that real sadness? He didn't know. He did know, however, it was quite a shame to live on this earth nearly twenty-three years and only have eaten waffles once, maybe twice. "We shall have to double that amount today."

"You do know I was jesting when I said I was being starved, right?" she said with a wobbly smile.

"Yes. Believe it or not, I do know a jest when I hear one."

"All right," she said uneasily. "I just wanted to make sure you knew."

"I know."

She looked flustered. "I cannot possibly eat two waffles for lunch," she burst out.

He stared at her and tried to keep his lips from twitching. "I didn't ask you to."

"No. But you said, we were going to double the amount of waffles I've eaten," she pointed out. "That would mean if I've eaten one previously, I'd have to eat two today."

"And you will."

"But I cannot possibly eat two at one meal," she explained, exasperated.

"And you won't."

"You mean—"

"I mean," he broke in. "We'll eat one now and we'll eat one later after our other activity."

"And what is our other activity?"

Grinning, he said, "I'm taking you to a bathhouse."

Chapter 13

A meal never seemed so daunting. And that included the ones she'd pretended to eat on her wedding day.

Benjamin was pleasant company during the meal, if not a bit unnerving. For some reason she couldn't understand, he had the host set their two plates right next to each other, rather than across the table from each other. Fortunately, they were seated in a private room and didn't have to endure the curious stares of the other patrons while they ate.

Many times before, Madison had witnessed—and pretended to be oblivious to—the actions between couples when they sat so close together. She'd caught sight of intentional hand brushing, or shifting in chairs to become closer, or once when she'd dropped her napkin on the floor and bent to pick it up, she'd seen a man's boot on the floor with no foot inside it. A quick glance to the right informed her where his foot had gone, under the lady's skirt to caress her ankle with his toes.

She'd personally played the female role in this dinner dance, but only a few times, and always with the ungraceful Robbie. Actually, that wasn't entirely fair. Robbie had been graceful, just not with her. She'd caught glimpses of him touching and caressing other women with much more skill and charm than he'd used on her. When she'd confronted him about it, he'd laughed and said she was jealous but had nothing to worry about since he was courting her, not them. Having spent so much time in the presence of gentlemen who only cared to compliment her beauty or some other superficial trait, she'd accepted Robbie's words and had forgotten the incident.

It wasn't that Robbie had told her he thought she was ugly but had a winning personality. No, it was that he'd never been one to talk incessantly about her looks, or anything else about her if she were being honest. That's what kept her attracted to him. At first, it was as Brooke claimed; she had a tendency to act as a lifeline to those in need of saving. Robbie had definitely been in need of saving and with his handsome looks and his easy charm, a girlhood crush developed. The crush changed into something else after she'd tried to catch the notice of another, only to have the other man dismiss her with nasty remarks and unflattering ideas. Not that she'd heard him say these things herself, mind you. Not even the worst sort of man would speak that way in front of a female, even one he thought was a tart. No, she'd only heard a sugarcoated version, but that was enough to know she'd best not stray from Robbie.

And so she hadn't, even if he had. She'd often caught him entertaining other girls or heard stories about his exploits. It had hurt, but he'd always soothed her with sweet words and reminded her he was courting her and they'd marry one day. What a joke, she thought. He'd only said that to keep her on a string. And like the puppet she'd been, she'd stayed firmly attached. Too afraid to trust another. Too afraid to trust herself with another. She'd thought she'd seen a real shimmer of something good in the man who Robbie claimed was a womanizer. She had no idea a wolf was hiding under that sheep's fur. The fear of finding another man who would view her as the equivalent of a challenging courtesan kept her safely with Robbie. At least he was toying with those girls and not her, she'd tell herself as she wept into her pillow at night. He'd promised her he'd marry her, not them. He was just having his bachelor fun and would settle down with her when he finished.

Mama, for all her sweet southern charm learned straight from growing up in South Carolina, had been rather blunt on the subject when she'd spoken to Madison about Robbie. She'd tried to discourage the match in many ways over the five years, but the only argument that seemed to hold water was her belief he'd be unfaithful to Madison after they married. Naïve girl that she'd been, she'd never considered the possibility before Mama mentioned it. A few days later, she'd casually mentioned it to Robbie and he'd assured her even though most men had affairs, he would not.

Now, sitting next to Benjamin, eating his favorite meal in the world, waffles and a cup of chocolate, she couldn't help wonder how long it would be before he sought the company of another; or if he'd already done so. She'd believed him when he'd said he hadn't on their wedding night. But that was several days ago. There were many servants at Rockhurst; perhaps he'd been with a maid. She frowned. For some reason, the thought of him sharing another woman's bed hurt more than the confirmation that Robbie actually had. She shouldn't let it, she told herself. She'd expected him to before they'd married and she'd practically given him her permission in the carriage on the way to Rockhurst.

She put her fork down. There was no way she was going to be able to eat now.

"You're not worried about our bath, are you?" Benjamin asked, genuine concern stamped on his hard features.

She shook her head. "No. I've been before. I'm looking forward to going."

"Excellent. Eat up."

"I'm quite full." She pushed her plate away.

He frowned down at her plate. "You've taken three bites."

"Yes, three very filling bites," she said with a weak smile.

He put his fork down and looked at her curiously. "Is something not to your liking?"

"No," she said hastily. "I'm just not as hungry as I thought."

"Would you care to tell me what you've been thinking about?" he asked, picking his fork back up.

She shook her head. "No." There was no use in denying she'd been thinking about *something*.

"All right," he said quietly before picking up his cup of chocolate and taking a gulp.

She glanced at the space between them. As close as they were to each other, he could easily have "accidentally" brushed against her at least a dozen times already. Why hadn't he? More importantly, why did she feel disappointed he hadn't? He'd better not have lost interest in her already, she thought somewhat bitterly. If he was just another man that only saw her pretty face and only dreamt of lifting her skirts and nothing more, she was going to be furious. And, quite frankly, she didn't know who she'd be more furious with: him for thinking of her that way, or herself for once again being attracted to a scoundrel. There was no denying it; she was definitely attracted to him. And that wasn't necessarily a welcome discovery, either.

"Are you ready?" he asked, standing.

She nodded. "As ready as I can be."

"Good. We'll walk to the bathhouse, it's just down the street," he said, offering her his arm.

She took his arm and together they walked down the street to the bathhouse.

The common room that was used as a waiting area had plain white walls and grey slate flooring. Madison found a seat in a plush red velvet chair and waited while Benjamin walked up to the lady behind the counter to make their arrangements. She'd been to a bathhouse only once before and enjoyed the experience greatly. The warm water and heated rooms created a relaxing atmosphere that she was certain she needed.

She needed to relax and sort out her feelings for Benjamin. It would be best for her to keep him at arm's length where neither would get hurt. Not that she thought he'd be too badly hurt in all this, but she knew she'd been hurt before and knew it was possible again.

"They're ready for us," Benjamin said with a grin that sent queer sensations through her body.

She got up from her chair and together they followed the attendant down the hall. The hall was long and had five giant wooden doors that lined both sides of the hallway. At the very end, there was one final door. The attendant opened the door, and Benjamin stood back and ushered her inside. She walked in and looked down at the bath. It looked the same as the one she'd seen before. As if a giant hole had been dug into the floor and decorated with tiles of different colors and shapes then the whole thing filled with steaming hot water. One end had a bit of a slope and even a handrail next to it that made it easier to step in. The only thing different was the size of the tub. It was gigantic. Almost like it wasn't meant to be used alone.

She spun around to see Benjamin's face right behind her. His face was split in two by a grin that rivaled the one he wore on their wedding day. She swallowed. He intended to share the bath with her. She looked around for the attendant.

"She's gone," Benjamin said, causing Madison's eyes to meet his. "I've already dismissed her. If you need help with your gown, I'll do it."

She swallowed again and nodded. "A—all right."

"Why don't you turn around," he murmured.

Her palms grew clammy and she hastily wiped them on her skirts as she turned around to give him better access to the back of her gown. One by one, she could feel him undoing the row of buttons that went down the back of her gown. When he'd undone the last button, which happened to be positioned just above her waist, he slipped his curved fingertips under the edges of the pale green fabric and ran his hands along the edge up to the shoulder caps, searing her skin through her chemise as he went. Once he reached the sleeves, his hold on the fabric tightened and with gentle ease, he slipped the caps off her shoulders and held onto them as her gown slid down her body.

"You're beautiful," he whispered, making her body tense. He brought his fingers up to trace her shoulder blade. "It was just a compliment, Madison, nothing more."

She nodded tersely and closed her eyes. She was nothing but a pretty face to him, and the confirmation stung. "Thank you," she said quietly and waited for him to remove her chemise like she knew he would.

Benjamin let his fingers lightly skim her back and the flare of her hips before giving her waist a light squeeze. "Could you lift your foot?" he murmured in her ear before sinking to his haunches in front of her.

Her blood was pumping through her body so furiously she had no idea how her body cooperated with his request, but somehow she found herself raising her foot a few inches off the floor. Benjamin's hand took hold of her ankle, and he pushed her slipper off. His other hand came to settle on her other ankle and without being prompted, she lifted her foot and allowed him to slip off her other slipper.

His hands stayed on her ankles for a moment before he slid them up her calves, past her knees and to the tops of her stockings, leaving a hot trail in their wake. She could feel his stare piercing her as he turned his head to look up at her while his thumbs tenderly caressed the skin above the tops of her stockings.

He took his right hand from her left leg and used it to bend her right knee and bring her foot to rest on his thigh. She watched in stunned silence as he lowered his head and placed a searing kiss on the inside of her right thigh before using both hands to unroll her stocking.

His movements were slow as he peeled off her stocking. He used his thumbs and forefingers to pull her stockings down and trailed his other fingers along the skin that was newly exposed. His big hand lifted the foot that was still resting on his thigh and gave it a squeeze before lowering it to the cold tile. With the same slow and patient movements, he silently removed her other stocking before standing up to face her.

"Why don't you get in," he said hoarsely. "I'll join you in a moment."

"Am I allowed to wear my chemise?" she asked, uncertain.

"I'd recommend that you do," he said raggedly, turning away.

She nodded her understanding, though she didn't understand at all. Last time she'd come, she hadn't worn anything in the water. Nobody told her it was recommended she keep her chemise on.

The water was just as warm as she remembered. She took a seat toward the middle of the slope. Her position was perfect, in her opinion. She was far enough into the water so she could lie down completely and be submerged up to the top of her chest, while her face stayed above water with only her hair getting a little damp.

She heard the water next to her splash when Benjamin's feet stepped in. She turned her head to look at him and grinned when she saw he was once again wearing his too tight drawers. "You wore your drawers," she said laughingly. "I thought they were uncomfortable."

"They are," he grumbled. "But women wear tight corsets in an effort to impress men, and I'm wearing these to please you."

She laughed. "You're absurd. Just take them off. Nobody's here to see but me."

"Exactly, and you're the one I don't want to see," he teased, lying down next to her.

"I assure you, the mystery you contain in there does not hold my interest the way you think it ought," she said bluntly.

"You speak as if you have vast knowledge of men's body parts," he mused aloud, reaching over and taking her hand into his.

"I've seen one before," she blurted out as he interlaced their fingers.

He scoffed. "Yes, but that was a little boy's. There's a difference."

"Fine, suit yourself," she said with a shrug. "But if you have a permanent red line that circles your waist because you're too stubborn about being mysterious and all that nonsense, you'll have no one to blame but yourself."

"'Tis a brand I'll wear with honor if it wins your heart," he said cryptically.

She shook her head. Men. They were such complex creatures it was really a wonder the human race had survived this long. "You're cracked."

"I know."

"How long do we have in the bath?" she asked after a minute of silence.

"As long as we want, duchess," he said with a grin. He broke their hand hold and stood. "Care to join me at the other end?"

She brought her head up to look down to the end of the bath. "It looks rather deep."

"It is," he confirmed, reaching his hand down to help her to her feet. "Probably too deep for me to touch and still have my neck above water."

"But you're tall," she reasoned. Surely it wouldn't be *that* deep, would it?

"Most aren't as tall as I am, and some rent this specific room to do light swimming."

"Oh," she said, gaining her feet and walking further into the bath with him. "You plan to teach me the breaststroke now, don't you?"

"If you want, I can. But I thought we'd just relax against the side." He wrapped his arm around her waist and pulled her closer against him.

They walked along in the water until they got to a part where Madison could no longer touch with her whole foot and stopped walking. "I need to stop," she said softly. She might be able to do the backstroke in waist deep water with someone watching, but she didn't like the idea of standing on her tiptoes just to be able to barely keep her chin above water.

"Come a little farther," he urged. "I'm not going to let you drown."

She looked at him keenly. She knew he wouldn't let her drown, but still the idea that for three seconds she could be thrashing around like a scared fish before he could bring her to safety didn't thrill her.

"Come on," he urged again. "I'll support you, I promise. I'll never be more than an inch away."

"All right," she agreed, inching closer to him and his protective hold.

A few steps later, she wasn't even able to walk on her toes any longer and he used his arm to lift her and bring her squarely in front of him. He wrapped his other arm around her and walked her over to the closest wall. "This'll do," he said, favoring her with a grin.

She looked down at the end of the tub. "But we're not at the end. There's still a good two feet before we reach the end."

"I know," he said, moving his hands to hold her about the waist. "I don't think I'd be able to support us at the end. Not unless I lean against the wall, too."

"Why not?"

"I don't float."

"I thought you said almost everyone floats," she countered. Her feet were a good six or eight inches off the floor and she was being suspended in the water only by his hands on her waist and her back lightly pressing against the wall.

"I did," he agreed. "But I'm not one of them. Actually, that's incorrect. I don't exactly sink, either."

"How do you not float and not sink?" she asked dubiously. It was simple really, you either floated or sunk. Which was it?

He moved his body closer to hers and brought his thigh up between her legs, resting his foot against the wall behind her. "To help support you," he murmured when she gave him a startled look after she saw the new position of his leg. "About the sinking and floating business, I don't float at the top and I don't sink to the bottom. It's strange really. My body cannot stay on top of the water, but it can't stay on the bottom, either. I seem to find myself sucked into the middle and struggle to come to the surface or stay on the bottom."

"Why would you want to go to the bottom?" And why would anyone want to *stay* at the bottom of a body of water?

He shrugged. "To look for things. As a boy, I didn't have anyone to play with for a few years and when I'd go swimming, I'd throw something in and dive to retrieve it. It's a great single-person game."

"Oh, that makes sense," she conceded. "I wonder why you can't float or sink. Is that common?"

"No," he said, shaking his head. "I've only met one other person that has the same difficulty. But I don't know what causes it. Something about the density of the body being more than the water, therefore, you sink. Or perhaps it's the other way around. All I know is my body—"

She cut him off with a quick kiss on the lips. "Sorry, you were starting to remind me of my overly scientific cousin, Alex, and I just couldn't bear you ruining this moment that way."

He looked to be in shock. "I'd say I'll be sure to keep my scientific talk to myself in the future, but if my punishment for talking about science is a kiss, I believe I may take up an interest in biology, astronomy, chemistry, physics, horticulture and perhaps botany as well," he told her with a grin.

"That may not be the punishment next time," she retorted, resting her hands on his broad shoulders. He was actually a rather big man. Not enormous and fearfully intimidating, by any means, but not small and powerless, either. The muscles in his shoulders, chest and arms were so pronounced they were visible through his clothes. She'd barely taken note of that fact before they'd married. Before her wedding day, he'd just been another man, nothing more. But in the past few days, she'd taken notice of how his body filled out his clothing. Yesterday, when she'd seen him in the water and lying on the grass, she'd noticed just how big he was but hadn't given it much thought. However, now that he was holding her so closely, she couldn't notice anything *but* his masculinity.

His chest was mere inches from hers and she had the strangest urge to reach her fingers into the middle of his small smattering of short reddish brown chest hair and feel his heartbeat under her fingers.

Many doubted he had a heart, but she knew he did. And just now, it seemed to be beating in time with hers.

"You know you still owe me a kiss," he murmured in her ear.

"I know," she said.

"Good. As long as you didn't think you'd gotten out of it just now."

"You mean that paltry peck didn't count as my Waffle Law kiss?" she teased, bringing her cheek to rest against his slightly hair roughened jaw.

He shook his head and moved his hands from her waist and brought them up to caress her lower back. "No, it doesn't count," he rasped, his voice barely audible.

Heat she didn't recognize pooled in her midsection as his hands continued their gentle and thorough exploration, climbing up her back. She may have been up to her shoulders in hot water, but she could feel every heated touch of his hands as if it were a brand. She closed her eyes and leaned against his powerful chest for the support she suddenly seemed to require.

Her body sank an inch or two farther into the water and she rested on the muscled thigh he'd positioned in between her legs. His bristled jaw tickled a path across her cheek just before his lips landed on hers for a tender kiss. His soft lips pressed hers with a gentle pressure that made her sigh with pleasure. His strong hands stopped roaming her back and came to rest on her shoulders, using their strength to pull her closer to him and hold her there.

His lips moved slightly lower to focus attention on her bottom lip, gently pulling it between his lips. Her fingers dug into his shoulders and she shamelessly pressed her entire body closer to his. She could feel his strong chest against her swollen breasts and the hard planes of his stomach against her softer one. Below that, her knee brushed the hardness of his desire for her and she abruptly pulled her face back.

Embarrassment and shame washed over her. She'd just acted like a wanton by pressing her body against a man she hardly knew.

"Don't pull away," he panted as she scooted away from his body and toward the wall.

She couldn't make herself look at him as she tried to scramble out of his embrace.

"Madison," he said softly, moving closer to her as she backed up completely against the wall. "There's nothing wrong with kissing me."

She closed her eyes and shook her head. "I know," she whispered. But even whispering it didn't keep her voice from cracking.

He repositioned himself to stand in front of her with one of his legs on either side of her and his body helping to keep her pressed against the side of the bath. Bringing his hands up to frame her face and tilt it toward his, he said, "There's no shame in enjoying it, you know?"

She swallowed. Had she been so obvious? Of course she had. She'd just pressed herself against him like a tavern wench looking for a quick coin.

"I enjoyed it," he said with a smile. "Why shouldn't you be able to?"

She lowered her lashes and mumbled, "I don't know."

"Yes, you do. You just don't want to tell me," he countered softly. He leaned forward and brushed a sweet kiss on her forehead. "You don't have to tell me today. You can tell me whenever you're ready. I'll be ready to listen."

"Thank you," she choked, bringing her fingers up to idly skate along the tops of his shoulders and down his clavicle.

He wrapped his arms around her waist, kicked off the wall to the middle of the bath and lifted her partially from the water before spinning her in a full circle that caused a large wave of water to spray around the room. With a smile, he rested his forehead on hers and whispered, "I'll always be there for you, Madison. Always."

Chapter 14

Madison felt like a fugitive as she and Benjamin snuck back into Rockhurst after another meal of waffles (which she ate) and chocolate. It was nearly ten before their carriage entered the drive and dropped them off. Not that their hosts would have locked them out for being out so late. No, that would have been a preferable fate than what Madison assumed they'd have waiting for them when they arrived: an interrogation.

Thinking it best to just sneak to her room and evade Brooke's questions in the morning, they took hallways that led them away from the rest of the house to get to her room. She'd told Benjamin to go to the gamekeeper's cottage and she'd worry about avoiding her sister by herself. Of course he pulled the gentleman card (as if he'd ever been one before) and insisted he'd see her to her room.

They were almost to her door when Stevens suddenly appeared. "I was told to have you report to the drawing room immediately, Your Grace," Stevens said with a bow.

Madison turned to Benjamin and shot him an apologetic glance. She had no idea why they'd want to see him, but at least she wasn't the one they were summoning and for that, she was eternally thankful.

Benjamin grumbled something she couldn't understand before turning to face the butler. "Tell them I'll be there in a minute."

"Very well," Stevens said. "And you, Your Grace?" he asked with a pointed look at Madison.

"Pardon?" she asked in confusion.

"Will you also be down shortly?"

She shifted her eyes to her snickering husband. "Oh, good grief;

they did not tell you to call me that, did they?"

Stevens coughed to cover up his own snicker. That wasn't an unusual habit for him. Before he'd become a butler, he was actually a footman. Due to Andrew's impoverished state a few years ago, he'd had to pension off the majority of his servants and he'd elevated Stevens to be his butlering footman here at Rockhurst. He had another, Addams, in London. Addams was always more professional about his butlering duties—actually he was quite snotty, if one were interested in the truth. Stevens, on the other hand, had a lot to learn about professionalism. "I do believe it was Mrs. Grimes who directed me to call you that," he said with a smirk.

Madison fought the urge to roll her eyes. Of course, Liberty did that. Until she'd married Paul—wait, that wasn't true, even for a while after she'd married Paul—she'd had a penchant for the rules of propriety to such a point that her husband still teased her from time to time, calling her Live-by-the-rules Liberty. Madison had warned Liberty the whole month of her engagement not to "Your Grace" her or she'd find a way to torture her. So far, Liberty had followed the rules, but apparently she'd found a loophole. "Which one of us do they require for this blessed family event?" Madison asked with a hint of sarcasm.

"Both," Stevens said promptly.

Was it her imagination or did Benjamin groan at the same time she did? No matter. She shot him another apologetic glance and together they turned to walk back downstairs. Blast; all that skillful navigation of the halls only to be found out at the very end by the butler. Perhaps next time, they'd just bore a hole in the ceiling and lower her in.

"It's about time," Andrew drawled as they walked in.

Madison felt a blush creep up her neck. "If we'd known you'd be waiting for us, we'd have stayed out longer," Benjamin said smugly, leading Madison to lightly elbow him in the side. This was no time for jokes, not that she thought her family would understand his humor anyway.

"Not to worry, I've been late once or twice myself," Paul said dismissively.

"No need to bring up the past," Liberty said lightly. "Now that everyone's here, tell us what you've been tantalizing us with all afternoon."

Paul reached into his breast pocket and retrieved a piece of paper. "There was a time when I was filled with dread upon receiving one of these," he announced with a grin directed to his wife. "But this time, I am proud to announce I have a piece of correspondence from one Mr. John Banks." He held it up in the air for all to see. "Gentlemen, control your wives," he commanded playfully a second later, when the three women in the room ran to his side to try to grab the missive from his hand.

"Why did he send it to you?" Andrew asked testily, not bothering to pull his wife off the man.

"Because I'm his favorite son-in-law," Paul retorted with a snicker, still holding the note as high in the air as he could.

Andrew frowned. "What makes you think you're the favorite?"

All the commotion in the room came to an abrupt halt followed instantly by four people giggling, howling, shaking and bending over in laughter. "Are you cracked?" Madison said between ragged breaths of laughter.

"No," Andrew said solemnly, shaking his head then turning to look at Benjamin who only shrugged in return.

"Putting aside that we're both men of the cloth," Paul broke in, still shaking with mirth, "you both married your wives due to scandals."

"So did you," Andrew retorted.

"Of her making, not mine," Paul corrected, garnering him a swat on his bottom from Liberty.

"And," Brooke said, still giggling almost uncontrollably, "If you think about it, you helped create the scandal that led to Madison's marriage to the very man who hired you to create the scandal involving me."

"I daresay, you just may hold the title of the least favorite," Madison quipped.

Andrew shook his head. "All right, I'm the least favorite, as always. Now, can we just hear what the letter has to say?"

"As soon as the vultures retreat," Paul said.

Realizing the man wasn't going to hand over the note to any of them, the girls backed away and waited in anticipation as Paul read the letter.

Most of it was a lot of agitated nonsense about how Andrew had botched his job as guardian and how disappointed Mama was she'd miss the one wedding that wasn't a five minute ceremony put together on a whim with only half a dozen guests in a private residence. Then Papa went on to explain they'd be returning on the passenger vessel that was set to depart three days after the one that carried the letter. That meant they were only three or four days away. Excitement skittered up Madison's spine. She'd missed her parents dearly the past few months. At the very end of the letter, there was a reference to three small chests that accompanied the letter.

Madison's heart pounded. She knew which chests her parents had sent. Each of the girls had a small chest, two feet high, two feet long and maybe a foot and a half wide. They weren't terribly big, just big enough to hold personal items that were special to them. Brooke's and Liberty's probably held such things as favorite ribbons, dance card slips from their first dances, or other innocent things like that. Madison wished hers held innocent tokens, as well. Instead, she knew it was stuffed full of missives from Robbie, sketches she'd drawn of a stranger and even a few paintings. Nothing she wanted. Nothing that held an ounce of appeal.

"Would you like yours?" Benjamin asked, startling her.

She blinked up at him and turned to where Paul had a cabinet open and was withdrawing the chests he'd hidden there earlier. She shifted her gaze to Brooke when she heard her laugh at the dance card slip that held the name of a Russian Prince she'd once danced with when he'd visited America. Andrew was sitting with his arm around Brooke and acting somewhat interested in what she was showing him, but kept turning his curious gaze back to Madison and Benjamin. "I don't believe so," she said at last. "I'd like to go to my room actually."

Benjamin wrapped a comforting arm around her and steered her from the room then down the maze of hallways and staircases that led to her room. "Madison, would you like to talk?" he asked when they reached her room. He moved to stand directly in front of her, resting his shoulder against the door.

She shook her head.

"I'll only listen," he said, taking her hands in his. His blue eyes looked curious and intent as they stayed locked with hers while she debated her choices.

She shook her head again. "I'd like to be alone just now, thank you."

He closed his eyes and nodded once. "All right. Will you come to where I'm staying tomorrow? I have something for you."

Madison swallowed visibly. "Can't you bring it here?"

"I could," he mused. "But I'd rather not. Just come see me."

"All right."

The corner of his mouth tipped up. He brought both her hands up to his mouth and feathered kisses on each of her knuckles. Lowering their hands, he leaned forward and ever so lightly pressed a kiss to her lips. "Sweet dreams," he murmured.

~*~*~*~

Madison sat on the edge of her bed, staring at the wall in front of her far longer than she should have. She just couldn't force herself to get up and get changed for bed. She'd already been unnerved by the crashing end to her bright day caused by the delivery of those blasted trunks with the blasted letters from blasted Robbie inside. But then to come into her room and find another blasted letter from blasted Robbie, only served to fray her edges. She might have stared at the wall for a week straight if Brooke hadn't arrived.

"Madison," Brooke said softly, coming into her room and shutting the door. "Do you want to talk?"

Madison handed Brooke the new blasted note from blasted Robbie.

Brooke's fingers snatched the unsigned note and she scanned it, moving her lips as she read the words. "Where did you get this?"

"On the bed," Madison said, pointing to where the note had been lying on her pillow when she'd opened the door.

Brooke sat down next to her. "Madison, the note was delivered by a paid messenger and isn't even signed. Why are you so upset over it?"

"It's from him," Madison said evenly, falling back to lie on the bed.

Brooke lay next to her. "Who, your husband?" she asked doubtfully.

Madison brought her hands up to cover her face in an attempt to stop from laughing and sarcastically said, "Yes, Brooke, Benjamin wrote me an anonymous note to warn me he was a murderer."

"You did know he was dangerous before you married him. He had to earn his title of Dangerous Duke somehow," Brooke quipped.

"I don't believe the content of that note for a second," Madison cut in before Brooke could make any more asinine comments. "It's the 'who' of the matter that bothers me."

"I haven't a clue what you're talking about," Brooke said, getting off the bed and going to Madison's chest of drawers. She opened one of the drawers and pulled out a cotton nightrail then tossed it on the bed next to Madison.

"Robbie," Madison said.

"What are you talking about?" Brooke asked with a hint of annoyance in her voice. She walked to where Madison was lying on the bed and motioned for her to get up.

Like the good younger sister that she was, she dutifully stood up and turned her back to Brooke so she could undo her gown. Having grown up in America without lady's maids, the girls had always helped each other dress and undress, if necessary. Having never had strangers help her disrobe, Madison had been slightly uncomfortable with Lottie's help and had given her time off until she was ready to leave Rockhurst. "The note; it's from Robbie," Madison clarified as Brooke quickly undid her buttons.

Brooke gave an exaggerated sigh. "Throw that in the fire. Robbie hasn't two thoughts to knock together in that empty space he calls a brain box."

Madison shook her head. "I just wish he'd leave me alone."

"We all do, trust me. He just cannot stand for you to be happy without him. Remember what happened w—"

"Do not speak of him to me," Madison cut her sister off sharply.

"All right, I won't. But the fact is, Robbie cannot stand for you to be happy with anyone else," Brooke stated flatly, stepping away from the back of Madison's gown and picking up her nightrail.

Madison stepped out of her slippers and got ready to pull her gown down. "And what makes you think I'm happy with someone else?"

"The fact that you're not wearing your chemise," Brooke said in a sing-song voice.

Heat rose in Madison's face. "It's not what you think," she said hastily. After their bath, she'd had to retire her wet chemise for the day.

Brooke shrugged. "I'm not passing judgment."

"Brooke, just leave it alone. Nothing happened." She quickly brought her nightrail over her head and turned to face her smiling sister.

"If you say so," Brooke said, disbelief filling her voice.

"Well, I say so," Madison countered with a hint of annoyance.

Brooke took a seat on the bed and patted the space next to her until Madison gave in and plopped down. "Say I believe you and nothing happened," she cast her a doubtful smile, "do you think it's possible something could happen?"

"It's possible," Madison confessed feeling slightly embarrassed.

Brooke tucked a raven tendril behind her ear and wet her lips. "If he makes you happy, I'm happy for you."

"Thank you," Madison said softly. "But that's what you said about Robbie, too."

"I know," Brooke said, nodding. "But I mean it this time."

"You're a good sister," Madison said, leaning her head on Brooke's shoulder.

"You are, too," Brooke said, "even if you do have abominable taste when it comes to men."

Chapter 15

B enjamin stared at the wooden chest. Who knew a little box no larger than six cubic feet could possibly fascinate him so? Madison had gone whiter than a corpse when she'd heard Paul's grand announcement about those chests. Something had to be inside that she didn't want to be reminded of, but what? For the hundredth time since he'd taken it from the drawing room, his fingers ran over the edges. All he had to do was flip it open and he'd know what she was hiding. But that wasn't his place, he reminded himself as he pulled his hands away and shoved them back into his pockets. She needed to trust him and she wasn't going to be able to if he searched her things as though she were a child.

Putting the trunk under his bed, he went about setting up the painting materials he'd purchased. He'd been pursuing her quite aggressively the past two days and hoped by asking her to join him here, she'd take a chance and trust him enough to come.

Morning couldn't come fast enough. And just like every other day in the last six years, it took its sweet time coming. But at last it arrived, and as the sun peeked into his windows, shedding light in the room, there was a soft knock at the door.

Wearing only his shirtsleeves and trousers, Benjamin tentatively opened the door and was rather surprised to see a perky Madison with a sleepy footman standing behind her holding a heavy tray. "Good morning, Benjamin," she said brightly before directing the footman to take the tray to a little table in the corner.

"Madison," he greeted, idly rubbing his jaw where he had a day's worth of bristle. He knew she didn't sleep until noon as she'd once claimed, but he had no idea she rose so early, either.

"May I come in?"

He looked at the position of her feet in the middle of the carpet. "It appears you're already in."

"I know," she said matter-of-factly. "Why don't you go finish getting dressed?"

He nodded and went to shave and finish putting on his clothes. He was glad she'd come, even if it was much earlier than he'd expected.

He'd finished shaving and was putting on his stockings and boots when she came to the bedroom doorway. "I'm almost done," he said, tying the laces of his boot.

"It's all right. Take your time," she said dismissively. "Breakfast is ready when you are." She shot him a winning smile and leaned her head against the doorjamb.

"Dare I hope it's waffles?" he teased.

Her smile slipped. "How did you know?"

"I didn't. But I do now," he said, taking to his feet.

She put her hands on her hips. "See if I ever try to surprise you again."

He smiled at her. "You do all the time and don't even know it."

"Leave the waistcoat and let's go," she said, walking out of the room.

He wasn't going to argue with that command. He tossed the waistcoat down by his waiting coat and cravat. "Thank you for the waffles," he said, sitting down. "I rarely eat them three meals in a row."

"Neither do I. Actually, I rarely eat them at all; and don't for one minute think I'll be eating them again for lunch," she informed him. "However, I had a brilliant idea in the middle of the night and I had to see if you'd like it. And I absolutely couldn't wait until our next trip to Bath to find out."

Benjamin smiled at her. She'd thought about him in the middle of the night! And from the sound of things, they'd been good thoughts. "All right, let's see what we have," he said, grabbing the top of the silver dome that was closest to him. He pulled the top off and looked at the waffles he'd just uncovered. They had little specks of brown sprinkled in them. "What's this?" He picked one up with his fingers and stared at it closely, barely resisting the urge to sniff it.

"It has chocolate powder in it," she said with a blinding smile. "I'm sure someone's thought of it before, but let's pretend they haven't and it was all my bright idea."

"Excellent idea," he agreed with a smile. "What made you put chocolate in it?" He noticed there was only one large round waffle on the plate that had been under the dome he'd removed, so he carefully cut it in half and slid a half onto each of their plates.

"You said you liked waffles and chocolate, so I thought, 'why not combine them?'. And if that doesn't taste good, I asked Cook to make one with chunks of strawberries cooked into the batter." She lifted up another dome that was hidden on the chair to her left. Pulling off the lid, she showed him the waffle with the strawberries. "I thought since you were putting strawberries on them yesterday, you might like them cooked inside, too." She shrugged and cut that waffle in half as he'd done with the other and gave them each half.

"Thank you. That was very thoughtful of you. I'm sure they'll be delicious."

And they were.

"I have something for you, too," Benjamin said after they'd finished eating and the conversation reached a lull.

"You do?" Both her voice and her bright blue eyes were so full of excitement Benjamin swore his heart rate increased.

He got up from his chair and walked back to the little bedroom. "Are you coming?" he called from inside the room.

"Aren't you going to bring it out?" she hollered back, still sounding excited, but perhaps a different kind of excitement.

He went to the vanity table located against the far wall and started to arrange the painting supplies a bit more. She'd come close to entering this room before breakfast, but the vanity was positioned so that she hadn't been able to see his surprise. "It would be easier for you to come in here." He fanned out several paintbrushes then arranged the tubes and jars of dye just right.

Slowly, he heard her feet scrape across the wooden floor as she walked across the great room to his little bedroom. "All right," she said in a weak, resigned voice. "I'm all yours."

"Excellent." He went to the door and flashed her a smile before grabbing her hand and pulling her inside. "I'm not the greatest at surprises, but I think you'll like this."

She stepped over the threshold and into his room. Her face looked a little paler than earlier and her body was tense as she looked to the middle of the room. At his bed.

"You're looking in the wrong direction," he said gently.

She blinked her eyes and slowly let them move from his bed to the window and finally to rest on the vanity, before she gasped. "How did you know?"

"Brooke told me you didn't bring your painting materials here. I thought now that England will be your permanent home, you could use some." He walked over to the table with her and watched as she picked up some of the brushes and dyes. "That was all I could find in Bath. We can get more next time we go to London."

"Thank you," she murmured, picking up one of the oil paints. "You didn't have to get both oils and watercolors."

He frowned. "Do you prefer one over the other?"

"No, I'm just surprised you'd go to such an extreme, that's all." She picked up one of the brushes that couldn't possibly have more than three hairs in it, and yet it had been almost the most expensive one, of course. "They swindled you, didn't they?"

"Absolutely," he agreed jovially with a "who gives a whit" smile. "I haven't a clue about painting and the clerk knew it. However, I don't mind how much it cost or what ridiculous piece of material I was tricked into buying. I bought this for you and I want you to enjoy it."

"I think I will," she mused. "You said you don't paint?"

"No," he confessed, "I couldn't even paint a stick."

"A stick?" she asked, favoring him with a curious expression. "Why in the world would you paint a stick?"

"I have no idea." He shook his head and grabbed a canvas. "When I was a boy of six or so, I got bored and found some old watercolors that belonged to my governess. She didn't want them and said I could have them. I was so excited to have something to do, I ran to my room to paint. An hour later, I still had a blank canvas. I had no idea what to paint. I looked out the window and saw what looked like a snake crawling on the ground and decided to paint that.

"First, I painted the entire canvas green to be the grass. Then I mixed a few colors together and painted the snake. When I showed it to my governess, her lips twitched a bit but she just patted me on the back and said it looked great for the first time. Inspired, I showed it to Lizzie and got a different reaction entirely. I believe her words were, 'Why did you paint a stick?' When I tried to explain it was a snake, she cocked her head to the side and said, 'It's hard to tell; it really doesn't look like either.' The only other time I tried to paint, I kept painting over the edges of the square canvas."

Madison didn't even try to hide her mirth. "Would you like to learn?" she asked, grabbing a few brushes and jars.

"I'll try, but I don't think I'm teachable." He brought one of the canvases over to the little table and chair by the window.

"That's all right. Just prop that up against the window, thank you. As Brooke mentioned, I haven't painted in a while. I'm probably not very good anymore."

"Rubbish," he countered. He left the room for a moment to go to the common room to grab another chair.

She had her back to him and was stirring paints when he walked back into the room. She looked so graceful standing there. He wanted to prolong the moment and watch her forever, but knew he couldn't do that; she was expecting him to return.

"I thought we'd use oil paints. They're far more forgiving than watercolors," she explained as he took a seat next to her. She finished mixing and poured small blobs of a few of the pigments on a pallet. "All right, Your Grace, shall I show you how to paint a stick or a snake?"

He grinned and shook his head. "Neither."

"Oh, a square, then?" she asked with a teasing smile. "Or would you like to branch out and do a circle?"

"Actually rhombi have always held special appeal to me," he said, edging his chair closer to her, hopefully without her noticing.

"Rhombi?"

"It's the Latin word for the plural of rhombus. I suppose it could also be rhombuses. I just like the word rhombi better." Boldly, he pressed his thigh against her skirts.

She looked at him curiously, which he interpreted to be a result of his words, not actions. "I don't mean to sound daft, but what on earth is a rhombus?"

"It's a shape," he said with a shrug. "It's a four-sided parallelogram whose sides are all equal in length. Kind of like a square. Except a square also has four right angles, therefore, it's called a square instead of a rhombus. The most common shape for a rhombus is the dia—"

She leaned forward and cut him off with another quick kiss. But he was too quick, and when she went to pull away, he moved his hands up to cup her face and brought her lips back to his.

He pressed his lips to hers and held them there, moving them slowly on top of hers, waiting for her to respond. And she did respond. Her lips moved to match his. Exerting pressure, then releasing. Carefully, he parted his lips more and ran his tongue along her bottom lip, flicking the corner of her mouth. She gasped his name and brought her hands up to rest on top of his fingers where they held her face.

Taking advantage of her parted lips, he slipped his tongue past her lips and swept her cheeks. She tasted sweet like strawberries and chocolate. He moved to touch her tongue and was sweetly rewarded by hers boldly following his as he swept her cheek again.

Hot desire shot through him, making his blood race and his temperature rise. She wanted this just as much as he did. Like him, she was powerless to stop. But rational thought returned and he knew he needed to stop. This wasn't the right time.

He withdrew his tongue and pulled back from her lips, eliciting a whimper of displeasure from her followed by a fetching blush. "You're so beautiful when you're blushing," he murmured, making her blush deepen.

She lowered her eyes to stare at the lower half of his face. "What were we talking about?" Her voice sounded strange. Lost. Dazed.

"Rhombi," he said with a roguish grin. "I was explaining wh—"

"Stop," she interrupted.

"Hmm, and here I thought you were enjoying our geometry lesson."

She shot him a pointed look. "You're not turning into Alex on me, are you?"

"No," he said, brushing a blonde curl out of her eye. "I only did that to see if you'd kiss me again."

She rolled her eyes. "If you want a kiss, just ask."

"You mean you'd kiss me if I asked?"

"Yes. I still owe you that Waffle Law kiss, remember?"

"Oh," he said, disappointed. She seemed awfully eager to have him collect on that and be done with it. But there was no reason to do so when she kept giving them to him without his having to ask. "I don't think I'm ready to use that yet," he mused. "However, I have decided what I want to paint."

"What? A waffle?" she asked sardonically.

"No," he said, matching her tone. "A landscape. I want a river running here," he ran his fingers in a curvy line down the middle of the canvas, "and trees here, here, and here," he tapped two fingers on three different spots on the canvas, "the rest can be rolling grass. You know, not flat, but not mountainous, either; just hills and such."

"For someone who looked at a blank canvas for an hour before deciding to paint a snake that looked more like a bad stick, you sure have high aspirations."

A half hour later, Benjamin had more paint on his shirt and hands than was on the canvas. Not that that was saying much. The canvas was covered in paint. No, it was slathered in paint. In fact, the paint alone had to have a thickness of half an inch off the canvas.

The picture itself was no masterpiece, either. The stream was black from far too many coats and colors mixed together. The grass looked like the wind was blowing it in different directions because of his uneven strokes. The trees resembled long skinny brown sticks wearing big curly green wigs. But he didn't care. He didn't care that it looked atrocious and he was covered in paint. No, he was grinning like an idiot.

The whole time he'd attempted to paint, she'd grinned at him. She'd touched his hand to help guide his strokes. She'd laughed at his asinine jokes. She'd even calmly answered his stupid questions. All that was well worth the horrific painting he'd produced.

"Your turn," he said, picking up his work of art and moving it out of the way to dry. He returned a moment later with a fresh canvas and saw Madison cleaning the brushes. "Can I help?"

"No, I'm almost done." She finished cleaning them and stared at the white cloth in front of her. After a few minutes, she finally said, "I have no idea what to paint."

"Hmm, how about a landscape? I'm sure yours would turn out much better than mine."

She shook her head. "I've never been good matching nature's hues."

"What about an animal? Have you ever been to a menagerie?"

"No. I've only seen small animals like dogs, ducks, squirrels, and mice. But, I've seen drawings of things like rhinoceroses and duckbilled platypuses."

He grinned at her animal choices. "All right," he said slowly, rubbing his jaw. "What did you paint?"

"People," she blurted out, turning red.

"All you needed to do was ask. How would you like me? Standing? Sitting? By the window? On the bed?" *Naked?*

"Anywhere is fine really," she said uneasily, "wherever you'd feel most comfortable."

"Hmm," he said, pretending to think. He already knew where he was going, he just didn't want to seem *too* eager. "How about I lie on the bed? That way you can turn around and have the window to your back for better light."

"All right," she chirped. Her hands seemed a little unsteady as she went about squeezing fresh paint onto the pallet and turning her supplies around to face him.

Against his body's demands, Benjamin slowly walked to the bed and lay on his side. He propped his elbow up on the pillows and leaned his head against his hand. He took the other hand and brought it to rest in front of his stomach. "Is this all right?" he asked, when he was in what he thought to be a nearly perfect position. It would be better if he and she were minus their clothes, but this would do for now.

She looked up and a burble of laughter passed her lips. "You're trying much too hard. Just relax."

He stared at her. He was relaxed. At least as relaxed as he could possibly be when just looking at her, made his muscles tense with desire and his body ache with need. "Is this better?" he asked, even though he hadn't done a thing to change his position.

"No. You haven't moved a millimeter. Here, let me help you." She walked up to him and pushed him onto his back. She took his right arm and laid it behind his head, then moved his left arm to his side. She looked down at his boots and pursed her lips. "I suppose you want to leave those on?"

"No," he exclaimed a little too loudly. "I mean, I've no problem if you want to take them off."

She walked down to his feet and undid the laces on his boots before yanking them off and letting them hit the floor with two loud thuds. She left his stockings on and moved to his waist. A hot coil of desire twisted in his stomach as she grabbed onto the bottom of his shirt and tugged it from his trousers. Her dainty fingers arranged his shirttails then went to the buttons at the top of his shirt. She undid the first two and let it hang open in the perfect V. "Now just let me do your cuff and I'll get started," she murmured as she undid the buttons on the cuff that was to rest above his head. She rolled up his sleeve two rolls and set it back down.

He scowled. "You cannot undo the cuff of one arm and not the other. It feels unnatural." He quickly undid the other cuff and laid his arms back the way she'd had them.

"Sorry. I wasn't going to have the full length of that arm in the picture," she said with a shrug.

"It's fine." Then shooting her a wolfish grin, he purposely moved both his arms a little and said, "Oh, you had better come reposition me now that I've moved."

Quickly, she came back and put his arms exactly how she wanted them. "Don't move again," she warned.

"Yes, Your Grace," he teased, making her flash him a warm smile.

Madison walked back to where she'd propped her canvas up against the back of the chair he'd been sitting on earlier (how odd that the little shop in Bath carried brushes with three hairs, but not easels). She took her seat and grabbed a nearby quill.

Using the quill, she made a light outline of his body and the bed before grabbing her brushes. Time seemed to evaporate as he lay there watching her. She'd peek up at him every few seconds then swish her brush on the canvas.

She was so beautiful, glowing in the sunlight that streamed in the window behind her. The beams of light caught her hair and surrounded her face, making her look like an angel.

He wouldn't mind looking at that image forever.

"All right, you can talk now," Madison said softly. "I can see you're dying to."

He smiled at her. "Thank you. But believe it or not, I'm content just to look at you."

She twisted her lips in irritation. "Of course. All right, if you wish to stare, that's fine."

"It seems to me that you're the one who wants to talk," he mused. "What do you want to talk about?"

"I don't know." She shrugged. "It just feels strange with you staring at me."

"You're staring at me, too," he pointed out.

"Yes, because I'm painting you."

"And I'm looking at you because you're painting me," he said, trying not to laugh. She must not like people to look at her.

She got up out of her chair and grabbed the canvas. "It doesn't matter anyway. I'm done."

Rather comfortable in his position, he didn't move as she walked over to him with the canvas. His gaze slid over the picture when she turned it toward him. "It's a perfect likeness. You have everything exactly right."

She pursed her lips. "No, I missed a few things. Like right here—" She pointed to something on his face and Benjamin swiped her hand away.

"No. It's perfect. There are no flaws."

"If you say so," she said doubtfully. "Shall we annoy Andrew and hang it up in his gallery once it dries?"

He chuckled. "Not this one. This one goes to *my* gallery. However, I have an idea for Andrew's…"

"By the look on your face, I get the impression it's not a nice idea," she said, giving him the best sharp look she could manage while trying not to laugh.

"It's not," he said with a grin. "However, I wouldn't let you hang that one up, either. I wouldn't want to deal with a jealous Andrew once Brooke caught sight of it."

"Oh, for pity's sake," she said, exaggerating her words and rolling her eyes.

He sat up and swung his legs over the side of the bed then pulled her to stand in between them. "You know I only tease you in that way because I know you like it."

"Yes. And I admit, I do enjoy such banter, even if I shouldn't," she said with a shy smile.

"You're rather peculiar for a vicar's daughter, you know?" He took the canvas from her and set it beside him on the bed, freeing both of her hands.

"I know," she said easily. "I always was. Papa used to despair about what would happen to me. I've always had a propensity for saying unsavory comments. But, as much as my parents tried, I just didn't absorb their advice."

He pulled her arms up to wrap them around his neck. "Madison," he murmured, wrapping his arms around her waist and pulling her as close to him as he could. "I think you're perfect just the way you are, naughty banter and all."

She smiled down at him. "And I like you, naughty banter and all."

"Stay with me tonight." His voice was quiet and steady, belying the rush of emotions and blood coursing through him.

"I can't," she whispered.

"Why not?" He moved his hands to caress her lower back.

Her blue eyes met his and locked. "I don't know."

"Then stay. We won't do anything you don't want. I promise." He moved his lips to her jaw and kissed its rounded edge. "We can kiss. I know you like to kiss," he murmured in between kisses. His lips kissed a path to her ear and softly nipped and licked the hollow behind it. "I can hold you tight as I am right now." He moved his caressing hands farther up her back, broadening his movements to cover her whole back. His lips left her ear and found their way to her mouth. "I'll only do what you wish, Madison. I'll not force you. Ever."

Madison's body might have fallen into a heap of bones and flesh if it hadn't been for Benjamin's hands supporting her. "Just holding and kissing?"

"Just holding and kissing," he confirmed. He flashed her a roguish smile, "and perhaps a little touching, too."

"Touching?"

"Just a little," he said with a wink. "But only if you want to."

"All right," she agreed with a slight swallow. "I'll stay."

Chapter 16

D inner dragged by slower than a twenty-five-year-old horse attempting to pull a phaeton in a race. But this time it wasn't the uncomfortable company that made dinner crawl, it was the apprehension that Madison might change her mind. Benjamin wasn't going to press her to share his bed tonight—well, in a literal sense she would have to, but not in the metaphoric sense.

"Are you ready?" he whispered after their meal.

"I just need to get some things from my room," she whispered back. Her eyes held no fear or uncertainty.

He walked with her down the hall to her room. "May I come in with you while you gather your things?"

She nodded and went inside, leaving the door open for him. He entered, shut the door behind them, and watched as she gathered a few items in her arms. Seeing her juggle her comb and other *toilette* items, he grabbed her reticule and carried it over to her. He held it and helped her fill it with the items she'd need, purposely not suggesting she add a nightrail to her travel bag.

"I think I'm ready now," she said evenly, not a hint of emotion in her voice.

They left both the room and the house together, making sure to avoid rooms that her sister and Andrew might occupy.

A broad smile spread across his face when they crossed the threshold to the cabin where they'd spend their first night together. He'd bungled their first attempt; he would not make a hash of things again.

"Where shall I put my reticule?"

"Anywhere you want, duchess," he answered, walking to the window and drawing the drapes. "Are you cold?"

"No." She withdrew several items from her reticule and placed them on the vanity. "I'm actually rather warm."

"Sorry. I forgot to shut the drapes when we left and it got hot in here." He stripped to his shirtsleeves and went to stand behind her while she arranged her things on the vanity. "I'm glad you agreed to stay," he murmured against her neck while he nuzzled it.

She mumbled an incoherent reply and her brush slipped from her fingers, making a loud noise when it hit the vanity. He moved his fingers to the top of her gown and pulled the edge down, dropping tender kisses across her shoulders and the top of her back as he went. He peeled the cap off her left shoulder and nipped the top with his teeth before soothing it with his tongue, making her gasp.

Her head lolled to the side, allowing him better access to her neck. He moved his moist lips from her shoulder to her neck, leaving a warm trail to mark his path. She sighed as he bent his head and kissed his way around to the front of her neck then licked the hollow by her clavicle.

He took his hands from her gown and brought them to her hair where he used his fingertips to gently massage her scalp. "May I play your lady's maid tonight?"

She groaned. "I don't have one," she said mindlessly.

"I know," he whispered into her neck. "Let me help you tonight." Without waiting for her to form a coherent response, his fingers started finding the pins in her hair and pulling them out. She had so much hair to free; but a man with a mission never takes long to complete his task, and in a matter of minutes, he was running his fingers through her blonde ringlets. "It's so long," he said inanely, before burying his face in its curly mass and kissing her on the sensitive spot behind her ear.

Madison's body fell limp against his when he pushed her hair away and pressed open mouthed kisses along her shoulder. His hands found the buttons on the back of her dress and slipped them free. Turning her around to face him, he grabbed the top of her gown and held it in place. Running his thumb over the skin next to the one sleeve that was still on her shoulder, he lowered his mouth to hers.

She responded immediately by brushing her lips against his and opening her mouth when he parted his lips. Deepening their kiss, he hooked his thumb inside her gown and dragged the fabric to the edge of her shoulder. Taking his lips from hers, he kissed the corner of her mouth before kissing a line to her jaw, then down her neck and over to her shoulder. Releasing the fabric with his fingers, the gown dropped to the floor and he took hold of her bare upper arms. "Put your arms around me," he murmured as he kissed her chest right above the thin line of lace on her chemise.

She obeyed his command and wrapped her arms around his neck. Her delicate fingers sank into his thick hair and twisted its golden strands. Wordlessly, he moved his hands to her waist and in one quick motion, picked her up and hauled her to the bed.

Remembering his promise to her, he rolled off to the side and murmured what he hoped sounded like a sincere apology. Cradling the far side of her face in his hand, he placed gentle kisses on the top of her chest. His face moved to the valley of her breasts while his hand pulled the top of her chemise down to expose more of her skin. His mouth explored her sternum and his hand drifted over to gently cup her breast.

She groaned and arched into his hand, pressing her nipple against his palm. He felt it harden through her chemise. He brought his other hand to her thigh and softly kneaded her pliant flesh as his mouth found her free breast and started kissing its soft slope.

"Ben," she gasped when his mouth found the crest of her breast and closed around it.

"Madison," he panted, laving her nipple with his tongue. His hand abandoned her breast and skated down her abdomen to her waist, then to her other thigh. Dropping lower, his mouth left her breast and kissed the undersides of her breasts, along the top of her ribs. His hands moved to her knees and he ran a lone finger behind each knee, drawing a shiver from her.

Her body was limp with her eyes only half open. Her head rested with one cheek on the pillow and her hair covering the other. She brought one hand up to rest in Benjamin's hair as he kissed his way down her abdomen and his hands spread her thighs. He came up on his knees between her legs and ran his hands down the gentle curves of her calves.

Benjamin's slow-moving hands came back to her knees then moved upward past her waist, bringing the hem of her chemise with them. "Madison," he rasped as his lips moved over her hipbone.

"Yes," she sighed, arching off the bed as his mouth traveled lower. The fingers she'd had in his hair tightened their grip while her other hand twisted in the sheets. "Ben," she moaned.

One of his hands came up to rest in the sweet dip between her thigh and hip and the other slid underneath her to cup her bottom. Bringing his mouth to her thigh, he moved his fingers to twist in her nest of curls before slipping them lower. Deftly, he massaged her sensitive flesh as she arched and bucked off the bed at his touch. He heard her groan his name again and murmured hers in reply as he slipped his finger into her warm, ready body.

Her fingers tightened in his hair as he increased his pace. Her breathing sounded shallow and her skin grew warm. Her hips moved to meet his rhythm as his palm rubbed her aching flesh and he slipped another finger inside.

Benjamin's eyes swept his wife's body. This was the most beautiful sight he'd ever beheld. Her face was relaxed with pleasure; her skin was pink and hot with desire. Subtle sighs escaped her lips, becoming louder and more frequent. And then, her face flushed and her body convulsed around him in completion.

After he felt the last waves of her pleasure, he withdrew his hand and leaned forward to drop a kiss on her flushed forehead. He pulled the bottom of her chemise back down and lay next to her, cradling her body so that her back rested against his chest.

A minute later, he heard her softly say, "No lady's maid has ever done *that* to me."

"I should hope not," he replied dryly, reaching forward to push a lock of her damp hair from her cheek.

She snuggled closer to him, and from a little mirror across the room on the vanity, he could see her pink lips curve into a sleepy smile. "Thank you," she whispered quietly, her face turning a fetching shade of pale pink.

"For what?" he murmured, leaning down to scatter kisses across her delicate shoulders.

"For, you know," she said, her skin turning warmer. "I've never felt that way before. Thank you."

He stopped kissing her and drew back. "You haven't?"

"No," she said, turning her head just enough so she could partially see him with one eye. "How would I have? Unlike your sex, mine doesn't typically go around touching their private parts."

A new wave of shame washed over him, causing the blood to rush to his head, his stomach to clench and his heart to ache. He swallowed hard, then again. "Oh, Madison, I'm so sorry," he whispered raggedly before wrapping his arm around her and holding her tightly against his pounding chest.

~*~*~*~

Madison tried to twist her head around to better see the nodcock who was holding her. He'd just given her the most intense pleasure of her life and he was apologizing? What was wrong with the man? And why on earth did he look more unsettled now than he had the night of their engagement when he'd been sucker punched in the breadbasket? "What are you upset about?" she demanded a bit irritably. He was most certainly ruining the moment with his reaction.

"It all makes sense now," he said, ignoring her questions.

"What makes sense?" she asked a bit louder.

He looked down at her and gave her another squeeze. "I'm so sorry about our wedding night." His voice sounded raw and ragged.

"Our wedding night?" she repeated. She thought that would be a subject they'd both gladly never discuss again.

He nodded. "Yes. I thought... I thought..." He broke off and cleared his throat. "I thought you did that because you didn't want to go to bed with me. But that wasn't the reason, was it? You just didn't know any better."

Madison's eyes went wide. "You knew?" she croaked.

He nodded. "Yes, I knew you weren't a virgin."

Heat flooded her face, shame and embarrassment warring for the position of its primary cause. "I'm sorry," she whispered. "If I'd known you before we married the way I know you now, I would have told you." She would have, too. They'd become so close in the last few days, she would have wanted to be honest with him. She would have known she could trust him to guard her secret. Even if he didn't want to marry her due to her lack of innocence, she would have told him. But apparently, it hadn't mattered as much to him as she'd thought and her heart squeezed. He'd known and had still wanted to marry her for some reason. How had he known, she wondered. She had her answer a split-second later: Andrew. Brooke must have told Andrew, and Andrew must have told Benjamin when they'd talked of betrothal contracts.

"No, Madison," he said fiercely, bringing her to the present. "I'm the one who ought to be sorry, Madison. What I said was bad enough, but to know you didn't do it deliberately to hurt me, makes it worse." His fingers lazily made shapes on her shoulder.

"Are you angry?" she asked tentatively, chastising herself for asking such a stupid question when she could look at his face and clearly see he was.

"Not at you," he said, giving her a tight, reassuring squeeze. "I'm angry with myself for what I said. And I'm even angrier at that selfish ass for taking all the pleasure."

She laughed. "Taking all the pleasure?" From what she could remember, there wasn't any other way to describe it. She'd never found an ounce of pleasure in the activity during any of the times she'd shared Robbie's bed. Women just didn't. So, why did he seem so upset about it?

"Yes," he said tightly. "Women feel pleasure, too."

She looked at him as if he were insane. "I assure you, they do not."

"I assure you, they can," he countered. "Did it hurt?"

Her eyes widened. Did she really have to answer that? "Yes," she said quietly.

"I mean after the first time?" he asked, swallowing hard. Surely this could not be an easy topic for him to discuss with her.

Of course it had hurt after the first time. It hurt every time. Wasn't it supposed to? Isn't that why women despised the activity? Except for her sisters, that is. For some reason she couldn't understand for the life of her, they both seemed to like the activity rather well. She felt him give her shoulder a squeeze and realized he was still waiting for her answer. "Yes," she said so quietly that she was only aware he'd heard her because his arms tightened their hold around her.

"It's not supposed to. If it does, it's because the man's a selfish ass. Some women can even enjoy it the first time, too. But only if she has a considerate partner."

She shrugged. "It's a little late now, isn't it?" she said, hoping he'd let the conversation go.

"Yes. It's too late for your first time, and I'm sorry it was so bad. But I can promise you that you'll find nothing but pleasure in my bed."

"All right," she said doubtfully. She'd shared Robbie's bed enough times to know that wasn't going to happen, but there was no need to tell him. She'd just lie there quietly while he went about his business, as she had with Robbie.

"Madison, that's a promise and I don't make promises lightly. You'll enjoy sharing my bed; I'll not take my pleasure until you get yours. I promise." His words were quiet yet firm; definite.

She smiled at him and buried her head in his chest. "Are you going to sleep in all your clothes?" she asked, turning her head to look down at his booted feet.

"I suppose I can take some off," he mumbled as she rolled away to give him room to get up. He sat on the edge of the bed and quickly kicked off his boots then peeled off his stockings. Next, he undid the top few buttons on his shirt before reaching up over his head and yanking it off.

"What about your trousers?" she asked when he went to lie down.

"Better leave those on."

She looked at him for a minute then laughed. "No too-tight drawers under them?"

"No," he said, shaking his head ruefully. "I left those off this morning. I don't like to wear them if I don't have to. It seems as though my waistline has changed drastically since the last time I wore them on a regular basis."

"Too many waffles?" she teased, patting his rock hard stomach.

He chuckled and gave her an affectionate squeeze. "No, pugilism. It's a great way to expend pent up energy."

She moved her head to rest it on his chest. "You haven't a lot of chest hair," she said, running her fingers over the small mat that ran down the middle of his chest.

"Do you have a penchant for chest hair?" he teased, rubbing his knuckles over cheek.

"Not really. Actually, I'm glad you don't. I don't think I'd like it if you had a bearskin rug on your chest like Andrew."

He stiffened.

"Oh, relax," she said, skimming her fingers over his abs, making them tremble in response. "I saw him in his dressing robe once, remember?"

"Right," he clipped. "But henceforth, I'd better be the only man you see in his dressing robe."

"Don't worry, you will be," she said lightly. "You're the only one I've ever actually wanted to see in his dressing robe." She pressed a soft kiss right above his heart and laid her head back on his chest, falling asleep to the steady beat of his heart.

~*~*~*~

Benjamin watched his wife sleep for more than an hour before rolling her to her side and climbing out of bed to put out the candles. He knew they'd burn out eventually, but after the fire that had happened at his house in Yorkshire several years ago, he'd made it a habit to make sure every candle was snuffed before falling asleep. He'd even gone so far as to not allow a fire to burn in his house without a screen.

He walked to the common room and made sure nothing was still burning there. Then he went back into the bedroom and walked to the vanity where a five-candle candelabra was lit. Before blowing out the candle sticks, he looked at the objects on the table. Madison had placed her brush and hand mirror next to his comb, shaving razor and strop. He liked the way their things looked together on a shared vanity. In a few days, hopefully no more, he'd take her to Glenbrook, the seat of his dukedom, and get to see this tableau every day. He had no intention of having separate rooms, especially not now that they'd become so close.

His fingers touched the pointy bristles of her brush and he wondered if she'd let him brush her hair for her in the morning. Reflecting back on the evening, perhaps he should have taken it slower by brushing her hair and slowly easing her into bed. But it really didn't matter; she didn't seem to mind his rush.

She let out a little moan in her sleep and he turned to look at her. She was beautiful, and best yet, she was all his. What was he doing staring at the vanity table when she was on his bed waiting to be held? Picking up the candelabra so he could blow out the candles, he accidentally knocked her reticule onto the floor, spilling the contents. He grunted and leaned over to pick up her things. He chuckled as he gathered the little pile of odds and ends and put them back inside. She was just like him. She carried quite an array of different things she just *might* need during the day. A small pair of scissors, sewing needles and three different miniature spools of thread, mints, loose coins, a couple of keys, and several hair pins seemed the most useful things. There were many other things, including bejeweled hair combs and a quill (but no inkpot in sight), that seemed a little less necessary. He smiled at her oddity, it was just like his. It was just one more thing they had in common.

A piece of vellum caught his eye and he reached out to grab it to stuff it into the bag. Picking up the paper by its corner, the note unfolded and the handwriting caught his attention. Why did she carry a note from Robbie in her reticule, he wondered as his jaw clenched. Knowing it was her private business, he thought about doing the right thing and shoving it back inside without reading it. But he'd never been one to be confused for a gentleman and felt only a sliver of guilt as he read the missive.

His sliver of guilt soon vanished and then panic that had nothing to do with him being termed a murderer, formed in his chest.

Chapter 17

Madison awoke with the strangest ache in her neck, almost like a crick. How on earth did she get a crick in her neck, she wondered as she fluttered her lashes open. The first thing her eyes caught sight of was Benjamin's white shirt. How odd. Hadn't he taken that off before they'd gone to sleep? Yes, he had. She remembered they'd talked of chest hair and she had run her fingers over his bare, well-formed muscles, delighting in how his body had reacted to her touch. So why was he wearing a shirt now? And why did it feel like they were moving? Moving? Yes, moving. She had the oddest feeling they were in a carriage.

She jerked her head up and blinked owlishly a few times. They *were* in a carriage. "Why are we in a carriage?" she asked bluntly.

"We're going somewhere. Don't worry, we're almost there." He brought her head back down to rest her cheek against his chest.

She groaned. "I hope you didn't kidnap me to go eat waffles again," she mumbled. She liked them well enough, but for goodness' sake, enough was enough.

"No," he said, chuckling. "We're not going to eat waffles. But if you want some later, that can be arranged."

"No, thank you." She sat up and brought her hands to the back of her neck.

His hand came to her neck and he gently massaged the sore muscles and tendons. "Better?" he murmured.

"Yes, thank you." She felt the blanket he'd draped over her slip and she almost shrieked when she realized she was still in her chemise.

"Relax," he said with a smile. "Where we're going, your chemise will be acceptable attire."

She eyed him askance. "And where is that?"

"Home."

"Home? Whose home?"

"Our home," he said as if that explained everything.

"Excuse me," she exclaimed in shock. "I don't remember agreeing to return to your home yet."

He shrugged. "You didn't have to."

Enraged, she scooted away from him and pulled the blanket up to her chin. "What are you about?"

"I could ask you the same," he countered, his voice held a sharp edge.

"What does that mean?" she demanded hotly, her pulse speeding to new heights. He'd abducted her. He'd seduced her and abducted her. How stupid could she possibly be to fall so easily into the trap he'd set? She'd known he was a snake. Look at the trap he'd laid for Brooke.

He reached into his pocket and withdrew a piece of paper. Without a word, he tossed it in her direction.

She unfolded the paper and stared at him in disbelief. "I'm not even going to ask how you got this. Obviously, you're not above going through things that are not yours if you're not above kidnapping," she said fiercely. "But I demand to know how you take this as my acceptance to return to your house?"

"Don't worry, we'll be there soon," he said, ignoring her demands.

"Soon? How soon? It's barely dawn," she pointed out. London was close, but not that close.

He shrugged, then dug into his pocket and retrieved his watch. Checking the time, he said, "Less than two hours."

"Less than two hours? Just how long have we been traveling?"

He shrugged again. "Since about midnight."

"Midnight?" she shrieked. They should have arrived in London by now, or at least have been closer than two hours away, if they'd been traveling since midnight; unless he wasn't taking her to London. Panic filled her chest. "Where are we going?"

"To the coast," he said evenly. "But that's all I'm saying."

"Stop the carriage this instant, Your Grace," she yelled. He had no business hauling her off to the coast. Not that this wasn't partially her fault. He'd charmed her, and stupidly, she'd trusted him.

"Don't," he said fiercely, pinning her with his razor-sharp eyes.

"Don't what?" she asked. "Don't yell? Don't argue? Don't demand you return me? Don't what?"

"Don't 'Your Grace' me," he said sharply. "You've used my given name often enough, I should think you know it well. You even called me Ben last night," he said with a wicked grin.

"That won't be happening again, Your Grace," she said sharply as shame washed over her. He was right; she'd been so caught up in the moment she'd called him Ben, and more than once if memory served her correctly.

He frowned. "Why not? I'm the same man now that I was then."

"No, you're not. You were nice and sweet then; and now you're abducting me!"

He shrugged. "Some people fall in love with their abductors," he said huskily, waggling his eyebrows.

"Not this unsuspecting abductee," she retorted. "I still don't even know where we're going."

He *tsk, tsked* and drawled, "That's the normal way of things, I'm afraid. The abductor wouldn't be very intelligent to tell his captive where he's taking her. And, unlike Robbie, my brain serves a greater purpose than just ensuring my skull doesn't cave in."

"That's doubtful. I always did seem to attract simpletons," she said dismissively. "All right, if you won't tell me where you're taking me, then at least tell me *why* you're taking me."

"I already did." He pointed to the letter she'd carelessly balled up and tossed on the floor.

She nearly groaned in agitation. "It's not like I believed his words and was keeping you at Rockhurst while we waited for the constable. Although," she looked at him more sharply, "now that you've gone so far as to abduct me in the middle of the night, I might put more credence in his words."

"Don't," he said simply. "Well, do."

"What?" she asked, exasperated. Was he saying he did or didn't commit murder? She shivered. What fantastic luck she had. She was now trapped in a carriage traveling at a hell-for-hide speed toward the coast with a man who may have just suggested a ridiculous note about him killing a harmless old woman in his employ was true.

He made a face she had not seen him make before. "About six, almost seven, years ago there was a little dustup in Yorkshire that ended in the death of a man dressed as a woman that was in my employ."

"And you were involved?" She tried to keep her voice from growing high pitched, she truly did; but try as she might, it was undeniable that her words had sounded like an opera singer hitting that high C note.

"Yes," he said evenly. "After school and Tour, I went to Yorkshire to live in between Seasons. One Season I was in London, and Lady Algen begged me to take on one of her maids that she could no longer employ. I didn't think much of it and hired the woman. A few months later, I'd spent all night pouring over estate accounts in my study and fell asleep on the settee that was on the far side of the room. An hour or two later, I heard a noise and watched in stunned silence as this 'maid' sat and tried to pick the lock on my safe.

"After ten unsuccessful minutes, I walked over to her to ask if I could be of some assistance. That's when I discovered it was a man. His reaction to seeing me was not at all how a lady would react. Don't give me that dubious look. He looked rather convincing in that dress. He was short and clean shaven with the wrinkly face of an old woman. Even had curves, which I later discovered were rolled up stockings.

Anyhow, we fought and fortunately I was able to overpower him. I found out Lady Algen and my mother, not Lizzie, but my real mother, had been corresponding for some time and had concocted this scheme in order to steal whatever jewels they thought I had." He scoffed. "If she would have just asked me, I would have given them to her."

"So you killed the man?" she asked curiously. It was all an interesting tale for sure, but that still didn't clear him of a crime.

"No. Not really," he said quietly, a dark shadow crossing his face. "After I found out what I needed to know, I let him go and told him I wouldn't call the constable if he would just disappear. At three and twenty, I didn't want to deal with the legalities; especially if they would bring about a scandal, which they would. He started to walk out the door, but grabbed a candle out of the double-candle sconce next to the door and flung it at me. I was able to dodge it, but it lit the carpet on fire. I was trying to stomp out the flame when I heard the man scream. I looked up and realized he'd been standing so near the remaining candle in the sconce that his hair had caught fire." He stopped, closed his eyes and shook his head as if he were trying to dispel the image that filled his mind. When he spoke again, his voice was dark and bleak. "There wasn't anything I could do to save him."

"Is that why they call you the Dangerous Duke?" she asked, feeling her chest constrict. He'd witnessed a horrific accident and had lived with the stigma of it for years.

"Probably; that, or Eton," he said with a cheeky smile. "That was the only scrape I ever got into that the old duke helped me with. He was able to get Lady Algen to confess to knowing the maid was a man with a 'possible' criminal history. In exchange for her testimony, she was free of legal trouble and I was cleared of murder, which I hadn't even committed. But since there was no way to prove my innocence with a charred body in my study and no witnesses, it was the best I could hope for."

"That's why you threatened Lady Algen when we got engaged?"

"Yes. I wanted to make sure she knew I was aware of her motives for getting me to hire him. Obviously, she'd known I'd found out the maid was a man, but she hadn't known I'd learned what he'd been after and that she'd put him up to it. But she does now."

"Why did you tell me all that?" she asked quietly.

He locked eyes with her. "Because I trust you and I want you to trust me."

"It's hard to trust a man who's dragging me away in the dead of night to who knows where without my permission."

His gaze sharpened and he shook his head then looked down at the note.

"Don't," she said sharply, crossing her arms across her chest. "Don't just look at it. That doesn't tell me why you took it upon yourself to take me away in this fashion."

"Doesn't it?" he countered, crossing his arms to match her defiance.

"No," she exclaimed in annoyance. "It doesn't. If you didn't murder that man, why are you so concerned about the note?"

"Because he knows where you are."

"What's the problem with that? Are you afraid I'm going to sneak out and ride off into the sunset with him?" she asked sarcastically. "I assure you, I've no plan to do any such thing. Just return me to Rockhurst."

"No," he clipped. "It doesn't matter anyway. I told Andrew before we even went to Rockhurst that if anyone found out you were there, I'd be taking you home immediately."

"Oh," she said, drawing out her word as she thought about his words. "I get it now. You're male pride was pricked."

"No," he snapped. "My male pride was not pricked."

She snorted. "It seems like it to me. You can't stand the idea that someone might think you, the Great Gateway, who entered into the Golden Gateway Marriage, has problems keeping his wife under his roof."

"That's not it at all," he countered, leaning forward. "Well, maybe a little," he admitted sheepishly. "When I first said that to Andrew, that was my reasoning, but it's not the reason I took you."

"Then why did you?" Honestly, she wanted to know what thoughts could have possibly gone through his mind that made him think it was perfectly acceptable to carry her off this way.

"I've already told you. He knows where you are. He may be a clodpole, but sometimes even the dumbest people can cause you harm. In fact, sometimes it's the dumbest people that cause the most harm. Typically more for themselves than others, but you never know, he might already know to point the gun away from himself before he pulls the trigger. And, on the off chance he already knows that, I'm taking you away to better protect you," he explained, confusing her even more. Did he honestly think Robbie posed any danger?

She started laughing uncontrollably. He did! His facial expression said he actually thought Robbie posed a threat to her! Robbie was only interested in one thing. And that one thing did not require a lot of brain activity. He couldn't possibly formulate a plan to harm anyone. "You're cracked," she said when her peals of laughter subsided to giggles.

"No, I'm not," he said sternly. "Men are determined creatures. And the more they want something, especially something they can't have, the more determined they become."

"You should know," she retorted, still shaking with mirth. "You abducted me because you wanted me all to yourself and used the excuse of a featherbrain knowing my whereabouts as a reason to justify it."

He let out a pent up breath. "Yes, I admit, I want you all to myself. But I'm not just making up reasons."

"Yes, you are. Now, take me back."

"No."

"Why not?"

"Because I'm not going to and we're not discussing this

anymore," he said in steely tones.

She pulled her blanket tighter around herself. It was the only barrier she really had against him. "I demand to know your reasons, Your Grace."

"Stop calling me that," he said through clenched teeth. "I don't like it and you know it."

"Well, I don't like being taken from my bed while I'm sleeping," she retorted. "How did you manage it anyway? Did you use chloroform? Did you drug me and take advantage of me?" she accused.

"No," he bellowed. "I've never drugged or taken advantage of anyone before and I won't be starting with my wife. I may have a reputation for being the Dangerous Duke, but even I wouldn't stoop so low."

"I don't believe you," she said, raising her chin a notch. He had to have done *something* to get her into his carriage and complete more than six hours of travel without her noticing.

"Believe what you want," he said flippantly. "However, despite your tendency to rise early, you sleep like the dead."

She pursed her lips. Brooke always said the same thing about her. That's how she used to sneak into her room and hide her favorite dolls when they were girls. "Be that as it may," she said archly, "I did not give you permission to remove me from my bed. Now return me."

"It was my bed," he told her smugly. "And I plan to return you to that locale as soon as possible, just in a different room." He sent her a wolfish grin that made her go pink.

"Absolutely not," she snapped, shaking her head. "There is no way I'll share your bed after this."

He shrugged. "Yes, you will."

"Only if you use force."

"I won't have to," he said with a shrug. "You'll come to me."

She scarcely heard his words as she looked down at her trembling hands barely holding the blanket under her chin. Her knuckles had gone white, either from rage or holding the blanket too tight, she didn't know. He'd told her the night before that he'd only find pleasure in their marriage bed if she did. Had he said that only because he was trying to get her to trust him? "You lying bastard."

He leaned forward and firmly held her chin between his thumb and index finger. "I didn't lie to you."

"Yes, you did," she yelled, swatting at the hand he used to hold her chin. "Everything you've done the past few days was all done in an effort for me to trust you, so you could steal me away without catching notice."

"In a way, yes," he admitted, leaning back against the red velvet squabs. "I was trying to get you to trust me and go home with me. However, I did not plan for your lovesick suitor to enter the picture. How did he know you were there anyway?" he mused with a pointed look in her direction.

"I don't know. But don't you dare accuse me of telling him or having some other connection to him. I haven't willingly laid eyes on the man in longer than I care to remember."

"I'm not," he said quietly. "He probably bribed a servant. Even if he's denser than a rock, he has the blunt to fund a minor investigation."

"Then won't he find us wherever you're taking me?" she asked, agitated.

"No. Since we left in the dead of night, it's doubtful we've been followed. Besides, if he does start searching for you at my estates, he'll never find you."

"Why?" she asked, shivering. So many questions were running through her head. Was he going to hide her in the attic? Was he going to chain her to the wall and lock her in the dungeon? Was he going to kill her, cut her body up into little pieces, and scatter her across the countryside? She shook her head. She had to quit reading Brooke's gothic novels; they gave young girls ideas that should never enter anyone's imagination.

He smiled a smile that made her blood unsure if it wanted to turn to ice or course through her veins like a racehorse. "Because nobody knows I own it."

"And what does that mean?" she demanded, scanning his unsettling facial expression.

"Nobody will be able to find it."

"What do you mean, nobody will be able to find it?" she demanded again, feeling uneasy.

He shrugged. "It's not easy to locate, that's all."

"You mean it's secreted off?" She'd heard of houses that were in such desolate places, people could scour the land and never find what they were looking for. Her heart sank. Was he taking her to a place like that?

"You could say that."

"You're a bastard," she repeated for good measure. He truly intended to kidnap her.

He leaned forward again. "That fact was established nearly thirty years ago," he said with a smug smile.

Chapter 18

Benjamin had never felt so relieved to get out of a carriage in his life. The first six hours had been wonderful; the last two, not so much. A viper would have been better company. After finding that letter from Robbie, he'd been unable to sleep. That little weasel knew right where they were and he didn't like that one bit. Not that he was afraid Madison would run off with him. He was more afraid Robbie would try to persuade her and when she refused, he'd turn violent. He'd been around Robbie enough during his month in America to know if Robbie needed to, he'd use force to get what he wanted. Benjamin had seen him use both physical force and emotional manipulation to get girls to bend to his will, which is probably what he'd done with Madison.

He'd probably used one of his famous, "You say you love me, why not show me?" or "How can you deny the love between us? You can't, I know it, so let's go show it," or some other ridiculous line he'd made up and used to play on a woman's emotions to get her to lift her skirt. He had a way about him. First, he'd have used his charm. Then, if that hadn't worked, he'd have shot those guilt arrows squarely at the person. And if neither of those methods achieved the desired result, he'd have used physical force. The very thought sickened him. Madison was such a good person, how could he have taken advantage of her that way? And why had she let him? She'd stood up to Benjamin just fine. Why didn't she stand up to that ass? Love. That was the reason. It was the reason so many intelligent people did stupid things. Things like pay someone to chase a whole family off the continent.

He now knew she no longer loved Robbie. No, now she seemed

to have transferred all that emotion directly onto Andrew. Lucky man. The admiration in her eyes when she spoke of him or teased him was enough to make Benjamin want to rip his own hair out. He always had a way of finding Madison *after* she'd fallen in love. Now that he had her all to himself in the middle of nowhere, perhaps his luck would change and she'd fall in love with him.

But first, she was going to be angry.

"Show me to my dungeon," she said fiercely, clutching her blanket for dear life.

He shook his head. "You're not going to a dungeon. You'll stay in my room."

"Your room, dungeon, same thing," she said pertly. "Just show me where I'm to be locked away, so that I may lie upon my bed and dream up all the ways you could torture me."

"I'm not going to torture you," he hissed.

"You already are," she retorted. "If you take me back right now, I might forgive you."

"No," he ground out, steering her into the house. "I'm protecting you. Until I'm informed he's sitting in his mother's family room drinking tea every afternoon at three thirty, you'll be staying here."

"And what if I don't want to?"

He let out a sharp bark of laughter. "You don't have a choice. The nearest town with a mail coach that passes through is more than ten miles away."

"I could walk there if I have to," she informed him as he led her down the blue carpeted hallway.

"You don't even know which direction," he said with a snort.

She jerked her arm from his grasp. "I don't need to. I'd rather wander lost in the forest than be stuck here with you, Gateway."

Fire boiled inside him. "I told you not to call me that," he snapped, piercing her with his eyes. He detested being called by his title more than 'Your Grace'. "You may call me Benjamin or nothing. Understood?"

"Understood, nothing," she confirmed with a laughing smile.

He closed his eyes for a moment. He wasn't in the mood to laugh. But he'd inadvertently set himself up for that and he couldn't blame her for taking advantage. "Now, this room," he opened the door and nearly had to drag her inside, "is the drawing room." He stood there for a minute waiting for her to walk around, which she never did.

"Could you please just show me to where I'll be spending my nights?"

Any other time, he would have asked a cheeky question about if she planned to pass the night sleeping or "sleeping" then directed her to the appropriate room. In either case, he would have directed her to his room. "This way," he replied.

They walked up the stairs and proceeded to the fourth room on the left. Without waiting for him to open the door, Madison found the handle and swung it open before pulling out of his grasp again and marching inside. She tried to shut—or perhaps slam—the door, but he blocked it with his foot.

"This will be our room," he said with a forced smile.

She whipped around and glared at him. "I think not."

"And why not?" he drawled.

"I'm not sharing a room with you. Especially one that has only one bed that's smaller than the one I shared with Brooke at that atrocious boarding house in Bath last spring."

"We don't need a big bed," he countered with a wink. "If I remember last night correctly, we barely used more than my body's width worth of space. This will be large enough."

"You're right. It will be large enough," she agreed, sugar dripping from her voice, "for me!" Her voice became less like sugar and more like vinegar. "You can sleep outside with the rest of your kind."

"My kind?"

"The animals," she said simply. "Now, where are my clothes? I should like to dress."

He coughed, "On top of the carriage."

"All right, go get them. I'm not some doxy who only wears her chemise all day."

She walked over to the window, presumably to wait for him to leave the room to get the trunks. She looked down and sighed. He knew she would. Right below the only window in the room sat several large sticker bushes. She let her blanket drop and opened the window. Poking her head out, she made a sound of frustration at the realization that thick sticker bushes lined that entire side of the house.

"Sorry, I haven't a gardener at present," he murmured, startling a little scream out of her.

She turned around and pulled her blanket back up. "Why are you not getting my things?" she demanded.

"That's what servants are for." He leaned back against the doorjamb. "You don't have to hold that blanket up. I won't mind."

"You are impossible," she said with a sigh. "You're rather full of yourself, aren't you?"

"I'm really not."

In the hall, one of the footmen, either the one who was skinnier than a bedpost and limped or the one who was so old Benjamin kept thinking he was about to drop dead, was making an awful racket dragging a trunk down the hall, so Benjamin went to lend a hand and brought the trunk into their room with ease.

"Where are the rest?" she asked, staring at the single trunk that he placed in the middle of the floor.

He shot her a hopeful smile. "This is it."

"That's not it. I brought three trunks to Rockhurst. Where are the rest?" She went to the hall and twisted her head around the corner to see if there were more in the hall.

"Everything's in here," he said, pulling her back into their room.

"No, it's not," she said, shaking her head wildly. "There is no way my things could all fit in there."

"Everything's in there," he repeated, staring at the chest.

She jerked the lid open, pulled out her blue muslin day gown from yesterday that was on the top and laid it carefully across the bed. Then went back to the chest and started digging through it. "These are your things. Where are my other clothes?"

"That's all of it."

"Where are my other clothes?" she repeated, her voice turning sharper. "Do not tell me you left them."

"All right, I won't tell you that I left them," he said jovially.

She let out an exaggerated sigh. "Are you a relation to Robbie?" she asked flatly.

His heart started pounding in his chest. Had she just put it all together? Did she remember him? He was about to answer her when she cut him off.

"Because right now, I'd swear you are. You both seem to have the same level of brain function," she continued.

He frowned. Now, *that* wasn't very flattering. Perhaps it was best he'd not mentioned Robbie's Cousin Leo after all.

"Could you have put enough thought into your plan to think of me a little? Or did you think once you got me here, I'd swoon at your feet and play the part of your trollop, rendering a wardrobe unnecessary?"

Her accusations fueled the fire to his rage. "Listen here, Madison," he said sharply, coming to stand directly in front of her, offering her no means to escape. "I don't appreciate you accusing me of thinking of you as a whore. I've warned you about that twice before; there will be no more warnings. I've told you repeatedly that I won't force you. Don't mention it again. As for your clothes, that's where I'm smarter than Mr. Swift. See, a fool like Swift, would have gone into Rockhurst to try to collect your clothes. And I say 'try' because that's all it would have been. It would have been nearly impossible to do that without being detected. And that was a chance I didn't wish to take."

"No? Why not? Why not just wait a few hours and ask me if I'd go with you? Or why not explain the situation to Andrew and have his servants be on alert for Robbie? There were so many better options open to you, and instead of thinking about anyone but yourself, you chose to abduct me."

"And would you have come if I'd asked?" In her eyes, he witnessed her inner struggle as she tried to formulate an answer to his question. "That's what I thought."

"No," she said fiercely, shaking her head. "It's not what you thought. The truth is we'll never know. We'll never know because you took it upon yourself to do whatever you wanted. Just like you always do."

"What's that supposed to mean?"

"You never ask me about anything important, you just decide it," she clarified.

"Like what?" What had he decided for her that she thought she should have been consulted about?

She crossed her arms and said, "Us marrying. I never accepted your suit. You never even asked. You just sauntered out of that dark hallway and announced we were getting married."

He stared at her unblinkingly. "You had just been accused of dallying with your sister's husband. I was doing you a favor."

"I don't need your favors," she returned. "And it was your fault anyway. If you would have told me your identity, I would have left."

"I didn't want you to scream. I thought if you knew who I was you'd give a blood curdling scream and draw attention to us."

She rolled her eyes. "Use whatever excuse you want. It doesn't matter now."

"Is that what this is about? You wanted a real marriage proposal?" He sank to one knee and sarcastically said, "Oh, beautiful Madison, would you please, please, please, do me the honor of becoming my wife? I don't know how I'll be able to live another day if you say no."

"You don't have to be condescending about it," she said, her voice mostly even with just a hint of hurt mixed in that tugged at his heart.

"I'm sorry," he said, getting up off the floor. "That wasn't very nice."

"No it wasn't," she replied. "But I wouldn't expect anything more from the man who hired another man to destroy a young lady's reputation."

"It seemed to work out well for them," he retorted. "And there was a reason I did that."

"Yes, I'm sure there was. And I'm sure it would have benefited you greatly if things had gone according to plan. But I'm not interested in hearing about it anymore," she said flatly. "Now, get out. I'd like to dress and I don't need an audience."

"It actually benefitted me more that things didn't work out the way I'd planned," he said quietly. "Do you need some help with your gown?"

"No. Now, get out," she snapped, pointing to the door.

Chapter 19

What in the world was she to do now? Benjamin seemed bent on the idea of holding her hostage. But that didn't mean she had to stay. She may not be able to find the nearest town on her own but surely one of his servants could help her. She'd just have to ask them when he wasn't around.

She walked around the house. It wasn't anything special. It was two stories high and made completely out of smooth grey stone. Not just the outside, but the inside, too. The floor was large smooth-sided stones with carpet runners placed in the middle of the common walkways. Around the edges of most of the rooms, the rocks could be seen. The walls were also made of rocks. Some smooth, some not so smooth around the edges, but not jagged or dangerous, just interesting. None of the windows were very big. They were all half windows that started about four or five feet off the floor and were about two to three feet tall and three feet wide.

Most of the rooms had large fireplaces and very few furnishings. No decorations or sconces hung on the walls. A few miniatures and candle stands were placed on flat surfaces throughout the rooms. She picked up a wax candle and noticed that it was fresh. Just like the last one she'd picked up. Apparently, he either replaced his candles after each time he used one, which wasn't likely, or he didn't come here often.

She crept into the library and frowned when she saw only five volumes on the shelves. That was only further confirmation he never came here. Where, in England, was this place? Was it truly so far out of the way, she'd never be found? No. She wasn't going to think that way. She'd find a way to leave, even if she died trying. She wasn't going to let him manipulate her like she'd let Robbie. In a way, those two were alike; it truly wouldn't surprise her to find out they were relatives. Like Benjamin, Robbie could manipulate anyone into doing anything, even if it took him five years.

Plopping down onto the settee that was positioned just below the only window in the drawing room, she closed her eyes, leaned her head back and drifted back in time. Back to a time when she'd let her vulnerabilities get the best of her and first started playing the puppet to Robbie's skillful manipulation.

~*~*~*~

Brooklyn, NY
March 1807

"Who was that?" she asked Robbie with a grin.

"Who's who?" he asked, leading her onto the dance floor.

"Stop that," she said laughingly. "You sound like an owl."

He smiled and took his place in front of her for their dance. "All right, I suppose you refer to the man I was just speaking to?"

"Yes," she said, putting her hand in his and casting a quick look at the handsome man with the unkempt and rather scruffy looking beard.

"He's my cousin," Robbie said blandly. "His name's Leo. He's from England."

How intriguing. "And what is he doing here?"

Robbie shrugged and spun her around, making her almost collide with Big Thomas. "Don't know. Don't care."

"Is he staying with you?" She sent Big Thomas an apologetic smile and watched as he nodded his little head and licked the drool that was forming in the corner of his mouth.

Robbie stepped on her foot, presumably to recapture her attention from watching Big Thomas and his partner in awe. Really it was amazing his partner's arms could stretch far enough to hold onto him. It was even more amazing the man didn't topple over to the floor every time he danced because he was so top heavy. "Why do you care?"

"Hmmm?" she asked. "Oh, about your cousin," she'd thought he'd read her thoughts about Big Thomas and his little twig of a dance partner. "Right, I just wondered. He's rather handsome."

"Handsome?" Robbie scoffed, twirling her even more wildly than the last time. "He's not handsome. He looks like a beggar. He's got that scraggly beard. His clothes are dreadfully out of date. And anyway, it looks like he has an interest in Brooke."

Madison craned her neck. Sure enough, her handsome fellow was talking to Brooke. Brooke looked to be laughing about something he'd said and he had the largest grin she'd ever seen on his face. She hadn't gotten a good look at him when she'd walked up to Robbie, but she'd seen him earlier from across the room watching the dancers and had convinced Brooke to walk with her to go stand by him. She'd

125

waited for him to ask her to dance. But he hadn't. Instead, Wendell Marshall had.

After enduring Whiney Wendell for five minutes, she decided to take matters into her own hands. Hoping for an introduction, she walked over to Robbie since he was talking to this handsome stranger. However, once again, her plans to dance with him crumbled and she found herself dancing with Robbie. Not that she didn't like Robbie, she did. But just not in that way. Not anymore, anyway. She had once, but thankfully Brooke had talked sense into her and she now understood that had been a girlhood crush, nothing more.

"They just met. Surely he's not smitten with her already," Madison said airily. Everyone said Madison might be the more stunning of the two, but Brooke had the more exciting personality. She liked to tell jokes and laugh. Whereas, Madison found she didn't usually think other people's jokes were funny and very few found hers to be. Mama used to tell her she had a dry sense of humor. And unfortunately for her, decent men didn't seem to like her dry wit or occasionally crude comment. That was something she was working on. She'd repeatedly been told she needed to watch what she said. And though she'd explained to Mama and Papa many times that she wasn't sure it was physically possible, she'd known what they'd meant. She needed to be more mindful of what she said and to whom she said it.

Robbie shrugged. "Ever hear of love at first sight?"

"Why, Robbie," she said teasingly, "have you become a romantic?"

"No," he said flatly. "I'm just saying."

"Hmm, well, I shall discover the truth tonight," she said cheekily. "I shall interrogate Brooke into the wee hours of the morning to extract the details if I must."

"Why should you care?" he said with a suggestive grin. "I'm not in love with Brooke." He gave her waist a light squeeze.

Her eyes met his. He thought she was still interested in him and now that she wasn't, he was interested in her. What a coil. "Robbie, you're not in love with me, either," she said evenly, not wanting to hurt his feelings. "I know I've embarrassed myself in more ways than one trying to catch your notice, but it was all a bunch of girlhood fantasies. I don't harbor those feelings for you any longer and I don't think you truly feel that way for me."

He stepped on her toe again. Except this time, it seemed to be more of an accident than before. "You what?" he asked, blinking owlishly at her. "But you've been in love with me forever." He flashed her his most charming smile.

She squeezed his shoulder in a friendly gesture. "I know. But as you always said, it was just infatuation, not love."

"I see," he said slowly. "And you think you love Leo, all of a sudden?" His voice sounded bitter and angry.

"No," she said softly. "Robbie, it's just not that way between us. But no, I haven't suddenly transferred my affections to him. He's a stranger. I just thought he looked handsome and perhaps I might like to meet him, that's all."

He nodded once and didn't say a word for the rest of their dance.

True to her word, Madison went to Brooke's room that night to ask questions about Robbie's cousin and see if he was smitten with her. Long ago, the two had decided if one had a marked interest in a particular gentleman, the other would not interfere. That had never been a problem before and she desperately hoped it wouldn't become one now.

Madison put her hand on Brooke's doorknob and went to twist it when suddenly the knob seemed to be pulling her. She looked up and blinked at Brooke. "I...uh..." She looked at her hand that was still outstretched and holding onto Brooke's doorknob. "Can we talk?"

"Yes," Brooke almost squealed with excitement. She grabbed Madison's arm and tugged her into her room. "I was just coming to find you."

"You were?" Madison asked, blinking at her sister.

"Yes. I met the most charming man tonight," Brooke said with a smile.

A wave of sadness washed over her. Too bad she hadn't gone up to him sooner. Now he was as good as snagged. All Brooke had to do was turn up the charm and he'd be tripping over himself trying to pay her court within a week. "Oh," she said, trying not to act too disappointed.

Brooke nodded enthusiastically. "Yes. He's somewhat handsome, in a rugged way. He was extremely friendly and was terribly funny when he practically begged me to—"

"I'm very happy for you," Madison cut in. She really didn't think she wanted to hear all this. Not that she'd set her cap on him, but it still hurt to listen to Brooke prattle on about him for a reason she couldn't explain.

"Me?" Brooke asked, her brows furrowing in confusion. "He wasn't interested in me. He was interested in *you*."

"Me?" Madison squeaked. Her heart started slamming in her chest.

"Yes," Brooke said, nodding. "He confessed to being a bounder of the worst sort and said he needed saving, specifically by you. But have no worries, he assured me he was savable."

Madison couldn't stop smiling. He'd seen her and had been just as interested in her as she'd been in him. Perhaps there was such a thing as love at first sight. "What do I do now?"

"Talk to him," Brooke suggested in a tone that made Madison feel like the simpleton Robbie was.

"Right," she clipped. "But when?"

"When you see him again, of course," Brooke said with a giggle.

"I know that," Madison said hastily, taking a seat on Brooke's bed. "I just wonder when we'll see him again."

Brooke sat down next to her. "In two days, when we go to church. Surely if he's staying with Robbie, he'll come to church. Mr. Swift cannot afford not to attend each Sunday. It's how he tries to convince everyone he knows that he's a fair banker."

"You're right," Madison agreed. "I just hope Robbie doesn't spoil it."

"How would he? You'd think he'd be happy to pass your attentions to his unsuspecting cousin," Brooke teased.

Madison shook her head. "I don't know. I think I may have made a mistake tonight when I told Robbie I'd moved on and inquired about his cousin."

Brooke cast her a questioning glance.

"I can't explain it exactly. His face changed and he actually looked disappointed," she said with a shrug.

"Do not feel sorry for the man," Brooke said sharply, skewering her with a stare she'd perfected as a way to cripple her younger sisters and bend them to her will. "He's a bad apple and rather slow at that."

"I don't know. He may not be as slow as you think." She shook her head. "I mean he seems to get girls with no problem."

"That's charm," Brooke corrected, "not intelligence. For goodness' sake, he cut a line in his trousers—and who knows what else—because he was using a knife to cut a piece of paper while using his leg as a hard surface for the activity."

"That was just a lapse of judgment," Madison said in his defense.

"All right. What about the time we caught him making change in the offering plate? Was that a lapse in judgment, too?"

"No, that was just flat out disrespectful," she said, trying not to laugh. "But that doesn't mean he's one wheel short of a carriage. It just means he's an idiot."

Brooke rolled her eyes. "How about the time he came to visit and excused himself at dinner and came back into the dining room with the chamber pot on his head? Does that convince you he's dimwitted or do you require more examples?"

Madison shook her head. "I still don't think he's as dumb as you think. I believe he just wants attention."

"Why are you defending him?"

Madison sighed. "I don't mean to. It's just that even though I don't have those feelings for him any longer, doesn't mean I think we should be cruel about him."

"As long as that's the only reason," Brooke said skeptically.

"It is," Madison assured her.

"Madison, I know you think he's just a man in need of rescuing. And, don't get me wrong, that is certainly the case, but let someone else do it."

"I know," Madison said, nodding. "That's why I was scouting elsewhere tonight, most notably, his cousin."

"Very good," Brooke encouraged. "I can tell he has a tender heart, Madison. He'll treat you much better than Robbie."

"Let's hope he's not as addled as his cousin," Madison mumbled. If he was, it wouldn't necessarily shock her. She always seemed to attract the strangest men.

She went back to her bed and slept not a single wink that night.

She was too anxious planning what she'd say to him the next time she saw him.

Sunday came and she tried to no avail to get Leo's attention. Every time she'd get close enough to talk to him, someone would show up and try to distract her.

For the next three weeks, it was the same way. She only managed to have a conversation with him a few times. Each time it never lasted more than a few minutes, but those few minutes were sufficient to keep her intrigued enough to look forward to their next chance encounter.

During their brief chats, she'd told him she volunteered, sewed and even painted. And he'd said he was more of an observer of art, liked to study war, hated parlor games and thought Robbie was a dunce. However paltry all those little facts seemed, it was enough to know she'd found someone with whom she could happily spend the rest of her life. At almost seventeen, she wasn't too young to think of marriage and if he'd asked, she would have agreed on the spot. Even if they'd only spent less than a combined thirty minutes talking, it was enough to know in her heart she'd be absolutely happy.

One of the things that most convinced her they could be happy together was that he didn't seem to mind her accidental slip of the tongue. On one of the occasions they were able to talk, their conversation had started because he'd overheard her tell a bawdy joke about a dockside tart.

"Do all young ladies in America talk that way? Or is it just you?" he teased with a bright smile.

She blushed. She'd had no idea she'd been overheard, especially by him. "Unfortunately, it's just me," she said as evenly as she could. She'd never been embarrassed by being caught saying something inappropriate before, but this time she was.

"I don't think it's unfortunate," he said, shaking his head. "I think it's great. It makes you who you are."

"You're probably the only one who thinks it's great."

He grinned. "Who else matters?"

"No one, I suppose," she said, feeling excitement course through her veins. He didn't mind she enjoyed a bawdy jest or a crass comment now and then? How odd; odd, but wonderful.

"Exactly. It's what makes you unique, distinguished." His voice was silky and smooth, a stark contrast to the scruff on his face and his wind-whipped hair.

"I don't know about distinguished, but certainly unique. I don't know if there's another vicar's daughter on the planet whose mouth has tasted as much soap as mine," she said cheekily.

He chuckled. "I like it. Don't stop. It makes you—"

"Ho there, Leo," Robbie cut in, sneaking up on them unnoticed. "I've been looking for you. I need a hand with something outside."

"I'll help you in a bit," Leo said tightly, his face becoming set like stone.

Robbie shrugged. "Just as well, I suppose. Why don't you meet me outside in say," he glanced at his pocket watch, "thirty minutes? It will be exactly ten. That will be perfect."

Leo frowned and pulled out his pocket watch. "No, in thirty minutes it will be ten minutes to eleven."

Robbie blinked. "Is there a difference?"

"Yes," Leo ground out, making Madison bring her hand to her mouth to stifle a giggle. "It's already twenty past ten now."

Robbie shrugged again. "All right," he said slowly, pulling his pocket watch back out and pointing it in Leo's direction. "How about when the short hand is close to the eleven, but not quite touching it, and the long hand is pointing straight out to the left?"

Leo groaned and possibly rolled his eyes, it was hard to tell. "All right. That's in twenty-five minutes. I'll be there."

"Excellent," Robbie said. Then, turning to Madison, he put his arm out. "Madison dear, remember you promised you'd explain to my mother how to yarn?"

"Knit, you mean?" she asked, flabbergasted.

"Yes, knit," he agreed offhandedly. "Anyway, she's expecting you. I'll take you to her now, if you don't mind." He took her hand and looped it through his arm then took her to see the shrill-voiced vulture he called a mother.

Madison ground her teeth. She didn't want to go with him; she wanted to stay and talk to Leo. And why exactly did his blasted mother not know how to knit? Wasn't that something all girls were tortured into learning? "All right," she said, suppressing a groan as they walked away.

Besides the annoyance of always trying to come up with new ways to snag Leo's attention during those three weeks, Madison also had to deal with the ever-present Robbie. It was as if the man had become a barnacle and thought her a ship. The man was always there. And if not, he'd show up just as soon as she and Leo started talking. It was infuriating. It would have been merely irritating if he'd only butted into the conversation. However, he didn't. He ended their conversations and that's what made it infuriating. He'd find some excuse to haul one of the two of them away from the other, usually her. Then he'd make unflattering remarks about Leo to her. Yet, instead of making her dislike Leo, it only furthered her dislike for Robbie.

The most infuriating time was when she'd agreed to go fishing in the Hudson only because she thought Leo would be joining them. When Robbie asked if she wanted to, she couldn't say yes fast enough. Images of Leo draping himself over her and helping her hold the pole correctly flashed through her mind. But right after she agreed, Robbie announced Leo wouldn't be joining them and disappointment washed over her. She tried not to feel hurt by Leo's blatant rejection of spending time with her while he just stood there doing nothing. He could have joined them if he wanted to spend time with her. But no, he just stood there and watched her go off with Robbie.

Not giving up hope, she acted completely reckless with the pole by swinging it all over the place. She hoped if she was deliberately bad at fishing, he'd come over and help her. However, he didn't, which only made her more desperate and she tried harder to get his attention. But that only led to her slipping on a rock and gashing her ankle against the sharp edge of one of the other rocks right before her foot slipped completely and landed in the water. Her perspective changed during the next moments. She knew she'd shrieked in surprise and was certain a person would have to be deaf not to hear her. However, instead of coming to her side and inquiring what was wrong, Leo stood by the tree scowling as Robbie scooped her up and carried her to a nearby bench to clean her wound.

That night she sought Brooke out in her room and asked for advice. Brooke had been the biggest champion for the match. She'd constantly reminded Madison of their initial conversation and had continuously sung his praises. Madison had believed her at first, but she was starting to doubt his feelings now.

"I don't think he's interested in me," Madison said dully.

Brooke put her brush down. "Why do you say that?"

Madison shrugged. "He barely talks to me."

"That's because Robbie's jealous and doesn't want you two to talk," Brooke pointed out.

"And here you thought he was a coxcomb," Madison said, shaking her head and digging her bare toes into the carpet.

"He is. He's a jealous coxcomb. He just doesn't want to see you happy," Brooke explained. "He'll get over it once he sees you're still interested in Leo. His pride was wounded when you told him you'd moved on. Give him time to gather the pieces."

"Perhaps you're right. But what if it takes Robbie too long to get over his newfound infatuation with me and I lose Leo? I really like him, Brooke. In fact, I think I might love him."

Brooke shook her head and smiled. "I hate to mention this, but you are aware you've only had a handful of conversations with him, are you not?"

"I know," Madison said with a smile. "But it's enough. Sometimes when you know, you know."

"Then ask him how he feels about you," Brooke advised, fixing the sleeve of her nightrail. "Tomorrow night we're going to the Flank's house for a dinner party. He'll be there, too. I'll try to distract Robbie for a minute and you go talk to Leo."

That night, just like every other night in the past few weeks, she barely slept. The next day she rehearsed exactly what she'd say to him at the party. She tried to condense it down to take less than a minute in case Brooke was unsuccessful in diverting Robbie.

The dinner party was packed. There were at least fifty guests and it was hard to find a moment to seek out Leo. Brooke noticed her inability to find Leo in order to have her conversation with him, so she devised a plan to help her. She'd suggested to the hostess they all hide and have someone find them. Of course, this suggestion was met with as much groaning as charades had been, but the hostess insisted she wanted to play and everyone went to find their hiding places.

Madison purposely walked slowly down the hallway in the hope he'd follow her. She knew of a room that had a private balcony and slipped inside to wait for him. A few minutes later, the door opened and she nearly jumped with glee. He'd come for her. Running out from behind the curtains where she'd been standing, she abruptly halted when she saw her guest was Robbie, not Leo.

"Oh," she said with disappointment in her voice.

"Madison, we need to talk," he said solemnly. "It's about Leo."

"What about him?"

"He's no good for you. I know you like him, and oh, how I hate that you do, but he's no good."

"What do you mean?" she insisted. He'd done nothing in the past weeks to make her think poorly of him.

Robbie came to stand by her and grabbed her hand. "He's using you," he said simply, squeezing her hand affectionately.

"What do you mean?" she repeated innocently.

"He's just trying to get under your skirt," he said with a sigh.

Her eyes went wide. "I don't believe it."

"Believe it."

"No," she said fiercely. "He's not like that."

"Yes, he is. The first night he came with me to the ball, he was searching out women he wanted to bed," Robbie told her.

She suddenly felt overheated and opened the door to step out onto the balcony. "How do you know?"

Robbie joined her on the balcony and shut the door. "He told me that he thinks women are only good for one thing: lifting their skirts."

"But why me?"

He shrugged again. "Why not you? You're beautiful." His statement was spoken as if it was an awful thing to be beautiful.

"There are lots of pretty girls around," she said defensively. "That's not a good enough reason."

"Yes, it is. He said he views you as a courtesan with a challenge. But that's a challenge he won't walk away from. He wants your virtue."

She felt all her dreams slip away. Was it possible he was only interested in bedding her and nothing more? He'd laughed at her naughty jest and even encouraged her to talk in that manner. Had he said those things hoping she'd discover the wanton he thought lurked in her soul and then join him in bed? She was going to be sick.

"Madison," Robbie said, bringing her out of her thoughts. "I'm not like him. I don't see women that way at all. I know there's more to you than your vibrant beauty. Actually, I don't even see your beauty. I don't care about it. I'll treat you right. I'll become a monk if you ask it of me."

His words, so comforting and soothing, were a balm for her breaking heart. He may not be the smartest man in existence, or even in the top ninety-five percent, but he'd just pledged to treat her right. What more could she ask for? It was obvious she couldn't follow her heart; it had led her to the wrong man. But perhaps she could follow logic. "What are you saying?" she asked.

"Let me court you," he said with a slow smile. "I know you said you don't love me anymore, but I don't believe you. Give me another chance."

Madison nodded. "All right," she agreed, allowing herself to be pulled into his embrace.

"Promise me, Madison. Promise me you'll give me a chance. Don't let him, or any other bounder for that matter, court you; only me." He pulled her closer. "Promise me, Madison. I want to hear you say it."

In for a penny, in for a pound, she thought. If this is what it took to secure a good man who didn't see her as only a bed partner, she'd promise him anything. "Not him, only you," she whispered weakly, winding her arms around his neck.

He brought his head down and pressed a slimy, unsatisfactory kiss on her lips. She tried to force a smile in return. A poor kisser was a small price to pay for the security of knowing she was wanted for herself and not her body. Although, if there'd been a musket pressed to her head, she would have admitted she'd have preferred her first kiss to be from that no-good bounder Leo. Oh well, the less she thought of *him* the better.

Later that night, she told Brooke of the change of events. To which Brooke's response had been total silence and to stare at her as if she needed to be packed off to an insane asylum post haste. Brooke then spent an hour trying to convince Madison that Robbie was wrong. Finally, Madison agreed to confront Leo about his words the next time she saw him. But, she never saw him again. After the night of the party, he seemed to have vanished into thin air. Madison had once asked Robbie about him, but after he'd erupted in a temper over her innocent question, she'd never asked again.

And so began the game of cat and mouse or rather puppeteer and puppet.

Over the course of their courtship, they'd had their share of disagreements about why they'd never formally announced their engagement. Or why he kept company with other women. He'd always used some excuse about being too young or getting to enjoy his bachelor freedom a while longer, but not to worry, he'd marry her.

No one in her family championed their match and it didn't take her very long to realize Brooke had definitely been right about one thing: the man had the intelligence of a goose. He was always adding incorrectly, using the wrong words in conversations, or dripping things on himself when he ate; he couldn't tell time on his pocket watch correctly; and he even hurt himself quite frequently because he didn't have enough sense to consider the repercussions of his actions. She typically brushed his actions off as something she could withstand; just as long as their children inherited her intelligence, that is. If not, she might go mad.

A few times over the years, she'd told him she was going to allow others to court her. His typical response was to remind her of her folly the last time she'd done that and reiterate that any man but him would only want her for her body.

After four and a half years, she was desperate enough to marry him that she'd do just about anything, including dropping subtle hints about her wanting to deepen their relationship. It didn't take him long to catch on and soon she found herself exactly where she didn't want to be: unwed and in his bed. She knew she was playing with fire when she dropped the hints. She just hoped he'd take them differently. But, he was a man, therefore, he did his thinking with the head that didn't possess a brain and interpreted her eagerness and curiosity as willingness to share his bed with or without a wedding ring.

In her naivety, she hadn't anticipated this. She thought he'd take the hints to mean it was time to get married. But he hadn't, and when she tried to back out, he wouldn't let her. He'd called her a tease and insisted she was correct; it was time to deepen their relationship. He'd even suggested that her feelings for him were not strong enough if she wasn't willing to go to bed with him. Wanting to prove him wrong, she'd joined him in bed, and not just once. No, she'd slept with him more than a dozen times before she'd realized the painful truth: he'd never marry her, nor did she ever actually want him to.

The sound of the front door slamming woke her from her time travels and she sat up and rubbed her eyes. Perhaps Benjamin was right in one respect, she thought, tightening the pins in her coiffure. Apparently, those who appear to be the dumbest people are truly the most harmful to others. Not that she could fault Robbie entirely on that score. She'd been the one stupid enough to believe his cock and bull stories for five years.

How ironic that she'd wasted five years of her life and her virtue on a man who was the exact bounder he'd accused his cousin to be. Not that she didn't still believe Leo to be a bounder, she did. She just knew now it was a trait that was bred, and they both seemed to possess it.

Chapter 20

Rockhurst
Later that day

"Brooke," Carolina Banks chirped when she saw her oldest daughter. "I'm so happy to see you!"

"It's good to see you, too," Brooke said, wrapping Mama in a big hug. "We weren't expecting you so soon."

"The wind was in our favor," John, her papa, said simply, embracing her so tightly she thought she might snap. "Now where is that rapscallion son-in-law of mine?"

"Which one?" Brooke asked, stalling for time. She hadn't seen Madison or Benjamin all day. She'd gone to Madison's room last night to talk and when nobody had answered the door, she'd let herself in. Nothing appeared to be out of place at first, but upon closer inspection, Brooke noticed Madison's brush and personal mirror were missing. She tried not to smile with excitement when she realized her sister had spent the night with her husband.

"Good point," John said smoothly. "Both of them."

"They're not in at the moment," she said, still stalling. Andrew was on his way to the gamekeeper's cabin to discuss the possibility that they were ready to go to Glenbrook. "Would you like to see Nathan?"

"Of course," Mama exclaimed, walking to the little basket by the window where Nathan was taking a nap. She picked him up and cooed in his ear while she swayed with him by the window.

Papa went over to see the baby. He idly ran his finger on Nathan's soft cheek. "Brooke, can I ask you something? Do you think there's something familiar about Gateway?"

Brooke almost choked. The night before she'd met Andrew, she'd been kissing Benjamin in the shrubs at a ball. "Ugh…not really, no. I mean, I've only seen him as much as everyone else here, I'd wager," she said evasively. Likely, her parents knew she'd kissed men before her husband, but she didn't want to start listing names and places for them.

"Hmmm," Papa said. "I just get the feeling I've seen him somewhere else."

"Perhaps you knew his father," Mama put in helpfully. "You did grow up in England. Maybe you went to school with him."

Papa shook his head. "No, I think his father is at least a decade, maybe more, older than me."

"What of a brother? Did his father have a younger brother?" Brooke asked, even though she knew the old duke wasn't really Benjamin's father, and if he did have a younger brother, he'd have no resemblance to Benjamin.

Papa shook his head again. "I think I've met the man before. I just cannot place where."

"Nonsense," Mama said dismissively. "Before we came to England last spring, you'd been living in America for twenty-five years. If you'd met him before you left, he'd have been what, four or five, and you'd have been nineteen. I hardly think you'd recognize him now."

"You're right," Papa acknowledged. "It would have been in America and I don't remember meeting any dukes over there." He took a seat on the settee and watched his wife as she swayed their grandson. "On a different note, I went and saw Theodore Swift after I received Andrew's missive."

Brooke nodded. She'd be willing to bet that wasn't a happy visit.

"He couldn't get rid of me fast enough," Papa continued with a laugh. "I told him he better retrieve his son and keep him on a tight leash because Madison's husband wasn't likely to let him live if he showed up here again. The man actually had the nerve to laugh at me until I told him who Madison's husband was. Apparently Gateway's reputation is known all the way to Brooklyn." He chuckled and closed his eyes, resting his head back against the wall. "Hmm, funny I never heard of him though," he mused with a frown. "I'd have thought if Theo knew of him, I'd have heard of him, too."

Brooke took a seat and watched as Mama played with Nathan and Papa took a nap. That was odd that Mr. Swift knew of Benjamin's dangerous reputation all the way to Brooklyn. Who in America would care? None of the girls she'd grown up with knew or cared about the reputations of titled Englishmen. But then again, the Swifts had connections over here, she remembered. They'd had their handsome English cousin stay with them for a while.

Oh, if only Madison would have ended up with him. She still didn't believe the things Robbie had said about him. Robbie had been jealous and grasping at straws to get Madison to return to his side like a lost puppy. Unfortunately, it had worked.

She'd even admit to herself Gateway was a better choice than Robbie. But still, nobody could compare to the handsome man who sat on the edge of the ballroom with his heart in his eyes as he confessed to being a bounder of the worst sort but promised he was savable.

She smiled and then froze. She'd heard Benjamin say something similar to that not too long ago. She frowned. Why had he said that? It was the night he'd come to apologize for his stupidity involving her ruination last spring. Was it just a coincidence he'd used the same words as Leo? It had to be. Leo was a lowly commoner and Benjamin was a duke. They were worlds apart.

She closed her eyes and tried to drag up an image of Leo. His uneven beard had covered half his face, but she remembered his vivid blue eyes and light blond hair precisely. He'd worn a face-splitting grin every time he'd caught sight of Madison, much the same way that Benjamin did. She nearly choked on her gasp. Benjamin was Leo. Leo was Benjamin. For whatever reason, he'd come to America dressed as a beggar and given his heart to Madison.

"Are you all right, dear?" Mama asked, breaking Brooke from her trance.

She nodded. "I know where we've seen him before."

Papa's eyes snapped open. "Where?"

"He's Leo," she croaked.

Mama stopped mid-sway. "You mean—"

"Yes."

"Are you sure?"

Brooke nodded. "Madison probably isn't going to like this revelation," she said numbly.

"Perhaps not, but Liberty will. She'll appreciate the irony," Papa said with a smirk.

Just then, Andrew came into the room mumbling and muttering words that are better left unmentioned. "They're gone," he nearly shouted. "That no-good filthy bounder abducted her. All his things are gone and there is nary a trace of her anywhere. When I get my hands on him—"

"No!" Mama and Brooke exclaimed in unison, waking poor Nathan up and making him cry.

"Why not?" Andrew demanded, crossing his arms.

"He's not going to hurt her." Brooke walked over to him and placed her hands on his broad shoulders.

"You bet he won't," he spat. "I'll kill him when I find him. I should have known I couldn't trust him. This is my fault. I should have tried harder to convince him to drop the engagement. But don't worry, Brooke. I'll bring her back—"

Brooke brought her finger up to stop her husband's lips from spouting any more nonsense. "Stop," she said in a small voice. "I've already told you he's not going to hurt her."

Andrew looked at her dubiously. "And what makes you so certain of that?"

Brooke smiled. "He loves her, the same way you love me."

.

Chapter 21

The middle of nowhere near the coast of England
Later that day

Benjamin walked into the drawing room and stood quietly inside the door while Madison rested on the settee with her eyes shut. He couldn't tell if she was sleeping or just resting. Either way, he didn't wish to disturb her.

The footmen had finished unloading the carriage. He'd had her painting supplies put into an empty room and everything else had been placed in the one they'd share, including that bloody wooden chest that was driving him to distraction. Twice already this afternoon, he'd had to remind himself he couldn't open it without her permission and had to remove his hands from the latch.

Maybe tonight he'd just ask her about it. She was already mad at him, how much worse could it get if he asked about the box?

He walked down the hall and into the kitchen to see if Cook had some biscuits he could snag. Taking a tray of fresh biscuits and hot tea with him, he walked back to the drawing room. Madison was sitting up now, but she didn't look overly happy.

"Can I interest you in something to eat?" he asked, placing the tray down on the squat table positioned in front of the settee.

She shrugged and took a biscuit.

"How about some tea?" he asked, waiting for her to take the hint and pour. When she didn't, he asked, "Aren't you going to serve?"

"No," she said flatly, grabbing another biscuit.

He stared at the teapot. It was so small and delicate he'd probably break it with his grasp if he tried to pour. "Would you like to pour me a cup?"

"Not particularly," she answered smugly, chewing her biscuit.

He snatched the teapot and started dumping tea into a cup, sloshing the liquid all over everything. When the cup was filled with as much tea as a thimble would hold, he brought it to his lips and drank it all in one exaggerated swallow. "Tea's delicious," he said with a smile.

"I'm sure the table thinks so, too," she said dryly, staring at the huge puddle he'd made.

Putting the cup down, he leaned forward. "Are you going to be angry with me forever?"

"No. Not forever. Just until you return me," she said pertly. "I knew one day I'd have to live in your house, but I didn't think you'd be so highhanded as to accomplish it this way."

He ran a hand through his hair. "I'm not being highhanded. I'm trying to protect you."

"As I said, I don't need protecting. The man is an imbecile. He can't even tie his own cravat, for goodness' sake."

"I understand that. However, he may lack common sense and enjoy acting like a simpleton, but he still poses a threat."

She waved her hand in the air. "No, he doesn't. I once thought he wasn't as dumb as everyone believed, but then I spent five years in his close company. Trust me when I say a rabbit uses his brain more than Robbie."

Benjamin pinned her with his eyes. "I don't care. The man isn't what he seems. A person doesn't have to have a lot of common sense to manipulate someone."

"I believe your theory," she said with a smirk. "I've met a person just like that before, you."

"Me?" he asked defensively. He crossed his arms and felt his body stiffen as he waited for her answer.

She nodded, "Yes, you. I've seen you manipulate people like a chess master moving his pieces. However, you lack common sense."

"How so?"

"You forgot my clothes, didn't you?"

He leaned forward. "That was not a lack of common sense. That was using common sense. I've already explained why I didn't collect your clothes. So please, find another example."

"You wear drawers that are too tight because you think wearing them will make me magically interested in what they conceal," she said smartly. "When, quite frankly, I could care less."

"I only did that so I wouldn't scare you," he countered.

"Yes, because it's *so* large," she said sarcastically, rolling her eyes.

"Stop," he snapped. "Stop the sarcasm right now. I left them on because I knew you weren't a virgin and I didn't want you to think I was trying to force myself on you. I wanted to give you the space and respect you deserved."

She just stared at him unblinking. "Thank you," she whispered. "I didn't mean to insult you…"

"Yes, you did," he retorted. "But that's all right. Just don't discount what I do for you, Madison. Everything I've ever told you has been the truth. I haven't lied to you about anything. Ever." The last word was added more for his benefit than hers. He'd never lied to her in New York, not that she'd ever know that. He honestly doubted she even remembered him. He'd been nothing more to her than a passing flirtation.

"I'm sorry," she said quietly.

"No need to be," he said dismissively. "Now pour us some tea."

With a weak smile, she poured their tea and they had a strained conversation.

In his quick, unplanned escape last night, he hadn't considered just how angry she'd be. However, thinking about it from her side, he could understand. He'd stolen her away without letting her say goodbye or gather her things or even know what was going on. How astonishing to discover he really was a scoundrel.

Conversation at dinner was nonexistent. She just glowered at him and shoveled her food into her mouth at an astonishing rate, presumably to be out of his presence as quickly as possible. After he finished eating, he went up to their room and found the door locked. He had the key in his pocket, all he had to do was slip it in and unlock the door. But she didn't want him there tonight and he respected her wishes enough not to push it. For tonight anyway, he'd just try again tomorrow.

But tomorrow wasn't any different. And neither was the next day; nor the next. It turned out to be nearly a week before she so much as let him cross the threshold. And once he crossed it, he knew it wasn't for a reenactment of the night of passion they'd had the week before. No, she was full of rage. And her rage surprised him. She'd been very quiet and withdrawn all week as she'd tried to avoid him. To actually see her in a temper was rather unusual.

"You requested me," he said, shutting the door.

Skipping any hint of pleasantry, she pointed to the wooden box Paul had brought for her. "What's the meaning of this?" she asked in a voice that bordered on hysteria.

He looked at the offending box. "I don't know," he said as if he were a lad being questioned for a prank at Eton.

"Why is it here?" she demanded hotly.

"I don't know," he repeated. What did she expect him to say?

"Yes, you do," she snapped. "Now get it out of my sight."

"Why?" he demanded.

Her eyes flashed fire like he'd never seen. "Because I don't want to see it again, that's why."

He walked up to the chest and put his hand on the latch. "Why not? What's in here that made your face go white and caused you to look as though you were about to swoon?"

"Nothing," she said, putting her hands on his to stop him from opening the lid. "Get your hands off of it."

"No," he said, shaking his head. "I'm going to open it."

"No," she yelled. "You have no right to. It's mine."

He smiled. "Didn't you know that in England when a woman marries, all her possessions then belong to her husband?"

"This is different," she argued. "There is no monetary value in this chunk of wood."

"No," he agreed. "But there is another type of value in this box. Now get your hands off."

Her hands didn't budge. "Not on your life," she hissed. "I shouldn't have called you in here. I should have just lit it on fire and been done with it."

"But you didn't," he pointed out smugly. "And now you'll have to expose your secrets to me."

"No, I won't," she said, tugging on the chest.

"Yes, you will," he countered, pulling it out of her grasp. Holding it above her reach, he fiddled with the latch and almost had it open when his eyes caught Madison's. "You really don't want me to see what's in here, do you?" he asked softly, lowering the box.

She shook her head.

With a sigh, he held the box out to her and just before her fingers had a good grasp, he let it fall to the thinly carpeted stone floor, silently watching as it splintered apart. He knew it was a cruel trick, but hoped she'd think it was an accident.

All hope of her thinking it was an accident flew out the window when he saw her bend down and start scooping up pieces of paper.

He dropped to his knees to help and noticed they were letters; letters from Robbie to be exact. He wasn't going to be such a cad as to read her love letters in front of her, or at all. He murmured an apology and scooped them up. There were a ton of them. But then again, they'd courted for five years. His shock was more that the man actually knew to write them in the first place, not so much because she'd actually kept them. His eyes scanned a sentence here and there. His writing was messy and full of spelling errors. Benjamin knew that already though from the letters he'd received from Robbie detailing his relationship with Madison.

They were near the bottom of the stack and his hands were full of folded papers when he saw the corner of a picture. His interest now piqued by the picture more than it had been by the scribbled declarations of like from Robbie. Without saying anything, he put the notes in a pile next to her and grabbed for the corner of the drawing. His fingers had barely closed around the edge when her cold, trembling hand found his wrist. He looked up into her face and saw her shaking her head before whispering, "Please don't."

"Let me see, Madison. Please," he said, gently shaking her hand off his wrist. "I don't care if it's of him. I just want to see." With her hand off his wrist, he yanked up the papers and didn't see a picture of him. He saw a picture of *him!* Him as in Benjamin Archer Leopold Charles Robert Collins, Duke of Gateway, Marquis of Channing, Earl of Iversly, Viscount Clairborne, Baron Drake, also known to her as Leo.

He scanned the picture. He recognized it immediately. She'd drawn him leaning against the tree the day of the outing at the Hudson. His eyes traveled over his drawn form. She'd captured him perfectly. Well, perfectly for how he looked then, that is. Looking at the picture made it easier to see why she'd not recognized him. He'd been nothing more than a boy at the time. Everything about the image in the picture said so. The expression on his unevenly bearded face; his posture; his body in general. It wasn't until he'd come back from America that he'd taken up boxing and thickened up. He'd been nothing but a skinny pole with legs back then.

He flipped to the next picture and blinked. It was a drawing of them dancing. But they'd never danced. Had she drawn this because it had been how she'd envisioned dancing with him? There were more pages and he wanted to see them all. What was he thinking? He wanted to frame them all.

"Could you please dispose of those in the nearest fire," Madison said tonelessly.

"Why?" he asked hoarsely, looking into her sad face. She'd obviously remembered him if she'd known these were in the chest and hadn't wanted him to see them. It was also clear to see she'd felt the same for him that he'd felt for her. Why did she want them destroyed?

She came forward and tried to take them from him, but he drew his hand back. She shrugged. "All right, since you want to know so badly, I'll tell you. I fancied myself in love with him," she said blithely.

"And he felt the same," he said immediately, his heart pounding in his chest.

She snorted. "Hardly; no, he termed me a challenging courtesan or something of the like."

"Excuse me?" he asked breathlessly. "I never—"

"Oh, don't," she interrupted coldly. "Don't defend him. Brooke did enough of that back in New York."

"Well, madam," he drawled, "It just so happens that I know this man. And, believe it or not, you do, too. *And*, I know for certain he never said anything of the like regarding you."

She paled. "You know him?"

"Yes," he said with a grin. "And I know he never said that about you."

"All right, what's his name?" she asked with a doubtful expression.

"You'd know him as Leo," he paused and smiled when he heard her gasp, "but his real name is—"

"Benjamin!" she screamed, cutting him off as a bullet zipped in the open window and hit him directly in the shoulder.

Chapter 22

Madison's heart almost beat out of her chest as she tried to get Benjamin out of his clothes. "Would you just cooperate," she said testily

He appeared rather irritated. "Well, excuse me," he said sarcastically. "If I had known I was going to be shot at by your lovesick suitor today, I would have dressed accordingly."

"Next time, see that you do," she countered sweetly, sliding his coat off his injured arm.

He shook his head and undid his cravat. "What was that window doing open?" he asked, frowning.

"I'm sorry. I needed some air and decided to open the window."

"No more open windows," he grumbled.

She went to work on the buttons of his waistcoat and shirt. "I said I was sorry. I didn't think there was any harm in it."

"It's not your fault," he muttered. "I just can't believe he found us."

"You don't know that it was him," she pointed out, pulling his shirt off and sucking in her breath at the sight of his wound.

He looked doubtful. "Who else would it be?"

She shrugged. "Andrew, Papa, Paul, just about anyone in England has a grudge against you."

"It was him."

"How can that be?" she asked, grinning. "You said yourself this place was secreted off. And, if by some chance, he got the direction, you seem to think him too dull to be able to use a map or any other navigational tool to find this covert place. So how do you propose he found us? Stuck his nose to the ground and sniffed?"

"That's enough of your insolence, woman," he said in mock irritation. "I'm really not sure how he did it. But I know it was him."

"How can you be so certain?"

"Because he missed," Benjamin teased.

Madison blinked at him. "You cannot tell me that you hit your target every time you aim."

"Always," he said with a smile.

She bent her head closer to his wound, not that she really needed to, it was as big as Brooklyn. "I hope you have a lot of brandy available," she said with a wobbly smile.

"Fresh out," he mumbled. "Is it that bad?"

She nodded. "The ball didn't come out."

He swore.

She swore.

They grinned at each other. There was nothing that compared to bonding with your spouse through swear words.

"All right, since I've no alcohol, there's no reason for either of us to leave the room. You're not squeamish are you?"

"No," she said, shaking her head. "I've volunteered in one hospital or another since I was fifteen. Your paltry wound is nothing."

"Thanks," he muttered.

She pushed him back on the bed and started ripping his shirt into strips. She took one of the strips, folded it several times, and pressed it to the wound. "Here, hold this." She brought his other hand up to hold the linen against his shoulder. "Keep pressure on it. I'll be right back. I need to go look for something to dig that ball out with."

He quickly sat up on the bed. "Do not leave this room," he barked.

She shot him an annoyed look. "What?"

"I said you may not leave. I don't want you out of my sight. For all we know, he could be stalking about waiting for another opportunity. I want you to stay in my sight." His words were starting to slur together as dark red blood soaked through the cloth and trailed down his arm, leaving a nasty stain on the counterpane.

"Fine," she said, shaking her head in exasperation. "Lie back down. I'll just use your knife. But if you get an infection and die, you may not blame me."

"I won't. I'll be dead."

She rolled her eyes at his asinine comment and grabbed the water pitcher and basin from off the vanity. She brought the two items over and put them on the table next to the bed. "Where is your knife?"

"In my pocket."

She picked up his coat and checked his pockets. There were all sorts of things from keys to coins to matches, but no knife. "Not here," she called, putting his coat back down.

"In my trousers," he said with a hint of a smile on his face.

"Of course it is." She shook her head. "Any opportunity you can find for me to touch you."

"I won't deny it."

She dug in his pocket and pulled out his knife. "All right, I'm going to put some cold water on your shoulder, then dig out the ball."

He nodded. His skin had gone quite pale and he truly didn't look so good.

Perhaps he should have considered the proximity of the nearest doctor before he brought her here, she thought cheekily, pressing cool, wet linen to his wound. Once the blood around it was wiped away enough to allow her to see where she was digging, she pulled the blade from his knife and stuck the point into his wound to fish out the ball.

Ideally, she would have preferred forceps, or even needle-nose pliers, to get this out, but since His Bossy Grace wouldn't let her leave the room, she had to make do.

Angling the knife blade just so, she was able to slip it under the ball, which fortunately was lodged in muscle and not bone. Using slow movements, she carefully brought the ball up enough to be able to reach it with the tips of her fingers. Even though it wasn't normal hospital procedure to dig one's fingers into a wound without at least rinsing them off first, she just shrugged and plucked the ball out of his wound, grimacing when she heard the squelching sound it made as it emerged from his body.

She put the ball down on the table so she could clean it later and give it to him as a souvenir like she had for the few men in Brooklyn she'd helped treat for gunshot wounds. Truly, it was absolutely amazing what men wanted to keep. If it were a woman, she'd just be glad she was still alive. But not a man; men liked to admire the scars and wanted to carry the bullets that injured them in their pockets to show everyone, of course.

Cleaning his wound with another wet cloth, she looked around for something she could use as a bandage. Aside from wrapping clean strips of his shirt around it, there wasn't anything. That would have to do she decided, right before her eyes landed on her reticule. She had a needle and several spools of thread in there. It was just skin. It couldn't possibly be any more difficult than sewing silk.

Quickly, she ran across the room and grabbed her reticule. Dumping the contents on the bed, she smiled. Who knew they were both walking emporiums? Selecting the black thread, she went back to his side. She pulled the needle out of the end of the spool where she kept it, and willing her hands to stay calm, she threaded the needle. At the hospital, the extent of her experience had been cleaning and dressing wounds, never sewing. But she'd seen it enough to have a good idea what she was doing.

It didn't take more than a couple of passes with the needle to get him closed up. She realized he probably didn't even need to be stitched, but she wanted to do it for him anyway. For some reason, it felt good just to be near him and help him, even if he had abducted her in her sleep.

Wrapping his shoulder in clean strips of linen, she heard him mumbling some incoherent words; something about strangling Robbie and not saying something derogatory about someone else. She smiled. He may be somewhat unconscious and mumbling nonsense from his considerable loss of blood, but at least he was still alive. She brought her fingers to his neck and felt his pulse. It was there; weak, but there.

Without thought, she leaned forward and pressed a soft kiss to his lips.

"That didn't count" he mumbled, startling her.

"What do you mean?" she asked quietly so not to wake him if he was just dreaming.

"That kiss. You still owe me one. That one didn't count."

She laughed. "All right."

A faint smile touched his lips. "Madison, about earlier—"

She pressed a finger to his lips to stop him. "Don't tax yourself. We'll talk later."

Weakly, he reached up and took her fingers from his lips. "No," he said, barely able to shake his head. "I want to explain."

Embarrassment flooded her. She shouldn't have acted like a lunatic when she'd seen that chest. She should have just tossed it into the empty fireplace and lit a match. Instead, she'd gone into hysterics like a little girl and embarrassed herself. "Please don't," she whispered. "I know you said you know Leo. But please don't tell him anything. It was a long time ago and I don't want to relive the past."

He closed his eyes. "What if you were wrong? What if he hadn't said those things? Would it matter?"

"No," she said, shaking her head. "Not one whit. I'm yours now."

He nodded slowly. "All right, I'll leave the past alone. But please save the pictures for me."

"Why?" she asked, flabbergasted. Why would he want pictures she'd drawn of another man? Especially one she'd thought herself in love with.

He opened his eyes and looked at her with a very serious expression, "Because you drew them."

Chapter 23

Benjamin's last rational thought before slipping into a deep sleep was about Madison and if she'd heed his advice and stay put. Under any other circumstances, he'd physically make sure she didn't leave the room. However, his extreme amount of blood loss made it difficult to control the little slip of a woman he called his wife. She might be small, but she was mighty, he thought while falling deeper into a dreamless state.

Using all the energy he could possibly muster, he tried his hardest to pry one eyelid open just to glimpse her one more time to make sure she was still sitting in the chair he'd made her put in the hidden corner of the room. It was the only place that Robbie couldn't possibly put a bullet unless he was in the room. He doubted Robbie would be bold enough to make another attempt to shoot him today. Knowing that weasel, he'd probably shat his drawers when the gun fired and he realized he was still alive. And then, he probably did it again when he realized, so was Benjamin.

After Madison had bandaged his shoulder, one of the few servants that worked there came in and Benjamin directed him to secure the house and stay close in the unlikely event Robbie dared come back again today. If not for his weakness from the loss of blood, he'd have gone out, run Robbie down and torn him apart with his bare hands. But he never did like to enter into a fight he didn't think he'd win; and just now, he didn't think he'd win against that twerp. It was a sad day when one had to admit that a man no thicker than a broomstick with all the starch of a cooked noodle could best him in a fight. Quite frankly though, Benjamin was a realist and at this moment, that was the reality of the situation.

Tomorrow was a different story, however.

Tomorrow, he'd hunt him down and, in less than a minute, the world would have one less pest polluting the air.

Thoughts ceased and time evaporated. Only blackness surrounded him. He heard noises and voices around him, but didn't know who they belonged to or what they were saying. He felt gentle fingers touching his body. He felt a cool cloth come to rest on his forehead. He felt his arm being moved and the pressure around his wound easing. He heard murmurs he didn't understand. He felt a hand come to rest on his chin and a bottle touch his lips. He felt the bottle move from his lips and the hand on his chin pull away. He felt fire being poured on his shoulder.

His eyes snapped open. "What the hell is going on?" he shouted, using his free hand to bat away the hand that was pouring liquid fire on his shoulder.

"Sorry, Your Grace," a grey haired man with a Welsh accent said.

Benjamin's eyes shifted to Madison. She looked very serious; too serious. "Madison, what's wrong?" he asked raggedly. She did not look good.

"I'm sorry, Benjamin," she said softly. "Your wound is infected."

"Infected?" How could that be, it had only been a few hours? How were there already signs of infection?

"I'm sorry," she said again. "I knew that knife wasn't clean."

Benjamin shook his head. "Don't," he said hoarsely. "It'll be all right. It's not your fault."

She picked up a bulb filled with water or some other clear fluid and squeezed it, flushing out his wound. "The doctor says it is a mild infection and you should be well in a day or two."

"A day or two," he repeated, nodding. "And dare I ask how many days it has been already?"

Madison cleared her throat and handed the doctor some cotton. "Do you want the truth?"

He closed his eyes. "That long?"

"Three days," she said hesitantly.

He groaned. He'd lost Robbie's trail for sure if three days had passed.

"You don't even know it was him," Madison said calmly. "I was thinking about it. Isn't it possible it could have been a hunter? We are surrounded by forest. And I daresay, forests seem to have plenty of animals lurking about, just waiting to be shot."

"It's possible," he conceded. "But not probable."

She sighed. "Why are you so sure it was him?"

"Because if it had been anyone else, they would have had enough foresight to take a shot when I was more vulnerable and not in a second story room they couldn't see inside of."

"Oh," she said quietly. "I guess you're right."

He smiled. There was no guessing about it. He was right and she knew it. "However, I still wonder how he found us," he mused.

"Well, what he lacks in sense, he makes up for in cents," she said, giggling at her own pun.

"You think you're funny, don't you?" he teased with a grin. Good thing he'd been to America or he wouldn't have understood her jest. "But, I admit, you make a good point," he continued. "Coins slipped into the right palm can get a man far."

"And Robbie has access to more than most," Madison added. "His father runs a bank and Robbie is the vice president."

The doctor got up and mumbled something to Madison about taking care of his shoulder so it didn't get infected again and quoted her some exorbitant price for coming out to the middle of nowhere to attend him.

Madison dug in his coat pockets and paid the doctor the small fortune he'd quoted.

"Unless he came over here with bars of gold or bags of money, all the money at his father's bank won't do him much good," Benjamin told her as she walked back to his bedside. "He can go into every bank in London and say he's the vice president of a bank in America until he falls unconscious from lack of air and they still won't give him one pound without him exchanging dollars, or more preferably, gold. And he'd have to have a hefty sum if he were able to fund an investigation that would have led him here so quickly."

Madison came to sit by his side, making him ache to take her into his arms and hold her close. "Does any of this matter?"

"Yes," he burst out. "The man clearly wants you back. He's not going to stop now. Once he realizes I'm still alive, he'll just try again."

"I think you're giving him too much credit."

"No," he said, shaking his head. "I'm just being careful, Madison. He's determined to have you."

"I don't know why," she said with a sigh. "He didn't seem to want me very badly before."

"Yes, he did," Benjamin muttered. The man had obviously wanted her bad enough to make up lies about him in order to win her affections back. Benjamin wished he could tell her that, but she didn't want to hear it. She wanted to leave the past in the past and perhaps it was better that way. He'd won her once. He'd just have to do it again. It would just take more effort this time.

She said something he missed due to his pondering.

"All right," he said, pulling himself up to sit against the headboard. "First thing, why exactly am I naked?"

Madison blushed, turning a bright shade of red. "Sorry, I… uh…I had to take you clothes off to take care of you," she stammered uneasily.

He smiled. "Madam, while I appreciate your concern for my health and wellbeing, I just hope you controlled your urges and didn't ravish me when I was in such a defenseless state. I do have my virtue to protect, after all," he teased before dodging the pillow she swung at his head.

"You're terrible," she said laughingly.

"I know," he agreed, setting his hand on hers. "Thank you for staying and taking care of me. I appreciate it." His voice was uneven and full of emotion.

"You're welcome," she said quickly. "Second?" she prompted.

"Right." He rearranged the covers around his waist. "We need to find out how he knew to come here."

"Couldn't he have just followed us?"

"No," he said, shaking his head. "First, that would mean he was at Rockhurst, which he wasn't. I know that because the carrier that delivered your note generally works in London. If Robbie was near Rockhurst, he would have used a messenger from Bath."

"Could the messenger have followed us?"

Benjamin twisted his lips as he contemplated that. "Not likely, but possible, I suppose. But remember, we left suddenly, too suddenly for his benefit. There was no time for him to ferret out information from any of my servants before we left."

"Because they didn't know we'd be leaving," she finished for him. "But what I actually meant was could the messenger or whoever have literally followed us?"

"I know what you meant. And you're right, that would be the only way possible," he agreed. "However, unlike you, who could sleep through a stampede, I cannot. If they'd been following us, I would have heard them."

"Not necessarily," she countered. "They could have stayed far enough back so you didn't hear them."

"Not at night," he said, turning her hand over and slipping his fingers in between hers. "At night the visibility is so limited, they'd not drift back that far. Not without the risk of losing us anyway, especially since we passed through Bath. There are several turn offs in Bath that lead in different directions. He'd have had to stay fairly close to see which way we went. Anyway, that's all assuming he followed us which also doesn't seem likely, because he'd have had to have been staying at Rockhurst to know we'd departed. Even Brooke and Andrew didn't know."

"So what you're saying is if he knew we'd left, it was only because he'd been staying on the property close to the gamekeeper's cabin and heard us depart," she said slowly.

He nodded. "Exactly, so there's no way he could have followed us."

"We're back to guessing who Robbie bribed, then," she said with a shrug.

"Which leads us nowhere, unfortunately," Benjamin said sourly. "And as you pointed out earlier, it really doesn't matter. The fact is, he's here now and I'll have to find a way to lure him out of his hiding place."

She let out a sigh and rolled her eyes to look at the ceiling. "If I was right and it doesn't matter how he got here, then why did we just have to discuss how he got here?"

"Because I wanted a reason to talk to you," he said simply with a hint of a smile. "I know it's not the most romantic conversation we've ever had. But you're my wife and I like talking to you. I like hearing your ideas."

"You seem to find a way to reject them all," she retorted playfully.

He moved his good shoulder up in a lopsided shrug. "Can't help that. Put the pillow down, Madison! All right, all right, you were right about the only way he could have followed us was if he'd done it in a literal sense. And I even acknowledged it. Now put that pillow down before you swing it at me too much and the feathers fly out. I rather like my pillows fluffy."

She closed her eyes and shook her head. "Are you certain it was even him?" she asked again, tossing the pillow on the bed.

"Yes," he said firmly. "And if it's not, then it's someone he hired to do the job for him."

She swallowed and nodded. "What do we do now?"

He grinned. "I'll just wait for him to strike again. In the meantime, you keep fussing over me until I'm better."

"Who knew the Dangerous Duke would want a woman to fuss over him," she said laughingly.

"Not just any woman," he said genuinely, "Only you; always you." He leaned forward and pressed a tender but chaste kiss to her lips.

~*~*~*~

It didn't take long for Robbie to strike again, only about five minutes from the end of their romantic moment to be exact. And, since the man lacked the sense God gave a flea and had less than an ink drop of creativity, he tried the same tactic again. Except this time, the window was closed and the ball shattered the glass before flying over their heads and straight into the wardrobe.

"That does it," Benjamin said irritably, ripping off the blankets and jumping out of bed. He ran to the door and almost had it yanked open when Madison gave a delicate cough.

"I believe you're missing something," she said, humor filling her eyes.

He looked down and saw he was indeed missing something. "Why is it the first time I'm naked in the presence of both you and a bed I have to chase your deranged, lovesick suitor?" he grumbled, trying to pull up his trousers.

"Don't worry," she said lightly, finding him a shirt. "You'll be naked in a bed with me again."

His eyes flew to hers. "And when will this be?"

"When you're about fifty and the time for you to sire an heir is running out," she teased.

He shook his head. "It had better be before then or I'll go mad."

She laughed and swatted him playfully on his good shoulder. "Are you sure you have to go?" Her voice had taken on a serious, strained note.

"Yes," he said without hesitation.

"But you're not well. You just woke up no more than an hour

ago. Your right arm is virtually useless," she argued.

"Madison," he leaned down to tie his boots the best he could with one hand, "I'm not going to wait for him to strike again. He may not be a good aim, but eventually he'll hit something besides my shoulder and a wardrobe. And if it's you—" His voice broke and he swallowed. "I'd never be able to live with myself if that happened."

"But he has to already be gone. It's been at least two minutes since that shot. He may not be very bright, but he's not going to wait outside for you to come find him. He's probably run off, see—"

"Madison!" Benjamin yelled, wrapping an arm around her waist and hauling her across the room. "Do not go near that window again. Now, listen to me. I want you to follow me down the hall. There's a room just a few doors over that I want you to stay in. I think you'll be safer there than you are here. Promise me you'll stay there. Promise me."

"Oh, all right," she said with a sigh.

Grabbing a handful of lead balls and his flintlock rifle from behind the wardrobe, he shooed Madison out of the room and led her down the hall.

"What are you planning to do with that?" she asked, her eyes becoming as large as tea saucers.

"Just some light hunting."

"Do you need such a large gun?" she asked, eyeing the gun in a way that resembled someone looking at a bug that dared crawl onto the table during dinner.

He nodded his head once. "Yes. I want to make sure I get him. This will shoot far enough that I can be back a few hundred yards and still get him."

"Do you think his is as big as yours?"

"No," he said with a chuckle.

"I meant his gun," she said, her lips twitching.

"Oh, in that case, probably; there's no way he would be able to shoot into our room if he had a pistol. They don't have the same distance. Nor can they get the same altitude. See, if it was a pistol, he'd have to be stand—"

She cut his words off with a quick kiss. "No more explanation necessary."

He smiled and opened the door to the room—or perhaps closet, depending on who you asked. "All right, in you go," he said, trying to get his gun ready for the first, and hopefully only, shot.

"I don't think so." She crossed her arms in defiance. "This isn't a room, it's a closet. It doesn't even have windows."

"Exactly, but you promised. So, in you go," he encouraged, giving her bottom a little swat of encouragement.

She groaned and he sent her his best ducal glance. "That look does nothing to cow me. If you want to see a look that gets results, you should get to know Brooke better."

"I believe I've seen the look you speak of," he said honestly, "Twice actually."

"And did it scare you?" she asked with a cheeky smile.

"Yes, and I'll be happy to tell you all about it when I return," he said quickly. "Now, get in there so I can go hunt the goose and get back to spend the rest of my life with you."

"All right," she said, resigned. "But you owe me for this." She stepped into the little space and scowled.

"I'll do whatever you ask of me. Just stay in the clo—room, please," he said with a quick kiss. He shut the door quickly and flew down the stairs, taking them two at a time. He swung the front door open and ran in the direction from which he was certain the shot had come.

Madison had made a valid point. Robbie wouldn't be such a fool as to lurk in an open field or even around the edges of the forest. He had probably scrambled away before the puff of smoke from his rifle cleared. Possibly one of the smartest things he'd done in his life. But Benjamin still had an advantage: tracks.

The coastal regions were always wet from rain. Even if it hadn't rained in a few days, the ground would still be soggy enough to leave his tracks.

He ran over to where he assumed the shooter had to have been standing in order for the bullet to have come inside at such an angle. He slung his gun over his shoulder, looked down at the ground and groaned. His bullet wound hurt more than he wanted to admit. Madison had been right on that point, too. His right arm was virtually useless. It hurt too much to even try to move it. Good thing he favored his left eye when he shot. He could just prop the end of the gun on something and fire against his left shoulder without causing any pain in his right. He hoped.

Scowling, he surveyed the land. The grass was a moderate length. It was taller than he'd have liked it to be while searching for footprints, but it was short enough that if he scoured sufficiently, he'd find them.

Walking closer to a little knot of trees, his heart rate accelerated. Not only were there boot tracks, but Robbie had carelessly left a small box of lead balls and powder on a fallen log. "Careless fool," Benjamin muttered, pocketing his find.

Following the trail Robbie had so thoughtfully—or thoughtlessly—provided, Benjamin walked with his gun cocked and ready to fire at a second's notice. He walked through the forest for a good half a mile when he abruptly stopped his feet and swore.

He frowned as he looked down at the small rock bottom creek that ran right in front of him. It was only three feet wide and couldn't be more than ankle deep. But that was deep enough; deep enough to lose a trail. The rocks on the bottom were large enough that they wouldn't shift around a boot to leave a print and the water flowed swiftly enough not to allow the mud from his boots to stick to the rocks. He shook his head. Either this was a stroke of genius or luck. Considering Robbie was involved, it was probably the latter.

With a sigh, he released the cock on his gun and sat down. He was tired and in pain. Robbie, it appeared, had gotten away again, and wasn't likely to return anytime soon. He looked at the offending creek for a minute and then tore his gaze away in irritation. Just as his eyes left the creek, something on the other side of it caught his attention. Another set of boot prints.

He jumped up and leapt across the little creek. He looked down at the ground and frowned again. These boot prints were side by side, not one in front of the other. How odd. Another oddity, the new set was considerably larger than the ones he'd followed to the creek.

He set his gun down and put his foot next to one of the boot prints that was on his side of the creek. It was big. Not quite as big as his boot, but close. He scanned the ground to see if there were any more. There weren't. Whoever left these had to have walked to the spot via the creek and just stood here.

Benjamin stepped back across the little creek and ground his teeth. There was only one reason for two sets of fresh tracks to exist: Robbie had an accomplice.

Chapter 24

Madison felt like an eight-year-old girl during a thunderstorm hiding in the hall closet. Surely Benjamin was overreacting. Robbie wouldn't shoot at them and then be so dimwitted as to try to come into the house to collect her. If he was, he was destined for a surprise. She'd sooner brain the man than go off with him.

Time crept by in that dark little closet positioned right above the kitchen. Voices and sounds from the kitchen drifted up to her ears. Apparently most of the footmen were taking a break and enjoying a game of cards in the kitchen. They were awfully noisy with their laughter and cheers. Cook was banging around pots and pans, getting ready for their evening meal and yelling at all the men for dragging mud into her kitchen on their shoes. She smiled. As angry as she had been about being dragged here against her will, she was beginning to like it.

All of the staff had been more than friendly to her since she'd come. Cook offered to cook anything she wanted. Hatley, the informal butler, commanded all the inside footmen to do whatever she asked, which they did. She hadn't been outside much, but she imagined Billings would act as her groom if she wanted to go riding. She knew one day they'd have to leave to go to Glenbrook, but hopefully not for a while yet. She rather liked it here.

"Madison," Benjamin said tightly, opening the door to the room she was in. "Grab your things, we're leaving."

Madison gasped. Had he read her mind? Shaking her head, she said, "What?"

"I said we're leaving. I just instructed Billings to ready the carriage," he informed her matter-of-factly.

"But, you're not well," she protested. Why did they have to leave now?

He hefted her stubborn body over his good shoulder and carried her down to their room. "I'm well enough," he grunted. "Now, the carriage will be ready in fifteen minutes. Will you?"

"Hmm, I don't know," she said caustically, blinking at the clock. "I sure hope so. Let me see. Clothes?" She looked down at the same wrinkled blue gown she'd been wearing since they'd left Rockhurst and kicked her foot out from under the hem to reveal her slipper and stocking. "Check. Personal items?" She grabbed her reticule and dropped her brush, mirror and toothbrush inside. "Check." She looked back at the clock. "Do I win a prize for being early? It only took me fifteen seconds!"

He shook his head. "Very good, now you can help me?" He started grabbing his clothes from the wardrobe and haphazardly threw them into a trunk.

She went to his bureau and opened the top drawer. Inside was a mess of cravats, stockings and drawers. She left the cravats and stockings and tossed the drawers into his chest. "Anything else I can help you with?" she asked saucily, trying to let on to the "help" she'd already given.

"Yes. Grab the drawings, please," he said, tossing clothes into the chest.

She tensed. Why did he want those? She'd hoped he'd forget about them when he woke up and she could burn them. "Why don't we leave these here, and I'll draw some more," she offered.

"No," he said firmly. "Bring them. I want them."

Scooping them up from where she'd placed them face down on the vanity, she handed them to him and watched in confusion as he took them from her and carefully placed them on top of his pile of clothing. The man was cracked. There was nothing else for it. Only a deranged man would want to keep drawings of another man dancing with his wife. "You're addled."

"Perhaps; are you sure you don't want me to tell you who that handsome fellow is?" He looked at her and grinned.

"No," she said vehemently, shaking her head for emphasis. "However, he had better not show up wherever it is we're going."

His smiled dimmed. "And why is that?"

"Would you really want to share a house with him?"

Benjamin shrugged. "He looks like a nice enough fellow."

"You know what I mean," she said tonelessly.

He nodded. "I believe so, yes. However, I feel obligated to inform you he will be there."

"Then you'll just need to redistribute him," she said sharply, crossing her arms.

"Madison," he said softly, wrapping his arm around her and bringing her close. "Are you unwell? Your face has gone whiter than snow."

She nodded. "Do we have to go?" she asked weakly.

"I'm sorry, darling, but yes," he said softly before brushing a kiss on her cheek. "Just waiting for Robbie to make his next move isn't a good plan. We're too secluded here. I think I can protect you better at Glenbrook. I have more servants there and a better land spread so it will be harder for him to climb a tree and shoot inside our room."

"Then why don't you take me back to Rockhurst?" she argued.

"No," he barked. "You're my wife. You will stay with me." He abruptly let go of her, grabbed the trunk and left the room.

Madison sank down onto the feather mattress and watched Benjamin leave. Her heart started to hammer so fast with what she hoped to be rage, not panic. She didn't want to go live near Leo. They may have only seen each other little more than a dozen times and actually spoken less than half that many in less than a month, but it was enough. She didn't want to see him again. Not that she was certain she'd recognize him anyway; it had been a long time. He was probably fat, bald and dandling babes on his knees by now. But still, the idea he could show up unnerved her. What if he wasn't bald and ugly? What if he was handsome and single? What if old sparks ignited again and turned to flames? She shook her head. She couldn't let that happen. She was a married woman now. She belonged to Benjamin and she would never betray him.

But that did nothing to ease her mind. The point was she didn't want to go see him. More than that, she really hated being told what to do. Everyone always told her what to do. She'd been the most biddable of the three daughters. Even Liberty with her love for propriety and following rules garnered more respect than she did. People always ran over Madison because she was quiet and usually considered a bit different. Well, not anymore. She may have been manipulated by Robbie for five years. Used by Leo to be some sort of bawdy mental image he hoped to make a reality. Forced to marry Benjamin because she didn't want to be tied to a scandal involving her brother-in-law, and stolen straight from her bed in the dead of night. But not anymore; starting today she was going to starch her backbone and take matters into her own hands. Starting with informing Benjamin she intended to stay.

He'd be up shortly and she'd inform him of her plan to stay then. To prepare for his grand entrance, she kicked off her slippers, peeled off her stockings then shoved the items under the bed before moving to the top of the bed and reclining at a forty-five degree angle against the pillows. "I feel like a queen," she said with a smile.

Footfalls thudded down the hall and Madison pasted a bright smile on her lips. This was it. In a second, Benjamin was going to round the corner into their room, causing the curtain to drop and the show to begin, so to speak.

"Let's go, Madison," Benjamin called, entering the room. He looked rather handsome just then with his disheveled hair, bristly chin, and unkempt clothing. Certainly not like the duke he was. He looked rugged, common, and familiar.

She shook her head to clear her thoughts. "I'll be staying," she declared airily. "I happen to like it here. I think I should like to extend my visit."

He snorted. "That will not be happening. Let's go." He frowned. "Where are your stockings and slippers?"

She wiggled her toes at him. "I shan't need them for the rest of the day," she informed him with a smile.

"And why not?"

"Because I've no plans to move from my spot," she declared, wiggling against the pillows behind her for emphasis.

He smiled and shook his head. "All right, have it your way."

"What's that mean?" she asked, bringing her hand up to inspect her attention deprived cuticles.

"You'll see." Then before she could do or say anything else, he picked her up with his left arm and hoisted her over his good shoulder.

"Put me down," she yelled, slapping her palms against his back. "I mean it, Benjamin. Put me down."

"I will," he said, giving her a tight one-armed squeeze around her midsection. "I suppose you'll require your reticule."

"No, leave it there," she ordered when he picked it up.

He wound the straps around his right hand and let it hang. "If I leave it then you won't have any of your things."

"Put me down!"

"I already said I would," he said flippantly.

"Now," she ground out.

He started walking down the stairs. "Soon enough."

She started wiggling her body, trying to break free and his grasp tightened. "Benjamin Collins, let go of me!"

The front door opened and she saw Cook and Hatley stare at the two of them with unhinged jaws as Benjamin carried her past them. "Here we are, duchess," he said, plopping her down on the velvet squabs of his carriage.

She scrambled to get up and he held her down. "I don't want to go," she said stubbornly.

"I know," he said quietly. "But you have to."

"No, I don't," she said fiercely.

He nodded. "Yes, you do."

The carriage lurched forward and irritation swelled in her breast. Why did this man always seem to be abducting her as soon as she was beginning to like being around him? She crossed her arms and watched in annoyance as he leaned forward to secure the extra latches on the inside of the carriage She fought the urge to roll her eyes. "I'm not so daft I'd try to jump from a moving carriage," she muttered.

He shrugged. "I can never be too careful where you're concerned, sweet."

She shook her head. His sarcasm was rather annoying at times. "Once again, you weren't too concerned about me," she said with feigned sweetness as she kicked one of her bare feet from under her skirt in order to catch his eye.

"That's not my lack of concern for you. That was your own doing."

She frowned. "How so?"

He shook his head. "I didn't tell you to discard your slippers and stockings and hide them from me."

"I didn't hide them. They were under the bed."

"You didn't tell me that when I asked," he retorted. "Therefore, I took that to mean you didn't consider them important enough to bring with you."

She repositioned herself on the seat, tucking her bare and slightly cold feet under her. "You had better stop in the first town and buy me more," she said coldly. "And while you're at it, I demand you buy me a new gown. I've been wearing this one for ten days straight."

"My apologies," he said tonelessly. "However, we will not be stopping before we get to Glenbrook except to eat and change the horses. Once we're there, I'll commission a modiste to make you an entire new wardrobe."

She crossed her arms and let out a defiant huff. "And just how long will I get to endure your charming personality and my frozen feet?"

"Two days."

"Absolutely not," she said sharply, scowling. "I will not be stuck in a carriage with you for two days wearing the same gown I've worn for nearly a fortnight and nothing to cover my feet."

"Yes, you will," he said flatly, propping his feet up on the seat opposite him.

She closed her eyes and took a deep breath. It did nothing for her.

"I know what you're thinking," he said calmly. "You're not going to be able to run away from me when we stop. So don't even try it."

She looked at him sharply. How did he know she was thinking that? "You can't watch me every second," she said airily.

"No?" he asked curiously, his lips twitching. "And how do you plan to run away with nothing to cover those beautiful but bare feet of yours?"

"I could buy slippers," she informed him, raising her chin a notch.

He scoffed. "That would take too long. I might find you before you could board the mail coach if you did that."

"You make a good point," she said, nodding. "I won't need to shop for slippers. On the mail coach, I can buy some from another passenger."

"And if there's not another female passenger?"

She shrugged. "Then I'll just go in bare feet. It's not as if I'm not doing that right now."

He shook his head. "It doesn't matter. You're not boarding a mail coach. You're coming with me to Glenbrook."

"Whatever you say," she said dismissively.

"Madison," he said sharply. "You're my wife. You're coming with me. End of discussion."

"All right," she agreed with a shrug.

Four hours of uncomfortable, deafening silence later, they pulled into the first coaching inn. Billings went to water and feed the horses after he opened the carriage door.

"Come along, Madison," Benjamin said, climbing out of the carriage.

"No," she said, shaking her head in defiance.

"If you think I'll leave you here while I go order our supper and use the necessary, you're mistaken."

She scowled. "I'm not walking across the yard in my bare feet."

He smiled. "No need. Now, come along." He reached his hand up to her, waiting for her to take it.

She didn't. "I'll stay here, thank you."

"No you won't. Now, let's go. I'll carry you."

She sighed. "And how, pray tell, do you plan to do that when you have only one good arm?"

"The same way I carried you before," he said with a grin.

"No," she hissed. "I will not be embarrassed because you want to show off your brute strength by tossing me over your shoulder like a caveman taking his captive bride to the bearskin rug he calls a bed."

He chuckled. "You have some imagination. Now get down here. I'm hungry."

She didn't budge. He mumbled something beneath his breath and climbed back into the carriage.

"Is that the way of it, then?" he asked, putting an arm around her and dragging her out of the carriage. "I wouldn't kick and move around too much if I were you. It just draws more attention to us."

"Put me down," she said through clenched teeth.

"I will," he assured her, "Just as soon as we get back into the carriage."

Never in Madison's life had she been as embarrassed as she was in the inn. Benjamin continued to hold her bent in half over his shoulder with her backside facing the clerk as he ordered their dinner. Thankfully, he didn't further mortify her by insisting they eat in the crowded dining room full of curious onlookers.

"Here you are," he said, placing her onto the seat inside the carriage.

She glared at him until their food was brought out by one of the maids. Then she glared at the food. She was hungry. No, starving. No, famished. But she didn't want to eat. She was too upset.

"Eat," he encouraged.

"No, thank you," she said flatly.

He grabbed a sandwich and offered it to her. When she pushed his hand away, he said, "You have to eat something. Madison, I know you didn't want to go; and I know you're angry with me for embarrassing you. But you're only hurting yourself by not eating."

She looked at the sandwich. It was roasted beef, one of her favorites. Licking her lips, she took the sandwich and devoured it.

"There's more," he offered.

"No, thank you," she said, shaking her head and turning to rest the side of her body against the squabs.

"There's another inn in four hours or so. We'll stay there tonight," he said softly, fruitlessly trying to ease her stiffened body to relax against him.

Chapter 25

"You may sleep on the floor," Madison informed him primly after he carried her to their shared room and set her on the bed.

"No, I won't," he bit off. "Now scoot over."

"No," she said, spreading her arms and legs out on the bed like a giant starfish.

"What happened to the woman who said she'd share my bed because it's what's expected?" he asked tersely.

"She grew a backbone."

He crossed his arms and shook his head. "Scoot over."

"No. You may find somewhere else to sleep."

"No, I won't. Now be the model English wife and make room for your husband."

"Wrong sister," Madison said laughingly. "If you wanted the model English wife, you should have married Liberty."

"I don't want Liberty," he said tightly, sweeping her from the top of her outstretched fingertips to the end of her perfect toes.

She giggled. "I daresay she doesn't want you, either. Although—" She broke off in a fit of giggles.

"What could you possibly find funny?"

"The night before Liberty married Paul, she tried to get me to take her place. Just imagine if I had. I'd have married Paul and you could have married Liberty," she exclaimed, breaking into peals of laughter.

He stared blankly at her. "Madison, did you have some wine I don't know about?"

"No. Why?" she asked, trying not to giggle.

"There's absolutely nothing funny about what you just said," he told her flatly.

She blinked at him. "I suppose *you* wouldn't think so."

"No, I don't think anyone would think so," he corrected. "What has gotten into you? Don't get me wrong, I enjoy seeing you laugh and have fun, but you've turned completely silly."

"Oh dear," she said with a giggle as she swung her far hand up to cover her giggling mouth. "Brooke always said the same," she said between giggles.

"What?" he asked, staring at her in disbelief. This is what he imagined a candidate for Bedlam looked like. She looked absolutely mad; fetching, but mad.

She had a fit of giggles again. "Act like a silly willy!"

"Excuse me?" What was this mad, fetching woman talking about?

"Right before I fall asleep," she said as if that explained anything.

He nodded. "Are you telling me that when you're tired you act like a madwoman?"

"Yes," she chirped, nodding so enthusiastically he thought her head might nod off.

"Then you had better move over so we can go to sleep," he said, not letting her theatrics deter him. Nobody acted this spastic when they were tired; restless, yes; insane, no.

Suddenly, too suddenly, her head lolled to the side and a soft snoring noise filled the air.

He shook his head and picked up the hand that was closest to him and tried to move it over, but was met with strong resistance and stopped. "All right, you win," he said ruefully. "If you'd go through with an act worthy of Drury Lane in order to get me to leave you alone, I will." He bent his head and dropped a kiss on her cheek. "But I'll be in the chair by the door. And don't forget, I'm a light sleeper."

He sank into the leather chair and closed his eyes. Today could have been better, he mused. It also could have been worse. Robbie could have hit one of them with his bullet. His infection could have been a lot worse. He tried to move his arm and stopped after it moved less than an inch. He'd never been shot before and he prayed it never happened again. At least she'd been kind enough to clean it two more times for him in the carriage.

He smiled. She may be angry with him, but she wasn't heartless. He hoped she didn't keep resisting him tomorrow.

But she did.

The next day was just as uncomfortable. He'd tried to talk to her in the carriage, but she wouldn't respond. Not that she had ignored him entirely, mind you. No, she just gave him simple one word answers, which were usually of the monosyllabic variety.

Leaving before dawn and not having a lot of luggage, they were able to make good time and he decided they'd push all the way to Glenbrook to avoid another uncomfortable round of bedtime theatrics at another boarding house.

Glenbrook was the seat of his duchy. It was a large E-shaped estate built of red bricks. Three floors stood above ground with the kitchen and unfinished rooms below. He'd been told the rooms below were once used as a dungeon, but he refused to acknowledge them as such. Just the idea made him shudder.

The inside hadn't been refurnished in nearly a hundred years. Some of the things were repaired or replaced if they'd become broken, but the majority of the things were ancient. Except the water closets; that was one thing the previous duke had thought worthy of his money. He'd wanted—nay, needed—a private privy. Therefore, he'd indulged himself and bought the best available.

The estate and surrounding duchy boasted over one thousand farmable acres. There were close to fifty tenants and nearly every service was available in the village he controlled. He had a stable full of thoroughbreds and some of the finest stable hands money could afford. He also had a conservatory and extensive gardens that he didn't give a fig about.

It seemed Glenbrook had the finest of everything, and now it would have the finest mistress: Madison.

His heart leapt. She was his wife and he was bringing her to his home. To her home. To their home.

She was asleep with her bare feet stuffed in between the cushions. She hadn't let him touch her all day and he was aching to. Even if it was only her feet, he reached over and circled his fingers around her ankle. Carefully, he slid her toes from where they'd been resting then placed her foot on his thigh. He ran his hands along the delicate bones, tracing her arch with his fingers all the way down to her toes. He frowned. Her foot was rather cold, freezing even. There hadn't been a warm spot on her foot, not even her toes which had been tightly nestled between two cushions. He gently reached for her other foot and brought it to his leg. This one was just as cold.

Earlier he'd given her a small lap blanket and she'd used it to cover the top of her. He stripped off his coat and laid it over her feet and legs. Then put his hands together and blew on his palms before chafing them together in an effort to warm them up before touching her feet again. He wished she'd have said something if she was cold. He would have given her his coat or bought a hot brick the last time they stopped. Nothing for it now, he'd just keep her warm this way. He rather liked doing it anyway.

Around midnight, the carriage came to a halt at Glenbrook and Benjamin was filled with bittersweet feelings. He was glad to be home and to bring Madison with him to the home they'd share for the rest of their lives. But at the same time, the intimacy they'd been allowed during the past few weeks would be lost due to all the intruding servants and responsibilities. Too bad he hadn't made better progress in his attempt to win her affections during that time, he thought glumly.

He climbed from the carriage and did his best to carry her into the house in a more dignified manner by using both arms. His right arm still hurt, and it was dreadfully difficult to move it a lot, but for the most part the infection was clearing and he was able to move it just enough to support her legs as he carried her.

At the top of the main staircase was one of the doors that led to the master suites. He kicked open the door and carried her through a darkened sitting room to his bed. With all the care he could muster, he untied the laces of her gown and peeled it off her deadweight body.

With a groan, he pulled the counterpane up to cover her and lit a candle that was by his bureau. Opening the drawers, he rummaged through the contents until he found what he was looking for: a night shirt.

He didn't trust himself not to wear something and have *some* sort of a barrier between them. A nightshirt would have to do. And so would sleeping on top of the covers.

But that didn't help. He was able to resist acting out his primal urges. However, he was not able to resist thinking them.

As soon as the first rays of sunshine glinted through the window, he jumped up, pulled on his clothes and went downstairs to bark out orders to his staff in hopes of keeping himself distracted.

After he was certain Madison would be taken care of when she woke, he arranged for a meeting with his most trusted staff. He explained the situation regarding Robbie and informed them of his speculation that Robbie had an accomplice. They were given explicit instructions on what should happen if they spotted him.

Jamison, his burly head footman, was charged with the great responsibility of trailing Madison. She was not to leave Jamison's sight unless she was with Benjamin. Though he didn't believe Robbie had intentions of harming her, he might stoop to abducting her. Shame washed over him and he felt guilty for a brief minute. He'd abducted her to keep her safe, he argued with himself. If Robbie were to abduct her, it would be for a different reason altogether.

Jamison left to go about his task and Benjamin dashed off a few notes. He sent for Mrs. Cowley, the local seamstress. He asked that she come right away and he'd pay thrice the going rate for the gowns Madison ordered. Then he wrote one to the staffing agency to have Lottie sent back to help Madison.

He sat back in his chair and debated if he should send one to Andrew. He didn't want Andrew to get involved in his relationship with Madison and wasn't sure if sending a letter would help or hurt his chances of keeping Andrew at Rockhurst where he belonged.

With a sigh, he scribbled out the beginning of a vague note explaining Madison was safely living at her rightful home, Glenbrook.

"We need to speak for a moment," Madison declared, barging into his study.

He nodded a dismissal to Jamison. "Yes?"

"I'm not going to be followed around by that behemoth!" she said sharply, her eyes alight with fiery rage.

Benjamin folded his hands and closed his eyes for an extended blink. "I'm sorry to inform you of this, but yes, you are."

"No. I'm not," she snapped, looking all out of sorts. "It's bad enough you dragged me here against my wishes. But I will not have my personal privacy invaded by him."

He shook his head and picked an imaginary piece of lint from his pant leg. "Personal privacy?" he echoed with a smile.

"You know what I meant."

"I do," he conceded. "You don't like him following you. I understand that. But it's not going to change."

She let out a sound of frustration. "Why not?" she burst out, "I don't intend to be cruel about him, but he sets my teeth on edge."

He shrugged. "You'll get used to it."

"I don't want to get used to it," she said through clenched teeth. "I want him to leave me alone."

"No," he said firmly, shaking his head.

"Then I'll fire him," she said with all the dignity of the fairest duchess in the land.

"You can't," he countered evenly, watching as her chest heaved in anger beneath the horribly wrinkled bodice of her gown.

She inclined her chin a notch. "Yes, I can. I am a duchess and the mistress of this house. Therefore, he is in my employ and he will be out of a job immediately."

Benjamin shook his head and chuckled. "No," he corrected gently. "He is in my employ. As duke and master of this house, I am above the duchess, just slightly, but enough. Therefore, he is in *my* employ and only I can terminate his employment."

She closed her eyes and swallowed. "And it continues," she whispered, shaking her head in disbelief.

"What continues?"

"Being treated as if I don't matter," she said quietly, sweeping from the room in what would have been a grand exit if her gown wasn't wrinkled from two straight weeks of wear and her feet had some sort of covering.

Benjamin raked a hand through his hair. She did matter. That's why he'd stationed Jamison to guard her with his life. If only she could understand that.

An hour later, Mrs. Cowley arrived and Madison spent the afternoon behind locked doors being fitted for gowns.

Fortunately, Mrs. Cowley had a few already made up that needed only minor alterations and could be ready on the morrow.

After dinner, Benjamin steeled himself to go into their room. He had no idea what kind of a mood she'd be in. He'd always thought her to be Mild-Mannered Madison, but recently he'd discovered his assumption had been wrong. Not that he didn't like her having starch, he did. He just wished she'd direct some of her fire at someone besides him.

"Are you ready for bed?" he asked, opening the door.

"No." Her voice was as hard and cold as a chunk of ice. She was sitting on the edge of the bed wearing all the clothes she currently possessed, her arms crossed defiantly across her chest.

He closed the door. "Why not?"

She gave a terse nod across the room to where an agitated Jamison stood with his arms crossed as well. It would appear as if the two were having a showdown.

"Jamison," he said evenly, "you're dismissed."

"Thankee, Yer Grace," Jamison said, walking from his spot.

"Are you ready for bed now?" Benjamin asked.

"No," she repeated, staring at him in a way that made him feel unwelcome.

He cleared his throat. "Can I help you with your gown?" he offered, ignoring her stare.

"No," she said, still piercing him with her icy stare.

"It will help you get ready for bed," he said inanely.

"I'm not going to bed."

He crossed his arms. "And why not?"

She nodded in his direction.

"Because I'm here?" he asked with a hint of agitation.

She nodded.

"Too bad."

She pursed her lips. "I want to be alone."

"No."

"Why not?"

"Because you're not to be alone, that's why," he explained in a sharp tone. "So, either you'll sleep with me in the room or I'll get Jamison and bring him back in here. Which will it be?" He knew his voice sounded hard and menacing. He also knew she didn't deserve to be treated that way. But she needed his protection, and this was the only way he could see to offer it. There was no other way.

Her face turned pink with rage. "Get out!"

"I'm sorry, but no," he said gently, starting to undress.

"Then I'll leave," she said, running to the door.

He wrapped his arm around her waist and brought her back to the bed. "No," he whispered. "You can't leave. I know you don't want to stay, but you have no choice."

"Yes, I do," she said, struggling. "I'm a person, Benjamin. You cannot treat me this way."

"I wish I didn't have to," he said hoarsely, holding her in place.

He held her firmly against him while she struggled for what seemed like forever. "It won't always be this way, Madison," he whispered in her ear. "After Robbie's been caught and transported, you'll be given free reign of things. You'll be able to do exactly as you wish."

She didn't respond and he realized she'd spent so much energy struggling to get free she'd fallen asleep in his arms.

To his dismay, the entire next week was much the same. She kept her distance during the day and fought with him before going to bed at night. The only difference was he'd gotten her to agree to his presence in the room without yelling, fighting or struggling as long as he slept in the chair. He didn't much care for the arrangement, but it would have to do. He only hoped Robbie struck again soon or he'd have to change tactics.

He didn't like living with an angry wife while waiting for a madman to strike. It was just damned uncomfortable, almost as uncomfortable as his trousers at present.

He groaned and tore his eyes away from his wife's sleeping form. Soon enough, he told himself. After this business with Robbie was over, he'd pick up where he left off at Rockhurst and not stop wooing her until she was won. By him.

Chapter 26

M adison's dreamless state came to an abrupt end when she heard masculine grunting and sounds of a struggle. Popping her eyes open, she scanned the room. It was fairly dark with no candles burning and only a dim fire in the hearth. Tentatively, she put her feet on the floor and lit a candle.

The noises were too distinct to be coming from another room. So whatever was going on was going on right here. An uneasy skitter ran down her spine. Where was Jamison when she needed him, she thought wryly. She still didn't like being followed by the man, but at a time like this she would have gladly accepted his presence.

Picking up the candelabra with shaky hands, she held it in front of her face as she did a slow turn of the room. Every second she turned added to her nervous apprehension until she thought she might have a fit of panic.

Her eyes did a slow and thorough sweep of the large room. There were several large pieces of furniture that offered excellent hiding places. She wanted to make sure she missed nothing from where she sat perched on the bed, looking from afar. A nervous laugh almost escaped her. Here she was sitting on the bed, waving a little candle around, trying to see shadows of people fighting. What did she think she was going to do if she saw two people fighting? Brain them with the candlestick holder? Actually, that was a good idea. However, it would work better if she got up and was actually closer to the fight.

She slid off the bed and immediately knew where the sounds were coming from: the door. It had been hard to distinguish that while sitting on the bed in the far corner of the room. But now, standing in the middle of the room, it was easy to tell where they were coming from. "I'm such a nodcock," she muttered to herself as she blew out the candle and tossed it on the night stand.

Holding the candleless candelabra above her head, she walked toward the door. That's where Benjamin had been sleeping in his chair, she thought as she crept over. It made perfect sense that was where the struggle was taking place.

She tiptoed on the carpet until she was only three feet away from the noise and froze. The moonlight was shining through the window just enough that she could see Benjamin's face. His skin looked pale and his movements were jerky as he struggled with himself. Madison had to fight the burble of laughter that built in her throat as she thought of the situation. She stood with a candelabra over her head and was about to knock an intruder unconscious when it was only Benjamin having a nightmare!

Dropping the candelabra to the floor, she grabbed Benjamin's arm. "Benjamin," she whispered, giving him a shake.

He didn't answer.

"Benjamin," she repeated.

He mumbled something she assumed was meant for whoever was invading his slumber.

"Benjamin," she said a little louder, shaking him again.

He tried to jerk his arm away from her grasp.

"Ben," she said in a voice louder than normal. "Ben, wake up. It's just a nightmare."

His eyes snapped open and he blinked at her. "Sorry," he murmured, running a hand down his sleepy face.

"It's all right," she assured him quietly. "And here I thought you were a light sleeper."

"I usually am. But occasionally, if I drift deep enough, I'll have a nightmare." He shifted in his seat and cocked his head to see her better. "I must have been dreadfully loud if I woke you," he teased.

"You were."

He chuckled and reached for her. She allowed him to pull her onto his lap. "Thank you for waking me," he murmured against her hair.

"You're welcome. Would you like to talk about it?"

"No," he said, shaking his head. "It's nothing really, just a recurring dream about the night of the fire."

"You mean the night your man-maid caught on fire?"

He nodded.

"Is that why you don't like to have a fire without a screen and insist every candle is snuffed before bedtime?" she asked, running her fingers through his light blond hair.

He nodded again and gave a sharp bark of laughter. "What would people say if they knew the Dangerous Duke was scared of fire?" he asked with a self-deprecating smile.

"Or had nightmares?" she added cheekily.

"Or that." He brushed a quick kiss on her cheek.

"Hmm, it seems to me there is more to you than most know," she mused, snuggling closer to his chest.

"There's more to me than *you* know, too," he whispered in her ear.

She nodded. "I know. And I am having a rather good time finding out your secrets."

"You are?" He sounded surprised.

She twirled her fingers into the mass of hair on his head. "With the exception of being twice abducted and followed around by Jamison, I've enjoyed our time together."

He squeezed her. "You have no idea how glad I am to hear you say that."

"You have no idea how glad I'll be when this is all over," she retorted. "That man won't leave me alone for anything."

"That's his job," Benjamin said, feathering kisses on her shoulder.

She scowled. "Apparently, he takes it very seriously. Normally servants can be bribed, but not him."

Benjamin's chest rumbled with laughter. "I shall have to give the man a bonus," he murmured in between kisses. He brought his fingers up and hooked his thumb under the strap of her lacy nightrail. Pulling it down off her shoulder, he followed its path with kisses.

She laughed. "There's no need to give him a bonus, he's already gotten one."

"Been keeping your coins, has he?" His hands came around her waist and repositioned her to sit on his lap with her back facing his chest.

"No," she said tartly as he lowered the other strap and placed feather light kisses on the top of her back. "His bonus came in the form of him sneaking peeks at me in the bath."

His head shot up and his body tensed. "What? Even I don't get to do that."

She shrugged. "As I said, he won't leave me alone for anything." She leaned back and wiggled her shoulders in an attempt to catch his attention so he'd kiss her again. "What are you doing?" she asked, when she felt his hands close around her waist and he was none too gently trying to push her from his lap.

"Firing Jamison," he said tersely, setting her on the ground. "You wanted him gone. He's gone. He has no business watching you bathe. That was not in the orders I gave him."

"Benjamin, calm down," she said, placing her hands on his chest. "He doesn't watch me bathe."

"You just said—"

"What I said is he peeks," she corrected. "There's a difference, albeit very little, but still a difference."

Benjamin crossed his arms. "What, pray tell, is the difference?"

She pulled the straps of her nightrail back onto her shoulders since obviously he wasn't interested in her anymore. Well, he was, just not in kissing her.

"I'm waiting," he prompted.

"Right," she clipped nervously. "Watching is standing there and well, watching. Peeking is more of not looking directly at, but not keeping your eyes away at all times. Kind of like they stray."

"I don't really see a difference," he said irritably. "His eyes have no business watching or straying to your naked form. That image is for my personal enjoyment only; no one else's."

"Do be serious," she said, shaking her head. "You could be enjoying me right now, but instead you'd rather go make sure nobody else peeks at what's yours."

He stared at her. "I will enjoy you," he promised, sweeping her from head to toe with his intent gaze. "I plan to enjoy every delicious inch of you, as soon as I fire that peeping footman."

"It's not his fault, you know," she said testily. Why did he have to let his possessiveness ruin the mood?

He scoffed. "I highly doubt you invited him to peek at you in the tub."

"No," she agreed. "But you're the one who ordered him to stick to me like glue. He was just doing what you told him to."

He closed his eyes. "Still that's no reason for him to let his eyes stray, as you call it."

"You told him not to leave the room. What did you expect him to do? It's not like he stands over me and offers to wash my back," she retorted. She shook her head. Why was she bothering to defend the man? She wanted him gone. This was her chance. She should just let Benjamin assume what he wanted. But no, she was too soft hearted to risk Benjamin sacking the man without a reference for doing the job he'd been ordered to do.

"He better not be," Benjamin said harshly. "If anyone is to be washing your back, it'll be me."

"Come on," she whispered saucily, pulling at his wrist.

Slowly he allowed her to lead him toward the bed. "Madison," he said huskily.

She threw him a sultry smile over her shoulder. She felt just as unsure as he seemed to be acting. But somewhere—perhaps her heart?—she knew this was what she wanted. She was tired of being angry with him; tired of fighting with him. She'd realized in the past week he'd only been trying to protect her, and even if she disagreed with his methods, the fact was he cared enough for her to risk her temper in order to keep her safe, and for some reason she couldn't name, it endeared him to her in a way she could no longer fight. It was as if he'd broken down the wall she'd built to keep him out and now she was ready to share more than just a last name and title with him. She wanted to share her bed, her body.

"Are you sure you want this?" he whispered.

She nodded slowly. "I'm sure."

"You don't look very sure," he countered, lightly encircling her wrist with his fingers to keep her from crawling on the bed.

"I am," she insisted.

"Madison," he whispered, cupping her chin. "If you're not ready,

I'll wait."

"It's not that," she said dismissively.

"Then what is it?" he asked, gently rubbing her cheekbone with his thumb. "You can tell me anything."

"Just nervous, that's all."

He swallowed. "Because it hurt before?"

She broke eye contact and nodded. "Yes. I mean, I knew it would the first time. But I didn't know it would every time."

"It shouldn't." He turned her face up to look into his eyes. "I told you that before and I meant it. It doesn't have to hurt. If it does, it's because—"

"The man is a selfish ass," she cut in. "I know, you told me before."

"That's because it's true and it's worthy of repeating. Madison," he said with an audible swallow. "When a woman is interested and is given the proper care and attention, she can enjoy the activity as much, if not more, than a man. I promise it can happen."

"All right," she whispered with a hint of disbelief in her voice.

"Let me show you," he murmured before dropping his lips to hers and stealing her breath away with his kiss.

Chapter 27

B enjamin thought he was about to die from some sort of coronary malfunction. His heart beat out of control with the love and excitement he'd held bottled up for more than six years. He had no idea how he was going to keep his promise of ensuring her pleasure before his when his body was about to explode with it already. But he had to. He had to slow down and make this good for her. He only had one chance at this and if he bungled it, she'd never want to join him in bed again.

His lips moved slowly and surely on top of hers and his fingers moved to the back of her head to massage her scalp. "Madison," he murmured, deepening their kiss. He slid his tongue along her lips and she gasped at the intrusion when he slipped inside to sweep the inside of her cheek.

"Benjamin," she sighed, twisting her fingers tightly in the back of his hair.

His hands left her silky curls and slid to her shoulders, caressing every inch of skin on the way. His lips left hers and kissed a path from her mouth to the hollow of her neck while his fingers inched the sleeves of her nightrail to the tips of her shoulders. He bent his head lower and using an open mouth, kissed a path down the middle of her chest as he lowered her nightrail at the same time.

Her body trembled and he heard her sigh when he kissed her along the valley between her breasts. His hands let go of her nightrail, letting it drop to the floor to form a forgotten pile of silk and lace. He dropped to his knees and brought his hands to rest on her bare waist where he stroked her hipbones with his thumbs as his mouth continued its descent toward her waist.

Stopping just above her waist, he pulled back. "Let me light the candle. I want to see you," he whispered.

She stiffened. "No." Her tone was strained and held a slight edge.

"Please," he rasped, tenderly stroking the sides of her abdomen. She put her hands on top of his and tried to push them off.

"It's all right," he said, tightening his grasp. He stood back up. "It's all right," he repeated, circling his arms around her and pulling her close. "Next time," he murmured against her ear before kissing the sensitive hollow behind it.

His hands moved to her ribs and traveled to the flare of her hips, giving them a squeeze. "Put your arms around me."

Her arms threaded through his and her hands rested on his shoulders where they kneaded his muscles. He walked her backwards to the bed and lowered her onto the mattress. Uncertainly, her hands left his shoulders and slipped down his back. Even through his shirt, her fingers heated his skin. He pulled her hands off and yanked his shirt off. "Touch me," he rasped, putting her hands back where they'd been.

Her fingers danced up and down his back in a light, unsure caress. "You can touch me, sweetheart. I want you to," he whispered against her neck in between kisses. He brought one of his hands up to shape her breast and desire shot through his body when her pliant flesh swelled beneath his touch.

Her hands pressed harder into his back and he groaned with pleasure. "Like this?" she asked, bewildered.

"Yes," he choked. "You can touch me however you wish. I'm yours." He abruptly stood up and removed his trousers. "There," he whispered, crawling back into bed with her and putting her hands back on his hips. "Now I'm dressed the same as you."

Benjamin settled his legs between hers and leaned to the side to support his upper body on one of his forearms. He moved his free hand to her breast where he shaped her until her nipple hardened against his palm. Taking the sensitive tip of her other breast into his mouth, he circled her nipple with his tongue, causing her to groan and arch her back in pleasure.

Her body quivered and trembled as he slid his hand from the side of her breast to her hip. He gave the tip of her breast a gentle nip then soothed it before releasing it and moving his mouth to the other to lavish it with the same attention. Her body arched again in response to his mouth's exploration of her supple breast.

Her hands tightened their hold on his back when he flicked his tongue on her budded nipple. "Ben," she gasped. "Yes."

His mouth left her breast and kissed down her body. Answering her whimper of protest at leaving her breast, he dropped lower and brought both hands up to cup and massage her breasts while his lips placed warm kisses at the points of her hips. Still caressing her breasts with his hands, he moved his mouth to nuzzle her at the dip of her hip and thigh.

"Ben," she sighed again, her body writhing in reaction to him.

"Madison," he murmured against her thigh, inhaling her scent. "Sweet Madison." He released one of her breasts and brought his hand down to massage her silky flesh.

Her hips bucked in response to his teasing fingers as he circled her sensitive flesh, adding more pressure with each stroke. "Ben," she gasped, digging her fingers into the skin on his back. "Ben," she shrieked louder, her nails biting into his back.

Knowing what she needed, he slipped lower and slid a finger inside her, reveling in how she moaned in response. Her head lolled back and she bit her lip as he continued his steady back and forth rhythm. He kissed his way back up to her neck, murmuring her name as he went.

"Yes," she gasped when he added another finger. "Ben, yes." Suddenly her body tensed and tightened around his fingers.

He continued his steady movements until he felt the last waves of her completion. Then he removed his hand and moved his hips to settle on top of hers, positioning the tip of his erection just outside her ready body. He took a deep, calming breath.

"Ben," she whispered.

"Yes, sweetheart?" he asked, his voice hoarse and full of emotion.

She brought her arms up around his neck. "I'm ready."

He smiled. That was all he needed to know. With one swift motion, he pushed forward, sheathing himself completely inside her. "Sorry," he murmured when she tensed beneath him. "I should have done that a little slower. Try to relax so your body can adjust to mine."

She brought her hands to his chest and fanned her fingers out over his muscles. "It didn't hurt," she whispered.

"What?" he asked, confused.

She swallowed. "The reason I tensed is because I thought it would hurt. But it didn't."

"Good," he croaked. "I was worried I'd hurt you."

She shifted beneath him. "You didn't."

"Are you sure," he asked, wishing she'd be still before he embarrassed himself.

She didn't answer.

"Madison," he prompted a bit more seriously.

"I…uh…I—" She broke off.

He started to withdraw.

"No," she said, digging her nails into his back. "Don't go."

He shook his head. "But I hu—"

"No you didn't. I rather liked it, all right."

He stopped and looked down at her. He couldn't see her very well because there was barely any moonlight illuminating the area of the room they were in. "Are you lying?"

"No," she said, shaking her head so fiercely he felt the pillow moving.

He pushed back in. "You had better not be lying," he muttered as he slid in to the hilt. Brushing a kiss on her lips and murmuring her name, he started moving in and out, trying to find the perfect rhythm.

Her hands moved to his sinewy shoulders and she squeezed them hard. "Ben," she gasped, her back arching, pressing her breasts to his chest.

"Madison," he replied, his voice thick with emotion. He brought his hand between them to caress her breast and rolled her nipple between his fingers.

"Yes, Ben," she encouraged, her hips matching his movements. "More, Ben."

He moved his hips faster. "Madison," he grunted. "You've got to—"

His mouth ran dry and his words died on his tongue as her inner muscles clenched around him, bringing him to grunt out her name again and join her in a shattering climax.

His body collapsed on top of hers and he felt powerless to roll off. He kissed her neck and murmured a soft, inaudible "I love you" against her skin before rolling to the side.

She didn't respond. He hadn't expected her to. He'd purposely said it where she'd never hear. He didn't want her to say it back only because he'd said it. He wanted her to say it when she was ready.

"You didn't have to roll off," she murmured, snuggling beside him a moment later.

"Yes, I did," he corrected, pulling the sheet up to cover their naked bodies. "You could have suffocated under me."

"That wouldn't have been so bad," she said, wrapping her arm around his midsection.

"For you perhaps," he retorted. "You would have died a very satisfied woman. I, on the other hand, would have had to live the rest of my life in misery knowing I killed the best thing that ever happened to me—literally."

"Always thinking of yourself, aren't you?" she teased.

"Except when I'm thinking of you."

She laughed. "I think we're a little past the flattery stage in our relationship."

"All right," he said, stroking her shoulders with his knuckles. "Honestly, did you enjoy that?"

"What do you think?" she asked. "Can a woman fake that?"

"Yes," he said honestly. "But I don't think you did."

"I didn't," she admitted shyly. "I was afraid I wouldn't like it very much though."

He gave her a squeeze. "I know."

"I thought you'd hurt me for sure with your large John Thomas," she blurted.

A harsh bark of laughter passed his lips. "I thought you said we were past the stage of flattery."

"We are," she agreed, propping her head up on her elbow to put her face near his as she idly ran her fingers over his chest. "I'm being truthful. I saw it last week when I took care of you while you were unconscious. And let me say a heartfelt thank you for keeping those too tight drawers on. I would have run for my life if you hadn't. When I saw it I nearly shuddered just think—"

He cut her off with a quick kiss that was interrupted with a spurt of laughter. "That's enough," he choked, trying to hold back his laughter. "I'm flattered, I really am. But please do not continue in this vein. I fear I will laugh myself silly if you do."

She shrugged and moved her head back to rest on his chest. "All right, but I was just being honest."

He shook his head. He didn't mind her crude comments. He rather liked them actually. He always had. No other woman would ever compliment a man in such a naïve and crass way at the same time. It was one of the things about her that held his attention in America. And it was one of the things he still loved about her now. As bizarre as it was, most men would have been appalled by her scandalous slips, but not him. No, he could honestly say he loved her more because of her crass comments and crude remarks.

He looked at her closed eyes and gave his sleeping wife a quick kiss on the crown of her head, and in the dead quiet of the night, once again whispered, "I love you."

Chapter 28

Madison awoke naked in her husband's arms and didn't know whether to snuggle closer or scramble out of bed and dress as quickly as she could. Not that she regretted having intimacies with him, of course. She was more embarrassed her mouth had gotten away from her afterward. She'd been so drunk in the afterglow that she'd said all sorts of embarrassing things that were better left in her head.

It was no big surprise Benjamin was so much better endowed than Robbie. But she needn't have told him so. Mortification flooded her. Normally, she said whatever popped into her head without a second thought. But to say such a thing to one's husband directly following the consummation of their marriage was not appropriate. And if she of all people knew that, it must be bad indeed.

She peeked up at him. Did he think less of her for her comment? Most people usually laughed or shook their heads in disgust when she said something bawdy. For the most part though, Benjamin usually encouraged her by saying something scandalous in return. But he hadn't last night. He'd just laughed. She smiled. Perhaps he wasn't quite as offended as she thought he might be.

She moved her head to the pillow to look at the profile of his face better. He was a very handsome man. She'd always thought so. They'd been introduced by Lady Olivia shortly after she'd come to London. At the time, she had no romantic notions and as kindly as possible dismissed him out of hand without more than a cursory greeting. She'd been too busy mourning the past to care about the future, or even the present.

Lying next to him this way, she almost wished she'd given him more notice before. He was actually turning out to be a good husband. Even if he had a scandalous past, his actions toward her, though not always to her liking, had all revolved around her wellbeing. She ran her hand through his hair. Looking at him thus, he looked familiar, kind of like...

She shook her head. She needed to clear *that* thought immediately. Ever since coming here, she'd been on edge with worry about running into Leo. Of course she knew he wouldn't be in Benjamin's direct employ, so she was safe around the estate. But feared she might run into him if she went into the village.

Benjamin said she'd met him again, but she didn't believe that. The only men she'd met were titled and wealthy. Leo was neither. Not that he'd specifically told her he was a chimney sweep or anything. He didn't have to. His clothes were common. His bearded face was common. Even his manners were common. No noble lord or wealthy merchant would go to America and dress like a peasant. No, Leo was a commoner and with any luck they'd never cross paths again, which was all right with her.

At one time, she might have wished for one more meeting with him to confirm if his intentions were honorable, as Brooke claimed, or dishonorable, as Robbie had. Robbie's argument seemed stronger at the time. No man—gentleman or cad—would tell the sister of the young lady he was trying to seduce anything that might jeopardize his plans. But, on the other hand, Brooke had always been a fairly good judge of character and Robbie was, well, Robbie.

She shook her head once more. It really didn't matter. She didn't plan to see the man, and if she did, she wouldn't ask. She didn't care to know anymore. She'd moved on. And to be quite honest, she was glad she had. Benjamin was a good husband and she knew if she were ever to be reckless enough to give her heart away again, she could trust him with it. He wouldn't do her wrong.

"You look rather serious," Benjamin said, pulling her out of her thoughts.

"Just woolgathering," she said with a stilted smile.

He rolled onto his side. "No regrets, I hope."

"No," she said, shaking her head. "No regrets."

He smiled. "Care to tell me what you were thinking about?"

"Just that you look familiar," she said with a shrug.

His eyes sharpened their gaze. "Yes?"

She waved her hand dismissively. "Yes," she said laughingly. "But it's because you're my husband. I've seen you every single day for several weeks now. If you didn't look familiar, we'd have a problem."

"Yes, we would," he added quietly. "And what does the duchess plan to do today?"

She laid her head on his chest and kissed his sternum. "The usual, I suppose," she said, letting her fingers slide down his abdomen. "Eat. Sew. Scowl at Jamison. Walk around the house in an attempt to lose Jamison. Eat again. Read a book. Try to bribe Jamison. Stare at an empty wall. Eat dinner with you. Put on a naughty show for Jamison while I bathe. Put on my nightrail. Have a stare down with Jamison until you arrive."

He chuckled. "It sounds like you have a busy day planned," he acknowledged. "Perhaps I can arrange a little less Jamison and a little more Benjamin. Would that be acceptable?"

She nodded. "I'd like that."

"I'd prefer to keep you in bed all day," he said, running his fingers through her hair. "However, I have an errand I'm probably already late for. How about if you put in your quality time with Jamison this morning and we'll spend the afternoon together?"

"I like the sound of that."

"Me, too," He said as he dropped a kiss on her forehead. "I'll talk to Jamison before I leave. Perhaps while you're bathing and dressing, he can stand outside the door as long as Lottie is in the room with you and you don't take too long."

"I can accept that."

"Good. But you're not getting rid of me that easily. I'll not be leaving the room when you dress or bathe," he said with a wolfish grin.

"I wouldn't want you to," she said, her hand moving dangerously close to his waist.

He covered her hand with his and groaned. "I want to. Trust me, I do. But I really must go," he said raggedly. "This afternoon, I promise."

She nodded and watched him as he got up and dressed. His body looked like it had been carved from marble with rounded muscles and chiseled edges. He was magnificent, and all hers. He'd told her so last night and she quite believed him. She'd never be able to share him with another. Never.

After he'd given her a goodbye kiss and departed, she dressed quickly and had barely gotten the door open when she nearly collided with Jamison.

"Hullo, shadow," she said playfully. She may not have liked the man at first, and still didn't like him following her about, however, now that Benjamin had promised to talk to him about boundaries, she supposed it wouldn't hurt to be a bit nicer to him. He was just doing the job he'd been given. He couldn't help if said job involved following her like a stray dog.

"Yer Grace," he replied.

"Have you seen His Grace this morning?" she asked, praying he'd say yes.

Jamison nodded. "Yes," he said, the tips of his ears turning a pale shade of pink. "I is ta keep me peepers ta meself."

"Good," she said pertly. "See that you do."

"Aye, Yer Grace," he said, looking perfectly chastised.

Madison smiled and waved her hand around the sitting room. "Please, make yourself comfortable. I want to write a letter or two then I'll be ready to spend the morning with you."

She went to the cherry secretary that sat by the window. The writing surface was on hinges and under the board was a little compartment that held a stack of vellum an inch thick, half a dozen quills and four pots of ink that were black, green, blue and red. She reached under the stack of blank paper and pulled out the corner of the page on the bottom. It was the note she'd written her first day here. She pulled the offending paper out and laid it on the desk, letting her eyes do a quick scan.

Dear Andrew,
Please come quick. I've been abducted! Again! The first time, he took me to some remote coastal place that I was never able to learn the name of. We were more than fifty miles from the nearest town! Or so he claimed. For all I know, we could have been on the outskirts of London.
Oh, and while we were there, Robbie shot Benjamin! It was a dreadful mess and I had to sew him up. Then, his arm got infected and I had to send Billings, his coachman, to fetch a doctor. And then, just as soon as the doctor treated him, a bullet flew through the window, barely missing our heads and whizzed straight into a piece of furniture. Of course, that only led to Benjamin's predatory behavior of locking me in a dark closet and going in search of Robbie with the biggest gun I've ever seen.
And if all that is not bad enough, he came back in, yanked open the closet, slung me over his shoulder like a sack of potatoes and hauled me barefoot from the house all the way to Glenbrook. Once here, he continued his madman methods and hired Goliath to follow me around. The man follows me <u>*everywhere.*</u>
I don't know how much more I can bear. Please come quick before he locks me in his dungeon!
Yours,
Madison

She shook her head. She almost couldn't believe she'd actually written it. But she did remember writing it. It was only a few short days ago. She'd been so upset by the events of the day what with Jamison becoming her watchdog and Benjamin's easy dismissal of her arguments, she'd sat and penned the exaggerated note, knowing she'd never send it. But even knowing that, she'd felt better after she'd written it. Sometimes it just felt good to vent, even if the truth was embellished a bit.

A noise from across the room caught her attention and she whipped her head around to see Jamison talking to someone at the door.

"Beggin' yer pardon, Yer Grace," Jamison called with an uneasy look. "Yer ta be me shadow tis mornin'. Tere's a pr'lem tat I need ta hep wit."

"All right," she said, opening the top of her secretary and haphazardly shoving the missive inside. She'd prefer to stay in her room and use Jamison's errand as an excuse to be alone, but knew Benjamin would not be happy if Jamison left her alone or if something bad happened at the estate because she wouldn't cooperate with Jamison so that he could take care of whatever the problem was.

Madison walked down the stairs and out toward the stables with Jamison. Outside the stables, they could hear some of the grooms yelling and fighting. Madison frowned. Why was Jamison being called to deal with the squabbles of the grooms? He was the head footman. Shouldn't it be the job of the head groom to deal with this?

Inside the stables, she saw Billings standing off by the far wall. He was too old to be involved even if he wanted to be, she thought as she murmured to Jamison she was going to go stand by Billings while he settled the fight.

"What's going on?" she asked Billings as she approached.

The old man shrugged. "They was fightin' 'fore I gots here. I sent fer Jamison cuz I canna fine Leer." He ran a hand through his hair and watched the fight with wide eyes.

Madison hadn't taken her eyes off the fight, either. Even with Jamison present and trying to break up the fight, the boys were being just as aggressive, if not more so.

"Pr'aps we oughtta step out," Billings suggested when a stool came flying in their direction.

Madison nodded. She didn't want to walk up to Jamison to tell him she was leaving. He appeared a smart man. He'd know she went outside where it was safer. "All right," she said sweetly and followed him out.

~*~*~*~

Benjamin rode his mount at breakneck speed to the village where he was meeting several members of his staff, the village constable and a Bow Street Runner. He was ready to be done with Robbie and his schemes and move on with his life with Madison.

Before leaving the inn he and Madison had stayed in on the way to Glenbrook, he'd sent a message to London requesting Finch, the Runner he liked to use, to meet him at Glenbrook. Finch arrived one day after Benjamin and immediately started to do a discreet investigation of Benjamin's staff.

Unfortunately, he'd been unsuccessful in determining anything. Of course, his staff knew nothing. To start with, only a handful of them had gone with him to Rockhurst and Plymouth. Of those who'd gone with him, none of them had been in any condition to have gone trolling around either property in order to have happened upon anything of interest.

Benjamin ran a hand through his hair. "I guess we'll just have to wait for him to strike again," he mumbled.

"Aye," Leer, the head groom, said. "I've asked me boys to let me know if they see anyone they shouldn't be seein'."

"Good," Benjamin said approvingly. He'd asked that the grooms be on alert, but not informed. He wanted nothing to tip off Robbie or his mysterious accomplice.

Finch put his tankard down. "Do you still suspect an accomplice?"

Benjamin nodded. "It makes sense, too. The accomplice has to be the intelligence behind everything. Though not *too* intelligent if he leaves his own footprints," he added ruefully. "But yes, there has to be another man involved. Not only is Swift not smart enough to think of a way to hide his tracks on his own, there's no way he'd be able to gather the necessary information by himself either."

"What do you mean?" Hunter, his estate manager, asked with a curious look.

Benjamin brushed the imaginary crumbs off the table before looking back up at Hunter. "What I mean is, Swift cannot do everything himself. He couldn't have camped in the woods outside Rockhurst just waiting to see my carriage roll by—even at midnight. Nor, could he have had access to Townson's servants, or mine."

"What are you suggesting?" the constable asked, knitting his brows.

Benjamin's hand came up to rub his jaw. "I'm not exactly sure. But the more I think on it, the more convinced I am that he has to have had an inside source."

"An inside source?" Leer asked.

Benjamin nodded. "Madison left her maid in London. I brought a coachman, two footmen and one groom with us to Rockhurst and Plymouth. As much as I hate to think ill of my own staff, I wonder if one of them might be working for him."

"Any motives?" Finch asked with a cool, disinterested look on his face.

"No," Benjamin said, shaking his head. "That's why I have such a hard time believing it myself. But it's the only thing that makes sense."

"How so?" the constable asked before throwing back the rest of his tankard.

"That's the only way Swift would know to go to Plymouth. Finding out we went to Rockhurst couldn't have been too difficult. All he'd have had to do was bribe one of my London servants, or even Townson's. But for him to know about Plymouth," he shook his head, "no one, save the few of my servants who went with me, even knows I own an estate close to there."

"All right," Finch said thoughtfully. "What do you know about these four servants besides the basic facts? Families? Debts? Grudges?"

"Williams is the groom. He's only seventeen or so, far too young to have a family of his own. He's been in my employ since he was fourteen. I've never heard a complaint about him. Have you?" he asked, looking directly to Leer.

Leer shook his head. "Nay. E's a good boy. Does wot I says."

"Stone and Massey are the only footmen I brought along. Stone's getting on in years. I offered him a pension last year around Christmas. He refused and claimed he'd die in my employ. Therefore, if money is what Swift is offering, I doubt Stone sees that as much motivation. Massey, on the other hand, has a need for money. He's younger, early twenties perhaps, and he sends money back to his family. But he's got a terrible limp that makes him walk at a snail's pace and can hardly speak more than two words without stuttering."

Finch frowned and nodded, "And the coachman?"

"He's ancient," Benjamin said dismissively, twisting his lips. "He was my grandfather's coachman if that tells you anything. With the exception of one incident, I've never had any type of problem from him."

"What was the incident?" Finch asked curiously.

Benjamin shrugged. "Last year, he used my carriage to help my sister-in-law flee her new and highly infuriated husband, leaving me stranded with said husband. But I don't think money was the motive in that circumstance. When he finally remembered to come back for me, I asked him for the money he'd gotten from her and he pulled out all his pockets, revealing not as much as a halfpenny rested in his coffers."

"Williams or Massey seem the most likely suspects, then," Hunter mused, mindlessly spinning his tankard around.

The constable put his hat back on his head. "Perhaps we should go have a talk with the boys."

"What are you up to?" Benjamin asked, eyes narrowing. Not that he had anything against the man, but sometimes Benjamin got the impression the constable liked to rule his jurisdiction with an iron fist and would go to any lengths to make sure everyone knew his power.

"Nothing," he said with a shrug. "We'll just see what they have to say."

Benjamin scowled. Perhaps it would have been better to get the constable involved *after* the incident.

After paying their tab, the five men hopped on their mounts and rode in silence back to Glenbrook.

"Massey's an inside footman," Benjamin said. "After we hand our mounts to the groom, I'll go get him."

"Aight," the constable agreed with an easy smile.

Approaching the stables, a racket caught the notice of the group. "Wot the devil is goin' on in there?" Leer asked, jumping from his mount.

The other four looked at each other in curious silence before jumping off their own mounts and running into the stables.

Unblinkingly, Benjamin watched as every groom he employed was engaged in a fight. His eyes roamed over the image of punching and hitting until they landed on Jamison who was right in the middle of the melee. *Jamison!* What was he doing here? He tore his eyes away from the fight and scanned the walls looking for Madison. He didn't see her and his heart started to race. Where was she? He scanned the walls again; dread, unease, and undeniable fear settled in his chest when he still couldn't locate her.

Leaving it to the others to stop the fight, he ran from the stables and circled the exterior looking for Madison. Surely she wouldn't have strayed far. He understood she probably hadn't wished to stay in the stable with the fight, but knew her well enough to know she wouldn't have wandered off.

He caught sight of Billings milling around outside the dairy barn, probably not wanting to get involved in a juvenile fight from which he'd never stand a chance at emerging alive. "Have you seen Her Grace?" he asked casually. No need to let on to the private terror coursing through him.

"Nay," Billings said, shaking his gray head.

"All right."

Benjamin turned to leave when suddenly the sound of a bullet rent the air followed a split-second later by a high-pitched, ear-piercing, heart-stopping, bloodcurdling scream.

Chapter 29

Madison shook out her green muslin skirt as soon as she stepped out of the stable. With all the fighting, hay had been flying everywhere and straw had come to settle all over her dress.

"Glad to be away from that," she said with a sigh.

"Aye," Billings agreed. He sagged against the side of the stable. "Ye ever seen a dairy?"

Madison followed his gaze to the building a hundred yards away. "Is that the dairy?"

"Aye," he said, shaking his head. "Wanna see it?"

"No," Madison said truthfully. "I shouldn't have left the stable. I don't think I should go into the dairy."

"Come," Billings encouraged, grabbing her arm.

"No, thank you," Madison said politely, trying to pull her arm free. "Let go, please. You're hurting me."

"Ten be a good gel an' come 'long," he said with an unusual smile.

Madison tried to pull her arm free, but his grip only tightened. "Help!" she screamed.

He laughed. "'E won't hear ye in tere." He started pulling her in the direction of the dairy and she dug her heels into the ground to offer as much resistance as she could. For an old man, he was awfully strong.

He wrenched the door open to the dairy and flung her inside before slamming the door shut and locking her inside.

She looked around the dimly lit dairy. There were no cows in their stalls. Buckets and stools lined the aisle between stalls. The stench was enough to make one struggle to keep their stomach contents down. Why had he tossed her in there?

"Hello, Madison," said a familiar voice behind her that told her why she'd been locked in there.

Turning around, she saw the owner of that voice. He was halfway down the aisle that ran through the middle of the dairy, holding a lantern and sitting on a stool with his back to the door of one of the stalls and his feet resting on the stool across the aisle, his legs blocking the walkway. "Mr. Swift, I have nothing to say to you," she said stiffly, clutching her suddenly cold hands together in front of her. "I'm sorry, but you've come to your senses too late. However, I've no regrets."

"Sure you do," he said silkily. "Remember how good it was between us? It can be that way again."

"No, it cannot," she replied, taking a step backwards.

He leaned forward and grabbed her wrist in a hard, almost bone-crushing grip. "And why not?" he questioned with a hint of disbelief.

She tried to pull her hand free. "I'm married to Benjamin now."

He scoffed. "Get it annulled. Or better yet, don't. Then he can claim any children we might have. Just think, I'll get to be the father of the next duke," he said excitedly as if it was some great boon that she'd cuckold her husband with him and his bastard would inherit Benjamin's title.

Bile rose in her throat. "Never," she said through clenched teeth. "You're despicable to even think such a thing."

He shrugged lazily. "Do you really think you two share some great love?" he asked with a sneer.

"That's none of your concern," she snapped, trying to back away from him.

He stood and grabbed her by the shoulders, his fingers holding her so tightly she knew she was bruising. "Do you know his past, then?" he asked with an intent stare.

"I know all I need to know, thank you."

Robbie scoffed and his fingers became even tighter. "Does he know yours, I wonder," he mused with a sickening smile.

Much to his dismay, she'd never been very ladylike and felt not a hint of shame as she cleared her throat and spat in his face.

As she predicted, his right hand released her shoulder and he wiped his face. "That's disgusting, Madison," he criticized. "I see even as duchess you still act like a fish wife."

Madison didn't care about his criticism of her. She took advantage of the situation by wrenching her body from his hold and running toward the end of the aisle as fast as she could. She knew Billings had locked her inside. But perhaps there was a window she could climb out.

She quickly realized there were no windows through which to escape, they'd all been boarded up. Instead, she found a dark corner that was blocked off by a trough in one of the far stalls. She squatted down in the corner and waited.

She could hear Robbie's footsteps coming closer to her. He'd

189

probably taken the time to properly clean himself up with a handkerchief before bothering to pick up his lantern and start his search for her, she thought sourly. The man had always been vain; immature, but vain.

"I know you're still here," he called from one stall away from the one where she was hiding.

Madison's foot slipped a bit and her backside hit the ground. She put her hands down to help push herself off the ground and stilled when her hand landed on something round and hard the size of an egg. Without thought, she picked it up and put it in her lap as she kicked off her slipper and peeled down her stocking. She'd hoped it wouldn't come to this. But apparently it had; and she needed to be ready in case she had to knock some sense into him—literally.

Robbie's feet shuffled down the hall and Madison's heart picked up its pace when she heard his hand hit the door of the stall she occupied. Aside from the slivers of sunlight sneaking in through the space between the wooden planks of the exterior walls, his lantern was the only source of light. She hoped it was dark enough in the room she was in that he'd just do a quick glance and move on.

The door creaked on its rusty hinges and Robbie came into the room. She dared not make any movements as she held her breath and waited for him to move on.

"I know you're in here, Madison," Robbie said tonelessly. "Just come out and we'll talk. Don't make me move that trough and pull you out."

Madison's mouth went dry and her breath caught in her throat. Was he bluffing? Or had he seen her? Very carefully, she clenched the hand that held the hard object and her stocking and moved them behind her back before standing up. "All right, Robbie. What do you want?"

"You," he said with a slow smile.

She shook her head. "As I already explained, that is not an option."

Robbie's face went red and he shook his head. "That's not the right answer," he said angrily, reaching into the back of his trousers. "I will have you, or no one else will."

Madison tried to keep panic from settling in her chest as he brought a pistol from his waistband and leveled it at her. "Now, Robbie," she said calmly, using her sweaty palms to work her stocking just right. "There's no need to be rash. You've a lot going for you in America. There's no need to ruin your life because of a temporary sense of disappointment."

He laughed harshly and the gun tip waved wildly. "It's not so grand, I assure you," he said roughly.

"And how is harming me going to change anything?"

"It's not," he said with a shrug. "But if I can't enjoy you, no one else will be able to, either." He cocked his gun and pointed it in her direction. "Anything you want me to tell your widower?"

"No. There's nothing to say. He'll not be made a widower today," she said firmly, her fingers still working her stocking behind her back.

She'd have only one shot at this and didn't want to miss due to her carelessness.

"What's behind your back?" Robbie barked. "Show me your hands."

Madison's hands stayed safely behind her back as she grabbed the two ends of her stocking and got ready to whip it forward and fling the rock at him.

Robbie's free hand reached out to grab her and Madison jumped back. "Get away or I'll hit you," she yelled.

"With what?" he taunted. "Are you going to throw a pebble at me?"

"As a matter-of-fact, I am," she said proudly, bringing her newly fashioned weapon out from behind her back. She knew she looked foolish holding a rock-like object wrapped in a stocking, but right now she did not have time to be overly worried about looking like a fool.

He laughed. "You'll never hit me with that. Watching Brooke doesn't make you an expert," he explained rather rudely.

Madison brought her makeshift weapon up above her head and gave it a hard spin. "And who do you think taught her?"

His eyes went wide and he jumped back in shock, accidentally squeezing the cocked trigger, making the gun fire. Simultaneously, Madison let go of one end of her stocking and the egg-shaped object flew out and hit the hand Robbie was using to hold his gun, eliciting the most excruciatingly painful scream she'd ever been subjected to hear as her victim lost his grip on his gun and dropped to the floor to wallow in pain.

"Madison! Madison!" a new voice boomed a second later as its owner ran through the door of the dairy, leading with his shoulder and taking the door, hinges and all, with him as he barged through.

"I'm all right," she said with a weary smile when she saw her frantic husband rush to her side. "It was this ninny you heard scream," she explained, pointing to Robbie who was rolling around on the ground, writhing in pain.

"I'm not a ninny," Robbie said with a sneer.

Madison snorted. "Yes, you are. You had a gun and I had a rock— or at least I hope it was a rock, it could have been a petrified piece of a cow pat for all I know." She wiped her hand on her skirt and grimaced. "You missed me by a good ten feet," she pointed to the bullet hole in the stall wall that was at ankle level and in the opposite direction of where she was standing, "and I hit exactly where I was aiming." She flashed her husband a bright smile, which he didn't return.

"We'll talk later about why you're not with Jamison," Benjamin said sternly to Madison before turning to Robbie. He placed his booted foot on the man's chest. "You have a lot to answer for."

Robbie made a choking sound in his chest and tried to use his uninjured hand to bat at Benjamin's foot.

Benjamin applied more pressure to Robbie's chest and a cracking noise broke the silence. When more moans and whimpers resulted, Benjamin swore and removed his foot from Robbie's chest. "Get up," he barked.

Robbie rolled around on the ground, making no move to get up.

Benjamin grunted with irritation, then reached down with one hand and yanked Robbie to a standing position before slamming him into the wall and holding him there with his hand squeezing Robbie's neck so tightly his mouth hung open and he made strangled choking sounds.

"Benjamin, stop," Madison said, placing her hand on Benjamin's flexed forearm. "He's not worth it."

Benjamin's cold eyes snapped to hers. "I know that," he spat. "I don't plan to kill him." He brought his eyes back to Robbie. "Not until I find out a few things first, that is," he amended.

Robbie's bloodshot eyes widened, in fear.

"Benjamin, the gallows," Madison whispered.

"I'll not be going to the gallows," Benjamin assured her, as he tightened his grip. "As for him, he's a dead man either way. If I don't kill him, he *will* go to the gallows for his attempted murder of both a duke and a duchess."

Robbie made a sound of severe distress and soiled himself.

"Not to worry," Benjamin said with a mock reassuring smile. "You'll not be alone. Your newfound friend will be dangling right along with you."

Madison's eyes went wide. *Billings.* Benjamin had to be talking about Billings since he was the one who locked her in the dairy. How had he known?

Robbie made another choking noise and Benjamin relaxed his grip—slightly. "Now, are you going to tell me who's been helping you, or am I going to have to beat it out of you?" He made a fist and pulled it back where Robbie could see it.

Robbie swallowed convulsively and looked down the aisle to where the door of the dairy once stood. Benjamin and Madison followed his gaze and their eyes went as wide as Robbie's when they realized the whole far end of the dairy was on fire.

"What do we do, Benjamin?" Madison cried, panic evident in her voice.

Benjamin dropped Robbie and stepped back as the weaker man collapsed to his knees. "We've got to get out the other end," Benjamin said firmly, his eyes searching the rest of the structure for an opening of some sort by which they could leave. He looked down at Madison's feet. "Go put your other slipper on," he barked. "I'll be right back." He scooped down and snatched up Robbie's forgotten gun then ran down to the end of the hall.

Madison quickly put her abandoned slipper back on and watched as Benjamin ran back down the aisle with an axe. Benjamin carelessly grabbed Robbie by the arm, dragging his body as he ran to the other end of the dairy. Madison was only a step behind and almost crashed into Benjamin when he suddenly stopped.

"Back up," he commanded. He brought the axe above his shoulder and got ready to swing.

"Stop!" Madison screamed. She pointed through the slats. Someone stood outside with a large flaming torch running it down the middle of the wall where Benjamin was about to axe.

Benjamin jumped back just in time to not get scorched by the fresh flames that licked their way through the old, dead wood.

Madison stepped back and hit her hip on a stray board. "Ouch," she said automatically, rubbing her hip.

"Good thinking, my girl," Benjamin said with a thin smile. "I don't know what I'd do without you," he added, brushing a quick kiss across her cheek. He bent down and grabbed Robbie off the ground then slung him over his shoulder as if he were nothing but a bag of feathers. "Come."

Madison quickly followed behind Benjamin as he went into a little dark space then climbed up a hidden ladder. At the top was a lighted loft covered in scattered hay. "A window," Madison breathed, standing motionless as Benjamin dropped Robbie's body by the window.

"Right," Benjamin said, nodding. Using his elbow, he broke the pane of glass in the middle and knocked as much out around the edges as he could. "This'll have to do. I'm going to jump down first. Then when I tell you to, you'll jump to me. Understand?"

A lump of unease settled in her chest. She didn't want to jump out a window. It had to be more than fifteen feet from the bottom of that windowsill to the rocky ground. That could kill her. "Is there no other way?" she asked, panic making her voice waver.

"I'm sorry, sweetheart, but no. You'll have to jump. You'll be all right, I promise. I'll be right there," he assured her, throwing his leg over the window. Without waiting for another protest, he dropped to the ground.

Robbie started moaning, reminding her of his presence.

"What do I do with him?" Madison yelled to Benjamin.

"Leave him, Madison," Benjamin called back. "He'll die either way. We haven't much time and you're all I care about. Are you ready?"

She bit her lip. "I think so." She held onto the edge of the window and looked down at Benjamin. He was a tall, broad man, but just now, he seemed so far away. "I-I don't know if I can," she stammered.

"Yes, you can," he encouraged. "Just jump. I'll catch you. I promise."

"I don't know," she breathed, tears forming in her eyes as fear and panic took over. The flames were getting closer to her. She could feel their warmth heating the loft behind her and the fire was climbing the wall beneath the window.

"You have to," Benjamin insisted. "Now, Madison."

Madison lifted her shaking right foot and brought it up to the windowsill; just then, Robbie's hand closed around her ankle. "I think not," he spat, yanking her ankle and making her fall backwards to the loft floor with him.

"Let me go," she screamed, trying to hit and kick him anywhere she could as he held her body down with his brutal grasp.

"No," he said cruelly, kneeing her in her ribs as hard as he could before rolling over her to position himself closer to the window. "I'm going first." He slid his hand up the wall and grabbed onto the bottom of the window. Using whatever muscle he possessed, he quickly pulled himself up the wall until his face was able to rest on the bottom edge of the window. Bracing his feet on the floor, he pushed up a little further until the middle of his chest was level with the edge of the window. Placing both hands on the edge of the window, he gave a feminine shriek and propelled himself forward just enough so the top half of his body went out the window and his waist teetered on the edge of the windowsill. With a mighty grunt, he started wiggling his hips and trying to slither forward, causing gravity to come into play and pulling him headfirst, straight down through the fire to the ground.

After a brief three-second scream followed by a crunching noise, silence filled the air. No more screams. No swearing. No scuffling. Nothing.

"Madison," Benjamin screamed hoarsely, bringing her back to the hellish reality in which she was currently trapped.

"I'm here," Madison croaked weakly, pulling herself to stand up at the window. Her body was bruised from her tussle with Robbie, but she felt numb. The fire was closer now and the loft was so smoky she could barely see in front of her face. Robbie was undoubtedly dead. And now it was her turn to jump.

"Now jump, Madison," Benjamin yelled. His gaze was trained on hers and his arms were wide open. Just like the day in the stream.

"What if you don't catch me?"

"I will," he said confidently. "I will. Just trust me. Please."

She went to the window and carefully put a leg over.

"Good girl," he encouraged. "Rest your foot along that ridge and bring the other one over to join it."

She did.

"Good. Now count to three, then let go of the sides of the window and push off."

Her lips trembled and her skin burned as she felt the heat from the flames that surrounded her, threatening to engulf the loft at any moment. "I…I…"

"Just jump, Madison," Benjamin pleaded. "I'll catch you. I promise. You just have to trust me. Please, just this once trust me."

Madison closed her eyes, counted to two, removed her hands from the edges of the window, and was about to jump when another arm snaked around her midsection.

She shrieked and started fighting, heedless to what was going on around her. Turning her head ever so slightly, she saw it was a very sooty and out of sorts Billings who was holding her.

"Let me go," she yelled, choking on the smoke that burned her throat and caused her eyes to sting.

"Nay," he yelled back, dragging her back into the burning hayloft. Fire surrounded them and the sweat which had covered her face from the flames was now dripping off her chin at a surprising rate. "There isn't any time. I need to jump." She tried to yell, but her words came out barely more than a whisper

"Nay," he said harshly with a nasty cough, pulling her to the floor of the raging inferno. "Yer hu'ban' took sum'un from me. I is gwine take sum'un from him."

"What are you talking about?" she croaked hoarsely. Her vision blurred from the smoke as her throat worked convulsively trying to keep from choking. "He's been nothing but kind to you. He'll give you a pension and a cottage if you ask."

"I donna wanna dat. E kilt me broter wit fire. I canna kill him. But I can kill ye," Billings spat, tightening his grip where he held her waist and one shoulder.

"Your brother was the man-maid?" she rasped, still fighting the vice-like grip that kept her pinned to the floor of the now smoldering hayloft.

Billings' eyes turned hard as steel. "Aye. An' I was ta git part 'o de blunt. But nay. Dat hu'ban' 'o yers had to git invol'd."

"So, because your brother accidently died trying to rob His Grace, you want to kill me?" she rasped disbelievingly, struggling to free herself from his tight hold.

"Aye," he agreed with a terse nod, digging his fingers all the harder into her skin. "I ruther kilt him. But 'tis not ta be."

"But why?" she cried, kicking him so hard in the shin he let go of her with the hand he had on her waist to rub his bruising leg.

"'Cause I canna kill him," he said, trying to deflect the kicks her foot was now trying to deliver. "I tried fer years ta fine a way to make it look ax'den'l."

It all made sense now. As his coachman, any number of opportunities to harm Benjamin could have presented themselves, from highway men to carriage accidents. However, he, Billings, would always look somewhat suspicious, especially if he didn't attempt to help Benjamin or if the incidents took place too often. Perhaps Billings had been the brains of the operation and Robbie the pawn who was to take the fall.

She kicked him again, this time with her knee in the stomach, causing him to violently flinch and pull back, giving her just enough room to break free of his grasp. Scrambling to her feet, she looked back to the window and saw flames were licking the inside edge of the window.

It was too late.

Standing frozen in shock and disappointment, Billings grabbed her again. His pant leg was on fire and he was purposely rubbing it against her skirt, trying to get it to catch fire.

Briefly debating between a death of burning with Billings or trying to imitate Robbie, she used what little energy she could muster and walked to the window, dragging Billings' burning body along with her. Right before she reached the edge of the window, a gunshot sounded. Billings' body went limp and her eyes caught sight of Benjamin. He was literally hanging by a rope outside the window. "Come, Madison," he called raggedly, extending a hand to her.

"How did you?" she asked frantically, hiking her singed skirt up and hobbling over to him.

Benjamin gestured for her to come closer. "The roof hasn't caught yet and I found an old ladder by the stable along with a coil of rope. I was able to lean the ladder against the eaves and climb up to the roof. But don't worry about that just now. I've tied this not-so-new rope to something up there that I think will hold, but I can't be certain so we need to be going, Madison. Now."

"It all sounds very heroic," she quipped quietly, reaching her shaking hand toward his. As her hand sank into his, she started hacking and coughing and trembling as never before.

Benjamin let go of her shaky, clammy hand. "Only the most dramatic display for you," he teased, his grim face belying his easy tone. "Just stand there and I'll get you." He leaned forward and wrapped his arm around her waist then pulled her from the hayloft.

"You're all right," he murmured in her ear. "You're going to have to hold onto me tightly."

She wrapped her arms around his neck as tightly as she could and buried her face in the crook of his neck. He pushed off the wall with his foot only an inch above the consuming flames. Together they swung out and away from the barn, then all too abruptly, Benjamin let go of the rope.

For Madison, time ceased to exist as they flew through the air. The fall may have been only a few seconds, but to Madison it felt like an eternity.

With a loud, jolting thump, Benjamin's boots hit the ground.

Not wanting to ever let go of him, she continued to hold him tightly and whispered, "Oh, Benjamin, I was so scared."

"I know," he said, hugging her closely and pressing kisses all over her face.

"Ben," she whispered, hugging him closely. "I—I—"

A delicate cough cut her off. "Your Grace, we need a moment," a man who looked far too self-important for his own good intoned.

"Right," Benjamin clipped. "Madison, this is the constable..."

Madison knew he was talking about something important, but she couldn't hear it. Not when her nerves were in such a tangle. Madison didn't care to listen to anything at the moment. She only cared that she and Benjamin were safe.

"Are you ready?" Benjamin whispered in her ear after his conversation with the constable.

Madison's eyes snapped to his. "Sorry, I was woolgathering."

"That's all right," he said with a light squeeze. "I don't mind. I know you're overset. Would you like a bath?"

"Yes," she said, nodding.

He grinned. "Excellent. I shall take the place of both Lottie and Jamison and join you."

"I'd like that very much," she said honestly. She looked into his blue eyes and felt a deeper connection with him now than she ever had with anyone else.

Without wasting another second, he scooped her up and carried her into the house. Only stopping to order a bath, Benjamin carried her straight to the suite they'd been sharing and gently placed her down on the settee.

He dropped to his knees in front of her and pulled off her slippers and remaining stocking. "It'll be all right now," he promised, rubbing her calves.

The sun was shining through the window and she squinted to see him. "I'm just glad it's all over."

He lightly kissed her and stood up. "I'll go draw the drapes," he murmured, walking in the direction of the window.

Madison nodded and watched him walk to the window. He was almost there when a little corner of paper caught her eye. Her heart slammed in her chest when she realized what that paper was. She jumped to her feet and rushed over to where he was, positioning herself in a way she could push the note back into the secretary.

"What are you about, duchess," he asked with his handsome grin. His arms wrapped around her waist and his fingers closed down on top of where hers held the paper. "Have you been writing me a love letter?" he teased, pulling the paper from her fingers.

"No," she said quickly, trying to grab it back. "Please give it back, Benjamin," she pleaded, her voice strained.

He flashed her a rueful grin. "It's all right if you weren't done. I'll give it back and let you finish it later." He winked and pulled it from behind her back. He kept one arm wrapped possessively around her waist as he held the note above her head and his warm, tender eyes turned to cold, hard pellets of ice as he scanned each and every one of those damning words.

Chapter 30

"What's this?" he demanded, holding the paper so tightly it was crumpling. "Why did you write it?"

Her lips parted in shock and she opened and shut her mouth like a fish.

"Answer me," he barked, giving her a tight squeeze.

"I—I—didn't like how you treated me," she said defensively. "You just hauled me here against my wishes."

"And you thought Andrew would come to your rescue?" he spat, letting go of her. "Why is it you always run to Andrew when things aren't going well for you?"

She swallowed. "I don't know," she admitted. "I suppose it's because I trust him."

"And you don't trust me," his words a statement, not a question. "What do I have to do to get you to trust me, Madison? Why am I not good enough for you?"

"I never said that."

"No? Then why do you run to Andrew to save you all the time? Why can't you just, for once, trust me?" he yelled, jabbing a finger to his chest. "Even today, you didn't trust me to catch you. I had to climb back up there to get you."

"That's not fair. Billings yanked me back into the hayloft."

Benjamin snorted. "You had plenty of time to jump before he got there. You just chose to take your sweet time about it."

She shook her head. "I'm sorry that, unlike you, I find it terrifying to jump out a window and it took me a minute to compose myself."

"You're forgiven," he said tightly. "However, that does not

198

explain why you always run to Andrew to solve your problems for you. I'm your husband. You should come to me."

"I don't always run to Andrew," she shot back, matching his tone.

"Yes, you do," he countered with a sneer. "The day after our wedding, you did. After only one night with me, you run to Andrew and plead with him to save you from the Dangerous Duke."

"I never called you that."

"You didn't have to. Your tone and body language toward me that day screamed it."

"I don't know what you're talking about," she said evenly. "I went to Brooke to ask her advice after *you* ruined our wedding night by calling me a whore and leaving the house."

He held a hand up to stop her words. "Stop right there. I never called you a whore. I said you were acting like one. There's a difference."

She rolled her eyes. "Pardon my slip," she said with a hint of hysterical sarcasm. "I just assumed when I heard the words 'disgusting' and 'whore' directed at me that you were talking about me in general. Next time, I'll be sure to scribble down your words so that when I'm over my shock, I can read them to make sure I heard you correctly."

"It's inconsequential now," he said angrily. "I've apologized for it. And, I thought I was forgiven for it; perhaps not. But that's not the issue here. The issue is that you always run to Andrew to solve your problems for you."

"No, I don't," she countered. "I went to see Brooke that day, not him. I wanted to ask her why you reacted that way to me. I didn't know what I did wrong. That's how I thought I was supposed to dress," she said with an uneven voice that cracked mid-sentence.

A knot formed in his stomach at being reminded of that. If Robbie wasn't already dead, he'd kill him for making Madison disgrace herself that way. "That's immaterial," he said sharply, trying to focus on the present. He could beg her forgiveness for their bungled wedding night again later. Right now they needed to get to the bottom of her lack of trust in him and her overwhelming trust in Andrew. "I'll accept you went to their townhouse with the intention of speaking to Brooke. But, you ended your visit begging Andrew not to make you return to me."

"Of course I did," she retorted. "You looked angrier than a mother bear does when one of her babies is in danger. It's not like I hadn't heard rumors of your past exploits."

"That has nothing to do with it," he said again. "I've never struck a woman and there are no rumors, true or false, to suggest I have. You had nothing to fear and you knew it. But you still begged Andrew to keep you away from me."

She favored him with a curious glance. "You're jealous."

"Of course I am," he burst out. "He has the one thing I cannot seem to gain no matter how hard I try."

Madison shook her head. "It's not his fault your mother left you and his mother couldn't act as yours in public."

"I'm not talking about that," he said tersely. "I accepted that years ago. At first, I didn't understand it. But, I soon realized she had no other choice."

"Then why are you still jealous of him?"

"You really have to ask?" he asked, snarling.

She blinked. "Apparently I do, since I have no idea what you're talking about. He has a wife and an heir. You have a wife who will one day give you an heir. What is there to be jealous of?"

He shook his head. "You."

"Me?"

He nodded. "Yes, you."

"I don't understand what you're talking about," she said coolly.

"You have built him up to sainthood in your mind. You idolize him as if he's some sort of hero, when quite frankly, he's neither a hero nor a saint."

"I didn't say he was," she retorted. "I know he's made mistakes."

"Do you now?"

"Yes, one of the most recent involved him agreeing to take money from *you* in exchange for shaming my family off the continent," she said matter-of-factly.

"Ah, yes, perhaps the most well-known of his errors," he drawled. "And isn't it strange that you've had many opportunities to know the reason behind that and yet you don't seem interested anymore when I offer to tell you?"

She shrugged. "Why should I care? It doesn't exactly shed a favorable light on you that you'd be willing to pay someone money to ruin an innocent, now does it?"

"Don't try to make this seem as if you were trying to protect the mental image you have of me," he said, shaking his head. "I know you don't think very highly of me, even if I do possess a few admirable traits that Andrew does not."

"Like what?" she demanded, her voice full of disbelief.

"Like not frequenting brothels," he said defensively.

Her face turned red and she glared at him. "Don't you dare accuse him of being unfaithful to my sister. I don't believe it for a moment. He loves her and would never be untrue to her."

"I never said he was unfaithful," Benjamin countered. "I'm just telling you that I've lived a more respectable life than he has in that respect. Except for you, I haven't been with a woman in more than six years."

"What does that have to do with anything?"

He shrugged. "Nothing really, but since you seem to believe Andrew has me surpassed in all areas, I was just answering your question by pointing out a way I have him beat."

"Is there some sort of a competition I don't know about?"

After an extended blink, he said, "Apparently, there is."

"What are you talking about?" she asked, her brows knitting together in confusion.

He took a step toward her, making her back up against the desk. "You need to let go of your romantic notions about Andrew. He'll never return your love. He's not even worthy of it. And yet, you have set him up as some sort of hero in your mind."

"That's not true," she protested.

"Yes, it is," he snapped. "Otherwise, you wouldn't be writing him exaggerated letters of your distress in hopes he'd come to your rescue."

"As I said, I didn't like the way you were treating me. When I tried to talk sense into you, you refused to listen. I was locked in here. I wasn't allowed to do anything. You confined me to the house and had a footman trail me. I couldn't even be alone to use the water closet. What did you expect me to do?" she asked fiercely. "Did you think I'd do whatever crazy thing you told me to do just because you're my husband?"

"I was trying to protect you," he shouted. "I couldn't have you wandering around the estate alone. Anything could have happened to you and I would have never known about it. I'm sorry you didn't like it, but that's what I had to do to ensure your safety."

"Then you should have taken me back to Rockhurst. I would have been just as safe there and I would have been able to do as I pleased," she countered, crossing her arms.

"You would have liked that, wouldn't you?" he said coldly. "Then you could have lain in the grass and dreamt of Andrew all day."

She closed her eyes and let out a deep breath. "I don't know what you're talking about. You need to get over your jealousy. Besides being petty, it's just plain annoying."

"I'm sorry you find it annoying," he said, feigning a polite tone. "However, I find your blatant love and adoration for Andrew annoying."

"I have no love or adoration for him," she snapped. "It's your jealous imagination that seems to think I do."

"Your actions seem to betray your words, madam," he drawled with a scowl.

"No they don't," she snapped, her eyes flashing fire.

He crossed his arms and clenched his hands into fists. "Then tell me why you wrote the note pleading for him to come save you."

"I already told you."

He shook his head. "No, I want to know why only his name is on the letter. Why didn't you write the letter to Brooke? She's your sister. You could have written to her and we both know she'd have sent Andrew for you before her eyes reached your signature at the bottom of the page."

She dropped her gaze to the floor. "I don't know why I only addressed it to him," she admitted quietly, swallowing.

"I do," he snapped. "Because you love him; there's no other reason for it. Let's have some honesty, Madison. Do you love him?"

"I—I—"

"No," he cut in. "Yes or no?"

"Yes," she said with another swallow.

He laughed in a way he'd often heard termed akin to an evil

villain's laugh. "You want to know something that you shouldn't find a secret, but might anyway?" he asked with what he knew to be a less than convincing smile. "He doesn't love you. And he never will. He loves your sister."

"I know that," she snapped.

"Then accept it," he snarled. "Accept that he'll never love you the way he loves Brooke. Accept that I do love you that way."

"What?" she asked, blinking so rapidly he thought she might have something in her eye.

"My turn," he said harshly. "You seem to want to leave the past in the past. But I can't do that. Not when so much of the past seems to keep surfacing in the present."

She shook her head. "I don't want to do this. I have no intention of discussing the past with you or anyone else."

He ignored her. "Do you remember our wedding?"

"Of course," she said irritably. "Even with all the drama that's ensued in the interim, I think I can manage to sweep the cobwebs from my brain enough to remember it."

He gave her a sharp look. "Do you remember my full name?"

"Most of it, yes," she said, annoyance in her voice.

"Allow me to refresh your memory. My full name is Benjamin Archer Leopold Charles Robert Collins. Most people call me my title, Gateway. You, and only a handful of others, call me Benjamin. But at one time, I went by a shortened version of one of my numerous middle names. Would you like to guess what it was?" His eyes bored into hers, daring her not to answer his question.

She flicked her wrist in an annoyed gesture. "Archer?"

"I suppose I'll let that pass," he mumbled. "I take it you've heard all the juicy details of my childhood with Andrew. But I said I shortened one of my names. Guess again."

"Robbie?" she asked with a shudder.

He shook his head.

She looked at him in confusion. Her eyes scanned his face. "I don't know," she said quietly.

"Leo."

Her eyes widened.

He nodded. "After the incident at my house in Yorkshire, the old duke suggested I go on Tour to America. He said there were some relations in Brooklyn. It seemed like a good idea to me, so I went."

Her eyes locked with his as she listened to his words and her body sagged against the edge of the desk.

"Madison," he said hoarsely. "You know why I haven't been with a woman in six years?"

"That's not true," she interrupted sharply. "You told Andrew you'd give his estate to your mistress if he didn't agree to ruin Brooke."

"You're right, I did," he conceded flatly. "Have you ever heard of bluffing, Madison? I had to say something to get his dander up. The man was being positively stubborn about agreeing."

"I don't believe you," she said coldly.

"Believe what you want," he said with a tight one-shoulder shrug. "But, I haven't been with a woman in six years because I lost my heart to you the minute you walked in front of me in that ballroom. Ever since that night, I haven't even had interest in another woman." He gave a harsh laugh. "I even told my gutter-minded cousin I'd become a monk if it meant I could have you. As it turns out, I became a monk anyway and I'll still never have you." He let out a ragged, tortured breath.

"You did have me," she pointed out.

"No, I didn't. Not really," he said in a hollow voice. "You only shared my bed because you wanted more privacy to use Lottie to slip a note out to Andrew."

"Benjamin," she whispered, "I didn—"

"Anyway," he said sharply, cutting her off. "After Robbie took you dancing, I pleaded my case to Brooke. I tried to convince her I was a better choice and she seemed to be agreeable." He shook his head and ran a hand through his hair. "I tried to talk to you every chance I got, but my dunce of a cousin kept interrupting. When we went off to hide the night of the dinner party, I tried to talk to you. I wanted to tell you how I felt. But when I found you, you were embracing Robbie and declaring yourself to him. After you kissed him, I knew it was over. I knew I didn't stand a chance. You'd made your choice and it wasn't me."

"Yes, it was," she whispered brokenly.

He shook his head, dismissing her weak statement. "It doesn't really matter anymore. When I saw you last spring, I thought I had another chance. I gained an introduction to you at the second ball I saw you at. But you didn't seem interested in even talking to me. I thought I'd just wait for you to be ready. But that never happened."

She tensed. "Please do not make some rude comment about my tendency to daydream."

"I'm not," he said coldly. "I thought you were upset things didn't work out with Robbie and decided to give you some time."

"Oh."

"After a month, I saw you were still sad and realized you'd only be happy if you were back with Robbie. That's why I orchestrated Brooke's ruination. I picked Andrew because he was easy to cast in the role since he owed me something and as a boon Lizzie would benefit from it." He pursed his lips and scuffed one of his boots against the other. "Actually, that's not entirely true. At first, I tried to do it. I didn't want anyone else to know what I was up to and I tried to shame her," he said, twisting his lips into a bitter sneer. "But, it just wasn't meant to be. My heart really wasn't in it and I couldn't feign interest well enough so she rejected me. That's why I sought out Andrew. I thought he'd have better luck since his heart wasn't otherwise engaged, specifically to her sister."

"Excuse me," Madison interrupted hotly. "I was under the impression Andrew was not specifically asked to ruin Brooke. I was told he was just supposed to bring some sort of scandal to one of us.

Why did both of you choose to target her?"

Benjamin snorted. "Are you serious? Ruination was the only type of scandal that would accomplish the goal. As for choosing Brooke," he shrugged. "There weren't any other options. First, you were not an option since you wouldn't as much as look at a man. Second, only an idiot would have chosen to pursue Liberty with such intentions. She'd throw a fit if a man even suggested they go to the veranda. She'd probably unman anyone who was bold enough to touch her."

"You're right," she conceded.

He shrugged and scratched his head. "My thinking was that if you were back in New York, at least you'd be happy. Of course, I'd be miserable knowing I'd lost you forever. But, I loved you enough that I was willing to suffer knowing you were happy."

She shook her head. "That wasn't..." she trailed off and dropped her gaze to the carpet.

"I know," he said bitterly, causing her eyes to snap to his.

"You do?"

He nodded. "I got letters. Robbie sent me letters a few weeks later detailing your courtship with him, his recent marriage to another and how he wanted you back as his mistress." He contorted his face in disgust and flexed his fingers. "That's when I realized you weren't unhappy because you were brought to England, but you were brought to England because you were unhappy."

"Oh," she said quietly, searching the patterns in his royal blue carpet with her downcast eyes.

He sighed. "I'd hoped this Season to court you, except an opportunity never presented itself. Then when one did, I jumped on it; even though it meant skipping the courtship stage altogether and marrying you. In fact, I liked that even better," he said with a sad smile. "There has never been a man who looked forward to his wedding day as much as I did." He swallowed and pursed his lips again. "And then, I bungled it. I let my emotions get the best of me and I ruined everything."

"That's not true," she protested calmly.

He let out a harsh bark of laughter. "Yes, it is," he said in an emotionally raw voice. "I tried my damnedest to woo you and win your affections." He closed his eyes and exhaled deeply. "But no, now it's happened again. I'm too late, again. You have Andrew on such a bloody high pedestal I could never compete. But you know what?" he asked, his voice turning cold. "I can't do it again. I can't wait for you to fall out of love again to try to win you once more. I love you more than any man has ever loved his wife, but my heart cannot take anymore. Now that Robbie's gone, you're free to go."

"But I don't want to go," she said quietly.

"Then stay. I don't care. I just don't care anymore," he said brokenly, walking to the door. He walked out of their room to his study where he sank into a chair, feeling deflated. Defeated.

Chapter 31

Madison sat numbly on the settee and stared at the steaming tub that had been brought in for her. In less than ten minutes, the entire relationship she'd built with Benjamin had fallen apart.

She closed her eyes and relived their conversation once again. She should never have written the letter in the first place. She was definitely wrong on that score. But, he'd never even given her a chance to explain herself. Instead, he'd jumped to the bizarre conclusion that she was in love with her brother-in-law. She shook her head. Perhaps when he calmed down, she could try to smooth it out.

As for him being Leo, unfortunately, that fact was far more obvious than she'd like to admit. She'd felt a familiarity with him on more than one occasion: in the dark hall when he'd spoken to her, at the coast when he'd looked unkempt and rugged, and as recently as earlier that morning. It also made sense why he teased her about wanting to meet Leo or refused to ensure their paths wouldn't cross; even wanting to keep those drawings of them made sense now. If she'd been slightly more open-minded, she would have put the clues together much sooner. She groaned. He'd even encouraged her to talk about things that weren't appropriate. Just like Leo.

She shook her head. She was such a nodcock.

Not that it really mattered anyway. If she were being honest, she'd admit that her unruly heart had even started feeling for Benjamin feelings she'd only ever had for Leo.

She stood up and redressed. She needed to talk to him. She needed to explain that the letter had just been penned as a way to deal with her anger and she'd never planned to send it. He might not believe her. But she at least deserved the chance to plead her case.

Downstairs, she learned his study was locked and she knocked discreetly at the door. He didn't answer and she knocked again. And again. And again. After more than ten minutes, she decided to approach him at dinner instead.

Dinner, however, didn't turn out to be any better. She sat alone in the drawing room for thirty minutes before the butler informed her dinner was ready. Heart racing in anticipation, she hurried down to the dining room and frowned when she realized it was empty.

She ate dinner slower than a turtle, hoping he'd get hungry and come to dine at some point. No such luck.

Later that night, she waited for him to come join her in the room they'd been sharing. She knew it was actually the duke's room they'd been using and felt confident he'd come there to sleep.

But he never came.

About midnight, she swallowed her irritation at his direct avoidance of her and went to the connecting door. With a nervous gulp, she opened the door. Her eyes scanned the moonlit room and must have been playing tricks on her. To confirm her suspicion of suddenly poor eyesight, Madison crossed the threshold and walked to the bed.

Running her hand along the smooth counterpane, a wave of disappointment washed over her. She turned and walked to the chair in the corner and saw he wasn't there, either. She opened the door to the duchess' sitting room and blinked in surprise to see the room was absolutely empty. There wasn't a single piece of furniture in the room. There wasn't even a wall sconce. She shut the door and went back to her bed.

The man was still at the residence, she reminded herself. He couldn't escape her. She'd just wait to see him at breakfast.

Rising as soon as the first sunray came through the curtains, Madison ran downstairs to request Cook make waffles for Benjamin. Perhaps that could be a peace offering, she thought with a cheeky smile as she left the kitchen. By hook or by crook she was going to see him this morning.

And like magic, it worked.

She saw him all right.

She was eating her waffles in the breakfast room and heard heavy footfalls in the hallway. Plastering a sunny smile on her face, she waited for Benjamin to come into the room.

"Madam, your tricks will not work," he said sharply, coming into the room. "I've a set menu at this house and you're not to tell Cook to deviate from it. Understood?"

Her smiled dimmed a notch. "Excuse me?" she said archly. "I was under the impression that as duchess and the mistress of this house I would be in charge of the menu."

He speared her with his stare. "That is normally the case, yes," he conceded coldly. "But not with you. You don't wish to be the mistress of this house. Therefore, your decisions are invalid, I'm afraid."

She crossed her arms. "You're being unfair. The truth is *you* don't wish me to be mistress of this house any longer for reasons, that to be quite honest, I don't even understand."

"Yes, you do," he snapped. "You know as well as I do that you'd prefer to be mistress of Rockhurst, not Glenbrook. Unfortunately for you, that's not possible."

"Stop it, Benjamin," she snapped. "You're being cruel. You didn't even hear my side of things."

"I didn't need to," he countered. "I know enough. Nothing you can say now will change what you've done."

"I haven't done anything," she retorted, her eyes full of defiance.

"You didn't have to do it," he shot back. "You intended to. That was enough."

She stared unblinkingly at his retreating form. Perhaps he needed a few more days to come to his senses.

A few days passed and her luck hadn't changed. She hadn't gone out of her way to grab his attention again, but she hadn't needed to. She'd occasionally run into him in the hall and he'd given a terse nod of greeting in her direction. Or she'd walked into a room he'd been occupying only for him to immediately excuse himself. It was infuriating and heartbreaking at the same time.

Finally, after nearly a week, she'd gotten a glimpse of him in front of the house talking to his coachman.

Interested in what was going on, she'd casually walked outside to hear the orders he'd been giving to Michaels, his new coachman.

In less than three seconds, she'd surmised they were going to London.

She ran inside and asked Lottie if she was ready to go. Lottie acted confused and Madison ran back outside to check for herself to see if her trunks were loaded.

"What do you think you're doing, madam?" a cold baritone voice asked behind her, making her skin prickle with awareness.

"Benjamin," she said, flashing him a smile. "It's nice to see you this morning."

"What are you doing?" he asked with a pointed glance at where she'd been climbing up the back of the carriage.

She smiled weakly at him. "I was just checking to see that my things are loaded."

"They're not."

"All right, I'm sure Massey will be right down with them. I'll wait in the carriage."

"No," he said, shaking his head.

"All right, I'll wait out here with you. I'd like that better anyway," she said with a grin.

He ran a hand through his hair. "You're not coming," he said in a tone she didn't recognize.

"Why ever not?"

"Because you're not invited," he said flatly, looking past her shoulder.

"Who would invite the duke and not his duchess to be guests at his house?" she asked with a sniff.

"Me," he said tightly.

"What?" she asked, bewildered. "Where are you going?"

"To London."

"I know that already," she said tightly. "Where in London?"

"To my townhouse."

"Why?" Was he so upset with her he didn't even want to be in the same house?

"Parliament has called for an emergency session and I must attend," he explained.

She nodded. "How long are you to be gone?"

"I don't know," he said with a shrug.

"Why can't I come?" she questioned, her jaw stiffening. Why did he insist on being so difficult?

"Because you weren't invited," he said simply.

She ground her teeth. "I may not be a member of parliament, but that does not mean I cannot go to London and stay with you."

He closed his eyes for a moment. "Why don't you want to stay here?"

"Because you'll be gone," she said automatically.

He snorted. "That's an interesting reason. Or perhaps, the real reason is that Andrew will also be in London."

She let out a huff of indignation. "Stop it. I don't like your accusations. I'm coming with you to London."

"And just how do you think to accomplish that?" he asked, crossing his arms and leaning forward.

"Either you'll take me in your carriage or I'll ride one of your horses," she said defiantly.

His mouth clamped into a tight line. "Fine, get into the carriage," he barked, then started barking orders to have her trunk packed.

It was well into the night before the carriage came to a stop and a pair of sturdy arms carried her up a flight of stairs and set her in the softest bed she'd ever felt.

The next two days, she wandered aimlessly around their London townhouse trying to do anything to occupy her time. Whenever she couldn't find any amusement, she'd go visit one of the friends who were still in town and even helped Mrs. Ingram's sewing circle for an afternoon. However, she was still no closer to breaking down Benjamin's defenses.

It wasn't until the evening of their third day in London that the dreaded note from Brooke requesting she call upon her first thing in the morning arrived. Madison sighed. When Brooke said first thing in the morning, she meant first thing in the morning.

Chapter 32

"All right, Madison," Brooke said, breaking into her thoughts as she walked into the room. "What's wrong?"

"Nothing."

Brooke shook her head and sat down next to her sister on the settee. She was holding a wiggling Nathan in her arms, trying to get him to sleep. "You can lie to anyone, but you cannot lie to me. I know you better than anyone. And I know you're upset. There is no use in not telling me."

Madison swallowed. If it was about anything other than an accusation of her having romantic feelings for her sister's husband, she would have told her. But there was no way she wanted to risk their relationship. "I'm sorry, I can't tell you."

"No," Brooke said defiantly. "You can. You're just choosing not to. Do you remember the night before I was to leave for America?"

"Of course," Madison burst out. She may have been a bit of a scatterbrain at the time, but she wasn't a complete dolt.

"Good," Brooke said firmly. "Then you remember charging into my room and demanding to know what happened. And I told you. I told you every single detail, save the bedroom intimacies." Her face flushed and for a split-second she broke eye contact. "Then you sat there for fifteen minutes trying to convince me to go to him and claimed every excuse I gave you was feeble. Then, when you thought all hope was lost, you dressed as a prostitute and went to see Andrew. Does any of that sound familiar?"

"Stop it, Brooke," Madison said sharply.

Brooke sighed and repositioned Nathan in her arms. "I just want to help. You saved my marriage, Madison. I will be forever grateful for what you did. I just want to help you, the way you helped me. Please."

Madison dropped her eyes to the floor. "I can't tell you, Brooke. I don't want to lose you."

"Lose me?" Her voice dripped with disbelief. "I'm your sister, you can't lose me."

"You know what I meant," Madison countered sadly. She wished she could talk to her. Brooke always offered good advice, even if Madison hadn't always taken it.

Brooke ran her fingers through her son's hair. "I do know what you meant, our close relationship. But as I said, I'm your sister. With the exception of you sleeping with my husband—which I know isn't happening—there is nothing you could do that would change my perception of you. I know every wrong you've committed before, and I assure you, whatever you've done this time probably pales in comparison to the mess with Robbie. So just tell me."

"Brooke," Madison said before taking a deep breath. "Do you think I'm in love with Andrew?"

Brooke made an unusual sound that sounded like she was trying to choke down a single high pitched, stunned giggle. "No," she blurted out, shaking her head for emphasis. "Why?"

"Benjamin does."

"He told you this?" Brooke asked dumbly.

Madison nodded.

"Hmmm." Brooke twisted her lips and stared at the far wall for a minute. "Can I tell you something that will most likely hurt your feelings?"

"Go ahead," Madison replied blandly. "Everyone else does."

Brooke flashed her a quick, rueful grin. "Madison," she started in a rather quiet and serious voice, "I can see why Benjamin thinks that."

"But—"

Brooke's hand shot up and her piercing gaze silenced Madison. "No interruptions. I mean it. Think about it from Benjamin's point of view for a minute. Andrew was your guardian. He's the one who told Benjamin to keep you occupied while he took care of Robbie. Not that it's Andrew's fault, mind you. I told him to get rid of Robbie that night. Benjamin couldn't have objected to keeping you company and he couldn't haul Robbie out of there himself because at the time it wasn't his place. You weren't his wife or intended or even someone he was courting. Instead, he was powerless to help you in the way he thought mattered."

"And, as usual, it worked out well for him," she muttered, remembering how he took advantage of the situation causing them to become betrothed.

"It worked out rather well for you, too," Brooke remarked dryly. "But that's not the point. Before you married Benjamin, he had to stand by and watch Andrew solve your problems for you. Then—and I'm not saying this was entirely you're fault, so don't get angry—you asked Andrew to help you pursue any avenue available to get rid of Benjamin. Madison, I said no interruptions. I see your mouth open. Close it. Very good. What was I saying? Oh, right. After you begged Andrew to save you that day, he did. He convinced Benjamin to allow you to stay at Rockhurst so he could court you.

"Which, I must admit, I was rather surprised to hear. But that's not relevant anymore. The truth is you always rely on Andrew to help you."

"But it's because—"

"*I* know why you do it, Madison, but Benjamin doesn't" Brooke said softly, cutting her off.

Madison closed her eyes and bit her lip to keep it from quivering. "So you think I should be more trusting of Benjamin?" The unspoken part of that question hung in the air.

"Of course," Brooke said with a smile. "He really hasn't given you a reason not to be."

Madison shook her head. "I'm afraid it may not be so simple anymore."

"Sure it is," Brooke countered encouragingly.

"What if it's not?" she asked brokenly, her voice shaky and raw. "He said he loves me, but was done waiting for me to feel the same. What if he doesn't love me anymore? What if it's too late?"

"It's not," Brooke assured her. "Any man who's carried a torch for a woman for six years, most of which time he'd thought she'd married another, is not going to stop in a matter of days."

Madison shook her head sadly. "I don't think it's possible. He won't even look at me. He barely speaks to me. He acts as if I don't exist. I practically begged him to bring me to London, and even then he refused to ride in the carriage with me. Brooke, the man would rather ride on the hard coachman's bench and endure a cold rain for more than twelve hours to avoid my company."

Brooke waved her off dismissively. "He's hurt, that's all. I'd say to give it more time and let him have his space, but we both know that's not really what either of you want. Instead, he needs a little shove in the right direction."

"Brooke, you're not planning to do something, are you?" she asked, trying to imitate Brooke's scary stare.

Nathan's nurse arrived and Brooke handed her a sleeping Nathan. "No," she said after the nurse left. She shook her head and grinned. "You are."

Madison groaned. "Have you been listening to a word I said? He won't talk to me. He leaves the room whenever I enter. Whatever you have in that scheming mind of yours won't work."

"Poppycock," Brooke said, waving her hand in front of her face. "Men are simple creatures."

"Not this one," Madison muttered.

Brooke snorted. "You'd like to think so, but they're all equipped the same."

Now it was Madison's turn to snort. "They may have the same

parts, but they're not all created equal."

Brooke giggled then she abruptly stopped and got a very serious look on her face. "Forgive me," she said, fidgeting in her seat and dropping her eyes to the floor.

"No need," Madison said with a shrug. "I don't typically make a habit of speaking ill of the dead, but in this case, I'll make an exception."

Brooke met her eyes again and looked like she was about to burst into laughter. "I'm glad it all worked out well for you on that score, too."

"It did," Madison confirmed with a blush and a grin. Then her smile dimmed and she swallowed hard. "Not that it matters anymore."

"About that," Brooke said thoughtfully. "Do you still have those nightrails I had you order?"

Madison nodded. "They're safely tucked into the back of my bottom drawer."

Brooke closed her eyes and shook her head. "You had better dig one out. You're going to need it."

A giggle passed Madison's lips and she clapped her hand over her mouth to keep any more from escaping.

"Do you find something funny about wearing one?" Brooke lifted her eyebrow in the way her husband always did to put people off.

Madison shook her head no, still holding her mouth and laughing even harder at Brooke's imitation of her husband.

"Out with it," Brooke demanded with her stare.

"The night of my engagement, when Benjamin and I were in that little hall together, he accused you of leading Andrew around by his—"

"Stop," Brooke clipped with a frown. "I do no such thing. And neither will you. I'm just telling you how to gain admittance to his presence long enough to get him to listen to you."

Madison's brows knit in confusion.

Brooke sighed. "I'll tell you a secret. Marriage is a game of give and take. It seems to me that you've done all the taking, and now it's your turn to do some giving. You wearing the nightrail is not the giving I'm talking about, either. That's just to catch his attention while you explain yourself and offer him your heart."

"Oh."

Brooke smiled. "And hopefully after you do that, you'll be able to discard that pesky nightrail post haste," she added with wink.

Madison blushed. She hoped Brooke was right and that Benjamin would accept the broken heart she had to offer.

Chapter 33

"You look like hell," Andrew said, coming to take a seat next to Benjamin for their parliament session.

Benjamin scowled. "Since my understanding of hell is a large mass of all consuming fire, I can hardly believe I look that way."

Andrew whistled. "Relax. It's just an expression."

"So is bugger off," he countered with a steely stare.

"Touché," Andrew said with a grin.

Benjamin crossed his arms. "What do you want, Andrew?"

Andrew grinned. "My, my, but I remember several conversations that started this way, Benjamin. Only the dialogue was reversed."

Benjamin flicked his wrist. "Perhaps if you'd taken care of business, we wouldn't be having *this* conversation just now."

Andrew's smile vanished. "I, for one, am rather glad things worked out the way they did. And I think if you'd get past your own pride, you'd be happy, too."

"I'm glad things worked out so well for you," Benjamin said offhandedly. Would the man take the hint and go away?

"As I said, they'd work well for you if you'd let go of whatever is holding you back."

Benjamin broke eye contact. It all sounded so simple. But it wasn't. The idea of sharing his wife with another man wasn't an easy tonic to swallow. Sure Andrew was right and they could be content together sharing a bed and having a family. But knowing he'd never have her heart was more than he could bear. Especially knowing exactly who held it. "It's not that simple," he said quietly. "There's more to the story than you know."

"I'm sure you're correct," Andrew conceded. "Although I have a feeling I'll know more of it tonight."

His eyes snapped to Andrew's. "Just what do you mean by that?"

Andrew shrugged. "I saw Madison this morning on my way out the door."

Benjamin stiffened. "Why was she at your house?"

"Brooke summoned her," Andrew said, shaking his head ruefully. "Don't feel bad. Brooke does this to everyone. You wouldn't believe the things I know about Paul and Liberty's relationship," he shuddered, "or the things I've been asked to do on their behalf."

"Wonderful. Are you saying this is an occurrence I can look forward to for the rest of my life?" Benjamin muttered. Why did families have to involve themselves in everyone's business? Perhaps in this one respect, he was better off without one.

"You can count on it," Andrew said earnestly.

"Is that what you wanted?"

"You mean to warn you about my wife's tendency to ferret information out of her sisters better than a spy? No. I wanted to tell you something that is actually rather hard for me to say to you." He shifted in his seat and ran a hand through his black hair. "I know we've had our differences, but I'm not opposed to the match. I think you two suit each other very well and I hope things work out."

"Thank you," Benjamin said graciously.

The session ended and Benjamin took his time about going home. He'd taken to eating his meals by himself in his study where he could stare at a book and wonder when his life had gone down the privy.

Like Andrew, he hoped things would work out, but between her lack of faith in him and his craving to possess her heart and soul, he doubted things would be resolved in a way that would be pleasing to them both. As it was, their current situation wasn't pleasing to either of them.

Benjamin walked inside, gave his hat to Todd, and walked to his study, catching a glimpse of Madison in the drawing room as he went. Once in his study, he slammed the door and cursed his traitorous eyes for looking her up and down so thoroughly. No question about it, she was still as beautiful as she'd always been. His heart squeezed. He wanted her. It was undeniable. It was insane.

What was more insane was she hadn't seemed put off one iota by his attempts to keep her at arm's length. Instead of leaving, as he thought she might do, she'd greet him with a smile and try to engage him in conversation, no matter how rudely he acted as a means to escape.

He sank into his chair. Would it be so bad to have only part of her, he wondered as he flipped through his book. He found the page he wanted and pulled out a blank piece of paper and dipped his quill into an inkpot. His lips twisted into a doubtful sneer and he squeezed his quill with just enough pressure to make it bend but not snap. It wouldn't work to have only half of her. If he couldn't have all of her, there was no point.

~*~*~*~

Madison's hands shook as she carried the dinner tray she'd ordered to have delivered to her room down to Benjamin's study. She'd fibbed to Cook about Benjamin's dinner plans and asked her not to deliver his meal to his study.

Lottie walked next to her, shaking her head and mumbling under her breath about working in a madhouse. At the door to Benjamin's study, Lottie knocked and together they waited for him to shout for her to enter.

Taking a deep breath, Madison nodded for Lottie to open the door and slipped in as quietly as she could with all the silver clinging and clanging together on top of the tray.

"Just set it down by the door," Benjamin muttered without looking up from his desk.

Madison put the tray on the table that was by the door and quickly slipped off her dressing robe, leaving her clad in a transparent red knee-length number that swooped dangerously low in the front, had twin slits from her knees to her hips and was trimmed with black lace.

"You're dismissed," he mumbled after a minute, still not dragging his eyes from his work.

She realized the door was still open, and using her foot, she gave it a kick that sent it slamming to the doorjamb.

He didn't react. He didn't look up. He didn't curse. He didn't even jump. He just sat motionless, clutching his quill and staring down at his precious paper.

She wondered if he knew it was her. Perhaps that was why he didn't react. She was not going to be put off so easily. She'd had more than her share of stare downs with Jamison. She could stand here all night if she had to.

A fire blazed in the hearth not ten feet away from her warming the whole room. No candles were lit except the five-candle candelabra on Benjamin's desk.

Her eyes studied him as he sat. His body looked rigid and uncomfortable. His fingers held the quill an inch above the paper, poised and ready to write. His eyes, which she couldn't actually see, were trained on the paper in front of him. It was hard to tell, but it didn't look like they were moving. His unshaven jaw was clenched and his mouth formed a tight line.

She had no idea how long she stood there staring at him. An hour. Perhaps two. Maybe even three. She didn't know and it really didn't matter. She'd stand there all night if that's what it took.

Finally, when the fire was almost too dim to see and the candles on his desk had melted to little pools of wax that threatened to put the flames out, Benjamin sighed, threw his quill down and ran a hand through his unkempt hair. He leaned forward and quickly blew out the four candles that were still barely lit on his desk then stood up to walk to the fire and froze.

"What do you want?" he barked.

"You," she whispered. Now that the moment had come at last, her voice was failing her.

He snarled. "You're wasting your time. Go up to bed." His voice was harsh and cold, causing a lump of panic to form in her chest. He really might not want her anymore.

Steeling her spine and walking in his direction. "No," she said, shaking her head defiantly. "I listened to your tirade the other day. Now, you'll listen to me."

He scoffed and tried to walk past her.

She brought her hands up to his chest. "Stop, Benjamin. Just listen to me."

He brought his hands to her wrists to pull them off and she flipped her hands around to grab his hands right before his fingers encircled her wrist.

Holding both of his hands palm to palm, she squeezed her fingers around his as tightly as she could. "Please, just let me tell you something. After I've finished, I'll do whatever you want. Even leave, if you ask it of me." That was the most difficult thing she'd ever said in her life. Panic gripped her when she realized that statement was nowhere near as difficult as what she was about to say to him.

"Fine," he said, pulling his hands away from hers and crossing his arms defensively. His face was unreadable and if she had to guess, she'd say he'd already made his decision and was only listening to her as a formality.

She swallowed. "I never planned to send that letter. I don't love Andrew, I love you."

He ground his teeth. "That's not good enough," he responded. "You may leave tomorrow."

"No," she said almost hysterically. "I wasn't finished. I wasn't even close to being finished." She took a deep breath and willed herself to stay calm. "As I've already admitted, I fancied myself in love with your alter-ego, Leo. But when Robbie lied to me about your dishonorable intentions, my heart was crushed. For goodness' sake, I had been so far gone I was planning the wedding and drawing pictures of us dancing together." She shook her head and tried to swallow the emotion that had formed in her throat.

"After that, I was afraid to trust my heart with anyone again, including myself. I'll admit when I was a young girl, I spun daydreams of marriage to Robbie, but it wasn't until I met you that I knew the difference between infatuation and love. It had only been infatuation I'd felt for Robbie. But after he told me you were only using me, I convinced myself I could settle for making a match with Robbie. He was the safe choice. If my heart wasn't involved, I wouldn't get hurt." Her voice turned bitter and her heart squeezed in the painful way it had for the past year and a half when she thought of Robbie.

"But I was wrong," she said quietly. "The idea of Leo's cold rejection of me was nothing compared to the hurt Robbie caused." She took a deep breath. "When I came here, it wasn't for the reason you think," she whispered, shifting her line of vision from his eyes to his shoulders. "As you know, a few months earlier I'd given my virtue to Robbie in hopes of marriage. And contrary to his assurance, his seed took root and I conceived." She swallowed a sob that caught in her throat and closed her eyes to stop the flow of tears she was almost certain was about to leak out.

"I went to him and he denied his participation. My father spoke to his father and he refused to get involved. Without many options left to me, I ended the courtship, watched him marry a girl he barely knew and with the support of my parents and Brooke, decided I'd keep the child even if it branded me a whore and him a bastard." She swallowed hard and rubbed her eyes with her fingertips.

Taking a deep, uncomfortable breath, she continued, "But then in early March, when I was little more than three months along, I was leaving a friend's house and ran into Robbie's wife. In front of the little group that was standing there, she made several indirect but obvious remarks about my condition. I was so flustered because the only people I'd told were my parents, Brooke and Robbie. Even Liberty didn't know at the time, and I still don't know if she does. She probably does now since Papa used to be such good friends with Paul before they married." She closed her eyes and shook her head again. Now wasn't the time to get sidetracked.

"Anyway, I was so upset by her words, I literally ran out of the house to the front steps." Her voice broke and she swallowed convulsively to find her voice again. "It was early March and we'd had an ice storm a few days before. In my hurry, I didn't grab the handrail and slipped on an ice patch that was on the first stair then fell down the rest." The dam that was straining to hold her emotions in check broke and she could no longer hold back the tears that spilled or the sobs that wracked her body. "That's why we came. I wasn't melancholy over the loss of blasted Robbie but because I'd miscarried."

Her knees buckled and she would have collapsed to the floor if Benjamin's strong hands hadn't come around her upper arms and brought her against his hard chest. He murmured something she didn't understand against her ear as her body shook with emotion.

"I'm sorry," she cried. "I'm sorry, Ben." She really didn't know why specifically she was apologizing. So many possibilities flooded her mind that she'd just let him pick one.

His arms encircled her and he ran his big hands up and down her back while his cheek rested on the crown of her head.

"Ben," she said, pushing away from his chest a bit. She brought her eyes up to look at his. It was too dark for her to see well enough to read his expression. "The reason I'm so close to Andrew is *because* he's in love with my sister. From the day he first showed up at our house, it was in his eyes. He never offered me more than a courtesy glance." She swallowed and tucked a stray lock of hair behind her ear. "He was the first man I'd ever met that was only interested in friendship with me. Ever since I'd trusted my heart to Leo and had it handed back to me, I've been afraid to trust any man with anything more than my handkerchief."

"Including me," he said raggedly.

"Yes," she whispered, "including you." She swallowed again and pulled his arms off of her. She stepped back to look at him. "Benjamin, I'm sorry I've been so closed off to you. It was never my intention to make you think you weren't good enough. You are. You're better than I deserve. I was just skeptical of you as I was of all other men who just seemed to see a pretty face."

"I—"

She shook her head and put her finger to his lips. "I know now that you don't see me that way. I started to see it at Rockhurst when you wanted me to draw our feet and taught me to swim. Then you willingly let me go about my activities without condescending remarks about how a person of my beauty or position didn't need to sew for the needy or teach a group of illiterate bastards to read. You've continued to prove it with the painting materials and even when I wore the same dress every day for nearly a fortnight; you didn't seem to lose interest in me as others would have done."

"I love you," he whispered.

"I know you do," she said with a sweet smile. "And I love you, too. I want to give you full possession of my heart," she whispered, pulling his hand up to her chest and resting his palm over her rapidly beating heart. "But only if I can have yours in return."

He stared at her and slowly reached his hand forward to take hers and move it to rest on his thudding heart the way his hand rested on hers. "You have it," he said hoarsely. "You've always had it."

"Does this mean you want me to stay?" she asked with a watery grin.

The corner of his mouth tipped up and humor glistened in his shiny eyes. "That's right, you said you'd do whatever I wanted, didn't you?"

She nodded and her pounding heart missed a beat. Surely he wasn't going to send her away now, was he? "Yes," she whispered.

"I think I'd like to collect my Waffle Law kiss now," he said with a roguish grin.

A new round of tears formed in her eyes. But this time they were happy tears. "As you wish, Your Grace," she said, coming up on her toes to bring her mouth to his.

His hands came to her shoulders and he pulled her as close to him as he could. "Madison," he murmured against her lips.

She wrapped her arms around his neck and with a sigh, parted her lips when his tongue traced the seam. His hands moved to her breasts and he lovingly shaped them as his tongue continued to sweep her mouth. She sighed, feeling completely boneless.

He pulled back and looked into her flushed face. "Madison," he said raggedly, "I want you. All of you. Now."

"I want you, too," she replied, arching her back to further push her breasts into his palms.

He swallowed. "I don't think I can go slowly like I did last time," he said hoarsely, his breathing shallow and strained.

She ran her hands across his shoulders and down his chest. "Then don't," she said coyly.

He groaned. "You have no idea what you do to me, sweetheart." She brushed the front of his trousers. "I think I do," she argued with a wink.

He groaned again. "You do indeed," he agreed, picking her up and hauling her to the settee.

Madison fell back against the cushions with his heavy body following right on top of hers. His crushing weight felt good against her swollen breasts. His hands roamed over her body. He touched and squeezed every inch he could before lifting the hem of the scrap of fabric she dared to call a nightrail.

His hands brought the nightrail up, up, then completely off. "Let me see you," he murmured, leaning back and hungrily drinking her in with his slow, intent gaze.

She blushed. She'd never been naked in front of him in a somewhat lighted room before and his hungry eyes coupled with his hard swallows made her shiver with anticipation.

"You're beautiful," he rasped when he finished his perusal.

She reached up and started to unbutton his shirt, kissing each patch of newly revealed skin as she went. She pushed his shirt off and scooted down to work the fastenings of his trousers. She could feel the hardness of his erection underneath her palms as her fingers worked. She'd freed the first button when his hands closed around her wrists and her eyes flew to his. "Enough," he said roughly.

Her eyes widened as he pushed her hands to rest on the settee above her head and his hands went to the fall of his trousers. In less than a second, he'd released the fastenings and his erection sprang free from his trousers. Intrigued by the sheer size and presence of him, she reached her hand forward and wrapped her fingers around the pulsating flesh. A little bead of fluid had formed on the tip and she used her thumb to rub it over his velvety tip. He groaned and she became bolder. She squeezed her fingers tighter over his shaft and moved her hand up and down, marveling at how he felt just like satin over iron.

He closed his long fingers around her wrist again. "Enough," he choked out. "If you keep doing that, this will be over too soon."

She smiled a sensual smile. "We could always add another act to this performance," she suggested, batting her lashes.

"I already planned on that. An encore, too," he said harshly, pushing her hands back over her head and settling himself between her thighs.

She wrapped her arms around his neck and closed her eyes as he filled her with one quick thrust. She sighed, lolling her head back just a little.

His blue eyes locked with hers briefly before his hips adopted a rhythm that sent hot sparks of desire shooting through her. Her hips rocked in time with his, adding to her pleasure. He murmured her name and she gasped his in return.

"Put your legs around my waist," he told her, reaching for her thighs.

She wrapped her legs around him and locked her ankles, enabling his strokes to go deeper. "Ben," she moaned as the waves of pleasure started to come over her.

His fingers dug into her hips and he lightly sucked on her neck. "It's time, Madison."

"Yes," she shrieked, moving her hands to hold onto Benjamin's shoulders. One more thrust and fire rushed through her veins as her mind spiraled away from reality.

The muscles in Benjamin's shoulders tensed under her hands and he let out a harsh growl before coming to rest upon her. "I love you," he whispered in her ear.

"I know," she said, idly stroking the back of his hair. She smiled. "I think I've always known."

"You have?" he asked, still not lifting his head.

"Yes," she said, pressing a kiss to his cheek. "Only a man who loves his wife would allow her more time to get to know him before sharing his bed."

He scoffed. "Or a man who's led around by his prick," he retorted in a mocking tone.

"No," she countered with a little laugh. "That is a trait of the most besotted man in England. Which, dear husband, is a title I think you now own."

He lifted his head and propped himself up on his elbows so he could look into her eyes. "I may be Duke of Gateway, but the title of Most Besotted Man in England seems to have a lot more appeal to me."

"What about Most Loved Man in England?" she asked with a grin.

"I like that one even better," he said, returning her grin.

She brought her hands to his face and ran her thumbs along his cheekbones. "Claim it with honor, my love. I love you more than any woman has ever loved her husband," she said with a kiss.

"And I love you, too," he returned before taking her lips in a searing kiss that would be the prelude for acts two and three.

To be followed by an explosive encore.

Epilogue

Christmas 1813
Glenbrook

Benjamin grinned at Madison as she did her best to suppress an annoyed groan at her mother's suggestion. "Mama, truly, we are not children. Can we not just sit in the drawing room and talk? Must we play a game?"

"Of course we must," Carolina chirped. "Parlor games are a tradition in this family. Besides, you never minded them before. Why now?"

Madison's blue gaze swung to where Brooke sat with a smug expression on her face, plotting revenge against her sisters for their last game of charades, no doubt. "Fine, but pick something else. Just like at Rockhurst, charades has been banned from Glenbrook, too."

"What a relief," Andrew muttered, shaking his head. "Sorry, darling. I know you had the perfect scene worked out in your head, but that's just where it will have to stay."

Brooke rolled her eyes and sighed. "Fine, but you two are not off the hook. And I daresay it would be much less embarrassing for the scene to be displayed here than at a house party I host."

"Ahem," Liberty interjected. "We had an agreement, remember? If you don't, I should be happy to refresh your memory." She dug in her reticule and pulled out a paper. "Ah, here it is. I knew I might need to bring this."

"Oh, put it away," Brooke said, shaking her head. "I know what it says."

"Very well; just don't forget."

Wondering what that was about, Benjamin nudged Madison.

She shrugged and shook her head. "I think I know, but I'm not sure," she murmured.

Silence filled the air. It might be Christmas, and the whole family may have gathered together to celebrate the holiday at Glenbrook, but sometimes old wounds take a while to heal and there was no mistaking that under the calm pretense everyone was showing, some traces of bitter emotions and resentment still lurked. Benjamin wondered if that would always be the case. If he'd made such a hash of things that every holiday or house party he attended, everyone would be uncomfortable. He hoped not, but all he could do was take Andrew's advice and let everyone see they had nothing to fear from him. He had no more intentions of doing anything underhanded or that would deliberately harm anyone else.

He sighed. He may have been able to persuade his wife to love him, but her family was another matter.

"I have an idea," Madison finally spoke up. "Why don't we all go hide and you two can come seek us out."

"Why do you wish to play a nursery game?" Benjamin asked his wife, taking in the blushes and giggles that were overtaking her sisters.

A saucy smile took her lips and she leaned forward to whisper in his ear, "You'll see."

Carolina cleared her throat. "That sounds like a superb idea. Everyone go hide and we'll come find you."

~*~*~*~

"Oh, John, they all got what I was praying for," Carolina said, snuggling up on the settee next to her husband.

"They did?"

"Yes," she said, smoothing his hair out of his blue eyes. "A love match. Remember I said I wanted them all to marry for love?"

"I remember," John grumbled. "It's just too bad two of their husbands aren't exactly lovable."

"Yes, they are," Carolina countered. "Andrew may be the scoundrel who agreed to take money in exchange for ruining Brooke's reputation and Gateway the wastrel who offered to pay him, but it all worked out. And if they love their husbands, then so do I."

"Goodness, Carolina," John said, shaking his head, "you make it sound as if you condone that reprobate's actions."

Carolina smiled. "He had good motives, it seems. I don't believe he'd have done that if he didn't love her; and there's no doubt about it, he loves her. He just wanted to see her happy, even if it wasn't with him."

"But to hurt another…" He shrugged. "Nothing for it now, as you said, it all worked out."

"It did. Are you ready to go upstairs now?"

John stood and extended his arm down to his wife. "Where shall I escort you?"

"To our bedchamber, of course," his wife said, swishing her skirts to air them out. "You don't honestly think those six are really hiding in hopes of us finding them, do you?"

~*~*~*~

And they weren't.

Off in their respective bedchambers, Brooke and Andrew and Paul and Liberty were off hiding—under the covers—with the expectation of not being found.

Meanwhile, Madison tugged Benjamin's hand and led him to their bed. "Come on," she urged when he stopped walking and wouldn't allow himself to be pulled any closer.

"Madison, I'm not exactly in your family's favor just now. I don't think it would be to my advantage for us to be caught…" he trailed off and waved his hand to gesture at the bed.

His wife grinned at him. "Oh, you have no idea," she said, starting to undo the buttons on his shirt.

He thought to protest, but just couldn't bring himself to do so as she slid his shirt and coat off. He blinked down at her. Now, more than ever, he loved her. He'd loved her when they'd first met, and he'd loved her all those years they'd been apart, but he loved her more now. He reached his hand out to rest on her stomach. "You're sure?"

Her fingers stilled and she looked up at him. "Yes, I'm sure, and so are Mr. Green, Mr. Folley, Mr. Abrams, *and* Mr. Clink."

Benjamin nodded. "Very well, I just wanted to make sure."

"And if I weren't?"

"Then, I'd take you to bed right this instant and not let you out until you were."

Madison's lips twisted in contemplation. "On second thought, I'm not so sure, after all. You see, my waist isn't *that* thick…"

"You little minx," Benjamin chided, wrapping his arms around Madison and hauling her to the mattress. Positioning himself on top of her, he brushed the hair from her face and kissed her check. "You're absolutely sure they're not going to remark upon our absence?"

"Yes," she said with a smile. "Nobody will be looking for us, particularly not Mama and Papa."

"Oh," he said, pulling the cap of her gown off her shoulder and dropping kisses along her clavicle.

"They're off in their room taking a nap," she explained with an overdone yawn. "Just like we're going to do."

"Oh no, we're not."

If you enjoyed *To Win His Wayward Wife*, I would appreciate it if you would help others enjoy this book, too.

Lend it. Feel free to share it with a friend.

Recommend it. Please help other readers find this book by recommending it to friends, readers' groups and discussion boards.

Review it. Please tell other readers why you liked this book by reviewing it at one of the following websites: Amazon or Goodreads.

Scandalous Sisters Series
    Three American sisters have arrived in England for a brief visit, but they're about to all find something they never bargained for: love.

    Intentions of the Earl—Faced with never-ending poverty, a gentleman is offered a handsome sum if he'll ruin a certain young lady's future—only she has other plans, and it might entail her ruining his.

    Liberty for Paul—There's only one thing Liberty Banks hates worse than impropriety: one Mr. Paul Grimes, and unfortunately for her, it's her own impropriety that just got her married to him!

    To Win His Wayward Wife—Not to be outdone by her sisters' scandalous marriages, Madison Banks is about to have her own marriage-producing scandal to a man who, unbeknownst to her has loved her all along.

Groom Series
    Four decided bachelors are about to have their freedom ripped right from their clutches with nothing to show for it but love.

    Her Sudden Groom—When informed he must marry within the month or be forced to marry the worst harpy ever to set foot on English shores, the overly scientific, always logical Alex Banks decides to conduct his courtship like a science experiment!

    Her Reluctant Groom—Emma Green has loved Marcus, Lord Sinclair for as long as she can remember, so when he slips up and says he loves her, too, it should all be so simple. But it's never that simple when the man in question was once been engaged to and jilted by Emma's older sister.

    Her Secondhand Groom—What Patrick Ramsey, Lord Drakely AKA Lord Presumptuous wanted was an ordinary village girl to be a "motherness" to his daughters and stay out of his bedroom; what he's about to get is something so much more.

    Her Imperfect Groom— Sir Wallace Benedict is a thrice-jilted baronet who is about to finally have his happily-ever-after, if only the family of his one-true-love, would stop being so darn meddlesome!

Banks Brothers' Brides
The first two are prequels to the previous series and the second two are follow ups.

His Contract Bride—Since just a lad, Edward Banks, Lord Watson knew Regina Harris would one day be his bride, he'd seen the paper to prove it many times; only someone forgot to inform Regina...

His Yankee Bride—John Banks wants nothing to do with the scandalous, sweet talking, ever-present, American beauty named Carolina, or so that's what he keeps saying...

His Jilted Bride—Amelia Brice has a secret...and so does Elijah Banks. Hers is big...but his is bigger!

His Brother's Bride—Presented with a marriage contract his twin brother has signed but cannot fulfill, Henry Banks has to form a plan to save the Banks name, even if it means pretending he's his brother, or worse yet, marrying a lady who holds a grudge against his family.

Fort Gibson Officers Series
American-set historical romance series that takes place in Indian Territory in the mid-1840s.

The Officer and the Bostoner—When Allison Pearson is stranded in at a forsaken fort in the middle of Indian Territory on her way to meet her fiance, what other option does she have than to temporarily marry the handsome, smooth-talking Captain Wes Tucker?

The Officer and the Southerner—Lieutenant Jack Walker sent off for a mail-order bride. Ella Davis answered the ad. Jack forgot to mention a few living details, and Ella's about to let him know it!

The Officer and the Traveler—Captain Grayson Montgomery's mouth has landed him in trouble again! And this time, a quick smile and a clever statement won't save him—only marriage to none other than the daughter of his sworn enemy.

Gentlemen of Honor Series
Secrets of a Viscount—Sebastian, Lord Belgrave might have eloped with the wrong sister, but ever-the-gentleman, he wants to make it right and help her find the perfect husband—never once thinking it just might be the one she already has.

Desires of a Baron—Giles Goddard, Lord Norcourt is odd. Odder still, he has suddenly taken a fancy to his brother's love interest, the fallen Lucy Whitaker. Lucy was once thrown over by a lord and she has little desire to let it happen again, but she's about to learn that his desires just might be enough for the both of them.

Passions of a Gentleman—Having been thrown over twice already, Simon Appleton has given up his pursuit for a wife—especially if his only choice is the elusive Miss Henrietta Hughes. But when he discovers a secret about her, he's not above helping to protect her...

If you'd like to stay current on Rose's releases, then sign up for her new release newsletter at http://www.rosegordon.net.

About the Author

USA Today Bestselling and Award Winning Author Rose Gordon writes unusually unusual historical romances that have been known to include scarred heroes, feisty heroines, marriage-producing scandals, far too much scheming, naughty literature and always a sweet happily-ever-after. When not escaping to another world via reading or writing a book, she spends her time chasing two young boys around the house, being hunted by wild animals, or sitting on the swing in the backyard where she has to use her arms as shields to deflect projectiles AKA: balls, water balloons, sticks, pinecones, and anything else one of her boys picks up to hurl at his brother who just happens to be hiding behind her.

She can be found somewhere in cyberspace on her website or talking about *something* inappropriate on her blog. You can also find her on Facebook, Goodreads, and Twitter.

Rose would love to hear from her readers and you can e-mail her at rose.gordon@hotmail.com.

If you never want to miss a new release, click here to subscribe to her New Release list or visit her website to subscribe and you'll be notified each time a new book becomes available.

http://www.rosegordon.net

Printed in Great Britain
by Amazon

54065684R00133